Arab Women Writers

SUNY series, Women Writers in Translation
Marilyn Gaddis Rose, editor

Arab Women Writers

An Anthology of Short Stories

Edited, Translated, and with an Introduction by
Dalya Cohen-Mor

State University of New York Press

Published by
State University of New York Press, Albany

For information, contact State University of New York Press, Albany, NY
www.sunypress.edu

Production by Judith Block
Marketing by Fran Keneston

Library of Congress Cataloging-in-Publication Data

Arab women writers : an anthology of short stories / collected, translated,
and introduced by Dalya Cohen-Mor.
      p. cm. — (SUNY series, women writers in translation)
   Includes bibliographical references.
   ISBN 0-7914-6419-9 (hardcover : alk. paper) —
   ISBN 0-7914-6420-2 (pbk. : alk. paper)
   1. Short stories, Arabic—Translations into English.   2. Arabic fiction—Women
authors—Translations into English.   I. Cohen-Mor, Dalya   II. Series.

PJ7694. E8A719 2005
892.7'301089287—dc22   2004015114

10 9 8 7 6 5 4 3 2 1

To Michael, my life's companion

Contents

꧁꧂

Acknowledgments

❦❦❦

his anthology owes its existence to the assistance and cooperation of many people and institutions. First and foremost, I want to thank the authors for permission to translate and print selections from their writings. The scope of this anthology made it at times difficult, despite all efforts, to locate some of the authors, their agents, or both. The editor and publisher regret any omissions or errors, which will be gladly corrected in subsequent printings.

I want to express my gratitude to all the authors whose individual stories appear in this volume: Sufi Abdallah for "Half a Woman"; Nura Amin for "My Mother's Friend" and "Let's Play Doctor"; Daisy al-Amir for "The Newcomer," "The Future," and "The Cat, the Maid, and the Wife"; Radwa Ashour for "In the Moonlight" and "In Need of Reassurance"; Samiya At'ut for "The Collapse of Barriers," Mozart's Fez," and "That Summer Holiday"; Samira Azzam for "Tears for Sale" and "A Virgin Continent"; Salwa Bakr for "International Women's Day" and "The Beginning"; Layla Ba'labakki for "The Cat" and "The Filly Became a Mouse"; Hayat Bin al-Shaykh for "A Worthless Woman"; Nuzha Bin Sulayman for "A Moment of Contemplation"; Nafila Dhahab for "Short and Sassy" and "The Smile"; Fadila al-Faruq for "The Woman of my Dreams" and "Homecoming"; Sakina Fuad for "Pharaoh Is Drowning Again"; Ulfat al-Idilbi for "The Breeze of Youth"; Ramziya Abbas al-Iryani for "Misfortune in the Alley" and "Heir Apparent"; Ihsan Kamal for "A Mistake in the Knitting" and "The Spider's Web"; Umayma al-Khamis for "The Parting Gift," "Restoration," and "Waiting for Hayla"; Zabya Khamis for "Bittersweet Memories"; Colette Suhayl al-Khuri for "Where To?"; Nadiya Khust for "An Old Couple"; Aliya Mamdouh for "The Dream"; Sahar al-Muji for "The Dummy" and "The Closely Guarded Secret"; Buthayna al-Nasiri for "At the Beach"; Emily Nasrallah for "The Dinosaur"; Suhayr al-Qalamawi for "A Successful Woman"; Mona Ragab for

"I Will Try Tomorrow," "A Helping Hand," and "I Will Never Forfeit My Right"; Fawziya Rashid for "In the Recesses of Memory" and "Questioning"; Alifa Rifaat for "My Wedding Night"; Nawal al-Saadawi for "The Picture"; Hadiya Sa'id for "Moonstruck"; Khayriya al-Saqqaf for "A Moment of Truth"; Sharifa al-Shamlan for "Fragments from a Life"; Hanan al-Shaykh for "The Persian Rug" and "Sun, I Am the Moon"; Rafiqat al-Tabi'a for "Man and Woman"; Suhayr al-Tall for "The Gallows"; Najiya Thamir for "The Slave"; Layla al-Uthman for "The Picture"; Zuhur Wanisi for "The Dreadful Sea"; Latifa al-Zayyat for "The Picture"; Mayy Ziyada for "Woman with a Story."

I also thank Sheba Press for permission to print revised translations from *An Arabian Mosaic*, which appeared in a limited edition in 1993.

In transliterating Arabic words and names, I have used a simplified system based on that of the Library of Congress. For greater ease in reading, all the diacritical marks have been omitted. The sign ' stands for both *'ayn* and *hamza*, which are denoted only when they occur in the middle of a word (with the exception of bibliographical references, where they are denoted in full). Anglicized forms of Arabic words and names have been retained in the translated text.

This anthology has evolved over a decade of teaching modern Arabic literature in various settings and institutions. My contact with students, and my recurrent observation that the life of women in the Arab world is poorly understood and inadequately described in the West, provided the main impetus to study and collect stories by and about women from different parts of the Arab world.

Collecting the stories for this work was a formidable task that was facilitated by the Library of Congress, Georgetown University's Lauinger Library, and the Arabic Language Institute at the American University in Cairo. My warm thanks to all those members of staff and faculty who have gone out of their way to help me complete this project.

While the main part of this research was conducted at these prominent institutions, additional—and most fascinating—texts were obtained through travels to Arab countries, where my favorite pastimes were going to book fairs, visiting publishing houses, and browsing in bookshops and bookstalls. By looking at what was placed on the shelves or displayed on the sidewalks, and by talking to bookshop clerks and street vendors, I could familiarize myself with new authors and new works that have not yet made their way to public libraries in the East or the West. I could also assess which authors were the most popular, respected, neglected, and obscure . . .

Hunting for texts became an especially adventurous activity in Cairo, where books printed in Egypt and elsewhere in the Arab world are sold at very low prices. From Maktabat Madbuli to Maktabat al-Shuruq to Maktabat Layla, and from Dar al-Hilal to Dar al-Kitab al-Lubnani to Dar Sharqiyyat (to name but a few bookshops), I walked many miles, climbed many dark staircases, waited endlessly in small and hot offices, and searched patiently through stacks of dusty books—all for the sake of a particular volume or edition. On some occasions, I returned to my hotel with interesting finds such as banned books, out-of-print books, or hard-to-find books; at other times, I returned empty-handed. A particular test of perseverance was a bookseller's promise to bring me a certain book the next day. "Are you sure you will have it tomorrow?" I would ask. "Inshallah," he would say. I would then return the following day only to discover that "tomorrow" is a very fluid concept ranging from a couple of days to a couple of weeks—"Middle Eastern time," as the saying goes. Nevertheless, I am profoundly grateful to all those unnamed individuals for their important contributions to this project.

Once I had obtained all the books I wanted, the process of selecting appropriate stories began. I had to read hundreds of short stories for the purpose of choosing texts for this anthology. Each of the stories I considered had to meet several requirements: tell the story well, reflect the current interests and concerns of Arab women, add a viewpoint to the myriad voices of Arab women writers, and help to represent the many countries of the Arab world. In addition, I preferred to include texts that have not yet been translated into English, and writers who are still alive, though I made a few exceptions.

In my translation of these stories, I have done my utmost to faithfully represent the originals. Rather than being literal, or conversely interpretive, I have tried to strike a balance between the two approaches, striving to make the translation as accurate as possible while at the same time meeting Western literary expectations. Reading and rereading the texts, I have tried to understand the authors' intentions and to fill the linguistic and cultural gaps, using endnotes where necessary. This arduous task was greatly facilitated by a fellowship at the American University in Cairo. I thank the faculty members of the Arabic Language Institute at the American University in Cairo for their kind assistance in clarifying the rich texture of many stories, elucidating complex linguistic items and literary images, and introducing me to some intriguing works by Egyptian women writers.

Above all, my deep gratitude goes out to the authors who appear in this anthology. Their narratives open windows onto Arab culture and society and offer keen insights into what Arab women feel and think.

Introduction

❦❧❦❧

his anthology contains short stories by forty contemporary women writers from across the Arab world. These multiple voices articulate the female experience over the past half-century in an area stretching from the Middle East to North Africa. They speak of old values, new needs, marriage, childbearing, love, sexuality, education, work, and freedom. They explore the relations between the sexes, and question traditional norms and bequeathed customs as they assert their own desires and aspirations. Invariably, they take a stand, be it romantic, rebellious, conservative, liberal, or radical. The intimate and vividly crafted portrait of the Arab woman that emerges from these narratives is not only fascinating but endlessly thought provoking.

The aim of this anthology is to introduce the English reader to Arab women's ways of life, currents of thought, and creative expression. The volume offers a rich cultural encounter in which the complex world of Arab women, as seen by these women themselves, is unveiled. One may hope that the wealth of material presented in this volume will deepen Western understanding of Arab society, illuminate the status and lifestyles of Arab women, and broaden awareness of the contribution of Arab women writers to modern Arabic literature.

The anthology is organized around the genre of the short story and its individual female practitioners. In this regard, it is the first of its kind, the traditional collection being generally centered on a single author, a particular country, or a variety of genres.

The scope of this anthology extends over several generations of women writers, beginning with the pioneers who published in the 1940s and 1950s, through the younger generation who followed in the 1960s and 1970s, to the present generation whose literary output appeared in the 1980s and especially the 1990s, thus

1

providing a broad spectrum of works of fiction by Arab women. While the authors are culled from diverse countries, there is an unavoidable balance in favor of Egyptian writers. For one thing, Egypt has always been the center of cultural activity in the Arab world. In addition, its population is the largest among the Arab nations.

The focus on the genre of the short story was guided by several factors, foremost among which is the fact that since the 1950s, the short story has become the most popular form of creative writing in the Arab world. The ready availability of avenues of publication for the short story, notably newspapers, journals, and magazines, and the relatively little amount of time and planning needed to produce a complete short story (as opposed to a novel or novella), have made it the favorite fictional genre among women, who often have to juggle the demands of a family with a literary career. In addition, the short story's brevity, as well as its ability to dramatize concrete issues and convey pithy messages, render it uniquely suitable for an anthology that aims to present unabridged texts, and a large number of them at that.

In selecting the stories for this anthology, the first priority was to ensure a wide range of subject matter. The stories had to reflect the current interests and concerns of Arab women, from feminist issues to social and political problems to cultural and moral dilemmas. Further, the stories had to illustrate different styles and modes of writing, with diversity of techniques and creative approaches. Aside from sociocultural content and artistic merit, the stories had to possess heuristic value, namely, show many points of view and various ways of solving problems and confronting situations in everyday life. Occasionally, the overriding factor was the "story behind the story," as in the case of "The Gallows" by Suhayr al-Tall, who was prosecuted and jailed by the authorities for publishing it. An additional feature of this anthology is the frequent inclusion of more than one story by the same author, thus affording a deeper glimpse into her creative work. While the stories had to fulfill any one of these criteria, the final decision was also influenced by personal taste—an unavoidable element in such a process.

The headings under which the stories are arranged represent some of the prevailing themes in Arab women's imaginative writings. While the stories in each section express similar concerns, their interpretive potential is rich and may well suggest or overlap other themes.

Moreover, many stories contain several themes and thus fall under more than one heading. In these instances, I have placed the story in the section where I believe its most intriguing theme is highlighted. Needless to say, there are common threads running through all the stories. On the whole, the present organization is fluid and meant to provide an easy frame of reference rather than a rigid set of categories.

Arab Women Writers: A Brief Sketch

Women in the Arab world have been producing significant fiction for the past half-century. Although the Arabic literary tradition had its narrative types, the short story and the novel were new genres adopted from the West in the late nineteenth and early twentieth centuries. Introduced during the process of cultural revival known in Arabic as *al-nahda*, the new forms underwent considerable experimentation before gaining acceptance and reaching maturity. The emergence of the short story in particular is closely connected with the development of the Arabic press, which offered authors an avenue of publication and thus a readership. Since the Second World War, when most Arab countries have gained their political independence and their newly formed governments have pursued policies of social and economic reforms, there has been a gradual improvement in the condition of women. The spread of free compulsory public education not only raised the level of literacy among women but also opened the door to new employment opportunities. Women's participation in public life increased, reaching into all areas of activity. In the domain of literature, women advanced gradually from the margins to the center of literary production and their contribution to modern Arabic literature has been invaluable. Fiction, which possesses the guise of fantasy and therefore entails a lesser degree of exposure and accountability, has become the most popular and powerful vehicle of self-expression and social criticism for women. In the last half-century, Arab women writers have brought the art of storytelling to a high level of accomplishment and achieved a remarkable development in theme, form, and technique. Prominent among the pioneer authors are the Palestinian Mayy Ziyada (1886–1941), the Egyptian Suhayr al-Qalamawi (1911–97), and the Syrian Ulfat al-Idilbi (b. 1912).[1]

While the presence of women on the Arabic literary scene has grown in number and influence in recent decades, there are still fewer female than male authors. In addition, they do not represent all segments of Arab society. Most of these women writers come from the middle and upper classes and have had the education and resources needed for intellectual pursuits. In a developing part of the world where illiteracy is still widespread, and where the overwhelming majority of women are preoccupied with the harsh realities of daily life, Virginia Woolf's basic assumption that "a woman must have money and a room of her own if she is to write fiction"[2] is of particular relevance. As Woolf elaborates, "Fiction, imaginative work that is, is not dropped like a pebble upon the ground, as science may be; fiction is like a spider's web, attached ever so lightly perhaps, but still attached to life at all four corners. . . . These webs are not spun in mid-air by incorporeal creatures, but are the work of suffering human beings, and are attached to grossly material things, like health and money and the houses we live in."[3] Owing to the privileged social background of most Arab women writers, their fictional works give inadequate attention to, and lack realistic solutions for, the plight of women from the poorer classes of society.[4]

Despite the increase in the number of women who are creative writers, only very few of them can devote themselves entirely to their writing. Family obligations, full-time jobs, or financial pressures are usually the factors that impede them. It should be noted that the writing of fiction in the Arab world is not a profession by which a person, male or female, can earn a living. Even the Nobel Prize laureate Naguib Mahfouz worked as a civil servant in Egypt's Ministry of Culture until his retirement. Of the women writers included in this volume, Nawal al-Saadawi, for example, has maintained a dual career as a physician and a writer. Radwa Ashour is a university professor, as were Suhayr al-Qalamawi and Latifa al-Zayyat. Aliya Mamdouh, Fawziya Rashid, Mona Ragab, Fadila al-Faruq, and Hadiya Sa'id are journalists. Ramziya Abbas al-Iryani is a career diplomat. The literary activities of these authors are conducted alongside their duties as wives, mothers, and working women.

Economic freedom, however, does not necessarily entail intellectual freedom. Arab women who have had the opportunity to embark on a writing career may still encounter opposition to their work, and may even find it impossible to publish it or acquire a readership. Nawal al-Saadawi published her first work of nonfiction, *Women and Sex*, in Beirut in 1972. The book deals candidly with taboos surrounding female sexuality, including virginity, circumcision, and crimes of honor. It caused such an uproar that she was dismissed from her post as Egypt's director-general of health education. As with other provocative works that she has penned, the book has been banned in several Arab countries. Layla Ba'labakki of Lebanon published her collection of short stories, *A Spaceship of Tenderness to the Moon*, in Beirut in 1963. The book led to her trial on charges of obscenity and endangering public morality.[5] The indictment was based on erotic descriptions that appeared in some of her stories. Although she was eventually acquitted, she stopped publishing works of fiction since then. Suhayr al-Tall of Jordan went through a traumatic experience following the publication of her story "The Gallows," included in this anthology, in Amman in 1987. The narrative, a surrealistic depiction of a public execution in which the hangman's noose is portrayed as a huge phallus, landed her in court on a charge of offending public sensibilities. After a long and bitter trial, she was convicted, fined, and sentenced to short imprisonment.[6] Zabya Khamis of the United Arab Emirates suffered an even harsher ordeal. In 1987 she was arrested in Abu Dhabi and jailed for five months without trial as punishment for writing allegedly transgressive poetry.[7]

Besides problems of censorship, Arab women writers may also encounter opposition to their work within their own families. Alifa Rifaat was discouraged from writing first by her father and then by her husband, who threatened her with divorce to enforce his will. Only after his death could she write and publish freely. Nawal al-Saadawi chose to divorce two husbands who were hostile to her literary activities. In most instances, the attitudes of family members—particularly fathers and husbands—whether progressive or conservative, play a critical role in shaping a woman's writing career.

The critic and writer Yusuf al-Sharuni cites the following explanation of this state of affairs in his introduction to *The 1002nd Night*, the first anthology of short stories by Egyptian women: "Man, especially in our Middle Eastern milieu, does not object to woman's emergence into public life in order to work alongside him, especially if this work relieves him of the burden of bearing the family's living costs by himself. But beyond that he strongly

objects to her having an independent social existence, just as he totally rejects the idea of the home becoming a secondary occupation
for her, subordinate to her outside, wider world. In other words,
man still asserts that the home, not external society, is woman's
domain."[8]

The sociologist Fatima Mernissi has another explanation. In
Doing Daily Battle, she writes about her experiences "as a Moroccan
woman who uses writing and analysis—two tools which are exclu-
sively male in our culture. And let no one tell me that 'in our heritage there have always been women scholars.' "[9] Mernissi states,
with an engaging sense of humor, that she has learned to distinguish
"the varieties of terrorist tactics that men, who monopolize the symbolic values of our society, use to stop me from expressing myself, or
to denigrate what I say—which comes to the same thing." She iden-
tifies two main "terrorist tactics": "Firstly, 'What you are talking
about is an imported idea' (referring to access to the cultural heritage); and secondly, 'What you are saying is not representative'
(referring to access to science)." Debunking these myths, Mernissi
comes to the conclusion that "the relations between the sexes are always inextricably and unconditionally linked to class relations."[10]

From the beginning, then, Arab women writers have had to
assert themselves in a male-dominated arena, from audience to pub-
lishers to critics to literary tradition.[11] The Egyptian author Salwa
Bakr acknowledges the formidable task facing an Arab woman
writer: "It is a heavy tax on many levels, especially in a society in
which most individuals are illiterate, a society which is conservative
by nature, whose values are static and which does not respect women
in the first place. All this makes writing seem like the task of Sisy-
phus, particularly if the writer stops to think for whom she is writing."[12] Yet despite the various obstacles that they encounter in the
path of their careers, Arab women writers continue to give literary
expression to their feelings and thoughts. Many of the authors presented in this anthology have produced a large volume of work and
achieved eminence, among them Ulfat al-Idilbi (Syria), Hanan al-
Shaykh (Lebanon), Layla al-Uthman (Kuwait), Nawal al-Saadawi
(Egypt), and Daisy al-Amir (Iraq). Others, such as Samiya At'ut
(Palestine), Nuzha Bin Sulayman (Morocco), Umayma al-Khamis
(Saudi Arabia), and Sahar al-Muji (Egypt) are rising young writers.
While most of the established authors have also received interna-
tional recognition by being translated into European languages, for

several of the new authors, this volume marks their first appearance in English.

Two groups of women writers can be distinguished in this anthology: those from the Arab East (Mashriq), and those from the Arab West (Maghrib). Historically and culturally, these parts of the Arab world have developed differently. Domination by European colonial powers in the nineteenth and twentieth centuries contributed to this division. The countries of the Arab East were mostly under British colonial rule (e.g., Egypt, Palestine, Iraq), while those of the Arab West (e.g., Algeria, Tunisia, Morocco) were largely occupied by the French. French colonial rule explains the problem of biculturalism facing North African writers.[13] Whereas British colonial policy did not impose the English language and culture on the colonized, the French embarked on an aggressive linguistic and cultural campaign that sought to replace the indigenous languages and cultures. The result has been the emergence of whole generations of intellectuals who are francophones and prefer to express themselves in French. The Algerian women writers Jamila Debeche and Assia Djebar, their male counterparts Muhammed Dib and Kateb Yacine, as well as the Moroccan novelist Driss Chraibi and the Tunisian Albert Memmi, all illustrate this phenomenon. It is interesting to note that North African authors who choose to write in Arabic occasionally show traces of French influence in their diction. For example, the Moroccan writer Khannatha Bannuna in her story "Suqut al-intizar" (Shattered Expectations) uses the phrase *'ilab al-layl* to mean "night clubs," which is a word-for-word translation from the French *boîtes de nuit*.[14] Similarly, the Algerian Fadila al-Faruq, in the story "Homecoming," uses the word *miziriyya* (French: *misère*) for "misery." On the whole, while the majority of literary works coming from the Arab East are in Arabic, those coming from North Africa are in French. In this volume, only women writers of Arabic have been included.

Thematic Aspects

This anthology is arranged in eight parts, each of which focuses on a major phase, event, or issue in the life cycle of Arab women. The diversity of the physical and social environments in which Arab women live, as well as the complexity of their situations and circumstances, are depicted in the stories. Narrated by forty women writers from across the Arab world, these sixty stories offer testimonies, observations, reflections, visions, memories, criticisms, and commentaries about life from the female perspective. The intellectual discourse that emerges from these narratives is insightful and daring. Eloquent, outspoken, and provocative, these literary texts undermine the stereotyped images often presented by superficial journalistic reports and selective social studies. Told through the eyes of insiders, the stories reveal the rich texture of women's lives, both private and public, throughout the many cultures and countries of the Arab world. They shed light on the status and lifestyles of Arab women, the way they view the world, address the challenges of modern life, and cope with daily dilemmas. At the same time, they expose abusive situations, raise controversial issues, and criticize many aspects of Arab society, with the goal of generating a constructive dialogue by both men and women.

In part 1, the stories depict the experience of growing up female in traditional Arab society. Certain commonalities emerge: while the early years of a girl's life appear to be relatively joyous and carefree, the onset of puberty puts an end to her childhood. When a girl reaches the age of puberty, she begins to wear the veil. She loses her freedom of movement and is confined to the domain of her home until she can be married off. The overwhelming desire to safeguard her chastity—and the family honor—may lead to her withdrawal from school and the end of her education. The abrupt and painful transition from childhood to adulthood is portrayed in the stories "That Summer Holiday" by Samiya At'ut, "The Parting Gift" by Umayma al-Khamis, and "Let's Play Doctor" by Nura Amin. The practice of marrying a girl off at the first sign of her menses is featured in "In the Recesses of Memory" by Fawziya Rashid. The phenomenon of child labor is highlighted in Radwa Ashour's "In the Moonlight" and Buthayna al-Nasiri's "At the Beach." The oppression of women by other women is dramatized in "The Slave" by Najiya Thamir. In this story, a fatherless girl is adopted by a selfish woman who enslaves her and deprives her of a life of her own, ultimately breaking her spirit. The story shows that a woman can be a worse tyrant than a man, especially in a relationship with another female who is subordinate to her and over whom she retains some power.

That mental breakdown may be caused by patriarchal oppression and socialization is suggested by Sharifa al-Shamlan's "Fragments from a Life." In this story, the protagonist, a young girl, is a patient in a mental institution. Her life has been marked by neglect, abuse, and victimization: a father who kept her illiterate, a greedy stepmother who sold her cherished palm-tree garden, a doctor who tried to rape her, a nurse who stole her medicine, and an orderly who pilfered her food. Faced with relentless acts of injustice, the girl's personality crumbles, and she loses her sanity. Paradoxically, her madness empowers her and gives her a voice that seems to be reckoned with in her confined environment.

In part 2, the stories explore the mysteries of love and sexuality. Arab women writers denounce the strict practices surrounding female sexuality: veiling, seclusion, social segregation, virginity, circumcision, and crimes of honor. At the same time, they offer a rare glimpse into intimate relations between men and women, which reveal that the sexual code is often violated in everyday life. Despite the sexual repression that predominates in traditional Arab society, the themes of love, passion, and erotic pleasure have always been celebrated in Arabic poetry, both classical and modern.

It is interesting to note that titles of works by Arab women writers occasionally echo each other, whether consciously or unconsciously. Nawal al-Saadawi, Latifa al-Zayyat, and Layla al-Uthman have all written a story entitled "The Picture." Not only are their stories woven around the same object—a photograph—but they also deal with the same subject—female sexuality. Each story, however, focuses on a different phase in a woman's life: in al-Saadawi's "Picture" it is adolescence, in al-Zayyat's it is adulthood, and in al-Uthman's it is middle age. Thus, taken together, the stories paint a vivid portrait of female sexuality over a complete life cycle. The connecting thread between the individual depictions of these particular phases is that each narrative features a traumatic event that captures a specific moment of truth, resulting in a flash of recognition and the acquisition of an indelible awareness.

"Suffering is the sole origin of consciousness," wrote Dostoyevsky: in al-Saadawi's story the teenage girl stumbles on her much-admired father raping the maid in the kitchen; in al-Zayyat's story the loving wife is publicly confronted with her husband's infidelity; and in al-Uthman's story the insecure middle-aged woman looking for reassurance in an extramarital love affair sees her own confused self in another woman. Each constructed around a photograph, all three stories express the idea that "true vision is always twofold: it involves emotional comprehension as well as physical perception."[15]

A controversial aspect of sexuality is depicted in "My Mother's Friend" by Nura Amin. The story recounts a lesbian relationship between the mother of a young girl and an unmarried woman. Not only is the story daring in its subject matter and explicit language, but it is also provocative in its treatment of female sexuality. In the absence of the girl's father, who often travels on business, the mother finds comfort and intimacy in the arms of another woman. Narrated from the perspective of the girl, the story highlights her sexual awakening and personal identification with her mother. Needless to say, in a society in which public discussion of sexual matters is generally discouraged, the depiction of a lesbian love affair constitutes a strict taboo. Yet despite censorship and the risk of ostracism, the topic has been explored by other women writers, notably Alifa Rifaat in her story "My World of the Unknown," published elsewhere.[16]

The miseries of unrequited love are portrayed in "A Worthless Woman" by Hayat Bin al-Shaykh. In this story, the heroine is tormented by unresolved feelings of longing, frustration, and self-doubt. In "The Smile" by Nafila Dhahab, love becomes a transforming experience for a girl who is infatuated with a young man in her neighborhood. Unable to reveal her feelings, she worships him from afar, until one day he disappears. Years later she meets him again and is shocked by his shabby appearance and incoherent speech. The military uniform that he wears suggests that he was drafted into the army and fought in a war; perhaps he suffers from psychic war trauma. She mourns the loss of her love and the fact that she will never know whether he loved her too. The intriguing perspective of this story is that it depicts the man as the primary victim of the prevailing social order and value system.

In part 3, the issue of gender relations serves as a basis for a feminist discourse. Arab women writers are deeply concerned with the inequality between the sexes, which is manifested in male domination and the oppression and marginalization of women. Their fictional works abound with female characters who are trapped in abusive situations in which their male kin—husbands, fathers, brothers, or uncles—act as the authors of their destinies. They protest their degradation at the hands of men, and rebel against the patriarchal institutions and traditions that keep them in bondage. Voicing anger, frustration, and alienation, they challenge the status quo and call for freedom, justice, and equality. Although there are instances in which male characters are presented in a positive light, they are more commonly portrayed as egotistic, insensitive, and vain, and as driven by greed, lust, and a primitive sense of honor.

Male hypocrisy, practice of double standards, and irrational expectations of women are exposed in "A Virgin Continent" by Samira Azzam. In this story, the protagonist proudly boasts about his romantic adventures to his fiancée, but insists on her being pure, virginal, and without a past. In "The Cat" by Layla Ba'labakki and "The Woman of My Dreams" by Fadila al-Faruq, women are prey to sexual exploitation. The men in these stories display a seemingly progressive attitude, but in reality their actions are deceptive and manipulative. The stories convey the message that in Arab society liberated women are more vulnerable than traditional women be-cause of a male tendency to view them as fallen, degraded, and un-worthy of being taken seriously.

A penetrating cameo portrait that captures the essence of male-female relations is "Mozart's Fez" by Samiya At'ut. In this vignette, reminiscent of a seduction scene from the *Arabian Nights*, the harem, represented by a tent full of women who are controlled by a single male, is the symbol of women's subordination and sexual exploitation. The juxtaposition of the name of the classical European composer, Mozart, and the traditional Muslim headdress, fez, is provocative, and serves to dramatize the erotic appeal and highly ro-manticized view of the harem in Western popular imagination. By contrast, in "Where To?" Colette Suhayl al-Khuri paints a romantic picture of a young couple passionately in love and deeply devoted to each other. The story, which is written in a poetic style, expresses both optimism and irony.

The strict code governing the relations between the sexes is relaxed in old age. Aging brings respect, prestige, and a certain mea-sure of freedom and independence. This situation is depicted in "An Old Couple" by Nadiya Khust. The story tells of a loving relation-ship between two villagers separated in their youth and reunited in old age. The woman, who was married off to an old man to pay her father's debts on his plot of land, returns to the village after she is widowed, and the man, who never married, renews his close friend-ship with her. The crucial difference is that at this stage in their lives, both the man and the woman enjoy more latitude in conduct-ing their personal affairs, which enables them to cultivate their rela-tionship without fear or interference.

In part 4, the institution of marriage is subject to a close scrutiny. In traditional Arab society, marriage represents the trans-fer of a girl from the authority of her father to that of her husband. The girl has no say in choosing her prospective husband, who is se-lected by the parents according to the custom of arranged marriage. After the bride price is agreed on, the marriage contract signed, and the wedding celebration held, the girl moves into her husband's household, ill-prepared for the tasks awaiting her—domestic, sex-ual, reproductive. As a result, many women experience marriage as a state of captivity and oppression harsher than the one they en-dured in their own homes. In the present volume, the protagonists' reactions to the institution of marriage range from acceptance, as reflected in "My Wedding Night" by Alifa Rifaat, to rejection, as shown in "Pharaoh Is Drowning Again" by Sakina Fuad, to rebel-lion, as depicted in "The Beginning" by Salwa Bakr.

A great significance is attached to virginity in traditional Arab society. The chastity of a girl represents not only her honor but that of her entire family. It is therefore imperative for a girl to pre-serve her virginity until her first marriage. Premarital sex is re-garded as a grievous offense, punishable by death. A bride who is found to be unchaste on her wedding night is the cause of a great scandal to her family. Her husband has the right to annul the mar-riage, and her male kin—father, brother, uncle—have the duty to avenge their honor by putting her to death. Public opinion permits honor killings and the courts treat them leniently. The issues of vir-ginity and crimes of honor are raised in "Questioning" by Fawziya Rashid.[17]

Another practice affecting the institution of marriage is poly-gamy, which emphasizes the inequality between the sexes: a man may take four wives, but a woman is allowed only one husband at a time. The stress, insecurity, and misery that polygamy inflicts on women are portrayed in "Sun, I Am the Moon" by Hanan al-Shaykh. In this story, the teenage, third wife of an ugly old man, unable to cope with her suffering, contemplates the murder of her abusive husband as the only way out of her predicament. While men who are dissatisfied with their wives can obtain divorce by the simple act of oral repudiation, women find that their right to divorce is severely limited. Moreover, child custody laws discriminate against them. The tribulations of getting a divorce or custody of the children are depicted in the stories "The Dreadful Sea" by Zuhur Wanisi, "Woman with a Story" by Mayy Ziyada, "The Persian Rug" by Hanan al-Shaykh, and "I Will Never Forfeit My Right" by Mona Ragab.

Despite the fact that the customs surrounding marriage place men in an advantageous position, they too suffer the consequences of the rigid social mores. In Alifa Rifaat's story "My Wedding Night," the groom, whose bride is as much a stranger to him as he is to her, is paralyzed with fear and confusion to the point that he is unable to consummate the marriage. In "The Dummy" by Sahar al-Muji, the husband—the authority figure in the household—is absent from the daily life of his family: he does not participate in any activity involving his wife and children. Taciturn and distant, he becomes increasingly isolated—the ultimate victim of his own position of power and privilege.

In part 5, the stories focus on the issue of childbearing. Traditionally regarded as the primary task of women in society and as the main purpose of marriage, childbearing has a great impact on a woman's life. For one thing, children provide a woman with a legitimate means of self-fulfillment. For another, children are the key to a woman's social standing, earning her respect in the family and the community. Across all sectors of Arab society, there is an overwhelming preference for boys. While the birth of a boy is greeted with joy and celebration, that of a girl is relatively ignored, or even met with a sense of disappointment. The desire for boys is so strong that a woman who bears only daughters is not much better off than a childless wife.[18]

In a culture in which a much-quoted dictum by the prophet Muhammad runs "Paradise lies at the feet of mothers," the position of an infertile woman is highly precarious. A husband whose wife is infertile has the right to divorce her or take an additional wife. According to popular belief—and in contrast to scientific evidence—the woman is the party responsible for a childless marriage as well as for the sex of the child. Hence the birth of a long line of daughters and the absence of sons are generally blamed on the woman. These attitudes are reflected in the story "Heir Apparent" by Ramziya Abbas al-Iryani. The psychological effects of the pressure on a woman to bear children are portrayed in "The Spider's Web" by Ihsan Kamal. "Half a Woman" by Sufi Abdallah shows that a woman's self-image is dependent on her children. The tragedy of infertility, which drives a woman into insanity, is depicted in shocking detail in Ghada al-Samman's story, "Another Scarecrow," published elsewhere.[19]

The vicious circle between large families and poverty is dramatized in "The Newcomer" by Daisy al-Amir. Told from the perspective of the eldest daughter who is burdened with the care of her siblings, the story highlights the perennial problem of overpopulation and lack of family planning in Arab society. That modern attitudes toward childbearing have begun to appear among Arab women is evident from Rafiqat al-Tabi'a's "Man and Woman," which tells of a wife who refuses to bring children into a world plagued by misery, poverty, and war.

In part 6, the stories address the issue of self-fulfillment. Arab women have traditionally occupied the private domain of the household. This domain afforded them limited roles, notably those of daughters, wives, and mothers. The opportunities for personal development and self-expression have expanded dramatically with the modernization of Arab society. The spread of free compulsory public education, as well as the economic necessity of contributing to the household income, has facilitated women's efforts to join the workforce and increased their participation in public life.

The new reality of women's presence in the workplace within the urban environment has created internal and external conflicts. On the personal level, women are torn between the desire to raise a family and the ambition to develop a career. On the interpersonal level, women find themselves at odds with authority figures within the family, usually husbands, who adhere to the traditions of the past, asserting that a woman's place is in the home. The tragic consequences of a failure to reconcile such differing expectations are depicted in "I Will Never Forfeit My Right" by Mona Ragab. In this story, a wife who chooses to work outside the home is divorced by her husband, who gets custody of their child. The woman's desperate efforts to appeal for justice in a court of law fall on deaf ears. In Layla Ba'labakki's story "The Filly Became a Mouse," the wife insists on her right to fulfill herself in her dancing profession. Her husband's lack of sympathy and cooperation drives her to take her little daughter and run away.

The search for self-fulfillment yields various results and solutions. In "The Closely Guarded Secret" by Sahar al-Muji, the heroine's thirst for knowledge is irrepressible. Despite oppressive conditions, she finds spiritual nourishment in reading a book, which she guards with her life. In Salwa Bakr's "International Women's Day," the protagonist juggles the demands of her family with a career as a school headmistress. Her life, though hectic, is full and rich in content. By contrast, in Umayma al-Khamis's "Waiting for Hayla," the boredom and emptiness of a life of leisure of women from the upper classes lead to apathy and depression. The characters' narrow existence centers around social gatherings, dinners, and gossip, all of which dulls their minds and personalities. That the external trappings of success do not necessarily bring emotional satisfaction and psychological equilibrium is depicted in Umayma al-Khamis's "Restoration." In this ultrashort text, the heroine's loss of her sense of self brings her to the verge of a mental breakdown.

In certain instances, particularly a francophone environment, women attempt to achieve self-fulfillment outside their culture. In Fadila al-Faruq's "Homecoming," the protagonist escapes the social limitations imposed on her gender in Algeria by emigrating to France. After a long stay, she is overcome by nostalgia for the haven of her childhood, and embarks on a journey back home. As soon as she arrives in her country, she is disillusioned by the gloomy reality of poverty, overcrowding, and discontent. The story shows her increasing isolation and alienation: she does not feel at home in France, and she is rejected by her own family members, who believe that she has acquired a different mentality and thus is unlikely to fit in.

The culture shock awaiting an Arab woman who returns to her homeland after a stay in the West figures prominently in Zabya Khamis's "Bittersweet Memories." In this story, the protagonist travels to Europe to pursue higher education. The forms of freedom that she enjoys there enable her to engage in adventurous and revolutionary activities unthinkable in her own country. Her journey of self-fulfillment ends abruptly when she returns to her country and is confronted by the authoritarian customs officers at the airport. At that moment, she realizes that the assets she has gained in the West are a liability in her conservative Arab state.

In part 7, the stories highlight the impact of custom and tradition on the lives of women. Arab culture abounds with time-honored customs and traditions, which serve as a source of communal attitudes and as criteria of individual and group conduct. While all members of society are bound by the rules of custom and tradition, it is the women who are affected the most. Veiling, seclusion, social segregation, circumcision, and crimes of honor are determined by local custom. Patterns of marriage, divorce, childbearing, and child rearing are rooted in custom. Popular attitudes toward women's education and work outside the home are based on custom. Custom dictates a woman's behavior at every phase of her life, from the cradle to the grave. Hence the forces of custom and tradition constitute the most difficult barriers for women to overcome.

The issues of virginity and crimes of honor are raised in the story "Questioning" by Fawziya Rashid. The sharp contrast between the sexual mores of the East and those of the West, especially as they relate to women, is depicted in the stories "The Dinosaur" by Emily Nasrallah and "Moonstruck" by Hadiya Sa'id. "Misfortune in the Alley" by Ramziya Abbas al-Iryani tells of the disappearance of a young village girl from her father's home, highlighting the grave threat that this incident poses both to his honor and to her life. The patriarchal values of Arab society, which underlie the moral and sexual codes, are denounced in Suhayr al-Tall's surrealistic story "The Gallows." In Khayriya al-Saqqaf's symbolic story, "A Moment of Truth," time, represented by a clock on the wall, and history, represented by a book in the hands of a rigid old man, are frozen in the oppressive presence of this authority figure, who, speechless and motionless, signifies the static values of traditional Arab society. The scene, which is marked by stagnation and death, illustrates the fundamental principle that life cannot be preserved without movement and change.

Civil war destroys the fabric of society, plunging it into chaos and anarchy, with tragic loss of innocent lives and great human suffering. Daisy al-Amir's story, "The Future," is set in the Lebanese Civil War of 1975–1990. The narrative depicts a woman's daily confrontation with the horror of explosions, shootings, killings, looting, and arbitrary death in a senseless, and seemingly endless, war fought by men. In an effort to transcend the devastation around her, the heroine buys a new spring dress. The dress symbolizes the future and her yearning for peace and normality.

The role of women in preserving traditional rites is dramatized in "Tears for Sale" by Samira Azzam. In this story, a village woman functions both as a mourner for the dead and as a beautician for brides. That the same woman performs both—opposite—rites, serves to highlight the pivotal position of women in the cycle of birth, life, and death.

In part 8, the stories focus on the improvement in the status and lifestyle of Arab women. The rapid social transformation taking place throughout the Arab world is reflected in the background of almost every story in this volume. Many of the female characters in these narratives drive cars, wear modern clothes, walk unaccompanied in the streets, travel by themselves to foreign countries, and live abroad for prolonged periods of time; they also raise families, study, work, run businesses, and engage in diverse activities no different from those of women in the West. Admittedly, the level of modernity varies from one Arab country to another. Saudi Arabia, for example, is a stronghold of conservative Arab-Muslim values, whereas Egypt is more liberal and affords women a greater degree of freedom and more access to means of personal advancement. The situation further varies within the same Arab country from region to region—urban, rural, nomadic. Nevertheless, the winds of change are blowing across the Arab lands. The impact of television, of the technological and communication revolution, and of the process of globalization, transcends linguistic and geographic boundaries, making inroads into all areas of life in Arab society.

That traditional norms and attitudes are giving way to modern ideas and values is evident from the stories "The Breeze of Youth" by Ulfat al-Idilbi and "In Need of Reassurance" by Radwa Ashour. Both stories depict a conflict between the old and young generations: in al-Idilbi's story, a grandmother clashes with her granddaughter in a middle-class urban family; in Ashour's story, a grandfather clashes with his granddaughter in a lower-class rural family. The changes emerging in the patterns of women's lives over three generations are dramatic: the granddaughters are neither cloistered nor illiterate; rather, they are free and educated; they study at the university, and map out their own futures. It is interesting to note that both the grandmother and the grandfather have a hard time adjusting themselves to the new realities, even though they recognize the benefits of these advances for their granddaughters.

Male-female relations are also changing. In Salwa Bakr's story "The Beginning," the protagonist, a married woman who works outside the home, is outraged by her husband's selfish attitude and tyrannical conduct. She gives him a piece of her mind—and a taste of her fist—and walks out on him fearlessly and resolutely. "A Successful

Woman" by Suhayr al-Qalamawi demonstrates that a woman does not need the protection of a husband or a male relative to survive—she can make it on her own. In Samiya At'ut's story "The Collapse of Barriers," the heroine is trapped in an elevator with a male operator, a situation that temporarily removes the barriers between them. As soon as the elevator begins to move again, she regains her composure and reasserts her position of master, rather than servant, vis-à-vis the elevator operator. In "A Moment of Contemplation" by Nuzha Bin Sulayman, a marital dispute between the protagonist, who suffers from the strain of juggling a job and a family, and her husband ends on a note of conciliation, friendship, and affection.

The burst of literary activity by women in contemporary Arab society is mirrored in "I Will Try Tomorrow" by Mona Ragab. In this story, the protagonist is a writer and the mother of two small children. She knows how precious the moments of inspiration are and how delicate the creative process is, yet she dutifully attends to all her tasks and tries to balance the various demands on her time with patience and a sense of humor.

While there is a marked increase in Arab women's participation in public life, and a growing level of awareness on their part, both collective and individual, the process of liberation is not complete. In their struggle for freedom and equality, Arab women writers at times encounter hostility and resistance and at other times solidarity and support. The depth of their vision is reflected in the fact that they perceive the liberation of their gender as inseparable from the re-birth of Arab society in general and the Arab man in particular.

Modes of Writing

The question of whether Arab women authors write differently from their male counterparts has stimulated a great deal of critical discourse. Some critics argue that the elements of imaginative literature do not differ from gender to gender. What differs is the concerns of each gender, resulting from their specific experiences and impressions of life and society. Hence one should not look for a distinct type of literature with particular qualities in women's writings, although one should acknowledge that women have different interests owing to their different social and psychological circumstances.[20]

A rather opposing view is expressed by Yusuf Idris (1927–91), one of the most influential modern writers in Egypt and throughout the Arab world. In an article on women writers in the Arabian Peninsula, he offers the following impressions:

> Over the last few years, collections of short stories have started reaching me from Saudi Arabia and the Arab Gulf States. It is true that most of them are by male writers, but a good number are by female writers. This is really amazing: the Arab woman in Saudi Arabia and the Arab Gulf States is almost secluded from public life. Many women there work as physicians, teachers, and bank employees (there are special banks for women), but their existence as an independent entity, and as a political or social force, is almost completely on the periphery of public life.
>
> Yet the Arab woman there is a live being, educated, well-informed, and moved by all the desires and aspirations of the human soul. However, her desires and aspirations have a very low ceiling which she is not allowed to break through. Because of this, she channels her energies into writing. She finds an outlet in it, and speaks through it. Her writing may take the form of either poetry or prose, but the short story takes up the largest share.
>
> One day not very long ago I applied myself to reading these collections of women's stories, poring over them not like a casual reader but like an expert who knows, or claims to know, the oppressive force which brings the word out from the depths of the soul and onto the page.
>
> And after I had finished reading a number of collections, I discovered that I was not reading short stories in the accepted sense of the word *story*, or even in the modern sense; I was reading something different, or a different kind of writing, which is not a story and not a poem, not a tale and not scattered thoughts. It is a new and strange kind of writing that the Arab woman who remains distant from the course of events has invented in order to do with it something that will affirm to her that she is a live being, indeed a person who possesses the power of action and reaction. It is a literary action arising under an overpowering feverish pressure that interferes with the creative process to the extent that the writing appears like a puzzle to the reader. She wants to say something and yet she does not want to say it. She wants to express something, and at the same time she does not want anyone to grasp her expression—I might almost say her secret.
>
> And thus I found myself giving a name to this kind of writing by female writers from Saudi Arabia and the Arab Gulf States: *the short story from behind a veil*.[21]

Idris illustrates his conclusion with the story "Scheherazade's Nights" by the Saudi writer Ruqayya al-Shabeeb. Written in a symbolic style, this enigmatic narrative is heavily laced with images from Arab heritage and plays on multiple associations and connotations in the reader's mind.[22]

It is interesting to note that the ever watchful eye of the censor does not prevent Arab women writers from expressing their thoughts, but rather affects the clarity and simplicity of their literary works. In fact, the need to escape the censor and still make sure that their voices are heard stimulates them to explore new forms of expression and presentation.

In many of the stories in this volume, the narrative voice is a woman's voice, often using the first-person form of narration. While this technique lends the stories a quality of eyewitness accounting, it also presents a peculiar problem to Arab women writers: critics, as well as readers, assume that the first-person pronoun refers not to the character in the story but to the author. Hence they tend to regard women's fictional works as self-revelations.[23] The assumption that the narrator and the author are one and the same and that she is necessarily talking about some personal experience can have serious consequences for the author's social standing, especially when the narrative deals with sensitive matters. A case in point is the Egyptian Nura Amin, who is included in this anthology. Her stories about lesbian love affairs damaged her standing in her family and her community.

One of the ways in which Arab women writers avoid the problem associated with the first-person narrator is the use of gender ambiguity in the narrative voice.[24] "The Gallows," by Suhayr al-Tall, illustrates this strategy. In this text, a first-person narrator tells his/her story to a silent protagonist. The first-person pronoun is used sparingly—only three times—and the protagonist is continually addressed as "you." While several adjectives and verb endings clearly indicate that the protagonist is a man, the gender of the narrator remains ambiguous. Throughout the story, the narrator's comments and observations continue to tease the reader concerning the narrative voice, but provide no clue as to its identity. In view of the daring social criticism that the story conveys, it is quite plausible that the writer deliberately set out to mask the identity of the narrative voice. Nevertheless, the writer did not escape the wrath of the authorities, who prosecuted her for offending public sensibilities.

The fact that a legal case was brought against al-Tall merits a brief analysis of the story. The narrative depicts a city in which a dark, gelatinous mass flows rapidly through the streets, causing fear and confusion. The protagonist is carried away by the flow, which takes him to the city square: a place where the city is divided into two feuding parts, and where an elaborate ceremony is in progress. There the protagonist's feet are shackled with a steel chain, and blood-red saliva begins to gush out of his mouth and cover his face, blurring his sight. Slowly, he is led toward a big gallows in the middle of the square, to which he surrenders his body. The noose that tightens around his neck is a gigantic phallus.

On the surface, the story appears to be a surrealistic depiction of the evil nature of human society. While the particular reference to the male sex organ may well be regarded as offensive by conservative readers, it cannot explain the extreme reaction of the authorities to the story. A closer look at the text suggests that it is a feminist account of the patriarchal system. The protagonist represents the male gender, which is unfavorably portrayed as a monstrous creature engaged in bloodshed and destruction. The gallows, an instrument of oppression, is also a phallic symbol. The male gender, whose control over society is achieved through the gallows, is both a victimizer and a victim. The dark mass that flows through the streets and pours into the city square signifies a large and excited crowd. The city square serves as the setting for the action because it is the place where all individual desires merge into one unanimous will; namely, it is the arena of custom and convention. The public execution resembles a sexual rite that culminates in self-annihilation. The absence of women and children from the narrative suggests that their existence is obliterated by the patriarchal system. It is not surprising that a story that attacks the core values of Arab society should lead to the prosecution of the writer by the authorities.

An innovative narrative strategy is also employed by Fawziya Rashid in "Questioning." In this instance, the story unfolds through the consciousness of the protagonist, who recalls a crime of honor committed against his sister when he was still a little boy. Throughout the text, it is the inner self or an inner voice that speaks to the protagonist in the second-person pronoun. The reader is privy to the protagonist's self-reflections, childhood memories, and nagging questions about his sister's tragic fate. The poignant story expresses strong criticism of the patriarchal values of Arab society, especially its preoccupation with virginity, its practice of double standards of morality, and its blind adherence to brutal, ancient customs, all of which are denounced through a male narrative voice.

Other techniques of narrative voice include the use of a first-person *male* narrator/protagonist, as in "The Collapse of Barriers" by Samiya At'ut, or an omniscient third-person narrator and a male protagonist, as in "The Dream" by Aliya Mamdouh. Yet another technique consists of a combination of a third-person narrator and a form of interior monologue, especially when the inner self or individual consciousness is depicted, as in "An Old Couple" by Nadiya Khust and "A Moment of Truth" by Khayriya al-Saqqaf. Despite such creative alternatives, a *female* narrator/protagonist remains the most common narrative voice.

Perhaps the most striking feature of the stories in this volume is the predominance of female characters who also figure as the heroines. By contrast, there are few heroes, and most of the male characters are either marginalized or presented in a negative light. This tendency is most conspicuous in "The Dummy" by Sahar al-Muji and "The Beginning" by Salwa Bakr. Herein lies a dramatic reversal of roles: in the fictional worlds of the stories, it is the women who occupy center stage, whereas the men are relegated to the periphery.

There are various types of stories in this volume. Some stories are mainly about situations and states of being; others are distinguished by an adherence to action and events; and still others display a more static form wherein atmosphere is the author's primary focus. While many of the stories exhibit a traditional narrative approach, a significant number are innovative and experimental. The authors' modes of presentation vary according to their visions and attitudes, as well as the theme and degree of censorship. Frequently, they use direct, concrete language and rely on detail to enhance the realism of their work. They also combine evocative language with symbolism to get their message across. Surrealism and the absurd are employed particularly in stories of biting social and political criticism. Occasionally, classical Arabic blends with the colloquial variety, creating the effect of spontaneity and liveliness, but usually the vernacular is limited to dialogue. On the whole, the stories reveal keen powers of observation and extraordinary boldness and outspokenness.

Arab women writers continue to hone their craft and experiment with new modes of expression and narration. That their creative efforts yield works of literary excellence is illustrated by

Salwa Bakr's "International Women's Day," which is one of the most accomplished stories in this volume. Among the various devices that Bakr skillfully employs in this story is intertextuality: there are allusions to great Arab women of the past (e.g., the poet al-Khansa and the scout Zarqa al-Yamama), a quotation of a well-known verse by the modern Egyptian poet Hafiz Ibrahim, and a recitation of a famous tradition attributed to the prophet Muhammad. In addition, the narrative is laced with colloquial phrases that dramatize the characters' thought patterns. Bakr's style is rich in irony, which draws attention to the discrepancy between the apperance of a situation and the reality that underlies it, or between what is said and what is thought. Her tone, though humorous, is serious, and both the man (i.e., the teacher) and the woman (i.e., the headmistress) are the butts of her criticism.

Several other stories merit brief mention. "A Virgin Continent," by Samira Azzam, is notable for its dialogue form, which produces the effect of directness and immediacy. Sharifa al-Shamlan's "Fragments from a Life" makes use of a sequence of subtitles to capture the fragmented reality and disintegrating personality of the heroine. Colette Suhayl al-Khuri's poetic prose "Where To?" dramatizes the theme of love through parallel dialogues between two stars in the sky and a young couple on the seashore. Insofar as ending devices are concerned, the more traditional stories provide a closure to the narratives of their protagonists, whereas the more innovative stories tend to remain open-ended. In some instances, such as Umayma al-Khamis's "Restoration" and Samiya At'ut's "Mozart's Fez," the story ends with a return to the beginning, thus assuming a circular pattern.

In isolating certain thematic aspects and modes of writing, I have neither discussed all the stories in this volume nor exhausted these topics. Rather, I have merely considered some fascinating facets in the fiction of Arab women writers. Needless to say, the contribution of these writers to modern Arabic literature continues to grow in volume, content, and form.

Arab Women: Old Images, New Profiles

In his provocative books, *The Liberation of Women* (1899) and *The New Woman* (1900), the Egyptian lawyer Qasim Amin (1863–1908) laid the foundation of feminism in Egypt by connecting the issue of national progress with the emancipation of women. In discussing the rapid development of the Western woman following the radical changes in her status, he writes:

> [The Western woman] was replaced by a new woman who was a sister to man, a companion to her husband, a tutor to her children—a refined individual.
>
> This transformation is all we intend. We hope the Egyptian woman achieves this high status through the appropriate avenues open to her, and that she will acquire her share of intellectual and moral development, happiness, and authority in her household. We are convinced that if this goal were achieved, it would prove to be the most significant development in Egypt's history.[25]

A century later, Amin's aspiration, boldly articulated and defended, is no longer a fanciful idea. Arab women have made great strides in freeing themselves from the bondage of illiteracy and seclusion, and have entered more productively into national life. While the liberation of women has not yet been fully attained, and many issues remain unresolved, major advances are clearly evident.

The stories presented in this volume reveal that the Arab woman is changing both in her role and in her self-perception. Allowed to study, work, and travel, the Arab woman has gained more access to power and more control over her life. No longer valid is the image of the Arab woman as silent, passive, and submissive. The contemporary Arab woman is outspoken, active, and assertive. She may be a salesclerk, as in "Homecoming" by Fadila al-Faruq; a hairdresser, as in "A Successful Woman" by Suhayr al-Qalamawi; a teacher, as in "The Woman of My Dreams" by Fadila al-Faruq; a headmistress, as in "International Women's Day" by Salwa Bakr; a professional woman, as in "The Dinosaur" by Emily Nasrallah; a ballet dancer, as in "The Filly Became a Mouse" by Layla Ba'labakki; or a creative writer, as in "I Will Try Tomorrow" by Mona Ragab. Whatever job she holds, the Arab woman has developed a new image for herself and conspicuous individuality. Admittedly, the traditional roles assigned to women still persist in great measure in Arab society, but at the same time, old barriers have been removed and social frontiers expanded.

The new status of Arab women is varied and complex. Some

areas of their lives, notably education and employment, show a marked improvement; others, especially the laws regulating marriage, divorce, child custody, and inheritance, still await reform. Moreover, certain segments of Arab society, such as peasant, village, and bedouin women, have not benefited equally from the process of modernization, which has mainly affected the urban population. Nevertheless, even in rural and remote areas women's self-awareness has increased, as illustrated by "The Closely Guarded Secret" of Sahar al-Muji. In this ultrashort text, the heroine's thirst for knowledge leads her to risk her safety by hiding a book from her family and reading it in secret. A heightened level of consciousness is also depicted in "The Dreadful Sea" by Zuhur Wanisi. The story recounts the tragedy of a young village woman who is abandoned by her husband after he travels overseas to work and marries a foreign woman. Despite her apparent compliance, there is constant questioning in the heroine's mind that someday might be translated into concrete actions. Significantly, women, especially educated ones who have succeeded in shaping their own futures, serve as role models for other women, and thus become instruments of social change.

As more Arab women pursue higher education and join the workforce, they inevitably have to grapple with new problems, social, moral, and emotional. Throughout the stories, the reader can sense concern, fear, hope, anxiety, optimism, disappointment, and criticism. The heroines try to combine the old with the new, adopt and adapt, and draw on their own resources to improve their lives. In some instances, they choose to break up their dysfunctional marriages, as happens in "The Beginning" by Salwa Bakr; in other instances, they reconcile with their husbands, as in "A Moment of Contemplation" by Nuzha Bin Sulayman. Whatever the solution, the myth of the Arab woman as totally dependent on—and subservient to—the Arab man is shattered.

The changing profiles of women in Arab society are portrayed in many different ways. In "A Successful Woman" by Suhayr al-Qalamawi, the heroine is a simple village girl who migrates to the city of Cairo, where she earns her living as a hairdresser. Twice disappointed in finding a husband—her employer, with whom she fell in love, marries a wealthy customer, and her cousin in the village marries another woman—she decides to be mistress of herself and her destiny. She works hard and opens her own hairdressing salon, which develops into a thriving business. As the years pass, she transforms from a gentle, sentimental girl into a tough, hard-nosed businesswoman. Planning ahead, she saves money for her retirement, having remained unmarried and childless, and thus without the prospect of family support. While showing the sacrifices that the heroine had to make, the story demonstrates that a single woman can take care of herself and achieve a sense of well-being. The heroine sets her goal, pursues it with great determination, and shapes her own future. Her success is a triumph for the Arab woman, who emerges as an independent, competitive, and enterprising individual.

In Salwa Bakr's "International Women's Day," the heroine is the headmistress of a public school at which she supervises the work of a male teacher. This situation entails a dramatic reversal of roles: the boss is a woman, and the subordinate a man. In this story, the issue of gender relations figures on several levels: the personal, the social, and the professional. Does the woman rise to the challenge? Judging by Bakr's critical tone, she has serious reservations about the measure of her success. For one thing, instead of paying attention to the lesson that the teacher gives his class, the headmistress is preoccupied with private matters, specifically a request for transfer to a school closer to her home so that she can spare herself the difficulties of public transportation. For another, when the teacher slaps a female student for using vulgar expressions—after letting a male student get away with the same offense—the headmistress does not rebuke the teacher or remind him that hitting is prohibited by law. As for the teacher, outwardly he shows respect and courtesy toward his female superior, but inwardly he is furious and resentful. In addition, he is obsessed with the thought of disciplining his wife and bending her to his will. He teaches his class about the equality of women, and then proceeds to discriminate against a female student openly and harshly. The fact that the story is set against the background of International Women's Day adds to the irony of the situation. What happens in the classroom—instances of displaced aggression, hypocrisy, and double standards of morality—mocks the idea of International Women's Day and contradicts the very spirit of it. Bakr's message seems to be that despite some improvement in the condition of women, basic attitudes have remained the same. There is no significant departure from traditional thought and behavioral patterns, which emphasize conformity, respect for authority, and adherence to custom and convention. As noted earlier, both the man and the woman are targets for the author's criticism.

Ulfat al-Idilbi's story "The Breeze of Youth" dramatizes the emergence of the modern Arab woman by contrasting the lives of two women in one family: the grandmother and her granddaughter. The progress depicted over three generations is remarkable. While the grandmother grew up veiled and cloistered, deprived of personal freedom and of the pleasures of reading and writing, the granddaughter is a university student, free to come and go as she pleases, mingle with boys, smoke, apply makeup, and wear fashionable clothes. The grandmother received her upbringing in a traditional household headed by a strict and conservative father who married her off at a young age to an old man. By contrast, the granddaughter receives her upbringing in a modern household headed by a lenient and progressive father—her grandmother's son from her short-lived marriage. In this story, the grandmother represents the past and the oppression of women, whereas the granddaughter represents the future and the liberation of women. It is significant that for both women, the father—the male—plays the key role in obstructing, or alternatively facilitating, their development.

The preceding examples illustrate that Arab women are shaping their destinies and redefining their relationships with family members and traditional social institutions. Most often, they seek solutions in their own culture and traditions rather than in Western ones. In the quest for authentic selfhood, they attempt to balance the major elements comprising their identities: gender, family, nation, religion. They see themselves as women, daughters, wives, mothers, Arabs, and Muslims (or Christians), but also as individuals—beings in their own right, with vital needs for self-expression and self-fulfillment.

In conclusion, the short stories of Arab women writers presented in this volume display a variety of themes, styles, and techniques. Whatever the approach, these women writers demonstrate that they are responding creatively and vigorously to existential dilemmas related to their gender and to challenges arising from rapid social change. They interpret their personal experiences insightfully and offer authentic accounts of the realities of their lives. The resonance of their literary voices transcends the dominant male fabric of their culture and conveys an aspiration to achieve recognition as valuable members of society, endowed with their own distinctive talents.

Part One

❦❦❦❦❦

Growing Up Female

That Summer Holiday

Samiya At'ut

❧❦❧

When she played with the neighbors' children in their old, narrow alley, it was as an important member of the group. Her pride in belonging was such that she boasted of it continually to her schoolmates. Her association with the group was not limited to playing marbles, seven stones, and soccer, nor to sharing innocent intimacies. She even participated with them in a war game, which was her favorite. It required fast running and muscular strength, as well as ferocity and rowdy behavior.

One day she came home from school happy because the summer holiday was about to begin. Her routine was the same at the end of each year: she removed her school uniform and put on a floral shirt and white shorts. Her slender body looked beautiful, well proportioned, and full of vitality, as would that of any healthy nine-year-old girl. She and her brothers prepared to go out to play. Her younger brother brought the stones that he had collected previously, her older brother fetched the sticks and slingshots, and then they all went down to the alley to play war.

They hardly noticed the time, which passed quickly as they ran excitedly between the alleys and the lanes, until evening, when their mother sent their little sister out to call them back.

They returned home exhausted and covered in dust. They entered noisily, full of good cheer and joy, despite their disheveled hair and dirty faces, limbs, and clothes. Their father was seated in the hall, which was unusual. He was silent, his head bowed, as if sunk in deep thought. They washed up and ate supper. As soon as her brothers had vanished into the bedrooms, her mother summoned her to the hall, whereupon her father rose and went into the kitchen.

"How was your game today?" her mother asked amicably.

"We enjoyed it very much, and we won. Fathi collided and bled from the head, and Samir threw me to the ground, but I didn't care. Tomorrow we have a final soccer match. We want to finish the game," she replied enthusiastically.

"Good, good," the mother said, in an attempt to silence her. Then she continued in a quiet and serious tone. "Today Abu Mahmud the grocer and Fahmi the greengrocer spoke with your father."

"What did they want?"

"They told him that you've grown and that . . ."

The mother fell silent for a moment, so the daughter asked, "And that what?"

"That your breasts have developed prominently. They were upset to see you wearing shorts and running in the streets with the children."

"What?"

"Dalal, from now on, you are absolutely not to go out into the street. That's what your father said. Also, from now on, you are forbidden to wear shorts. You can give these clothes to your brothers."

Thunderstruck, Dalal tried to protest. "But Mother, I like to play, and I like to wear shorts. What's the connection . . ."

The mother interrupted her resolutely: "The discussion is over. I don't want to hear another word." And she left the room.

Dalal stood for a moment as if rooted to the spot. She dragged herself to the bathroom and locked the door. She sat on the floor and seemed unable to think. Suddenly she got up, lifted her shirt, and looked at herself in the mirror. Running her hands over her chest, her fingers felt two small round buds sprouting, almost escaping, from her body. She remembered that Abu Mahmud had tried to touch them during the previous week. Unable to control her feelings, she covered herself with her shirt and burst into hot tears.

The Parting Gift

Umayma al-Khamis

❦

The swift winter winds had brought some gray clouds to the sky, but the morning sun was calm and tender, while the air was saturated with the smell of imminent rain.

The schoolyard was filled with young, blossoming girls, whose movements in their school uniforms were lively and nimble, as if they were preparing for a vigorous dance. The shoes were black and smooth, and remained firmly on the ground. The Muslim calendar by the headmistress's office stated that it was the year 1411 following the Prophet's emigration from Mecca to Medina.

The girls formed scattered circles. Some of them used their free time to chat; others were busy with schoolbooks. There were quick footsteps, voices that had outgrown youthful frivolity and had assumed a slow feminine rhythm. The whispers rose higher and higher to become large circles of laughter filling the schoolyard. The footsteps met, parted, and then assembled at the crowded school cafeteria. Many hands with riyals rose in the air to buy cans of Pepsi and tins of potato chips.

Al-Jazi's thick black hair was arranged in a knot at the back of her head. Her slender and delicate figure often provoked whispered comments when she walked past a group of friends. She slipped her hand into the bottom of her schoolbag, expecting to grasp the five-hundred-riyal note. She pushed her hand deeper. Nothing. Trembling, she checked her pockets, emptied her schoolbag, and then turned it upside down. She even searched between the pages of her books. Still nothing. She hastened to collect the contents of her schoolbag, after eyes had begun to notice her confusion. Munira approached her quietly, and she rushed toward her, reporting that the five-hundred-riyal note had vanished.

"Did you search well?"

"I turned the schoolbag inside out."

"Check your pockets and your bra."

"Nothing."

Munira was chewing calmly and occasionally sipping her Pepsi, with which she washed down the food stuffed in her mouth.

"Check again, and be quick. The break has ended, and the fourth class is about to begin."

They walked around the schoolyard, searching the ground and scrutinizing every piece of paper. The girls' voices had filled the school with a confused background noise of rarely intelligible words. The stairs were packed with girls climbing up to the classrooms on the second floor. Before long the voices subsided, and the schoolyard began to empty. There was no sound except for the recess teacher's whistle, which startled those still chatting in the corners. Then the cleaning staff spread throughout the schoolyard, picking up bits of paper and empty cans.

Al-Jazi stood by the door of the counselor's office. School activity seemed remote and vague today. She had remained sleepless throughout the previous night, and when she had dozed off at dawn, she had felt as if she had arrived from a distant world or had circled the globe that night. In the morning, she had gone to school.

The day before, as he had approached her by the outer wall of her house, he had looked so handsome that she felt an ache of desire for him. She had leaned against the wall, trying to push him away with her hand, which was weak from tension. His features became blurred in her mind. She remembered only his brown, high cheekbones and his headdress. Her memory transformed into small, colorful scraps of paper floating in a crystal bowl of water. Each scrap evoked in her a particular sight, shade, taste, and smell. But since morning she had been unable to piece together the entire scene. That wall with flaking paint ended in a small back door to the left side of which was an animal pen containing pigeons, hens, a rooster, three goats, and a billy goat. The rooster had climbed to the top of a wooden post and closed its eyes, while its neck had sunk into its feathers. She watched it attentively, hoping that it would not call, and it seemed as if the rooster reluctantly kept quiet for her. The only light came from a distant street lamp, casting a pale gray shadow over everything. She put down the froth-filled milk bowl, after she had finished milking the goats, and opened the door a crack. Through the narrow opening, the streetlight looked like a thin, white thread.

His pickup truck was carefully parked by the opposite wall. He crossed the narrow street, carrying a package in his hands. He tried to walk at a steady pace, but his steps seemed cautious and anxious. She opened the door slightly, and he slipped in quickly. She became confused, and her heart beat wildly. What should she say? Should she talk to him or embrace him passionately? Frightened, bewildered, and ashamed, she suddenly asked him to leave. She thought that was the most appropriate thing to do.

He drew close to her. How alluring and handsome he was, with his body drenched in perspiration from fear! He gave her the package and put his arms around her waist. He told her that she was his joy in life and that he had found a job. Suddenly, without speaking, she felt that she was his wife and that he was returning home tired from work. He embraced her and kissed her on her lips and neck. She fell silent, dazed, and offered little resistance. She was awakened by the voices of the muezzins calling for the evening prayer from the neighborhood mosques. One of the voices sounded loud and angry, another old, and the nearest was vibrant and youthful.

She held the milk bowl in her hands and shoved the package under the stairs. She turned on the stove and boiled the milk. Her paternal half-sister asked her why she looked so somber. She replied softly that the billy goat had committed a shameful act before her eyes.

At night, when a television commercial announced that Camay soap would make a woman's complexion as fresh and radiant as the morning dew, she crept quietly under the stairs and opened the package. In it she found several pieces of fabric and a five-hundred-riyal note. She hugged the pieces of fabric, wondering which one she would bring to the tailor and wear the next time.

She spread out her mattress on the floor by the window. The room was crammed with her sisters' bodies. The lights of Riyadh were distant, shining, scattered. The television tower flashed as if it were the red eye of some fearsome beast. At that moment, she tried to think of where he might be. She contemplated those tiny spots of light and imagined that his sweet breath rose high above the city and formed that misty golden cloud which she could see from afar.

She was slightly alarmed by the sound of stealthy footsteps on the roof. Before long she guessed that it was her unmarried uncle sneaking into the room belonging to the Indonesian maid. She had spent the rest of the night trying to reconcile the incongruity between his large body and the petite frame of the maid.

Al-Jazi waited for the counselor to complete some paperwork before entering her office. She contemplated the palms of her hands while waiting. Suddenly she felt warmth coursing through her body when she remembered how, the day before, the atmosphere had become intimate and affectionate when he had kissed her hands, and their conversation had flowed rapidly, tensely, and breathlessly, like the steps of a startled partridge.

The counselor noticed al-Jazi's shadow by the door and asked her why she was standing there.

Al-Jazi entered, confused. The counselor took a pen from above her desk and began to play with it. Between the girl's disjointed words, she inquired, "Why did you bring the five-hundred-riyal note with you?"

"My mother put it in my schoolbag."

The counselor took a sheet of paper from above her desk, gazing at al-Jazi from behind her big, dark-colored glasses. Al-Jazi felt that the counselor was trying to establish eye contact with her. In a low voice, resembling a murmur, the counselor asked her for her home phone number.

A terrible noise rang in al-Jazi's ears. She felt suddenly on slippery ground, trying to hang onto something, find an escape, any plausible excuse. But the counselor sensed that she had discovered something important enough to break the monotony of the school day and the tiresome rhythm of the class bell.

"My mother might be taking my little brother to the clinic today."

The counselor gave her a suspicious look, got to her feet, and went to the telephone. Al-Jazi felt a burning heat, as if there were a hot iron on the soles of her feet. She remembered the girl who had fled with the truck driver and had brought shame on her entire family, and Nura, who had suddenly vanished after a long journey to the countryside, and the secret gossip that had floated around, arousing both curiosity and fear. At that moment, when she thought of him, he was a weak, pale entity. He would be of no help to her. She imagined him driving his pickup truck and fleeing from their street, leaving her and a cloud of dust behind. She jumped with fear and screamed, "Don't call anyone. I'll try to find the money."

The counselor responded to her scream with increasingly animated movements. She pushed up her glasses, which had slipped to the tip of her nose, and left the office quickly.

Desperate thoughts ran through al-Jazi's mind: Where can I go? Shall I hide behind the school? Run to my uncle's house? Where? O God, I will devote myself to prayer. I will fast the remaining days that I owe from Ramadan. I will even fast another month. I will join the religious class. But would she give him up? She hid him quickly in the innermost recesses of her heart, as if she wanted God not to find him.

When the counselor returned, al-Jazi was pallid and trembling.

"Where did you get the five-hundred-riyal note? Your mother is on her way to the school now," the counselor said.

Al-Jazi was seized with a new wave of fear. She wondered whether fate had forsaken her.

"My brother gave it to me."

"Is he really your brother?"

"No. He's my brother in suckling. He's the son of my maternal uncle."

"Are you prepared to sign such a statement?"

If only the gas pipe would explode in the staff room so that everything would come to an end. . . . If only the water reservoir on the school roof would burst and the water would gush out in a flood, dissolving everything, even the counselor's black glasses. . . .

When her mother arrived, the veil covering her face was billowing with muffled, angry words. She was a stout, firmly built woman, whose body showed no signs of having borne children. When she saw al-Jazi sitting with bowed head on one of the chairs, she rushed at her furiously, her long cloak ballooning behind her. The counselor intervened between them with an elegant and nimble gesture.

The mother kept staring at her daughter with swollen eyes that had old traces of kohl. At that moment, it didn't seem that she remembered her daughter as a red lump of flesh that she had nursed, or as a little girl whose fine hair made only a small braid.

The counselor rushed to shut the door on the inquisitive students, while the mother pulled al-Jazi by the hair and shook her head violently. Al-Jazi thought of him at that moment and felt that she was despicable and lowly, and that she had lost the coquettish glamour that made her act arrogantly when she saw him.

Suddenly, as if the constant shaking of her head had stirred up her memory, she remembered her sister who lived in one of the villages in the north. Should she involve her? The image of her sister's shriveled and emaciated figure flashed across her mind. Would a third wife, and not the favorite one at that, be so lavish with her gifts for her family members? Nevertheless, she uttered her name mechanically and vaguely.

Her mother calmed down a little. The sister's name seemed to allay her fears and restore her sense of safety.

One of the staff fetched al-Jazi's schoolbag from the classroom on the top floor. Al-Jazi put on her cloak and walked slowly with bowed head behind her mother. With downcast eyes, she gazed at her mother's cloak gathering threads, dust, and bits of paper as she walked quickly ahead.

In the main street leading to their house, they passed the Pakistani tailor's shop. Al-Jazi feared that he might call out to her. She noticed that her dresses were ready and hanging in the shop window. She knew for certain that they would remain hanging there for a long time.

Let's Play Doctor

Nura Amin

❦

*L*et's play doctor."

That was what Alya used to shout on those summer days that we played together—she and I and her sister and the neighbors' daughter.

Alya was the leader of the group. She decided when we played, ate, slept, and met at the entrance of the apartment building in which we all lived. Her favorite game was "doctor."

"Every one of us must be completely naked and Umniyya will play the doctor." She never tired of issuing her daily orders. She never wearied of seeing the naked bodies of her girlfriend and little sister. As a favor, she always let me keep my clothes on, perhaps so that I would fit the doctor's role, which I had to play every day with gravity, composure, and severity, or perhaps so that I could face my mother when she suddenly opened the door of the room to check on us. "Completely naked or else you won't be playing!" was what Alya would say.

Hana, the neighbors' daughter, always held onto her underwear. Sometimes she obeyed the orders of our leader silently and complied with the rules of the game so as not to be excluded from the group. But eventually she insisted on obeying the orders of the real leader—her mother—in keeping on her underwear at all cost. That was after her mother had once discovered that she had come home without it, and after the severe beating that she had deservedly received. Nothing could save her from being punished with the belt that day but her tearful confession that her underwear was in my possession—although I was not sure where it was.

Alya took delight in mimicking her father's voice as he yelled angrily and made a great effort to terrorize the entire household, an effort matched only by that of his daughter when mimicking him.

38

"Shut up girl, you and her, or else I'll make your life miserable!" The three of us laughed a lot at this expression, which we used to hear each night from Alya's father, and each morning from Alya herself. As for her little sister, she hastened to remove her clothes mechanically whenever the tone of Alya's voice rose, as she masterfully mimicked her father. Sometimes the little sister stood naked throughout the entire game, regardless of the risk of catching influenza—from cold or from fear—until it was her turn to be examined.

All too soon the game of doctor was over, and with it the era of Alya's leadership. Her father's voice reverberated long afterward, with neither her mimicry nor our laughter. In fact, his voice rose higher and higher every day. Gradually, Alya, the eldest and most courageous of her sisters, stopped her mocking act, "Show us what you're going to do, you showoff!"

Gradually, too, our little group dispersed. Hana traveled with her parents to Saudi Arabia. Occasionally she returned during the summer holiday wearing the veil—which she had donned as soon as she had reached puberty—without casting so much as a glance at us, even if we met on the stairs or at the entrance to the building. Alya's little sister no longer left the apartment, and I had no idea what had happened to her. As for Alya, she began to sing Latifa's popular songs with amazing persistence every morning. This usually occurred after her father had left for work and before his return to perform his regular yelling session. I could discern the pattern of her life through the daily routine of her father's morning and evening yelling sessions and her own singing sessions of Latifa's tunes. I also knew that she had fallen in love for the first time when she had stopped playing Latifa's tapes and started to sing songs of her own composition with great zeal.

It was during this period when one evening we heard a terrible noise, as though their apartment were being turned upside down. Then the showoff uttered a legendary scream, unlike anything ever heard before, and began throwing household items on Alya's head. He also heaped numerous curses and insults, not only on Alya but also on her mother, for failing to rear her properly. This time, the voice of Alya—the victim—rang out spontaneously, revealing for the first time abilities that exceeded her talent for mimicry. Her voice shook the very corners of the building in a way that we had not experienced since the earthquake of 1992.

We could easily hear the pieces of furniture as they were thrown at Alya's body, which had not grown much since we had last played doctor. After the father had finished throwing the butane gas cylinder, the nightstand, and the shoe rack, Alya ran to the apartment front door, asking for help from her mother and sisters. They began to cluster around her like a human shield near the door, repelling the father's assault. The door was shaking from the weight of the people assembled behind it, as though it too wanted to escape the aggression of the showoff.

Over the next two and a half hours, we naturally discovered what had happened and got the details of the story from the very mouth of the showoff, who scandalized himself when he began lamenting his disappointment in his eldest daughter. She had brought shame on him because she had fallen in love with a fellow student at the university and had walked with him daily on the banks of the Nile while her father was taking his evening naps. She deceived her entire family by claiming that she was attending private tutoring because she had failed the first year final examinations four consecutive times and had been threatened with dismissal.

Two days later, we learned that her father had vowed to divorce her mother or kill Alya, if she set foot outside the apartment. He had also forbidden her to attend the university and complete her studies. Just then Alya rang our doorbell for the first time in twelve years. Her face was badly bruised, her back was hunched, and her eyes were sunken. Her facial features were obscured by swelling and discoloration, and her right arm was wrapped in bandages. I wanted to hug her and shelter her in my room, which looked exactly the same as it did during my childhood. But I didn't know what to say to her. My tongue stuck in my mouth. Before Alya crossed the threshold, she said sadly and feebly, "Come on, let's play doctor. . . ."

I embraced her and laughed to myself.

In the Moonlight

Radwa Ashour

❧❧❧❧

J saw them through the open window, three figures in the moonlight. It seemed as if the man and the woman were one body;
they both moved slowly and feebly, as is customary for those of
advanced years. There was nothing to their left or to their right;
then the little girl, all alone, trailed along behind them.

The man and the woman had come to visit the lady in whose
household I worked. I served them tea and cake that I had baked especially for the occasion, and then went out to the balcony to bring
in the washing. As usual, the wind whipped the balcony, as the apartment building was located in a street overlooking the seashore.

I removed the clothespins, picked up each piece of clothing
separately, folded it, and placed it in a big basket, as I did every
night. Suddenly I heard a noise coming from the direction of the
staircase. I thought it was a cat, but when it continued, I leaned out
of the balcony to make sure. The apartment was on the first floor
and its balcony faced the street. On the right side, it overlooked
a flight of five stairs leading to the door. I did not notice anything,
but when I looked closely I saw her—the same little girl—sitting on
the stair.

"What are you doing here?"

"I'm waiting."

"For whom?"

"For my mistress and master."

"Your mistress and master?"

"Yes, they're at your home now, visiting."

"But why are you waiting? If you want something, knock on
the door, ask for it, and then leave."

41

The girl rose from her place and stood directly under the balcony.

"I don't want anything from them. They took me along with them and said to me, 'Nadya, wait here until we finish our visit.' May I pick some jasmine flowers?"

"Aren't you cold?"

"I'll have fun picking jasmine. I won't take many."

"Turn in this direction. I'll open the door for you."

I pointed to the garden path which ended at the kitchen door.

"But my mistress and master!"

"I'll tell them that you're with me in the kitchen."

I opened the door for the girl who, in the light, appeared to be younger than I had thought. She was thin and frail, six or seven years of age. She was wearing a blue cotton robe patterned with dainty, orange flowers, and had a dark blue scarf tied around her head and rubber slippers on her feet.

I went into the living room and leaned toward my mistress, informing her that the girl was with me in the kitchen. My mistress turned to the guest, whose face was filled with wrinkles.

"Uncle, why didn't you tell me that you had brought the maid with you?" she asked.

"We left her playing on the stairs."

"Saniyya will take her with her to the kitchen because the weather is cold and the wind is strong outside."

Lifting a black woolen scarf decorated with big red flowers from her knees and wrapping it around her shoulders, the guest's wife said, "Indeed, the weather is cold. Close the window, Saniyya."

The woman had a small frame, narrow shoulders, and huge buttocks that emphasized the contrast in size between her upper and lower body.

"Yes, madam."

I closed the window and went back to the kitchen. I put the tea kettle on the stove, set up the ironing board, and plugged in the electric iron.

"Can I help you?" the little girl said.

I laughed and asked her whether she knew how to iron. She answered seriously that her mistress had said that she lacked nothing but cooking skills, which she still needed to learn. I poured her a cup of tea and placed it before her along with a slice from the cake that I had baked.

My mistress called out, asking me to inform the girl that her mistress and master were ready to leave. The girl got up and hastened to join them. I went to the living room to clear up the cups, plates, and ashtrays. The room was filled with smoke, and its air was stifling. I flung the window wide open, and a cold sea breeze blew in forcefully. Then I saw them moving away in the moonlight.

At the Beach

Buthayna al-Nasiri

*T*he three children jumped down the beach until they arrived at the water's edge, where Layla submerged her toes and entered anxiously. After he had scooped a little water and splashed it on her back and she had screamed as though she had been stung, Mahmud followed her. As for Ahmad, the youngest, he kept running along the beach hesitantly. His mother, who was walking behind him, removed his clothes piece by piece and threw them into Fatima's hands. After she had pushed Ahmad gently into the water, she turned to Fatima.

"Pull up a chair and sit here, and don't you dare take your eyes off them!" she said.

Fatima let her ten-year-old body sink into the chair opposite the sea. She smoothed down her flowing yellow dress and gazed unblinkingly at the three children playing in the water.

Again she smoothed down her dress, spreading it out on the chair. Originally the dress had belonged to her mistress. One evening, she had sat at her sewing machine and altered the dress: she had shortened the sleeves, tightened the bodice, and cut a long piece from the hem, fashioning it into a belt that wound around the waist. After she had finished sewing, she asked Fatima to try the dress on. Fatima was beside herself with joy. She stood in front of the big mirror in her mistress's bedroom, swaying from side to side, then she quickly removed the dress, for fear of spoiling it. She decided to wear it only at the summer resort, after she had discovered that her mistress was buying new clothes for her children for this journey, as if they were going to a religious festival.

On the day of the journey, she had approached her mistress hesitantly, holding a headband that Layla had not worn in a long

44

time, and asked shyly, "Can I wear this instead of the headscarf at the summer resort?" The mistress looked at her in amazement, as though seeing her for the first time. She pondered awhile and then said, "Okay, but only at the beach." Overjoyed, Fatima rushed to open her bundle of clothes and placed the headband in the middle of the yellow dress. She didn't feel the need to try it on, for she had often worn it secretly when everyone was asleep, and the lights were turned off. She would remove it gently from under the pillow, put it carefully around her head, and drift into dreams until she was overcome by sleep.

And now her dream was fulfilled. She was sitting opposite the sea, adorned with her most beautiful things: the dress, the headband, and the glass necklace. All she had to do was watch the children playing in the water.

She imagined that on the first Friday after returning from the summer resort, she would visit her village—as her mistress had promised—and her little friends would gather around her and ask her insistently:

"Did you see the real sea, Fatima?"

"What did you see at the seashore? Tell us."

"I saw naked women . . . and little children building castles in the sand, and men playing in the sea. I saw big ships, white and black, carrying flags of different shapes and colors . . . They passed from a distance."

"Did you go into the water?"

"Every day . . ."

How could she possibly admit that she had merely sat on a chair near the water, with a towel and a lunch bag in her lap, watching the movements of the children in the sea without blinking her eyes? From time to time, one of them would approach her, dripping wet and trembling, and she would put the towel around his shoulders and give him a sandwich, which he would devour ravenously. It pleased Layla, whenever she came out of the water, to run to Fatima and say, "The sea is delightful, Fatima. Come into the sea with us." And Fatima would immediately reply, "No, my dress would get wet." She disdained telling the girl, who was only one year younger than her, that she had to remain chained to the chair like a watchdog.

She turned around and saw that her mistress was busy talking with her neighbor while showing her the needlework in which she was engrossed day and night. Then she looked back toward the sea.

The soft waves advanced from afar to break up leisurely at the shore. The longer she gazed, the more she felt that the sea was calling her, for today was their last day at the summer resort. What a pity not to go into the water like the other children, if only once!

Her glance fell again on her mistress, who was still absorbed in her embroidery, her glasses slipping down her nose. Fatima rose and advanced hesitantly toward the sea. She lifted the hem of her dress a little and waded into the water near Ahmad, who was sitting in the sea filling a tin can and then emptying it.

"What are you doing, Ahmad?"

"I'm selling juice. Play with me."

She stood bewildered. She glanced around her, then swayed as she plunged into the sea with all her weight. "Oh . . ." she screamed as the cold water stung her thighs and soaked her underclothes and belly. Her dress billowed like a tent above the waves, then, saturated with water, it collapsed and floated. Gazing at her mistress, she said in a voice loud enough to be heard, "Ahmad pushed me. Ahmad pushed me into the water . . ."

When her mistress did not react, Fatima stretched out her legs and rolled in the water while moving her arms about, as though she were swimming. Then she crawled on her belly until she drew near Layla and Mahmud.

"The sea is . . . beautiful," she said in a drawn-out voice.

"Fatima! But your dress! Take it off so it will dry," Layla shouted.

"Your mother would kill me!"

"Fatima! Fatima!" The mistress's voice rang out angrily. "Where are you, Fatima?"

Fatima jumped out of the water and ran toward her mistress, her dress clinging to her body, dripping wet.

"What have you done, crazy girl? Have I not warned you not to leave your place? Look what you've done to yourself! Good heavens! You'll surely catch cold. Wring out the dress. What on earth has happened to you? You've been so sensible until now!"

Fatima listened to the rebuke with bowed head, hiding her confusion by wringing the hem of her dress. The water flowed in little streams to the ground, forming small puddles around her feet.

"Go now. Fetch the kids from the sea so I can take the last picture."

Fatima breathed a sigh of relief as she ran toward the sea, her steps hindered by her dress, which gathered between her thighs.

"Layla, Mahmud, Ahmad!"

And she plunged headlong into the sea for the last time, pretending that they had not heard her.

"Layla, Mahmud, Ahmad!"

She felt a pleasant sensation as the water caressed her belly. She swung her arms about vigorously, and when she came close to Layla, she splashed her with water, just as she had seen Layla do with her brothers earlier.

"Layla, come to have a picture taken. Mahmud, get out of the water. Ahmad, hurry up!"

The children stood in the frame of the camera lens with the sea behind them. Layla put her hand on Mahmud's shoulder, as he stood frozen in a karate posture. Ahmad sat on the ground with his neck twisted around, half looking at the camera, while Fatima stood behind him. Her beautiful dress had been ruined by the water, which was dripping from the hem to the ground and collecting in puddles around her feet. Her wet hair clung to her temples and neck, the headband had slipped to her forehead, and grains of sand were stuck in her glass necklace. She looked like a soaking wet dog that had not yet shaken itself off.

But she was the only one in the photograph whose face was lit with a smile stretching from ear to ear.

A Helping Hand

Mona Ragab

*H*e was playing ball in the quiet street. She was drawing hop-scotch lines with chalk on the ground of the alley across the way.

He approached her and asked, "Can I help you?"

The girl, whose body bore signs of budding femininity, blushed in embarrassment as she refused.

"I'll be nearby," he said.

She smiled, radiating youthful joy, and asked, "Why is it that when you play, you keep both feet firmly on the ground, whereas we were fated to play on one foot?"

His voice broke as he spoke, "That's the law of life."

"Then I'll change this law. I'll destroy its foundation. Now. At once. From this very moment."

He yielded to her wish, but stood prepared for her. She played hopscotch, jumping on one foot. She continued to play until her face was drenched with sweat. She became tired but kept on playing, determined to persist by sheer stubbornness. She did not give in to her exhaustion. Suddenly she slipped and fell on her side, tearing her clothes. She burst into tears from exasperation. He bent over, stretched out his arms, and helped her to her feet. She leaned against his shoulder with her right hand, while with the left one she fastened her torn skirt so that it would cover her bare legs.

In the Recesses of Memory

Fawziya Rashid

His swollen face frightened her. She paid no attention to what his glances concealed. She was about to flee like a leaf tossed by the wind.

"He'll beat me. He's no different from other men!"

When she heard him call out to her, she approached him cautiously. She had come to know him well by now. The last time he had given her money with which she had bought a piece of delicious candy.

"Come closer."

She extended her hand, and as soon as he touched her finger, the coin came to rest at the bottom of her palm. She rushed off, filled with happiness. She knew exactly what to do with this coin. She wouldn't tell her mother. She would hide whatever she bought so that no one would know. She quickened her step as she neared her house, and her naive eyes became more confused and frightened.

In front of her door, a middle-aged woman grabbed her and slapped her cruelly. She remained standing, shrunken between the woman's hands, like a terrified cat in the claws of a dog. Then she burst into tears.

"This crazy girl!"

The mother spoke to her husband, fixing him with a piercing stare.

"She'll bring shame on us!"

The girl bowed her head, and a dreadful fear of something unknown gripped her.

She found her doll, which was her only toy. One of them—she didn't remember who—had given it to her. She stretched out in the small space between the door and the dirty piece of furniture. She usually paid little attention to what people said, especially her mother. But this time, she became aware of something she had not heard before.

They're talking about me! she thought.

She also noticed her mother's angry gesticulations as she yelled at her father, who stood there like a dry date-palm tree without roots or leaves.

"Don't you see that her breasts have started to develop? We have no other solution. It's too good an opportunity to miss."

Her father made no reply.

"Why are you as silent as a stone? You're not going to spend a penny of your own money. The man will take care of everything."

She felt disappointed as she hugged her silent doll. Why didn't it speak? If only her mother would hush up so that she could hear her little doll. Suddenly, quick as the whistle of the wind, she rushed out of the house, without looking back.

"Come back, crazy girl . . ."

She stared at his face in astonishment as he gestured to her with another coin, which he held between his fingers.

"Come closer to me. Don't be afraid."

Silent, she huddled in the shade of one of the walls after she had fled from him. She was seized with a sudden desire to weep.

"Beware of men! All of them are wild beasts."

He beckoned to her. She watched him in alarm as she began to rise to her feet.

"I want my mother."

He grabbed her by the shoulder, touched her, and felt her breasts. They were small and budding, like wild mushrooms after a rainy season. He tried to put his arms around her. An obscure sensation crept into her body. Finally she slipped from his grasp. He stood bewildered for a moment, then tried to chase her.

"This crazy girl. How wonderful her body is!"

She went to her room, but she could still hear her parents talking.

She wept, and then asked for a piece of candy. Her mother, cursing angrily, gave it to her.

Strange figures were surrounding her . . . besieging her . . . tightening their grip around her neck. . . . One of them kicked her in the belly . . . She screamed in pain . . . She awoke frightened from her dream.

Her parents were cleaving together when she entered their room. They rose startled, raining curses around them.

"Come closer, crazy girl. What on earth has happened to you?"

Suddenly she stared at her legs in dismay. Her mother, too, stared in astonishment. Blood was trickling down between her thighs.

"We must rush the matter, man. Don't you see?"

Her fear intensified when her father shook her violently.

"You are forbidden to go outside the house from now on. Is that understood?"

And he slapped her hard across the face.

She didn't understand.

The broad face gazed at her body, then approached her, and even touched her.

She wanted to scream.

How could her mother see her standing near this man and not rebuke her? Instead, she urged her, "Move closer to him, sweetie. This man loves you. He'll give you candy and money. You'll get a real flesh and blood doll!"

Her frightened glances settled on his face again.

And the sound of her weeping suddenly rang in her own ears.

The street was empty. She was running to an unknown place, fleeing far away.

He said, "I'll give you money and candy. No one will beat you again."

She had come to know him well by now. The last time he had given her a coin and . . .

But he was no different from all the other men. He would not stop beating her.

The street raced faster under her heavy steps.

He was just like all the other men. Didn't her mother say so herself?

She swept the street with her eyes, sensing that someone was following her. She was out of breath, tired, running far away to an unknown place.

And her face gradually vanished on the road.

Fragments from a Life
Sharifa al-Shamlan

First Fragment

I'm twenty years old, I'm sure. My mother died when I was ten. I was brought here when I was seventeen. I can figure out my age because I used to plant a date-palm tree each year. I've been here for three years now. I know that from the number of my father's visits. At the end of every Ramadan, he visits me.

Another Fragment

Today is the Waqfa.[1] Tomorrow is the Great Festival. They are decorating the place not because of the Great Festival, but because the director is coming for a visit.

I requested pen and paper. I wanted to write a long letter to my mother and a greeting card to my father. They refused my request. They were afraid that I would write a complaint to the director. I laughed at them a lot in my heart, because I don't even know how to write.

And Another Fragment

I laughed a lot as I watched the director. He seemed puffed up, extremely puffed up. The male nurses lined up on either side of him, looking clean and shiny. When the director approached me, the chief doctor whispered audibly in his ear, "She's dangerous."

I tried to stretch out my hand to touch the director's cloak. He forced a smile onto his face and said, "What do you want, young woman?"

"To touch your cloak," I said.

"Why?"

I gestured to him to bring his ear closer, and then whispered to him, "I want to see how much it would fetch if it were sold. Would the money be enough to buy candy for the children in my village?"

He laughed, and then went away.

The chief doctor's eyes were popping with fear.

A Rear Fragment

The sight of the chief doctor makes me laugh. He has maps on his face that I drew with my fingernails. One day he wanted to break my pride. I tried to break his nose, but I could not. All I did was paint his face with his blood.

A Small Fragment

The orderly brought my food. I asked no questions.

She said, "I gave the piece of meat to the neighbors' dog. He was hungry."

"I hope he deserved it," I said.

A Horizontal Fragment

The nurse comes as usual, carrying a syringe in her hand. Instead of injecting it into my arm, she empties it into another vial, which she promptly hides in the front of her dress. I don't care. True, the injection transports me to beautiful worlds . . . to a vast universe, but afterward it leaves me in a dark world—and with a terrible headache.

I said to the nurse, "I wish you would bring me a lot of palm prickles."

"Why?" she asked indifferently.

"I will use them to make a fence around my bed," I replied.

Then I pinched her belly. She gasped. She wrapped her cloak around her, and went off in a rush.

A Painful Fragment

One day my father bought me some bangles. I was very happy with them. I showed them to my girlfriends. My stepmother bought necklaces and anklets and many bangles. I didn't care. I was happy because my father had become rich. I sat down looking at my bangles. They glittered in the sunlight. I heard a loud noise. A huge tractor was digging up the garden. It was approaching my date-palm trees. I screamed . . . and screamed . . . and then ran and sat on the ground in front of the tractor. My stepmother dragged me away, saying, "We've sold the garden. They're going to turn it into a street." I pulled her hair and scratched her face. She said, "Shouldn't you ask where the bangles came from?" I threw the bangles under the huge tractor. After that, I was brought here.

Last Fragment

The orderly came to me and said, "They wrote about you in the newspapers."

"Why?" I asked.

"The director sent candy to the children in your village."

"Were the children happy?"

"Yes," she said. "They sent a telegram thanking the director."

The Slave

Najiya Thamir

❧❧❧

I don't know my father. I know that I have an uncle with a large family, who was obviously unable to bear my presence, for he brought me to a family to care for me as a daughter, and I grew up among them.

The family consisted of two married sisters who lived in the same house. One gave birth to two daughters, while the other turned out to be barren after years of marriage, so she chose me. I've heard them say that my mother, who is alive, remarried a few months after my father passed away. At that time I was a year old and understood nothing about life. My uncle was furious because my mother didn't complete a full year of mourning after my father's death, so he took me away from her. She didn't offer much resistance. But the angry uncle was poor, and perhaps he later regretted his action. He began to search for a family that would care for me, until he found what he wanted. He preferred strangers to relatives. I've also heard that my mother bore other children, was delighted with them, and no longer inquired about me.

Since the time that I became aware of the facts of life, I've realized that I am a stranger in this house, and that no bloodline connects me to it. When I was little, I felt sad whenever I saw my aunt's daughters go to school and heard them talk about their teachers and lessons and classmates and books and notebooks, while I washed the dishes, mopped the floor, and cleaned the stove and soot-covered pans.

I never suffered hunger or lack of clothing, but I did notice that I had few clothes and that my food was plain and ordinary. I often ate a piece of bread with a few olives when we had unexpected guests, while my aunt's daughters ate from the cooked meal before it was served to the guests. Once I asked my mother, "Why don't I go to school like my aunt's daughters?" She replied that my father preferred that I stay at home, and requested that I refrain from raising this subject again. On another occasion, she rebuked me angrily and said, "You don't have a birth certificate. Your father is dead, and your mother is absent. Applying for a birth certificate is a long and laborious process. Your adoptive father cannot undertake this task because he has a lot of work." I was then seven years old. And why didn't I get my share of food like the others? She explained that there was a small amount of food, and that there wouldn't be enough for the guests if I ate any. As for the two girls, they had to be well fed because they went to school and expended a lot of energy in learning their lessons and doing their homework. Doing the house-work, by contrast, required little effort, which could be fully compensated by a piece of bread, even without olives . . .

I was more daring when I was little. I would ask myself these questions and then pose them until I got an answer. As I grew older, I was repeatedly rebuked by my family, who criticized me for being ill-mannered and outrageously inquisitive, so I gradually became silent.

My soul, however, continued to question. Occasionally I found sensible answers, but usually the answers were weak and unconvinc-ing. Many questions arose, and then slowly sank to the depths of my heart. I decided to silence these questions and bottle them up, be-cause they tormented and embarrassed me.

Shut up, Amina. No one here will satisfy your desire for an-swers. Instead, you'll be yelled at and scolded. Only after I turned thirteen did I obtain my birth certificate. I found out that the liter-acy center offered special classes for children. After hearing it on the radio several times, I mustered the courage to ask my mother to help me attain my goal of learning to read and write. "One or two hours in the afternoon will suffice, after I finish doing all of my household chores. There are holidays and Sundays when I won't have any classes. Just two years during which I'll learn enough to liberate myself from the bondage of illiteracy. Then I'll continue to study by myself, using whatever newspapers and books are available at home." My mother gave me an angry look and replied, "Do you think it proper for a grown-up girl like you to go out into the street and be absent from home every day for two or more hours? Who-ever sees you thinks you are older than your age. You look like you're sixteen."

"So what?"

"Your father won't permit you to walk alone through the alley-ways to attend classes at such a center. He fears for your safety."

"My safety? And why doesn't my uncle fear for his daughters' safety when both of them are older than me?"

"Every father has his own view about raising children. And besides, who will help me when my guests arrive?"

"I'll prepare the teapot before I leave. You will only have to heat it up and pour it into the glasses. This is in the event that one of the visitors arrives in my absence. I won't be away for more than two hours, especially as the literacy center is not very far from the house."

"I'll ask your aunt's daughters to teach you how to read and write. As for going to the literacy center, the subject is closed. You mustn't bring it up again. Your father will be angry, understand?"

My aunt's daughters refused to teach me the alphabet, excusing themselves by saying that they had a lot of homework, but they promised my mother that they would help me during their holidays. That made me really happy, especially when they began to keep their promise—at my mother's insistence—and take turns teaching me. They treated my lesson as an entertainment, laughing when I mispronounced a letter or misspelled a word. The joking would continue for several days in front of relatives and neighbors, while I blushed and raged inside. However, I bore it patiently and returned to the next lesson, until I learned to write and pronounce all the letters, and moved on to the texts.

Yes, I bore it patiently and succeeded in learning to read and write fluently through my willpower and determination, but I had to wash and iron their clothes, as well as perform other services for them, in return for their help. Whenever I made a mistake or overlooked something, my mother rebuked me: "You and your studying. What have you gained? Now you are even more stupid and ignorant than you were before!"

I am twenty years old now. I clean the house, prepare the food, and comply with the requests of all six members of the family. In addition, there are relatives and children who visit us frequently, and I'm the one who must attend to them. I know how to do all the housework, from cleaning to cooking to ironing, and I can sew, read, and write well. I am pretty, tall, and slender. Several young men came to ask for my hand in marriage, but they were refused on the pretext that they were unsuitable for me. My mother says, "Amina lacks nothing. She is pretty, tall, and well-mannered, and she can do women's chores skillfully. She is worthy of the son of a cabinet minister. She shouldn't act hastily because all those who have asked for her hand were beneath her." Then my aunt's daughters whisper in my ear, "Our aunt doesn't really understand that no matter how pretty and accomplished you are, no one but a simple civil servant or a day laborer will ask for your hand. The fact of the matter is that you're nothing but a stranger for whom our aunt felt pity and whom she raised like her daughter." Like her daughter? Her *daughter!* That's what I hear all the time, but I know that I'll never be like her daughter. I also realize that she refuses the men who ask for my hand only because she wants me to continue to serve her and the others.

I'm nothing but a servant, with no pay, no less and no more. Worse yet, I'm a servant forever. I know that for certain, and I will always keep that knowledge concealed in my heart.

I've become habitually silent and submissive.

I know everything, but say nothing. Perhaps I will reach the age of thirty or forty and still be tongue-tied, not uttering a word, while I remain in the service of this family.

I'm nothing but a slave with a bowed back, and my slender figure and attractive appearance are merely a mirage. I alone know the truth. What a terrible truth! I realize now that a little learning and beauty are in themselves not enough to liberate anyone, and that escaping from slavery is difficult for a person who has become accustomed to humiliation, subordination, and oppression.

My hands will remain chained even though they appear to be free. My pretty face is no better than an ugly face because it's a stranger to this house, and whatever skills I've learned and mastered will benefit only the lucky owners of this house.

My back has become bent under the stick, while I have neither the determination nor the power to rebel against slavery and injustice. I have to suffer forever, like any obedient slave girl whose tongue has been silenced and whose feelings have been branded with a stamp of burning charcoal to keep her at her master's beck and call, with no thought of escape, until the day she dies and is laid to rest.

And then? . . . What's the difference between these bars that surround me and a grave? Wouldn't a grave be more merciful and gentle?

Part Two

Love and Sexuality

The Picture

Nawal al-Saadawi

❧❦❧

*E*verything could have gone on as before in Narjis's life, had her hand not collided accidentally with Nabawiyya's backside, and had her fingers not hit a soft curve of flesh, and had her amazed eyes not seen a pair of small protrusions wobbling along under Nabawiyya's dress in time with the jerking of her arms as she stood washing at the sink. She had realized for the first time that Nabawiyya had buttocks. Nabawiyya, the village girl who had come to their house the previous year, was a little servant whose body was as thin and dry as a stalk of maize; you could hardly tell her back from her front, and had it not been for her name, you would have thought her a boy.

Narjis found herself looking in the mirror in her room, and she turned around in front of it. Her eyes opened wide in amazement when she saw a pair of small protrusions shaking under her dress. She stretched out her hand inquisitively, exploring her rear. Her trembling fingers came across a pair of soft curves of flesh. Was she growing buttocks too?

She lifted her dress from the back to reveal them, then twisted her head around to look at them, but they turned as her body turned and disappeared behind it. She tried to steady her lower half in front of the mirror and look right around it, but she couldn't. When her head turned, the upper part of her body turned with it, and when that happened, the lower half of her body followed. She was slightly baffled. She could see Nabawiyya from the rear, but not herself. At that moment, she imagined that she had discovered a new human misfortune: you could see other people's bodies but not the body in which you were born and which you always carried around.

An idea flashed across her mind: to go to the kitchen and ask Nabawiyya to look at her from the rear and describe her buttocks to her precisely. What shape were they? Round or oval? Did they shake when she was standing still or only when she walked? Did they protrude and attract attention or didn't they?

She set off, but then she stopped. Could she ask Nabawiyya something like that? Nabawiyya the servant, with whom she never exchanged a word? The most she ever did was to issue orders to her, and the most Nabawiyya ever replied was "Okay" or "Yes," spontaneous reactions, coming out regularly at a speed and pitch reminiscent of the vibrations of a machine, each sound the same as the next.

She felt slightly angry, and she resolved to get to see her rear by her own efforts. She pulled up her dress and bared herself completely from the back. Then she steadied her legs on the floor, twisted her head around, and ran her eyes over her body. Before long, her head stopped moving, her eyes not managing the full sweep around her body. She strained her muscles and tried once more to twist her head around. She had her head turned in front of the mirror and her rear completely bared, when her gaze met that of her father, and she shuddered. She knew they were not his real eyes, only his picture hanging on the wall, but her little body continued to tremble until she had pulled down the dress and covered up her rear. She couldn't take her eyes off his. She wanted to see them. Every time she looked at her father, she felt that she was not seeing enough of him, that she wanted to see more of him. For thirteen years, since the day she was born, she had seen him only from the back. When he had his back to her, she could raise her eyes and contemplate his tall, broad frame. She never looked him in the eye, and never exchanged a glance or a word with him. When he looked at her, she bowed her head; and when he spoke to her, it was not words he uttered, but instructions and orders, to which she responded with "Okay" or "Yes" mechanically, in blind obedience. When he told her to leave school and stay at home, she left school and stayed at home. When he told her not to open the windows, she didn't open the windows. When he told her not to look out from behind the shutters, she didn't look out from behind the shutters. Even when he told her to perform ablutions before going to sleep, so that she would have noble dreams, she began performing the ablutions and having noble dreams.

Her eyes were still riveted to his. She wanted to look at him without bowing her head, to fix her eyes on his eyes and see them, know them, get acquainted with them. But she couldn't. There was always a distance separating his eyes from hers, and she was unable to see them close up, even though her nose was almost touching the picture. His head looked big, his nose large and crooked, and his eyes hollow and wide, almost swallowing her up. She hid her face in her hands. A picture of the big desk flashed across her mind, and behind it her father's crooked nose peeping out from amid the many papers. From time to time, he would look at the long line of people standing in front of him, gazing at him pleadingly, submissively. His big head would move among the piles of papers, his long thick fingers twisted around the pen as it raced across the paper. She would draw her slim little legs together as she sat in the corner, and withdraw within herself, trying to breathe quietly. Could she really be the daughter of this great man? When her father stood up, his tall, broad frame towered over the desk, and his nose almost touched the ceiling. She carried her head proudly as she walked beside him on the street. She could almost see that all eyes were fixed on her father, and that all lips were parted in good wishes for him. Her little ears could almost catch the soft whisper that always floated among the passersby on the street: "This man is vested with supreme authority, and that's his daughter, Narjis, walking at his side!" And when the two of them crossed the street, her father would hold her by the hand, and wrap his big fingers around her little fingers, and her heart would pound, and her breathing would quicken, and she would bend her head to kiss his hand. As soon as her lips touched his big hairy hand, that powerful smell, her father's distinct smell, penetrated her nostrils. She didn't know exactly what it was, but she smelled it wherever he was; and when she went into his room, she smelled it in all the corners, in the bed, in the wardrobe, and in the clothing. Sometimes she would bury her head in his clothes in order to smell it even more; she would kiss his clothes and stroke them and kneel in front of the big picture of him above his bed, almost praying. Not the usual prayer that she performed quickly to a god she had never seen, but a real act of worship to a real god whom she could see with her own eyes, hear with her own ears, and smell with her own nose. He was the one who bought food and clothes for her, and possessed a huge desk with a lot of papers, and knew the contents of these papers, and provided for people's needs, and most importantly, wrote with a pen at eye-dazzling speed.

Narjis found herself kneeling in front of the picture as though in prayer. She rose, her head bowed low in humility, and kissed his hand, as was her custom every night before she went to sleep. As she lay on her back, her protruding buttocks rubbed against the bed, and a new, pleasant shudder ran through her body. She stretched out her trembling fingers to feel her backside. Two rounded mounds of flesh were crammed between her and the bed. She turned over onto her face to avoid feeling them and to try to sleep, but they rose up into the air, their weight pressing down on her stomach. She turned over onto her side, but they continued to rub against the bed every time she breathed in or out. She held her breath for a moment, but the breathing soon resumed at a rapid rate, sending tremors through her little body, which shook the bed, causing it to creak softly. It seemed to her that in the silence of the night the creaking was audible, that it could reach her father's ears as he slept in his room, and that he would know for sure where it came from and what had really caused it.

She shuddered at this thought and tried to suppress her breathing so that the bed would stop creaking. She almost choked, but the air suddenly burst out of her chest, and her body shook violently, as did the bed, emitting its harsh creaking in the silence of the night. Finally, she jumped out of bed.

As soon as she set her feet on the floor, the bed stopped creaking and all she could then hear was the sound of her heavy breathing. Little by little, it began to calm down, eventually becoming completely quiet. The customary silence had hardly returned to her room when she remembered that she had not performed the usual ablutions before going to bed. Having discovered the cause of all the sinful sensations that had crept into her impure body, she felt a sense of relief.

When she was standing in front of the sink, performing her ablutions while uttering the formulas "In the name of God, the Compassionate, the Merciful," "There is no power and no strength save in God," and "I seek refuge in God from the accursed Satan," she heard a faint noise coming from behind the kitchen door. Was Nabawiyya only just going to bed? She pushed gently on the kitchen door, but it didn't open. Once again she heard the faint noise, so she put her ear to the door and clearly heard the sound of confused and rapid breathing. She smiled with relief. Nabawiyya was awake like her, exploring her new buttocks! She instinctively turned her head toward the door, and her eyes came to rest on the keyhole. She peeped into the kitchen. The small sofa on which Nabawiyya slept was empty, and something was moving on the kitchen floor. She peered hard through the keyhole. Her eyes opened wide as her gaze settled on a naked two-headed heap of flesh rolling about on the floor. One of the heads, with its long plaits, was Nabawiyya's, and the other, with its high, crooked nose, was her father's!

At that moment, she almost fainted onto the floor, far away from the keyhole. But her eyes remained there, glued fast to it, as though a part of it. Her gaze froze on the big naked heap as it rolled about, as Nabawiyya's head came down onto the floor, bumping against the garbage can, and as her father's head rose up and hit the bottom of the sink. But they had soon swapped positions, and it was Nabawiyya's head that was hitting the bottom of the sink, and her father's head that was striking the garbage can. Before long, both heads had disappeared under the shelf where the cooking pots were kept, and she could no longer see anything but four legs, with their twenty toes jerking rapidly; some of the toes were entangled with others, making a strange shape, like a water creature with many arms, or an octopus.

Narjis didn't know how she had managed to tear her eyes away from the keyhole, or how she had gotten back to her room to look in the mirror. Her little head was shaking as her gaze swept over her body. Her wandering eyes fell on her protruding buttocks, moving in time with the rapid jolting of the rest of her body. She stretched out her hand spontaneously and bared her rear, looking at her father's picture out of the corner of her eye. She almost felt the same old shudder run through her arms, and she almost pulled down her dress to cover herself. But her arms didn't move, and she kept staring at her father's face without bowing her head. His wide eyes were bulging, and his sharp, crooked nose sliced his face in two. A long spider's web clung to the high and pointed tip of the nose, moving to and fro in the night breeze that was rushing in through the shutters.

Narjis went up to the picture and blew on the spider's web to clear it away, but drops of her spittle spread over the picture, and the spider's web stuck to her father's face. Again she tried to blow it away, but it only stuck on all the more. She stretched out her hand mechanically, and with her long sharp nails began to rub the spider's long thin threads off the picture. She managed to remove them, but at the same time she destroyed the picture, which had become wet with her spittle, and it fell from between her fingers to the floor in little fragments . . .

The Picture

Latifa al-Zayyat

✦✦✦✦✦

*A*mal's eyes settled on a splash of wave that moved on the
horizon, leaving behind a spiral lit up in rainbow colors
by the sun's rays. It was a splendid rainbow, visible only if
you tilted your head at a certain angle and looked hard. She pointed
out the rainbow to her husband, who was sitting across the table
from her in the casino[1] overlooking the point where the Nile meets
the sea at Ras al-Barr. But he couldn't see it. If only he could see it.
The rainbow seemed to disappear when it was still there, and
seemed still to be there when it had already disappeared with the
waves as they pulled away from the rocks of the Tongue, stretching
out where sea and river met. Once again the waves would come and
thrust against the rocks, and again the rainbow would rise up.

"There it is, Izzat, there it is!" Amal cried out in delight.

Her son, Midhat, grabbed the hem of her dress and followed
her gaze.

"Where, Mama, where?"

The look of boredom vanished from Izzat's eyes, and he burst out
laughing. A man wearing a fez and a full suit with a waistcoat shouted,
"Double five, my dear sir, double five," and he brought the chips down
onto the backgammon board. The fat man who was playing with him
swallowed hard and pulled at the front of his white cotton-and-silk
robe to wipe away the sweat. An old photographer in a black suit took
hold of his boy and shook him as he sat fast asleep, propped up against
the developing bucket. Brushing the sand off his bare feet, the man
selling raffle tickets shouted, "You never know your luck!"

Amal gave her shy, apologetic smile. The contagious laughter
took hold of her, and she burst out laughing without knowing why.
Suddenly she stopped, realizing that she was happy.

Midhat asked for ice cream, and Izzat was turning to look for the waiter when his gaze halted, glued to the casino entrance. He smiled, drawing down his thick, moist lower lip. His hand moved instinctively to open another button on his white shirt, revealing more of the copious hair on his chest.

The table behind Amal was now occupied by a woman in her thirties, wearing shorts that exposed her full, white thighs, and with her dyed blond hair fastened with a red georgette scarf decorated with white jasmine; with her sat another woman in her fifties, wearing a dress that revealed a tanned and wrinkled cleavage. Izzat clapped his hands, shouting loudly for the waiter, although he was nearby, and just a sign would have done.

"Three, three ice creams."

Amal was alarmed by her husband's unusual lavishness.

"Two's enough, Izzat. I don't feel like any," she whispered, blushing.

Izzat seemed not to hear her. He repeated, in a feverish voice, "Three ice creams of mixed flavors. Have you got that?"

When the waiter moved away, he called to him again, enunciating every word, "Make one of them vanilla. Yes, vanilla ice cream."

Amal smiled triumphantly as she relaxed in her seat.

"Where will you get the money to go on summer vacation?" her mother had asked her. "From the meager salary of fifteen pounds a month that he earns? You've been putting money aside. That's why your hands are chapped from washing. That's why you've lost weight. If only he was a decent man who understood and appreciated what you do. But he neglects you like a dog, and goes fooling around."

Amal pursed her lips together in an ironic expression. She and Izzat were finally together, the whole time, on vacation, at the hotel in Ras al-Barr. Fifteen days without cooking or cleaning, without waiting up, without the heat and humidity. She leaned her head back proudly, brushing a lock of pitch-black hair off her tawny forehead. She noticed Izzat's eyes and felt a lump in her throat.

The fire was burning in Izzat's eyes again. Those eyes, which for a long time seemed sightless, gliding over things without noticing them, had begun to see. They were once again lit with that fire, both fascinating and bewildering, the fire that burned and begged. Had she forgotten that gaze of his? Or had she deliberately tried to forget it so that she would not miss it? The fact was that it had returned, as if he had never lost it. Was it the summer resort? Was it the vacation? The only thing that mattered was that it had returned to envelop her again in a fever of excitement. Amal noticed Izzat's dark brown hand, with its protruding veins, and she was racked with a desire to lean over and kiss it. Her eyes filled with tears. She drew Midhat close to her with fumbling hands and planted kisses on him from cheek to ear. She hugged him, and when the fire that had invaded her body had subsided, she let him go and began searching for the rainbow through her tears, tilting her head to one side.

She must be sure. Was that really the rainbow or just a rainbow produced by her tears? . . . "Tomorrow you'll cry blood instead of tears," her mother had warned her, and her father had said, "You're young, my daughter, and tomorrow love and all that nonsense will vanish and nothing will remain except toil . . ." Amal shook her head as if to dislodge a fly that had landed on her cheek, and muttered to herself, "You don't understand anything. I found what I had been looking for all my life." She held the rainbow in her gaze, then awoke to a metallic clinking sound, as the ice-cream glasses chafed against the marble of the table.

"Three ice creams, two mixed and one vanilla."

"The vanilla's for me, sir. The vanilla's sufficient for me."

Izzat enunciated his words carefully, flashing a meaningful smile in the direction of . . . Which direction? A lewd female laugh rang out in response. In response to the smile? Amal cupped the frosty glass with her hands and stared at it, bewildered. *Strawberry, pistachio . . . and the yellow? Mango? Apricot? Dye, just dye . . . It can't be . . . It can't be . . .*

"Come on, eat up," Izzat cajoled her.

Amal picked up the spoon and was about to dig into the ice cream when she abruptly put it down and cupped the glass with her hands once again. Izzat turned to his son.

"Is the ice cream tasty, Midhat?"

"Yes, tasty."

"As tasty as you are, sweetie."

Another burst of laughter rang out behind Amal. Her hands tightened around the frosty glass, from which ice-cold steam was rising. She raised her eyes and turned her head without moving her shoulders, so she could see the woman in shorts. She did it reluctantly, slowly, afraid someone might notice her. And then she saw her . . . *white as a wall . . . as a candle . . . as vanilla ice cream?* Amal's eyes met the woman's for a fleeting second. Her lower lip trembled, and her gaze fell back onto the ice-cream glass. She raised her head and shoulders and sat stiffly, eating.

The woman in shorts took a cigarette out of her bag and left it dangling from her lips until the woman with the exposed cleavage lit it for her. She began to puff out smoke provocatively toward Amal, but Amal didn't turn to look at her. *The woman's cheap. Izzat only has to open his mouth, and she laughs. Cheap, no doubt about that. It's not fair to Izzat.*

Midhat finished eating his ice cream and started fidgeting around from boredom. He puckered his lips, as if he was about to cry.

"The Tongue . . . I want to go to the Tongue."

Amal heaved a sigh of relief: a great worry had been removed. This cheap woman would vanish from her sight forever. She tilted her head to one side, smiled, and, carefully enunciating her words as if playing a role in front of a large audience, said, "Of course, sweetie, right away. Mama and Papa will take Midhat and go to the Tongue." She pushed back her chair, giving a short forced laugh as she prepared to get up.

"Where to?" Izzat said in an unduly harsh tone.

"The boy wants to go to the Tongue."

"And after the Tongue? Are we going to be cooped up in the hotel from now on?"

Midhat burst out crying, striking against the floor with his feet. Amal jumped up nervously to hug him. *Izzat? Izzat wants to sit here because . . . It can't be . . . God, it can't be.* Midhat was alarmed at the force of her hug, and his crying grew louder.

"Shut up!" Izzat shouted.

Midhat didn't shut up, so Izzat jumped up, pulled him out of his mother's arms, and slapped him twice on the hand. Then he sat down, saying, as if justifying his position to others, "I won't have a child who's a crybaby."

Amal returned to her chair. The tears flowed silently from Midhat's eyes, gathering at the corners of his mouth. As if she had just awakened, the woman in shorts said in a hoarse, drawling voice, "Come on, sweetie, come to me." And out of her pocket she took a piece of chocolate in a red wrapping.

"Come on, darling, come and take the chocolate."

Amal pulled Midhat toward her. The woman in shorts tilted her head to one side, crossed her legs, and smiled faintly as she threw the chocolate onto the table so that Midhat could see it. Amal rested Midhat's head against her chest and began to stroke his hair with trembling hands. Midhat let himself be cuddled by his mother for a moment, then he lifted his arm to wipe away the tears and began to steal glances from under the arm at the chocolate. The woman in shorts gestured to Midhat and winked sideways at him. Amal buried Midhat's head in her chest. *It can't be . . . He can't possibly go to her . . . Izzat . . . Midhat . . . Izzat can't be ogling her.* With a sudden movement, Midhat slipped from his mother's grasp, and ran to the adjacent table. The lewd laugh rang out again, triumphant, reverberating.

"Go and get the boy," Amal whispered, her lips turning blue.

Izzat smiled defiantly. "Why don't you go and get him yourself?"

"We're not beggars," she said in a choked voice.

"What's begging got to do with it? Surely you don't want the boy to turn out as shy as you are!"

Amal didn't turn to look at the table behind her, where her son was sitting on the lap of the woman in shorts, eating chocolate and smudging his mouth, chin, hands, and shirt. She wished she could grab him and hit him until . . . But what fault was it of his? The fault was hers alone.

"Well done. You finished the chocolate. Now let's go and wash your hands," the woman in shorts said in her hoarse, drawling voice.

Amal jumped to her feet, her face pale. The woman in shorts walked away with a swinging gait, dragging Midhat along behind her. Izzat placed his hand on Amal's shoulder, saying softly, "You stay here. I'll get the boy."

Amal remained standing, watching the two of them: the woman holding Midhat by the hand, the woman with Izzat behind her. She watched them as they crossed the casino terrace, then through the glass door, as they crossed the inner lounge and disappeared inside the building. The woman's buttocks were swinging as if disconnected from her, and Izzat followed her, his body bent forward, as if about to charge. On they went, step after step, step close to step, step clinging to step. Amal's hand stretched out mechanically to wipe away the drops of sweat that had gathered at the corners of her mouth.

"No Izzat, don't be like that. You frighten me . . . you frighten me when you're like that, Izzat." She had uttered these words as she collapsed onto a rock in the cave at the Aquarium. It was during their engagement. Izzat was out of breath as he said, "Oh, Amal, you can't imagine how much I love you." His lips were pursed and his eyes half-closed, giving him the look of a cat calling its mate, a look that burned and begged. *Izzat and the other woman? Izzat wanting to . . . It can't be . . . It can't be . . .*

"A picture, madam?"

Amal dropped onto the chair in exhaustion, signaling to the old photographer to go away.

"No Izzat, don't put your hand on my neck like that. What will people say when they see the picture?" "They'll say I love you, Amal." "No, please don't." "Here it is. The picture shows us with my hand on your neck, and now you'll never be able to get away from me." That was what he had said that day, triumphant.

"A postcard picture for ten piasters, and no waiting, madam."

"Later, later," Amal replied, annoyed.

The old photographer walked away, repeating in a dull, listless chant, "Family pictures, souvenir pictures." Behind him, the barefoot seller of raffle tickets wiped his hand on his khaki pants and called out, "You never know your luck! Three numbers and we'll draw. A valuable Chinese tea set for just one piaster. It's a giveaway!" Amal lifted her hand from the table, as the chill of the marble had suddenly stung her.

"I'm lucky, Mother. I married a real man." "You married a scoundrel!" her mother had said. "Work! Is that what he says, work? It's a strange office that stays open till one and two o'clock in the morning!" Saber Effendi, their neighbor, had remarked. And Sitt Saniyya, pouring out the coffee, had added, "My poor child, Saber Effendi has been in government service for forty years, and nothing happens that he doesn't know about."

Izzat returned with Midhat. Sitting him down on his lap, he said softly, "The boy took ages. He didn't want to wash his hands."

Amal gave him a cold, scrutinizing look, as if seeing him for the first time. Then she turned her gaze away from him and focused on a chocolate stain on Midhat's shirt. Izzat seemed totally absorbed in teaching Midhat to count from one to ten. Midhat stretched out his hand and covered his father's mouth. Izzat smiled and leaned toward Amal.

"You know you look very attractive today. Pink really suits you," he said.

She felt a lump in her throat, and she smiled faintly.

The old photographer said again, "A group picture, sir? It'll be very nice, and you get it right away."

"No, thanks," Izzat replied.

Amal noticed the woman in shorts coming toward them with her swinging gait.

"Let's have our picture taken," she said in a choked voice.

"What for?" protested Izzat.

The other woman passed them with an aloof air, looking neither at her nor Izzat. She sat in her chair and began to talk to her friend.

Amal leaned toward Izzat and whispered, "Let's have our picture taken, you and me . . . Let's!" She pointed a finger at him, a finger at herself, and then joined the two fingers together.

Izzat shrugged his shoulders and said resignedly, "Take a picture, fellow."

When the photographer had slipped his head into the black hood, Amal stretched out her hand and grabbed her husband's arm; and when the photographer gave the signal, her hand tightened its grip. While waiting for the picture to be developed, Izzat didn't look at the woman, nor she at him. When the photographer returned with the picture, Izzat rose, looking for change.

Amal grasped the picture eagerly and held it firmly in her hands, as if afraid someone would snatch it from her . . . *Izzat at her side . . . her darling . . . her husband.* The woman in shorts stood up, pushing her chair back violently. When she passed by their table, her eyes met Amal's for a brief moment—a fleeting moment, but sufficient—and Amal let the picture fall from her hands.

It fell to the ground, not far from her. Without moving from her place, Amal rested her elbows on her thighs and her head on her hands, and began to scrutinize the picture with a cold, expressionless face. The picture of a strange woman looked up at her, a feverish woman feverishly grabbing the arm of a man whose face was grimacing with pain. Slowly and calmly, Amal stretched out her leg, and with the toe of her shoe, then with the heel, defaced the picture. She drew her leg back and bent her head, scrutinizing the picture once again.

The sand had obliterated the main features, but some parts remained clear: the man's face, with its expression of pain, and the woman's hand, grabbing the man's arm. Amal stretched out her leg again, and with the toe of her shoe drew the picture close to her chair, until it was within arm's reach. Then she bent down and picked it up.

When Izzat returned with the change, the picture had been torn into small pieces that were blowing about in the wind. The rainbow had disappeared. The sun had reached its zenith, and people were running on the hot sand so that it would not scorch their feet.

Amal realized that there was a long road ahead of her . . .

The Picture

Layla al-Uthman

y birthday party was over. I was a woman of forty-five celebrating her birthday . . .

I looked around me. The pale night had become completely still. The guests had started to disperse, each group heading off in its own direction. Some people had left their good sense at the bottom of their glasses and staggered out happily. Everything in the room was in disarray, waiting for the morning, when the servant's hands would work to clean it up. Silver and gold paper decorations lay scattered about or hung from the ceiling like lifeless caterpillars.

Empty, dry glasses stood as tokens of the avid thirst of those who had held them. Other glasses contained half-melted ice that mixed with the remains of the drink. It seemed as if the scent of the drinker's breath emanated from each concoction. The table was overflowing with leftovers, most of which lay spoiled and untouched. Perhaps the visitors had suffered an attack of indigestion—they had a habit of overindulgence. Every small table held several bowls full of cigarette and cigar butts. The contents gave off a strange aroma. Some people hated the smell, but I had always liked it. It gave me a dazed feeling, sending a kind of longing through my body for a moment of evening rest.

Alone . . .

I stood in front of the big mirror with the golden frame. It gleamed. My face and half my body were reflected in it. I drew closer and closer, until my face filled the mirror. I looked at my face closely. It was only then that I decided to be unfaithful to my husband.

I was neither taken nor daunted by any of the people at the party, despite the fact that some women had prominent bosoms with

73

cleavage like a warm riverbed, exuding splendid fragrances. Some of the perfumes I liked; others I had an aversion to. The aversion had developed along with the cravings that had accompanied my first pregnancy, and it had persisted to this day.

The men sidled up and sniffed, lust and hunger in their glances, forgetting they were in someone else's home. Friendships formed, and perhaps with a single glance, it was agreed . . . a time and a place.

No face excited me, except the one I was now following—my husband's face: his wrinkled forehead, and the two deep furrows dividing the space between his eyes like two juxtaposed numbers, giving him a slightly wicked look that was inconsistent with his nature. His body was tall and full; his hair was thin at the front and thick at the temples, like a halo of snow on a wintery night; his nose was long, scattered with a few old scars; and his lips were big, the upper one half-covered by a thick, silvery mustache.

My husband's face aroused my curiosity. The smile, the thoughtfulness, sometimes the harshness and distractedness, and a lot of charm . . .

And what about my own face, which I was now looking at in the mirror? The mirror was reflecting the truth to me. The damn mirror was gloating over me, as if saying, "This is you, and that's the truth you're trying to ignore. You're a woman of forty-five, and your husband is still keen on celebrating your birthday, as if you were a little girl. Perhaps he loves you. Or perhaps he does it to remind you that the years are passing, one by one, coming and going and consuming your life, bit by bit, carrying away with them your freshness and vitality and youth and beauty."

My face was not terribly ugly, but of course it was less charming and attractive than my husband's. Wrinkles surrounded my eyes—unlike his eyes, around which the skin was still tight, although he was over fifty-three.

This was my face, and that was its truth. A truth that suddenly provoked a strange feeling of rebellion in my soul.

I made a resolution: to be unfaithful to my husband.

How? When? With whom? I wasn't concerned with finding answers to these serious questions. I was at a moment of resolution. I resolved to embark on an adventure—I felt I needed it. An adventure that would bring back feelings of youth. A woman of forty-five, but desired, longed for. She has another man. He dreams of her, thinks about her, cares for her. Just like those other women, the ones who attracted my husband's attention. Perhaps they had engaged him in a moment of fleeting pleasure, or perhaps the relationship had lasted several months without my knowing. After all, I was confident of my charm and sex appeal.

Tonight was unlike any other night—it was the beginning of a new journey across my mental horizons. It would transfer me from my husband to the embrace of another man whose features I didn't know yet . . . Who *was* this man with whom I was now contemplating to deceive my husband?

I went to bed and huddled under the covers. It was cold. My husband had fallen asleep before me and was snoring. Every time he breathed out, his mustache trembled. His eyes were relaxed, and the furrows between them had softened a little and become less visible.

I felt cold biting my fingertips. I thought of snuggling close to him. I started to slide my feet under his warm legs, but then I backed off. For a moment, a vague feeling tormented me. What a coward I was, resolving secretly to embark for the first time on a journey which my husband wouldn't share. I was moving away from him, detaching myself, making a strange decision, without any sense of shame about what I was contemplating. Before long, I felt rebellion surge up inside me again, disrupting my calm, rebuking me. Why shouldn't I have another man? He would become an intimate part of my life. I would meet him the day my husband left me for another, younger woman. He, of course, had no thought of having another woman—as a standby—because he could find one whenever he wanted. There were many women available out there, waiting for a signal. But I was a woman who needed a long time to build a bridge between herself and a man, a woman cautious in her choice, who didn't rush into things, who didn't beg a man.

At this point I paused, wondering. Who could I replace my husband with when his desire died out? What kind of relationship was I capable of developing with this person? And could I guarantee that my husband would not find out about the affair?

I looked at him again. This man, asleep, his head resting on the pillow, recovering from his daily toil. Was he not dreaming about what I was thinking?

What of me? What stupidity had got into me? Shouldn't I be ashamed of all this idle talk—a woman who had bid farewell to her forty-fifth year?

In the morning, I felt the urge to return to the previous day's unsuccessful debate. My resolution began to challenge my mind, and my conscience.

I reviewed the names of other men linked to me by chance or necessity. I also reviewed the names of my husband's many men friends. Why shouldn't I? Perhaps he had been involved in some kind of adventure with one of my women friends. But I didn't find a single face among them that my soul desired, and none of them set that cord of longing stirring in me.

I became very calm, but my mind was racing. I felt a continuous sense of rebellion. I was driven by boredom, drawn from one room to another, from wardrobe to drawer. I searched for something to do. All the things that might need tidying up or dusting suddenly looked in perfect order. I loathed everything around me. The house was rejecting me. I decided to go out.

I got into the car in a state of bewilderment. Traces of the heavy makeup I had applied the previous evening were still visible on my face, filling the wrinkles.

The sun was hot, burning my face. It felt as if it were melting the oil in my face cream, and the gold eye-shadow.

I felt reckless. I was a woman looking for some kind of adventure, some frivolous dream. I searched for something in my soul to restore my confidence and tranquillity, but I could find nothing. I unleashed the fury of my failure on the gas pedal. The car flew along, defying everything, even the red lights.

I stopped at the central market. My eye chanced on a face. I turned away from it. It was not the face I wanted, not even to chance on. My gaze crossed many others. But the faces were ordinary. They didn't stir anything in the soul of a woman who wanted a man. A man whose description she herself could not give.

Hurrying into the market, I collided with a woman and stood back to apologize. *Oh, this face! Haven't I seen it before? Where was it?* I stared at the face inquisitively, attracting the woman's attention.

Did I really know this face?

I was certain that I had previously met this woman of about fifty. Her face was familiar. *O God!* The woman looked at me with a mixture of anger and amazement. She moved away, but her face lingered in my memory.

I roamed around the market, laden with all sorts of things I didn't need, my mind elsewhere. Where had I seen her?

Suddenly I remembered a picture of a woman. It had come with one of the letters that my son, who was studying abroad, used to send me, telling me news about himself, and even about his adventures with women. The letter had said:

"Please, Mother, don't be angry. I've spent an unforgettable night with a middle-aged woman. She likes to enjoy herself like a young person, even though her own young days are over for good. I was traveling by train to a distant city which hosts a festival of flowers every year at this time. The people there love flowers, Mother, and celebrate them with a festival. You know how fond I am of flowers, and of 'beauties.'

"This woman sat beside me. She chatted to me about her young days. To be honest, although she was rather silly, what she said was amusing, especially when she told me about her marriage, and her husband, and her awful life with him. She really made me forget the long journey. And after that she made me forget the departure time of my train back. And then she was inviting me to spend the night with her.

"I'm used to drinking, but with her I drank a little more than usual. The drink went to my head, and the woman got drunk as well, and lost what sense she had. I suddenly found myself embracing the flabby body on top of an antique rug. She had told me about this rug on the train, stressing the price she had paid for it and how she had competed with others to buy it. I don't know how many men before me had slept on this rug. Anyway, I did my duty. When I had had a rest, things started coming back to me. I felt disgusted: her body was sweaty and her joints bony, and there was a smell of old age from the parts of her body that were untouched by cosmetics. I had irrigated a dead land. I asked myself, 'How long had it been since this elderly woman had touched a man's body?' In any event, it was an experience. When she saw me off at the station, she made a point of giving me her picture, saying with a smile, 'Maybe you'll remember me, and come back soon.' And so as *not* to remember her, I'm sending *you* her picture."

Oh, her picture . . . I turned around, looking for the face of the woman I had bumped into. I didn't find her. I felt anger flare up in my chest as the picture haunted my imagination.

I dashed out of the central market and flung my trembling body into the car, which by then was as hot as a furnace. I put my foot down nervously on the gas pedal. Images of myself, including the smallest details of my body, flashed into my mind. In the rearview mirror, I saw a car. In it was a familiar face. I slowed down. As I drove away, I gradually forgot the woman's face, and so . . . the picture.

The Smile

Nafila Dhahab

❀❀❀

I used to see him every morning. I would run into him daily as he carried his books under his arm, wearing a smile. I didn't look for him because he always emerged before me like a lotus flower on the water's surface.

My mother would urge me to eat my breakfast, but I would forget it and dash out, not caring about anything, as if I had a date with him, which was not the case.

I was in the springtime of life, and I was afraid that it would pass me by.

Morning after morning I received his smile, until one day I didn't see him. I missed him. Thinking that some misfortune had befallen him, I imagined that I would meet him again in a few days. His face would be pale, and perhaps his smile would be pale as well.

But he didn't show up. I looked for him for a long time. The days passed. The sky cleared and then darkened again, the facades of buildings whitened and then blackened again, and the asphalt hardened and then softened again. But he never returned.

Eventually I grew accustomed to the loneliness. I was no longer in a rush every morning. I arose slowly, ate my breakfast slowly, and even closed the wooden door behind me slowly. I walked unhurriedly through the streets, gazing at the pebbles and the dirt that had accumulated on the pavement and in remote corners. Time stood still, and then I felt it was passing me by. I saw myself outside real time.

Finally, I decided to adopt his smile.

I began to walk through the streets with a smile. I smiled when I met people whose faces were wrinkled with misery. I smiled when I listened to a falsehood as plain as the stars at night. My smile was real and visible to others. I practiced wearing it. It became an integral part of me, and I of it.

At that time, I felt that his light had gone out and that I had become the illuminating torch. I no longer waited to see him because he dominated my imagination day and night. I cultivated "our" smile and became accustomed to this new look.

The days passed, and then months and years went by, while I remained in the same state of mind. The smile had become a permanent feature, my daily bread, and the mask with which I faced the people around me.

One day I went for a drive along the coast. I enjoyed the view of the sea along the road. There were birds flapping their wings on the right, and a few ships at anchor on the left. The day was sunny, dust collected in the air, and a breeze gently stroked the surface of the sea and shook the leaves on the trees. Suddenly my smile froze. Something seemed to have been forcibly snatched from me. I slowed down, and my right foot trembled a little. The sight was a reality surpassing both the truths and the lies that I knew. He was standing there, smiling, his hair blowing in the wind. He was dressed in a uniform with metal buttons and waving a cap the color of which I forgot. I pulled up at his side and got out of the car to greet him. He looked at me without seeing me, and smiled at me and the cars.

He spoke words which were far removed from reality.

I didn't understand what he said. His clothes were dirty, his shoes were faded, and the shoelaces were missing from them. His eyes were dull and expressionless.

I left him there and drove away hurriedly. I continued to look at him in my rearview mirror as he faded into the distance. His hair was blowing in the wind, and his head was tilted to the left. Suddenly I hated the sea birds, and the shining sun, and the ships at anchor. I had the feeling that the smile that I had adopted from him—the smile with which he had faced me every morning and with which I had faced others for years—was little more than morbid pretense. I was filled with remorse and overcome by a passionate longing to weep . . . because now I would never know the truth.

My Mother's Friend

Nura Amin

Abla Safa was very beautiful and graceful. She never married and never fell in love, despite the fact that all the young men in the neighborhood could not take their eyes off her. I used to think it strange that my mother would not let me talk to her or visit her, even though Abla Safa lived alone. As for my mother, she herself showed little inclination to talk to her, although it was clear that in every household Abla Safa had a woman friend—even if not a close friend—whether a young girl, a wife, or a mother. Some fascination made these women cultivate friendship with her, although she did not visit all of them regularly. Once, as I was coming home from school with my mother, we saw Abla Safa at the entrance to the adjacent apartment building. She was cupping her hand around the breast of Auntie Asmat's maid and taking it out of her robe in broad daylight. I decided to call out to Abla Safa but my mother jerked me so hard that she almost dislocated my arm and began to rush nervously toward our apartment. I didn't understand why my mother was behaving this way. Was Abla Safa harming the maid or was she committing a shameful act which I had better not witness so that I would not go to hell? I knew that Abla Safa was not harming the maid because the two of them seemed completely calm and at ease. Auntie Asmat's maid was not screaming or crying as she did every day when Auntie Asmat beat her. I also knew that the two of them were not committing a shameful act because all infants cup their hands around their mothers' breasts while suckling, even on the street or during a visit. So why did my mother continue to sob and angrily toss things around the apartment until Abla Safa came by to reconcile with her? Abla Safa did with my mother what she had done with the maid, then they vanished into the bedroom and

locked the door, emerging only at midnight, before my father returned from his trip abroad. All I knew was that afterward Abla Safa
stopped visiting other women friends, and came only to our house.
Nevertheless, my mother would not let me talk to her. Perhaps this
is the reason that today I still dream that Abla Safa is cupping my
breast with her hand and taking it out of my school uniform, and it's
as if my breast is budding and blossoming in her hand . . .

A Worthless Woman

Hayat Bin al-Shaykh

When he saw me the first time, he looked at me admiringly and said I was pretty, sweet. When he spoke with me, he said I was enticing, wonderful. When he tried to put his hand on my shoulder to kiss me, he said I was complicated, because I pushed his hand away and refused his kiss. And when he invited me to his apartment and I said no, he said I was abnormal. So I left him, with his insults ringing in my ears: "Crazy girl . . . conceited." I rushed off in search of a drink and a cigarette. I wanted to blot out my frustration, and downfall, and the bewildering questions, buzzing in my head.

As I began to drink from the first glass, I said to myself that it might be true that I was abnormal. Why was I abnormal? I really didn't know. Perhaps because I didn't want anyone else but you, because I couldn't forget you. By the second glass, I felt I wasn't abnormal, just rather unruly, like a wild tigress that needed to indulge in physical activity. By the third glass, I realized I was an exemplary woman, a wonderful woman. How was I wonderful? Never mind . . . but I was wonderful, and the men I knew were all stupid, fatuous. They didn't understand me. I laughed . . . I wasn't laughing because they were stupid and fatuous; I had always known that. I was laughing because I was certain I was wonderful . . . perhaps. By the fourth glass, the thoughts began to battle in my head; obvious truths began to crowd in front of my eyes. I tried to shut my eyes in order not to see the red warning light flashing in front of them. I was in the process of discovering something else: I wasn't wonderful, I wasn't exemplary; I was a stupid, failed woman . . . a desperate woman. I didn't know how to live or what to do. I was heading for madness, that was all. This was the plain truth I had pretended not to see for years and years. Only now did it finally dawn on me. By the fifth glass, I had become convinced that I was nothing, that I couldn't possibly amount to anything as long as I loved you, because my love for you destroyed every sensible thing in my life, and my desire for you put a slur on my name and what was best in my life. I smashed the glass and dragged my feet to the darkness of my house, weeping for my failed life, the life I had discovered was nothing. In the alleyways, on the walls, on the quilt and the pillow, I could see words written in a red as dark as the blood coagulating on the chest of a slaughtered bird: *a worthless woman.*

I couldn't bear the effect of these words for long, so I threw the pillow and the quilt and the papers and the books onto the floor and trampled on them. Then I went in search of a drink that would tell me I was a wonderful woman, not abnormal or stupid. But I found nothing. The words, dark red like the blood coagulating on the chest of a slaughtered bird, kept dancing in front of me. I saw them in every corner of the house: *a worthless woman.* . . . So I hurried away, running from the hateful words, from the constant buzzing that split my head.

I began to walk along the empty street, chewing over my exasperation, disgorging my hesitation, gulping at the cups of my failure and despair. I looked at the sky. The bright moonlight dazzled my eyes. I stood still, gazing at the moon, and asked myself, "Why can't I have the moon? I want it. How can I reach it? Would I be able to reach it if I tried to?" I began to laugh, convinced that I was a stupid fool. What was there in the moon for me to desire? The moon shed its light from far away, but in fact it was just a solid rock with nothing on it but frost. The frost that I hated. The moon deceived us with its pure light. The vast distance disguised the truth about it. And so it attracted silly girls like me, who were fond of absurdity.

Once again I began to chew over my exasperation, to disgorge my hesitation, and to gulp at the cups of my failure and despair. I remembered that when I was a naive little girl, I had wanted the sun. My mother used to hit me when she found me spending hours gazing at it, my eyes red from its rays, my body sweaty from its heat. My father constantly rebuked me, saying that if I didn't stop looking at the sun, it would one day tumble down on my head, burn me up, and leave me a pile of bones. But I would laugh and make fun of what he said. I would bounce off resolutely, break up one of my mother's necklaces, and throw the beads up one by one toward the sun, trying to hit it. I would carry on until I felt almost blinded by the burning rays, until my eyes were overflowing with tears, and the buzzing in my head grew louder and louder with the intense heat. The beads of the stolen necklace would be scattered here and there, having failed to hit their target. I would then look at the sky and scream, cursing the sun and the moon and my thoughts, teetering on the edge of madness and absurdity.

I was certain now that I wanted you, no one else but you, no matter what had happened or what would happen. Through the veils of darkness your bright face appeared—charming, handsome, and sweet—just as I knew and loved it. I saw your eyes, constantly filled with wonder and amazement, and felt I could almost drown in their sea of honey. I also realized that you were lovlier and sweeter— and farther away—than the sun and the moon.

I knew I wanted you and no one else but you; therefore, I was a stupid fool. I could have been a remarkable woman if I hadn't loved and wanted you. So I would carry on living as I did, following you like a faithful dog following its master. I was also certain that you were stupid like me, weak and vain, unable to say openly what you wanted, because you didn't know what to do or what to look for. And perhaps that was why I worshiped you.

I went home, dragging my tired feet, running away from the sun and the moon and you. I was no longer afraid of reading the words, dark red like the blood coagulating on the chest of a slaughtered bird, inscribed in the alleyways, on the quilt and the pillow: *a worthless woman.* We had become *two worthless people, you and me.* And I couldn't figure out which one of us had dragged the other down.

I made my way back, trying to paint your picture. How would you look, I wondered, if I painted your picture? I imagined you without a body, without a heart or face, just two beautiful eyes, a sea of honey in which I would drown the frustrations of my life and the confusion of my thoughts. I would drink it down to the dregs, until the source ran dry and . . .

But what if I painted you as a face without eyes? Like the moon without light, or the sky without a sun or moon, or springtime without flowers; like a rose without dew, or a river without water; like the statue of a blind god standing high up on a distant hill, and I a little pebble rolling between your legs, tossed about by the hurricane winds, flung to and fro against my will, darting about with the current. But

I would always come back to throw myself under your feet, to kiss the dust on the soles of your feet.

I threw the paintbrush to the floor, tore up the paper, and flung myself onto the bed to try to sleep. I had persuaded myself that you were a sly, mean god, made of mud and clay, who didn't deserve at all to be worshiped; that the honey that filled your eyes was bitter, mingled with a poison that killed anyone who tried to get a taste of it; that I was stupid and stubborn for loving you; that the whole world was fatuous, hateful; that people were silly, trivial, duped; that everyone had ten horns blazing with fire, and six eyes dripping with poison, and three open mouths waiting to bite anyone who dared to approach.

People constantly said I was rash, that I didn't know how to live. My women friends said I was conceited, hesitant, that I didn't know what I wanted. And men, observing me from a distance, said I was sweet, wonderful. But when they got closer, they said I was strange, abnormal. And you always said I was stubborn, crazy. I knew you were saying that because I loved you and wanted you. But I hadn't yet understood who I was. All I knew was that I was a failed woman, a desperate woman, *a worthless woman*. A woman who was looking for herself but who hadn't yet found herself.

Perhaps I *would* find myself—if I could forget you someday. Perhaps?

Part Three

❦⟡❦

Male-Female Relations

Where To?

Colette Suhayl al-Khuri

❧❀✦❀❧

*T*he isolated stella[1] gazes at the star and sparkles. Doesn't he realize that she's closer to him than he is to himself? Doesn't he feel that the light of her love defies the great studded distance between them, and fills it?

"Why don't we meet?"

The question is absorbed by the rays of the tender star.

"Why don't we meet?"

The call is drowned in her tears.

Her constant reply is a sparkle. How can she tell him that she fears for him because of her love? How can she explain to him that they have to fly above the stars and leave the sky altogether if they are to meet? The sky! She didn't ask to be a diamond in the nocturnal darkness, and the fact that she is a source of light doesn't dazzle her. She hates the sky. She hates the frost of the sky. But she will not remove her beloved from his luminous world. It was decreed that they should be separated in the sky. For his sake, she will yield to the sky's will.

"Why don't we meet?"

Her pride forbids her to reveal her inner conflict. She twinkles ironically: "We were created to adorn the sky!"

The star shines brightly: "And to illuminate the earth!"

The rays well up from her sorrowfully and pour down onto the earth.

There, on the seashore, a young couple are walking side by side, holding hands. They sit on a rock, clinging to each other.

The tender stella twinkles, and her wounded twinkle excites the star.

"They're human beings," she says. "But we live in the heights and can't do what earthly people do."

He glares: "We can if we want. If we want."

The stella fades, frightened. Does he know the price? The stars must pay for happiness. And the price of their meeting is high.

She suppresses her yearning: "But we don't want to. Our duty in life is loftier than we can pretend to forget. Ordinary people need you to stay in the heights. Passersby need your light."

Sparks of scorn fly from the star: "We stars delude ourselves that ordinary people need us. It's an illusion with which we console ourselves. We seek the warmth of this illusion in order to forget the frost of our existence."

The stella calms down, agreeing: "Yes, we give, and passersby don't understand the meaning of giving."

The young couple on the seashore are enthralled by the dual agonies exploding in rays above them.

The man raises his face to the sky, saying, "Look how wonderful our stars are, and how pure our sky is!"

Lost in thought, the woman murmurs, "How narrow the earth is! I wish we lived in the vastness of the sky! I wish we were two everlasting stars!"

The man regards her admiringly, his gaze lost in hers. He puts his arm around her shoulders, whispering, "I love you!"

The stella glitters, and the star flares: "Love, love. A word that ordinary people constantly repeat without understanding the meaning of it."

He turns toward the stella and glares out his confession: "I love you. I love you the way no human being can love. I love you with my fire and my light. I love you with every heavenly treasure and gift there is in my existence."

The stella is moved to tears, and her glow increases. Should she tell him that her only wish is to fly to him? No!

Her grief pours down in blazing strands, enveloping the wide-awake couple on the seashore.

The woman leans her head on the man's warm shoulder and asks him flirtatiously, "How much do you love me?"

He embraces her. "So much that I'll give you everything I own. I want to marry you!"

The star twinkles: "How stupid earthly people are!" Suddenly he shines anxiously. How much does his stella love him? His hopeful glow engulfs the stella, and she shimmers: "I love you . . . I love you even to the point of giving up my place in the eternal frost so that you can stay in the sky!"

The star shudders, amazed, and sprinkles the seashore with silver rays. Who told her that he wants to stay in the sky? Should he confess to her that his luminous world is miserable without her because it lacks an inner light?

He darkens: "How unhappy I am!"

The stella dims. What point is there in her sacrifice if it doesn't deliver him from his misery? What sense is there in her pride when it makes her a coward? Her misgivings ebb away. Why not turn his constant misery and her unending unhappiness into a moment of joy?

She lights up: "Won't you be sorry to leave the sky?"

He sparkles: "The moment of our meeting will be greater than the sky!"

"So why don't we meet?"

The question makes her tearful.

"Why don't we meet?"

The call has now become part of her.

The star shines fearfully. Does he have the right to stand in the way of her eternity? As long as he is far away from her, she is eternal. Their being together means conflagration!

"We shall burn up!"

She beams ecstatically: "What point is there in my eternity if I live in loneliness?" Then she opens her embrace, determined: "The moment of our being together will live forever! At that moment I will discharge my light. It is of no importance to me that I'll be extinguished afterward!"

The star trembles with longing and happiness.

"Let's leave the sky!"

She flies above the stars.

"Let's meet!"

They meet.

"Let's burn up!"

On the seashore, the woman sighs deeply.

"What's the matter?" the man asks.

"Nothing. I saw a shooting star!"

"It's a wishing star! Did you make a wish?"

She laughs shyly, "Yes."

He embraces her and asks tenderly, "What did you wish?"

"I wished . . . I wished our love would shine and last forever like the stars!"

The Cat

Layla Ba'labakki

W̶e are now at the beginning of summer. In February, the cat gave birth to her kittens on a small road where the municipal workmen were laying asphalt and had thrown away their leftovers and dirty handkerchiefs. The mother spent the first days licking the blood from the little bodies. One night, when the rain was beating down mercilessly on the street, and the cold was creeping into the mother's limbs and the kittens' paws, and the thunder was drowning every voice on earth, and the lightning was slashing the face of the sky—on this particular night, the kittens' mother heard soft footfalls on the paving stones outside the iron barrel, and they startled her. She pulled her kittens closer and rubbed their bodies to warm them up. Then she slowly sniffed them. The soft footfalls were hovering, hovering. The kittens' mother knew them. She had heard them at the window of the house where she used to live, and her heart fluttered. That was a few months earlier, when she had lived with an old couple, their unmarried, only son, and their maid. Everybody had spoiled her and was proud of her. She had the most beautiful eyes, sometimes violet, sometimes grayish-blue. She was slender, and her white fur, spotted with honey-colored circles, shone like a mirror reflecting the rising sun. She lived like a princess, sharing in the household's simple, quiet, and pleasant life. "What shall we cook today, Jasmine?" "The old man's smoking a lot, Jasmine." "The boy's late, Jasmine." "Jasmine."

The mistress had explained to her that her name meant a white flower that lives only for a short time and then disappears. Its fragrance, she said, was the strongest, softest, and best of all flower perfumes. Why hadn't the mistress told her that she resembled the jasmine flower only in its fleeting life, which faded like stars on a bright night? Anyway, what mattered was that she had seen his stubborn, giant figure filling the window. She had stolen glances at him, and whispered to herself that he was the most beautiful cat she had ever seen, that she felt weak and numb when she saw him, and that love with him would be wonderful. So she left the house one evening, followed him in his meanderings, and gave him love. Lots and lots of love. He showered her with love, overwhelmed her with love, smothered her with love. She was the richest cat in the world. At the very least, she had tasted this experience and felt the sensations, colors, and pulse of those magic moments, filled with pleasure and trembling and fear. And he, this cat who was hovering around the barrel now, he had given her more than love: he had given her the babies. And she, on account of the babies, would continue to respond to him, to follow him, to dream of him.

The soft footfalls of the kittens' father died away, and the storm intensified. The kittens' mother listened, alert. The kittens looked up at their mother's face, questioning, and she reassured them that all was safe again in their refuge, and that they would find another hideout the next day.

When the storm abated and dawn broke, the cat began to move her kittens. She thought it best to scatter them in different places, and so it was that one of them ended up in a lighted kitchen window.

The little cat didn't know what had happened to her mother and sisters. All she knew was that there was a smell of milk escaping from the open window, and she craned her neck toward it. A fat woman spotted her. She dragged her in savagely, threw her on the floor, and said in a mean and raucous voice, "This cat's arrived at the right time. She's going to clear the house of mice, and she'll get nothing to eat except what she catches!" To begin with, the mice didn't come out of their nests. Even if they had, the cat wouldn't have recognized them, because she had never encountered a mouse before. As a result, she was forced to steal a lot of milk so she would not die of hunger before the encounter with the mice took place. One night, she was dozing off in the darkness on a chair in the corner of the kitchen, when she heard a light, unusual movement. She opened one eye and saw a group of mice, big ones and small ones—perhaps a whole family. She got ready to challenge them, but then she closed her eyes and felt fear and disgust at the mere thought of ever having to eat these revolting creatures. She asked herself how she could possibly swallow a creature that size. Why, anyway, did she have to treat them as enemies? Who knows, perhaps they were kinder than the fat woman. She jumped down from the chair onto the tiled floor to welcome the guests, but they dispersed, startled. She looked around, and on one of the shelves, she saw a sack over-flowing with flour. Then she understood. She stole away into the living room, clearing the mice's way for a safe assault.

In the morning, the fat woman discovered the conspiracy, and she beat the cat and threw her out. After that, the cat wandered in and out of many houses, where she was beaten, imprisoned, starved, and forced to kill even rats and worms and gnats. Finally, she dis-covered a neglected garden and settled there, eating whatever the wealthy and wasteful dropped from their balconies. She roamed about in this plot of land, singing and rejoicing. Now she was on her own territory, free and nameless.

As for me, when my mother was pregnant with me, she was in love with a man who was not my father. Because she loved this man so passionately, I turned out very, very pretty, and everyone who sees me just keeps saying, "She's so pretty. She's so pretty." I'm now nineteen years old. I'm determined not to become pregnant unless I'm drown-ing in a stormy sea of love. Then the face of my child will look out onto the world like the moon. The moon? No. The moon is cold, stupid. It has no meaning. No. The face of my child will radiate warmth, like the sun. Had I lived in the age of paganism, I would have been one of the sun's slave girls, worshiping it in the temple and burning incense. And then the earth. This is the first time I've thought of the earth. The earth doesn't interest me: the soil, the trees, the rocks, the springs. What interests me is to be loved on this earth. And now I have a man who loves me. This is the only thing that gives me satisfaction.

I know what I want. Meanwhile my feet sink into the earth and my face embraces the sun in anticipation that someone will reach the moon to wipe it out and relieve me of its stupid light. I know I won't struggle to be a free woman and a heroine and immortal. It gives me pleasure to be going to the university this year, and to share in the clamor, boredom, superficiality, and sweet dreams of my fam-ily, and in the depravity of some of its members, and their cow-ardice. I relax at home and melt away in the street, and with this I feel that I'm safe, and I dream calmly, calmly, and with pleasure.

No. I'm not like those legendary women who can live alone. Loneliness? It kills me. Places empty of human beings frighten me.

That's why I intend to get married and have many children. In the meantime, I'm unable, unable to breathe, if there isn't a man at my side who loves me. As for myself, I haven't been in love yet.

This person sitting next to me in the car, listening carefully and alertly to the mewing of the cat, he's the man with whom I roam the city these days. Although his age is twice my own nineteen years, he is happier than I am. He's the one who taught me to laugh, and the one who discovered that my laughter betrays longing, that my smile is the blossoming of a tulip, that my complexion is the red, velvety petals of a rose, and that my eyes are a harbor guiding sailors to the shores of pleasure, to the prize diamond, to victory.

What I like about him is the gray hair on his temples. It's the only thing that makes my fingers go numb. Once he asked me what I wanted from him as a present. I said, "Your gray hair." His eyes grew pensive, and his cheeks paled. He pulled me toward him and showered me with kisses. He didn't leave one atom of my body un-kissed. When he kisses me, I feel as if I'm bathing in a rivulet under a walnut tree, while far away on the rugged road a villager carries a load of wheat to the mill. And the mill is on top of the mountain.

I made him understand from the start that I know what I want, and that I don't intend to fall madly in love with him and abandon my world, riding behind him on horseback to some unknown forest. That's why we've never talked about his wife, home, or work. And I haven't told him anything about my life. We go out to dinner, we dance, we swim, we climb mountains. I'm his spring, and he's my summer. We have fun.

But he surprises me.

He surprised me just now in the car. Instead of putting his arm around my shoulder and letting my head rest in the hollow between his chin and shoulder, then moistening my eyes, my mouth, and my neck with his tongue; instead of driving the car wildly with one hand through the city streets, he sat stiffly, his eyes exploring the court-yard of the club and the neglected garden. "Can you hear a cat mew-ing?" he asked. "Yes, I can," I answered. He jumped out and ordered, "Go on slowly. I'll pick up the cat and take her to my father so he can play with her." He disappeared behind a hedge of bright flowers and eventually emerged, clutching a skinny little cat that was rend-ing the air with her mewing. He threw the cat onto the back seat, closed the window, then drove like a maniac through the streets. I shut my eyes, afraid that any minute he would crash into a wall or knock someone over. I hadn't seen him so proud, triumphant, and happy, as he was just then. Without turning to me, he repeated, "I'm going back to give the cat to my father so he can play with her. After that we'll have dinner." At that moment, I felt lonely, so lonely, and sad; I almost suffocated. I wanted to weep but didn't open my mouth. I gave vent to my emotions in a sudden, magical movement: I stretched out my hand in the darkness of the car to the back seat. The cat had calmed down and stopped mewing, and I couldn't make her out behind me. I ran my fingers over the rough carpet, at the same time scrutinizing my man's face out of the corner of my eye. He was ecstatic, his glance wandering beyond the houses and the lights and the people on the street. I opened the window on my side, and continued to search the carpet with my other hand. As if anticipating her salvation, the cat drew near my fingers. I seized her, then squeezed her soft body with my fingers. This time she let out a scream. I drew my hand back and began to tremble. I breathed in relief when he didn't turn around but merely said, "My father will be so happy with the cat. He'll have fun with her." I smiled secretly in exhaustion. I shut my eyes, placed my hand on her belly, lifted her up carefully, and threw her out of the window into the street. Then I hurriedly closed the window and passed a cold hand across my flushed face. I didn't dare look at his face after that. My hair was getting in my eyes, and I wished it were as long as palm leaves, so I could hide myself behind it. I struggled for words. "Drop me off at a café," I said. Judging by his voice, he wasn't surprised. "We'll have dinner on the mountain, as agreed," he said, "after I've taken the cat to my father so he can play with her." But I shouted, "Drop me off at a café!" The pain was creeping farther into my hand, my chest was getting tighter, and the sadness was paralyzing my feet.

"Drop me off here!"

He pulled up at a café, saying, "What's the matter? Wait here until I've delivered the cat."

I dragged my feet to the door of the café, but I didn't go in. Instead, I hurried away to wander in the silent, deserted alleyways.

The Woman of My Dreams

Fadila al-Faruq

I like to call him "philosopher," for the simple reason that he really is a philosopher. Life, in his opinion, is an egg, and the egg
resembles the world, and the world is a point, and he's a point,
and I'm the most important point in his life. That's what he tells me
anyway.

Sometimes he calls me "Egg." When I ask him flirtatiously what
an egg means to him, he replies without hesitation, "Life is an egg,
Egg." We've known each other for five years. Now the time has
come to choose a direction for our relationship.

He teaches philosophy, which is lost in the jelly of this "egg,"
in a secondary school, and I teach chemistry, which means nothing
to my students except for the process of making a bomb.

My troublemaker student, Umar Hassun, constantly asks,
"When are we going to make ourselves a bomb, teacher?" In fact, I
don't know when we will have an opportunity to make a bomb together, and even the philosopher fails to give me a concrete answer
to this question. He stares at me, as if he has lost something in my
features, and doesn't utter a word for an entire hour. Instead, he
keeps rubbing his beard, which he hasn't shaved for a long time.

He's a philosopher, and it's his right to behave in an eccentric
manner, so long as I'm not yet his wife. I want to whisper this simple truth to him because I've been thinking about it for a while. But
Umar Hassun's question silences the words on the tip of my tongue.

Recently, I've decided to present this question to him again:
"When can we make a bomb, my ugly philosopher?" This is not a lie
that I've fabricated against him one day, because he is rather un-
attractive. His eyeballs are protruding from so much contemplation,
and his long teeth resemble the great Chinese wall. As for his hair,

it's been hanging loose over his shoulders since he was a university student. I still can't understand the physical attraction, because he's really ugly, although there are times that I never tire of looking at him.

He prefers to discuss matters in the order of their importance. He classifies them, invents strange names for things we know, and poses many questions about what we consider self-evident. He's different.

He's still gazing at me, while I'm waiting for an answer with which to satisfy Umar Hassun the troublemaker. It's my chance to delve beyond his eyes into his innermost thoughts. I wonder whether he'll make up his mind today and set a date for our engagement, a date for our wedding, a date for ending all our secret meetings in the Studio of Lights. Will he make up his mind today?

"Are you thinking about our marriage, philosopher?"

"Egg, darling, when you talk about marriage you appear to be as stupid as all the other women who allow the idea of marriage to dominate their thoughts."

"But marriage is the true relationship between—"

He cuts me short: "We're unable to make a bomb because we always think about establishing true relations between us. We think . . . think . . ."

What is this crazy man saying? He fills me with anxiety. In the twinkling of an eye he changes my identity to a prostitute—according to the customs and conventions of our society.

"But I love you. I love you," he declares. "I want to continue my life with you. Can't you understand? It's difficult for me to stop at this point, which doesn't represent the proper ending to what I've begun with you . . .

"Why can't you be an unconventional woman? Why can't you be an extraordinary woman who doesn't change with the purchase of a document that supposedly confers respectability? Why can't you be a dream woman, one who plays a big role in my research and studies, as well as in history? Yes, I want you to be the woman of my dreams, Egg. I want you to remain vibrant forever. I don't want you to be a wife whose concerns revolve around food, children, tantrums, and dinner invitations—a woman for others. I don't want you like that."

All men lie. They lie in general. Even the philosopher, a year after this speech, married another woman and had children by her, while granting me the permanent label of fallen woman as a result of my relationship with him in the Studio of Lights. I didn't find a husband to help rid me of the complexes that the philosopher bequeathed to me, so I returned to him to be a woman for his dreams. Oddly enough, after his marriage, I could no longer bear Umar Hassun's question, "When can we make a bomb?" It seemed to me that he was asking, "When will you establish a true relationship with your lover? When will you get married?" I began to hate his question, hate his face, hate his presence. So I gave him a recipe for making a traditional bomb, and put an end to his question. Later, I forgot him completely, when I became merely a woman of dreams.

Mozart's Fez

Samiya At'ut

When the sun rose, his stout figure appeared in the distance, beckoning me to come to him. I went, perfectly content with what would happen between us—Mozart, and perhaps other melodies of greater warmth than music.

When I arrived, he removed his fez and placed it carefully on the ground. Then he took a flute from the pocket of his harem pants and began to play. I found my body involuntarily bending in preparation for the dance. I danced for a long time, until I became exhausted. Hardly had I finished dancing when my speckled skin flaked and fell off. He opened the flap of his tent, which was pitched behind him, and let me in. Darkness enveloped me, and through the threads of luminous dust inside, I saw the tent filling with hundreds of Eves. I lifted the tent flap to go out and ask him for an explanation of what was happening, and perhaps to get a breath of fresh air. I was surprised to see him putting his red fez on his head and moving away. His sinuous movements were like those of a viper as he approached another woman in the distance.

A Virgin Continent

Samira Azzam

❧❧❧

"Do you know, darling? I used to feel that you were near me when I was busy composing my letters to you and writing at length. It annoyed me to receive your replies, for they were brief and cryptic like telegrams, as if you were only fulfilling a duty."

"Is this a rebuke?"

"You might call it that. How would you justify your behavior?"

"I don't know. Perhaps it's laziness. Or perhaps I suffer from a 'letter complex' which makes me feel that I'm no good at writing them."

"Were you once good at writing letters?"

"Yes. In fact, one of my girlfriends used to ask me to write her letters for her."

"Couldn't she write them herself?"

"No, she wasn't accustomed to writing. Writing requires keen understanding, and my friend could only read."

"I still don't understand this complex of yours."

"Well, since you insist that I tell you. I could feel her hypocrisy when she clothed her feelings with my words. The phrase, 'Oh, my first love,' with which she insisted on beginning every letter, seemed trite to me."

"Was he really her first love?"

"I don't know. The letters were addressed to a different person each time."

"That's hypocrisy!"

"I don't want to criticize unfairly. Let's call her a 'fortune hunter.'"

"Did she marry?"

"Her father was not one of those with the proper qualifications."

"Strange. I wonder if I . . ."

"It's not what I meant. I was talking only about my girlfriend."

"Is it possible for a woman to have more than one love in her life?"

"Perhaps a woman has no more than one love in her life, but it's possible that she has more than one man in her life."

"What do you mean?"

"Nothing."

"As you wish. Let's leave aside the riddles for now. I expected you to refer in your letters to specific things, because people are more daring on paper. You didn't try, for example, to ask me about my past."

"Why should I?"

"Doesn't my past interest you?"

"You'll tell me about your past even without my asking. You'll dig up every event, big and small. And even if you have no past, your imagination will come to your rescue with many stories."

"You mean that I excel at fabrication?"

"It's not a question of fabrication, but of translating adolescent dreams. Your eyes would shine—as would those of any Middle Eastern man—when you tell me about the dark-skinned woman and the blonde one and the tall one and the plump one, and the rich one whose wealth you flatly rejected because you hated the idea of being bought by a woman, and the divorcée whom you refused because you didn't want damaged goods, and the prostitute who learned moral excellence from you. The neighbors' daughter will be among them, and the bar girl, and your classmate in college. Dozens of them. Don't be angry, darling. Have I offended your manliness?"

"You are . . ."

"What? Say it!"

"I prefer not to."

"Then let me call myself frank."

"Still, I love you."

"I must believe it, or else you wouldn't be engaged to me."

"I fell in love with you for more than one reason."

"I don't doubt that at all."

"We're talking in riddles again."

"Never mind. Tell me. Why did you fall in love with me?"

"First of all, I must confess that you're pretty."

"I'm not prettier than any of your female cousins."

"And you're educated."

"Perhaps I deserve this attribute, as long as I don't go to my girlfriends and ask them to write my letters for me."

"And you're virtuous."

"Oh, come now! Stop here for a moment."

"Why? You possess everything that can be called a virtue according to our moral code."

"We are virtuous to the extent that others do not know us. Shouldn't we define this concept first?"

"I don't suppose that the word *virtue* has more than one meaning."

"You talk like my mother."

"What does your mother say?"

"About what?"

"About the virtuous woman, for example."

"Exactly what you say."

"Namely, that the virtuous woman is polite, composed, sensible, and without a past."

"A past which is written down!"

"What do you mean?"

"I mean that women, in contrast to men, are quick to forget, darling."

"All of them?"

"Yes, because it's not easy for them to gamble with the word *virtuous*. This word constitutes a thick passport, as you can imagine."

"You've aroused my curiosity."

"That makes me happy."

"Would it annoy you if I ask you a question?"

"Not at all. But I'm afraid that you might be annoyed by my answer."

"You're talking to an educated man."

"You do well to remind me."

"Have you . . . have you ever gambled?"

"Oh, stop beating about the bush. Speak plainly as I do."

"Were there letters?"

"Certainly."

"Let's suppose that you were to use your girlfriend's opening phrase in your letters to me. How would it read?"

"Oh, my second love!"

"Really? Then . . ."

"Yes. Once."

"Go on. Speak."

"Don't get excited. Or should I remind you that I'm talking to an educated man?"

"Were you in love with him?"

"It wasn't like my girlfriend's love. I loved him to the extent that I would feel ignoble if I started my life with you without letting you know the real me."

"When did it happen?"

"Seven years ago."

"And you still talk about him with such passion?"

"When a person dies before his time, he remains young in the memory of his loved ones."

"Would you have preferred him to me?"

"If I myself had chosen."

"Who, then, had chosen, if not you?"

"My mother, my father, my brothers. I felt weak. I also felt pressured by people's questions about why I hadn't married yet, and by my relatives' insistence that I get married. I'd begun to sense that they were weary of me."

"And why didn't your 'first love' end the way you wanted?"

"He was young and poor and could not be a husband—according to my mother's criteria."

"Was it important to you that your mother should approve of him?"

"I was afraid to lose her love. I knew how she could harass me and dispel my fantasies. It wasn't easy for me to imagine my father walking with his head bowed, as she would say, and my mother dying of grief, and my life destroyed at the hands of a beggar."

"She knows better what's good for you. Did you want her to go along with your illusions?"

"It wasn't an illusion. It was a true love and its memory is still alive in my heart."

"You're bold!"

"Bold, frank, insolent—say whatever you wish. But I told a truth that needed telling."

"As if the matter doesn't concern you . . ."

"On the contrary, it concerns both of us—you and me. I want you to recognize me as a whole that cannot be divided into parts, not as a creature whose life history began the day you deigned to notice her. This is my right. I didn't fabricate a story to test the depth of your love for me."

"Weren't you afraid of losing me?"

"Losing you? You're funny. I know the motives that propelled us toward each other. Why the hypocrisy? Don't you think that in our situation—or at least in my situation—sincerity is more conducive to building a life that so far possesses none of the essentials except for the facade?"

"You're cruel."

"I don't blame you for saying that. In fact, I forgive you."

"Forgive me?"

"Yes, in the same way that I forgive the landlord who hung plaques with his name on all four sides of the building that he had bought, because it annoyed him to see that the tenants received letters bearing the previous owner's name."

"Do you think that I'm jealous?"

"Perhaps there's more to it than that."

"Don't act rashly. I don't believe a word of what you've said."

"You're a landlord, too!"

"Don't provoke me. Say that you concocted the whole story."

"I didn't concoct anything."

"Then why do you mention this now?"

"I don't know. It has infuriated me at times to hear you talk about your experiences with such arrogance, as though you were speaking to a person with no right to experience anything nor to taste life's triumphs and defeats, a person who was not born until the day you met her."

"This, then, is an act of revenge."

"You can call it that as long as you insist on stripping the issue from its moral aspects. I call it frankness and openness."

"Your frankness and openness are unbearable! Don't you know that I hate such jokes?"

"Yes, as much as you hate losing the sense of being the discoverer of a virgin continent!"

An Old Couple

Nadiya Khust

❦

"The prickly pears have covered the land."

"I heard that the municipality has decided to cut down all the prickly pears."

"All of them? That's a shame. People have cut down the olive trees, and now the prickly pears as well?"

The woman was sitting on a stone bench near a mud house. In front of her, within her sight, were valleys of olives and figs. The man was sitting on a small wicker chair, and his eyes, like hers, were riveted on the blue-green horizon.

"The daffodils have sprouted, and we haven't pruned the grapevines."

The man looked at the woman, then turned his gaze toward the valleys. He thought to himself: At the time when I was able to prune the vines and peel the prickly pear for you, you refused me, Maryam. Today, other people wait for the trees to grow, and strew fertilizer around them, and watch the rain, and fear for the crop from the frost. In our plots, the vines have attacked the fig trees, and there's no one to prune them. The hand that could reach the farthest branches has weakened. Now, when the season of figs and prickly pears arrives, we can only pick the closest fruit.

The old couple fell silent, their faces turned toward the panoramic view. They were a man and a woman of the same age who knew each other well and could speak without words. Neither of them pretended to be kind to the other, or expressed special concern that betrayed old age, or showed any repressed anger. Each of them remembered the other as a young person with a firm body, picking olives and grapes, plowing and sowing the land.

106

"Shall I pour you another cup of tea, Abu Dib?"

"After a single cup, I'm unable to sleep, Maryam."

A silence followed. He said, "I have to go. People are waiting for me." But he did not move from his place.

He usually went from house to house, asking people what they needed and supplying those items. This work was all he could do in his old age. The small village had grown. Many households were added to it, and they needed someone to fetch vegetables, fruit, and meat from the shops. As for the shops, they sold cans of milk, juice, pineapple, and meat, as well as bottles of water. They needed someone to deliver the groceries to the customers.

The old man would carry his basket, knock on doors, and call out to the owners of the houses from the windows. He served the old, the women who remained in the village during the winter, and the absentees who returned during the summer and on holidays. He accepted small tasks, such as buying a bottle of Coke or a bunch of parsley. But he took these tasks seriously, as if he had reached an understanding with his customers that he would earn his payment with effort.

On his rounds he called on the old woman. He would sit on the wicker chair and talk to her, or remain silent, his basket at his side. Sometimes he charged her for what she wanted, and sometimes he bought her groceries as a gift: two bananas, an ounce of meat, and four eggs. She never refused what he brought her, nor did they discuss the matter, as if they were husband and wife.

"What do you need today, Maryam?" he asked her.

But he continued to sit, his eyes fastened on the scenic view. Today, in this weather, he wanted to stay here. He wanted to lean his head against the mud wall, and leave his basket by the pomegranate tree until the next day. The snow had melted. It seemed that the old couple had survived the winter and welcomed the spring. Indeed, the man feared the winter. At his age, he could not shovel snow to clear a path from his house, and the cold no longer turned his cheeks rosy.

The sun had climbed in the clear blue sky, and the distant sea appeared on the horizon. Umm Hanna emerged from her house on the other side of the street. She placed a large basin of water on the ground and began to wash her hair. The old man looked at her attentively, then turned his eyes toward the dramatic view. His mind filled with a vivid recollection. Long ago, when he had stood by the pomegranate tree, Umm Hanna was a little girl playing in front of her house.

"Maryam, Maryam," he called out.

"Go away. Go away," she replied.

"Maryam, let's run away."

"You're crazy Abu Dib. My God, you're crazy. Go away."

"Am I crazy, Maryam? No one's crazy but you!"

That day he retreated from his spot by the pomegranate tree, and stole away through the vines, figs, and olives.

Of all the places in the village, this spot was like a thorn in his side, a thorn which he felt however he moved. It was inevitable that he should settle his account with Maryam.

But old age did not encourage settling accounts. Nor was he the sort of man to carry a gun or a stick and lie in wait for his enemies behind a tree or between the rocks. Instead, he had stood in the wilderness in front of the mountain and screamed, "Woe unto you, world. Maryam went away, and who will bring her back? He screamed on and on, and then composed a love song from his screams and sang it plaintively.

"The world is full of girls. Forget her."

"No. There's no one like Maryam. I feel for you, Maryam. Your days will be black, Maryam."

He knew that her days were dismal, that her father was paying of his mortgage with the bride price, and that he had sworn not to marry off another daughter except in the village—as she wanted. But, could he have done all that without Maryam? Maryam was a jewel. After she had returned, he said to her, "How often have I told you, Maryam, let's run away? Are you better off this way? You're alone, and I'm alone."

She let him blame her. It was inevitable that he should blame her. But here they were now, meeting in their old age. Safe. Who would say that they were not husband and wife when they sat together in the morning?

"People have lost people. We have found each other, Abu Dib."

(You still don't understand why I didn't run away with you, Abu Dib? My father had to pay off the mortgage on his tiny plot of land. The old man came along. He wanted a blonde and tall girl. I was blonde and tall. He married me, and I wept. But could I say no to my father, and let my brothers go hungry? Once, I passed through this village with my husband. I squatted on the ground, placed my hand in the irrigation canal, and became lost in thought. Woe is me! I no longer belong here, and I don't belong there. After the old man had died, I returned to the village.)

"I never married."

"What's the use of dwelling on the past, Abu Dib? What's the use?"

(Yesterday, I saw girls walking with young men at night. The village girls have returned from the city on their school break, and there is a festive atmosphere everywhere. The world has changed, Abu Dib.)

"And what about our lives, Maryam?"

(Sadness, however, does not hit so hard in old age as it does in early youth, when you think that your soul will expire, that you will suffocate and die of grief.)

"Sit, Abu Dib. Sit."

(In old age, you are a witness, and everything seems complete to you. You know the fruit since its time as a flower. You know people from birth until today. You know the tree that was little and flourished, and the tree that grew old and dried out, and the houses that were built, and those that collapsed. After you sit down and rest, you continue to walk along the paths of your village. You leave one path and take another. Leave your path, Abu Dib, if it is rocky. Leave it behind you spread out like these valleys, and follow a well-trodden path.)

Abu Dib did not rise from his chair. The old couple talked about the olive grove that Adil had sold in order to buy a house in the city. Sand and gravel were laid on the land, and the olive trees were cut down. They talked about Jabbur's daughter who was studying at the College of Medicine, and about Hasan's son who had traveled to Moscow for a flight training course. It was as if they were sitting on a rock. The world in front of them was wide, blue, pure. Springtime had just begun, and the mountain air was fresh and fragrant, laden with the scent of the earth and the grass.

The woman was wearing an old woolen jacket over her long robe. The man was wearing shoes without socks. They both appeared smaller than their clothing. It was clear that the greater part of their lives had passed; nevertheless, the last cup of life seemed to have a special flavor. The little place where the man met the woman every day seemed like a spot on a high mountain where those who arrived could breathe deeply. The secret prayer they shared was that night would pass quickly and dawn would break.

The old man rose to his feet and took his basket.

"What do you need today, Maryam?"

"Nothing today, thank you. May you always be safe."

Part Four

Marriage

A Mistake in the Knitting

Ihsan Kamal

J told my sister many times that I didn't like knitting. It required a lot of patience, which I didn't have, to make a complete garment stitch by stitch. She would then philosophize and say, "A journey of a thousand miles begins with one step." I also reminded her that since childhood, I had been terrible at knitting and excellent at sewing. Sewing was really fun. The material was there from the start, and all I had to do to turn it into a complete dress was to sew up the sides and shoulders. But my sister insisted, saying it was now almost a tradition that one had to follow: every girl must give her fiancé a sweater she had knitted herself.

"What about a ready-made one?" I asked. "What's wrong with that?"

"He'll feel your affection for him more if you knit it yourself. Also, a ready-made one won't fit him," she replied.

"Then do me a good turn and make it for him yourself. Knitting is easy for you. Think how often you've presented us with your masterpieces!"

"Suzanne, my darling," she said. "Are you really stupid or do you just pretend to be? It was not for nothing that the woman who first came up with this idea carried it out. When you decide to knit a sweater for your fiancé, making a front and back and two sleeves out of nothing, you'll naturally think of him while you're working, stitch by stitch, and with every stitch he'll get closer to your soul, and his love will steal into your heart."

She was right. As I knitted, I thought of him. But with every stitch, I cursed the day I had met him. When some friends and I heard about the way my mother had married—which, I discovered, was the same way all their mothers had married—I felt sorry for her

112

and them. It was not a marriage but a gamble, even though my mother tried to play it down by calling it "a closed watermelon."[1] Why shouldn't it be "an opened watermelon"? But even we—the few girls who are university educated and claim to be liberated and sophisticated—cut with a knife that doesn't go very deep. We may discover the color, for example, whereas taste, smell, and hardness will remain a secret in the heart of the watermelon. After all, what person reveals all his character to his friends? Even after our engagement, I went out with him for a whole month before I discovered how despicable he was. Yes, he was despicable; I could not describe it otherwise. He said he wanted details of my salary from now on, and when I expressed astonishment, he tried to appear tolerant.

"You can enjoy the months left until our wedding."

"And after that?" I pressed him further. His attitude astounded me.

"The wife's time belongs to her husband and her home. If she uses it to do work, the pay goes back to the original owner of the time. The owner of a car, for example, is entitled to the revenue if it's used as a taxi."

I almost felt sick. He tried to be charming, but was it really charm? I may allow a person to rob me, if he steals in soft words. "Entitled," "revenue," "owner," "time," "car," "use"—he wasn't talking, he was throwing bricks, and it wasn't the first time either. On every visit, he had brought a brick to throw at me. Perhaps I hadn't noticed them because they were small, but that day I stacked them on top of one another, and suddenly they turned into a barrier between us.

I thought seriously about breaking the engagement, although I knew this act wouldn't be a simple matter for my father and family. Their roots lay in Upper Egypt, and they clung to certain beliefs. In fact, it wasn't simple for me either. There was my reputation to consider, and the gossip. I knew that kind of gossip very well. I had heard it on previous occasions. I had even taken part in it once—among us, the educated girls. The girl in question had hardly left the room when a female colleague winked.

"She says she's going to meet *him*, the man who broke the engagement."

"It's unlikely, but then she has to say that."

"I wonder why he left her."

But families and neighbors aren't satisfied with assumptions; they look for certainties. They don't inquire about reasons; they're ready with speculations. Why? Is it because in the marriage game, men are the strongest, and society is always in the grip of the strongest? Or do they consider a man to be a treasure and find it inconceivable that a girl who has stumbled on a man would give him up? For some men, this is true, but others are worth no more than a straw. Perhaps our society regards a girl as a drowning person who has to clutch even at a straw. And we may indeed be drowning girls: we've left our old traditions and plunged into the sea of life, striking out for the opposite bank—liberation. But it seems we haven't reached it yet. Perhaps our daughters will manage to get there. Our generation is the generation of sacrifice. If only we hadn't left the first bank, despite its emptiness!

Well, when I insisted on not having family supervision and raised objections on the basis of my age and sophistication, I got what I wanted. We began to go out alone, without a chaperon. There was only the promise of marriage, confirmed by two rings. So that gave us quite a lot of scope. Nothing much happened, but who can prove that to people? My mother told me, "From now on every young man will hesitate a hundred times before asking for your hand."

I knew all the difficulties I would have to face even before my mother listed them for me. She looked at things through a magnifying glass. Could it be that she had convinced me? Of course not. It was impossible. But when he came to see me the following day, I didn't say anything. I didn't even tell him how angry his views had made me. I pretended I was sad because a movie star I adored had died. Perhaps I was afraid *he* would be the one to break the engagement. It would be a disaster. It seemed that my mother had given me her magnifying glass along with her love and jewelry.

I thought I'd knitted enough: my sister had told me that the border had to be ten centimeters deep, and assured me that the border was the only difficult part; the rest was very easy. But what did I see? A mistake in the middle of the border! The right stitch was where the left one should be, and the left stitch was where the right one should be. How ugly it looked, like a chessboard! But to fix it I had to undo everything above it, about six rows, every one containing more than two hundred stitches that I had strained my eyes to produce. Every time I had completed a row, I had looked at it, reassuring myself that the sweater had grown. Was it absolutely necessary to undo all of this? And what would happen if his excellency wore a sweater with one mistake in it? It was unthinkable for me to start all over again: I disliked knitting, just as I had started disliking the intended recipient of the sweater. But why should I tell him that? Perhaps he had changed. Yes, why should I be so negative that I had to withdraw at the first setback?

The following day I went out with him, and when he headed toward the pastry shop, I firmly made him understand that I would never allow myself to be ridiculed in front of the staff there, from the manager down to the waiters, as had happened on previous occasions. He didn't buy pastries, but it was a hollow victory. All the time we sat on the terrace talking, it was clear that his views remained as strange as ever.

"They're thieves! Selling a piece of cake for five piasters, when outside it costs half that amount! We'll order tea so we can sit here, and that'll be enough. I'm not bothered if the waiters look at us disapprovingly or the manager objects. Let them go to hell. Those who buy people's respect by forking out more money are stupid and hypocritical."

I had tried every argument, but I couldn't convince him. On the other hand, *I* became convinced—convinced that this was not a positive outlook at all.

Being positive means overcoming obstacles with a view to improving the future. The positive approach encourages one to crush any mountains that stand in the way of the future—as is happening now in Aswan,[2] for example. But changing someone's character is an impossible task. Our ancestors rightly said that character leaves the body only after the soul. How on earth did I think I could change him? Take me, for example. Although I was younger and belonged to the so-called weaker sex, could anyone change my values and turn me into a slave of materialism? Impossible! Being positive, in my personal situation, meant courageously and decisively severing the ties that connected our two lives, refusing a marriage that from the outset clearly seemed bound to fail, and choosing a route to happiness that differed totally from his way of life.

"Valentine leaves the earth's orbit and circles in space." I pushed the newspaper aside. I thought it would distract me, but it only increased my anger. I was unable to break through the stupid notions that prevailed among people here. Only *here*. Everywhere else in the world, people regard an engagement as a trial period for the two partners and assume that if they break up, it means they lacked mutual understanding. But in our country—or in our conservative circle, to be precise—my mother, for example, said that the trial should *precede* the engagement. My God, Mother. Where on earth did you get hold of this idea? Suppose he were my classmate, even then much of his personality—the very part that concerns the future sharer of his life—would remain hidden from me. How much more so, then, when he was not my classmate! How could he be? He had graduated from the university a year before I joined it. He was a classmate of Afaf, my spoiled friend who had a relaxed attitude toward studying, took two years to complete one year's program, and graduated with me. A few months before her graduation, she introduced me to Shukri Abd al-Aziz. He had used the opportunity provided by his transfer to Cairo to come to the department to register his master's thesis as the first step toward a doctorate. The faculty regulations allowed only those who had obtained at least a grade of "good" to register for postgraduate work, and he tried to overcome this obstacle by making frequent visits to the department.

He saw us every time he came to the department. Afaf seemed to be expecting him to ask her to marry him, but he approached me instead. Our superficial acquaintance meant that I knew very little about him, and this little appealed to me—until I discovered that I had misunderstood his behavior and that the truth was quite the opposite of what I assumed. I admired his academic ambition in trying desperately to overcome the faculty regulations—until he told me sarcastically that he hadn't given a thought to ambition or status, and that his only motive was the high salary which the degree would bring. I also liked his unselfishness and his lack of that complex, latent in most Middle Eastern men, which pushes them to try to appear superior to their wives. That was when he started introducing me to all his friends as a doctoral candidate. I later realized that he was motivated by vanity. I was even wrong about the way I thought he viewed me, the woman who would share his life. I believed he preferred intelligence and equanimity to beauty, for there was no denying that Afaf was much prettier than I. In fact, I was merely a more lucrative deal, because of my expected degree. So I started to hate the degree, having originally felt so enthusiastic about it. His calculating attitude was not something that I figured out after getting to know his personality: he revealed it to me by a few slips of the tongue.

How could I marry a person I didn't respect? How could I live with him day after day, year after year, when our views clashed every time we met? Married life does not consist only of a union of two bodies, or else we would be just like animals: it would be enough for a male, any male, to meet a female, any female. Married life is first and foremost dependent on the compatibility between the characters and minds of two people as they set out together on the long journey of life.

What about the other option? Gossip, rumors, and the conjectures of envious people. As long as I was successful in my study and work, it would be unavoidable. My female neighbors and relatives whose scholastic scores were not high enough to get them to the university, or who went there and then dropped out (to the relief of their mothers, who said, "Our daughters won't be working alongside male colleagues!"), and my cheerful, sentimental girlfriends from whom I maintained a reserved and dignified distance—they would all talk about "his deception," even those who didn't dislike me. Everywhere I would encounter burning question marks in the eyes of my male colleagues and scorn in the eyes of my female colleagues. No sooner would I turn my back than pairs of heads would draw together, and the chitchat would begin. Our liberation has only been external. Our thoughts still wear the veil.

What would be my own position on all of this? Should I rise above all the gossip and toss it aside with indifference, or should I try to clarify things to everyone?

Why does the human soul have a predilection for mocking other people's misfortunes? Why did fate cause that white-suited old man with the elegant fly-whisk to fall down in front of our balcony the previous day? When he got up from the muddy ground, his suit was spotted like a leopard's skin. Everyone on the street and on our balcony burst out laughing. Wouldn't it have been more appropriate for them to show sympathy? And when an engagement is broken, either by the woman or the man, doesn't it imply the failure of a plan which the woman dreamed would bring her happiness? One would think, then, that she would receive commiseration, compassion, and cooperation from those around her. But I, too, had an excuse for attaching importance to gossip. Regardless of how developed and civilized we have become, we are unable to ignore people's views or what they say about us, as long as we live among them. I had even read in foreign novels about people who were overcome by despair or afflicted with complexes because of unfair rumors.

After that little incident at the pastry shop, the scales were balanced, although the scale for breaking the engagement was beginning to tilt downward. So I was still hesitating when he came to see me the previous evening. I didn't end our relationship, but I didn't go out with him either. I was like someone who has encountered some danger on the road in front of her, but who knows the road behind her is not clear either, and who chooses to stand still, in the middle of the road. Yet nothing in the world can stand still. Even the knitting in my hands was growing.

If that piece of wool had become so dear to me, then it's no wonder that psychologists ascribe a mother's love for her children to her efforts in carrying and bearing and rearing them. I looked at the knitting fondly. It had come into existence through a lot of effort involving the collaboration of my hands and eyes. It was also a big secret. He hadn't seen the sweater in my hands until the previous day. Initially, I had attempted to hide it, wanting it to be a surprise, but now I no longer cared. Of course he had to express his joy.

"You're making it yourself? That's wonderful! You can't imagine how much cheaper it is than the ready-made ones!"

Despite his "encouragement," I was still working on the sweater this morning. Alone. I no longer felt bored, sitting by myself. I worked in complete silence and a deep serenity that were hardly disturbed by the friction of the needles or the movement of the ball of wool. When I pulled the thread, the ball jumped around, like a happy, lively bird. The needles worked by themselves, or so it sometimes seemed to me. Like two magician's batons, their touch changed the loose thread into a solid weave. In my mind, they resembled a writer's pen, creating a story from separate words, or a composer's quill, combining scattered tunes into a symphony. The needles embraced each other, then disengaged, only to embrace again. They could not be separated. The woolen weave united them like an inescapable destiny. And they were contented with their intertwined lot. I heard no violent clash when they met, only a soft rustling, like a light kiss. The bird on the thread continued to dance in spite of the approaching end. It was as though it were happy to give its blood, drop by drop, so that a love story or symphony could be written. How far I still was from all that—at the other end of the world! He was delighted about the sweater and showed a lot of appreciation for my knitting it, just as you predicted, sister. But you meant one thing, and he meant another. . . . I wished my sister would come to see us, so I could argue it out with her in front of our

Lord in heaven. She had made me struggle for nothing. Talk of the devil!

She came along, cheerful and carefree. "Amazing!" she exclaimed. "You've almost finished the front."

"Yes. Yesterday I decreased the stitches for the arms, and now I'm starting to decrease for the collar."

I laid it down in front of her, and she looked at it closely, delighted. Suddenly she let out a great groan of dismay.

"There's a mistake in the middle of the border," she said ruefully.

"Yes," I replied indifferently. "I only noticed it after several rows."

"You have to undo everything up to that row," she said, and acted on her words. She drew out the needles, then pulled the thread. Her action so startled me that for a while I just stared at her, taken aback, unable to speak or move. Finally I awoke from my amazement, rushed at the sweater, and tried to snatch it from her.

"No, no," I screamed. "You can't do that! I worked so hard on it and put so much effort into it. I slaved day after day, night after night. You can't destroy all that in one second."

"It's your fault!" she retorted. "You should have gone back to the row with the mistake as soon as you discovered it, while you were still at the beginning, so that you could do it again correctly. How can you build anything on faulty foundations? Once you discovered the flaw in the knitting, you should never have continued. Never!"

My Wedding Night

Alifa Rifaat

〄〄〄

*T*he dream of my youth was the dream of every virgin whose body has been touched with the magic and exhilaration of youth, turning it into a luscious figure intoxicated with desire. All her songs revolve around the moment when she will give herself and all her delights to her chosen man on her wedding night.

And here was my wedding night. It arrived to find me sad, my spirit broken, my wings clipped, my heart fluttering with fear and confusion. In front of me a dancer was swaying, moving slowly on the floor to the rhythm of the loud music and the beating of the reverberating drums. She clashed her cymbals, and all the guests became enraptured and swayed with her happily. I was the only one annoyed by her shameless nakedness and the dissolute story she was telling, her belly trembling, until the tremor of excitement took hold of those surrounding her, and they began to clap their hands enthusiastically. I was the only one who was feeling upset, so upset that I was twisted in pain and had difficulty breathing. Perhaps the fear that gripped me had sparked my imagination.

Roses surrounded me, forming a large bouquet around my seat and the seat of the man to whom they were giving me away. But this throne over which I presided seemed to me nothing but a bier packed with frozen roses. Suddenly it would tumble with me into a bottomless grave, dark, like the obscure future that I faced. I was suffocating . . . suffocating. I wanted to jump to my feet amid the large crowd gathered around me. I wanted to run away. I didn't think anyone shared my suffering or paid any attention to it. I couldn't understand why the guests didn't take pity on me and leave. What was the benefit, anyway, of inviting them to my wedding night? I felt shy and confused at the thought that they all knew what would happen to me. I was so anxious that I couldn't move or rise. I didn't feel time passing; it passed as I played the heroine in this ongoing comedy they called the wedding celebration. Why should I rejoice when I was about to take on a heavy responsibility and a lot of hard work? Everybody had been preparing for this celebration for days, right up to the promised night. The house, decorated with lights and flowers, was filled with people. Large quantities of drink were poured, and piles of splendid sweets were served. But I felt that this house, my father's house, where I grew up, had become alien to me. The moment I signed the marriage contract, I became a guest in it; nothing there concerned me. Grief squeezed my heart at the thought that I would be leaving it in a few moments. "Why, then," you might ask, "did you agree to the marriage, if deep in your heart you had reservations about it?"

The reason, simply, was that I was obeying my father; and our family circumstances were such that I was duty-bound to agree to this marriage. I knew full well that my father wanted to lighten the heavy burden under which he had been laboring all these years. And I was the eldest in a long line of daughters; it was my duty to clear the way for the younger ones, as our traditions dictate. Besides, I wanted to make my poor, sick mother happy; she had put up for years with a hard life for our sake. It makes mothers happy to see their daughters married, despite the difficulties and problems that marriage brings their daughters later on.

In fact, I didn't have any great hopes about the man who, on this night, became my husband and master, a man suitable for me, as my father had assured me when he congratulated me. He had given his approval after an elaborate investigation of the man's background and circumstances. My father discovered that he was a hardworking engineer from a middle-class family like ours. His father was a devout, honest man, and his mother a good, respectable woman. Together, they had brought him up to be moral and principled. After graduation, he worked for the government, but then a voice urged him to visit the holy places. He obeyed the call and went off, leaving behind all the temptations of life, searching for the light, trying to get near to God. His journey lasted a long time. He forgot himself, living a life of asceticism and abstinence in a humble tent on top of a mountain.

But youth was obviously still stirring in his young body, because it had woken him from his delusion, and he realized that true faith meant struggling and being ready to grapple with the temptations of the devil; it didn't mean deprivation, introversion, and confinement. So he went back to his family and looked for a wife.

His mother, who was a friend of my mother, asked for my hand on his behalf. I consented, content with my lot. After all, I wasn't expecting to find anyone: my sweetheart had died and left me when we were still children. We were children, but we had known true love, in all its sincerity and devotion.

We used to hide our best pieces of candy and our best toys in order to surprise and impress each other. We would enjoy them together in complete innocence. We often stood in the garden, looking at the flowers dotted around the little fountain, and wandered about, chasing the butterflies and hornets that flew over the treetops and through the branches in blossom. Our hands were linked, and our hearts would beat in union to a tune that sang of unspoiled joy at the radiance of nature.

Our souls silently expressed deep gratitude to the Creator of the universe for having filled magical cups of beauty on which we drew without ever drinking our fill. We would stand side by side, humble and entranced, as if praying to the Great Creator. Then our emotions would overflow and we would embrace, quite openly, not caring that someone might see us.

We never thought that embracing might be forbidden. We would stretch out on the grass in each other's arms, rolling over on the carpet of dew and trying not to let go of each other. We would track little insects to their nests. Eventually we would tire of playing, and then we would lie in each other's arms, panting with exhaustion, and tenderness would flow between us, gently, serenely. Sometimes when we were together I would feel a warm, pleasant shudder, like the shudder the dancer was now trying to send through people's bodies. I would forget myself and cover my sweetheart's face with kisses, unaware of my true feelings. Our families saw us and understood; they were unable to separate us because of the strength of our love and our resolve. Once, as they were both watching us with a smile, his mother—our neighbor—promised my mother that I would be his bride when we grew up. We were overjoyed and laughed, and the laughter came from the bottom of our hearts. He whispered, "You're my bride from now on," and I pulled him by the hand and shouted delightedly, "Come on, let's play the marriage game with our sisters."

I grabbed my mother's veil and gown, which she kept folded in the prayer rug, and draped them over my little body. That was after I had smudged my face with her crimson lipstick, turning it into a small red rose with chaotic petals . . .

The sister who succeeded me in the long line of daughters that my parents had enthusiastically borne and jealously guarded stood banging the copper coffee tray and singing the song of the wedding procession. My other sisters swayed happily to her singing, repeating the song in their soft voices: "Walk proudly, pretty girl, beautiful rose from the garden." And I strutted along and offered myself to him like a real rose that blossoms in a garden. I moved majestically, though stumbling a little on the hem of my long gown. My hand lay in my sweetheart's hand; my eyes were fixed on his eyes, which sparkled with joy and happiness. Ecstatic, I couldn't help but join in the singing, my loud voice eventually rising above the voices of the other singers. All at once, my sister came to a halt and stopped banging the tray; the procession paused, and its orderly formation disintegrated. Then she rebuked me, shouting, "Don't sing. The bride's not allowed to sing." My joy suddenly dried up, and a vague sadness swept over me. I kept asking, "Why can't I sing happily like them? Why can't the bride be happy?"

And here I was now, a real bride, and it was my wedding night. But I wasn't singing for joy, and I didn't share people's joy for me. My heart was torn apart and shaking with fear, and my spirit was broken. A mysterious voice penetrated to the depths of my soul, urging me to refuse everything fate had brought on me, and begging the angel of death to rescue me from my unknown destiny.

The shrieks of joy suddenly became louder. The drums beat more rapidly as the dancer whirled faster. I was astounded at her ability to create happiness and to keep smiling all this time. Everybody stood up. The knight of my night stood up too and stretched out his hand to help me to my feet. My mother, feeling shy like me, signaled to me to obey him. I stood up, my heart falling to my silver shoes, and walked, led by candles dancing in the girls' hands.

A little girl stepped on the edge of the long veil that was fastened to my hair with flowers. I almost twisted my neck. She burst out laughing, thinking of the night—*her night*—when she would be in my place. I walked, rode in a car, then walked again, until I found myself in a closed room with the man who had become my husband, he and I, all alone.

I stood still, bewildered, my eyes lowered in anxiety. Having sat for so long so rigidly, I didn't know how I should behave. He too stood still, confused and baffled. Then he went over to a table crammed with food and sweets. Men never forget their stomachs, no matter what the circumstances are. Or perhaps his flight to the table was a way of relieving our embarrassing situation. We had met many times before tonight. We had gone for walks together during our engagement and talked about various subjects; but this was the first time that we were meeting as man and woman, with the family all waiting for the encounter. He took a handful of food, put it in his mouth, then said in a hoarse, trembling voice, "Hungry?"

"No." My head was still lowered, and now and again I would steal a glance at him.

"You must eat something. It's going to be a long night," he insisted.

I shuddered, feeling isolated and lonely. I wished I could run to my father's arms and be rocked until I calmed down. I stumbled hurriedly behind the screen and took off the veil that was weighing down my head. I removed my white wedding gown and folded it carefully, so my mother could keep it for my sisters after me. My father had paid a huge sum for it. Then I put on the white embroidered gown, prepared especially for my wedding night.

I crept into bed quietly, hoping to sleep and so to escape the long night that hung like a threat over me. He finished eating, turned to me, and whispered from a distance, "Kiss me." I turned my face away, anger at the ready, waiting to see what he would do.

When he reacted distantly, like a stranger, I mumbled an anxious "Good night." He turned off the light, lifted the blanket, and pulled me toward him. Fear gripped me, and I began to shake. As I closed my eyes in resignation, I remembered the story of Ishmael, peace be upon him, when he gave himself as a sacrifice to please his Lord and was tied to the stone by Abraham, God's friend.[3] He took off my underwear. Up to that moment, this had been one of my intimate secrets. The mere thought of my father seeing it accidentally hanging in the bathroom to dry was enough to embarrass me. The blood flowed hot through my veins, my head throbbed, and I felt dizzy.

He became absorbed in a long series of attempts, and I suppressed my pain and fear, waiting, expecting him to remove the barrier between us. But the nightmare dragged on endlessly. Suddenly he let go of my legs, hurried over to the light, and turned it on. I opened my eyes startled, and looked around, half expecting to see the sacrificial ram, brought down from heaven by the angel. What I did see was a man standing in the middle of the room, naked. His shapely body aroused me, but he was wailing and tearing at his hair.

"The sons of bitches did this to me."

At first I didn't understand what had happened. I dried my martyr's tears and said fervent thanks in my heart for having been saved by God's hand. Then the truth dawned on me: my own life was the sacrificial ram, and I had to guide my naive, innocent man, and make him play his proper role. Like me, he was a virgin; no female body had ever been near him before, just as no man's hand had ever touched me before. I got up, straightened my clothes, and drew him close to me. Then I wrapped the silk coverlet around him, so that I could talk to him without feeling embarrassed. He calmed down a little and buried his head in my chest.

"My uncle's wife did this to me because she wanted me to marry her daughter Samiya, but my mother chose you for me because you're gentle and pure," he said, with tears of sadness streaming down his face.

"What you're worrying about doesn't bother me," I consoled him. "Let's live together like friends, with love and compassion. That's a thousand times better than what you intended."

"But how shall we become husband and wife?" he said in despair, beating his breast with his hands.

"I'll tell you frankly," I said tenderly. "When I was a little girl, I had a sweetheart. We used to hug each other, quite innocently, and he would lay his head on my chest, and we would lie there for hours, cozy and peaceful. Why don't we do that now, until we fall asleep?"

"You think that fulfills the marriage contract?" he replied angrily.

"Can you manage anything else at the moment?" I asked teasingly.

My nonchalance had infected him, and he said, "Certainly not! I'm tired."

"Then let's hold each other, and try to get in tune with each other, and just let things develop with time," I said cheerfully.

"Will I be able to, one night?" he asked hopefully.

"Love works miracles," I said elatedly, as my anxiety vanished.

"Come on, then. We'll start our life together as children," he said, happy.

As he took me in his arms gently and affectionately, I laughed knowingly and said, "I think we're going to grow up quickly tonight."

We lay in each other's arms on the bed, exchanging kisses and ignoring that persistent flicker. As soon as he had calmed down, we turned off the light and surrendered to the hoped-for dream. As you know, it was my wedding night . . .

The Dummy

Sahar al-Muji

❦❧❦❧❦

*A*fter she had dressed him in his favorite pajamas with the dark brown stripes, she began to think about the best place to seat him. It was inevitable that she should seat him near the living-room table, where the newspapers, the ashtray, and the telephone were at hand, and where watching television was easy and clear.

It was difficult to move him from the bed to the living-room sofa. Until that moment, she had not realized how heavy his body was. As soon as she had completed the task she noticed that he was unable to sit upright, and kept leaning to the left. It was absolutely necessary to balance his body. She prevented his head from slumping to the front by propping it up with a pillow she had brought from the bedroom.

She fetched his reading glasses, placed them on his face, and put today's issue of *al-Ahram* newspaper in his hand. Then she walked to the other side of the room and took a look. It was essential that anyone entering the room should believe that the scene was real. To ascertain that she had done her duty skillfully, she called the children to bid him good night. As soon as they finished, she rushed them to their bedroom.

She bolted the front door and made sure that the windows and the cooking gas cylinder were shut. The house simply had to be safe. She pondered whether to move him into the bedroom at night or leave him where he was. She opted for the latter solution owing to the difficulty of implementing the first. To avoid problems that might arise should one of the children awaken at night and go into the living room, she locked the door. Then she went to bed.

The following morning, the usual daily routine began. No sooner had the children wished him good morning than she sent

127

them off to school. Then she had to air the house. In the living room, the sun's rays shone on the walls, the carpet, and the man who was still sitting in the same position, holding the same issue of *al-Ahram* newspaper. She dusted the bookshelves, the living-room table, and his reading glasses. It was absolutely necessary that he should look clean and . . .

The Cat, the Maid, and the Wife

Daisy al-Amir

❧⟡❧

er visit to her friend was delayed for months. The friend had begged her to come, and she had promised to look her up when she had time.

The friend had time for visits, but she had to work. How could her friend understand that what prevented her coming was the fact that she had so much work? How could a woman who didn't know how to pass her time understand that someone else's time was completely taken up?

But the friend's pleas and insistence on the need to see her were embarrassing. So that day she had put off some of her work, knowing that as a result the following day would be fuller.

There was no one else at her friend's house. The children were at school, or so the visitor thought, until the friend said that she had tired of them and sent them to her mother-in-law so that she could have a rest from them.

"A rest from them? But they're your children!" said the visitor.

"I'm tired of everything," the friend said.

"You've got a diploma in psychology. Why don't you bring them up properly, so they don't tire you or upset anyone?"

The friend laughed tearfully. "Do you think it's only up to me to bring them up? What shall I tell their father? And their grandmother? What shall I tell all the members of my family, and their father's family? Every one of them has a say in their upbringing!"

There was a brief pause.

"I hate my husband. I despise him," the friend continued with a total lack of inhibition.

The visitor was astonished. A wife who hates her husband yet continues to live with him? But before she could make any comment, the friend went on, "My husband respects me because I'm the daughter of a cabinet minister. He hopes he'll be appointed director-general. I myself don't actually respect my father. I have a very low opinion of all the people who praise him, because I know as well as they do that he's a thief!"

The maid came in, carrying two cups of coffee. The friend stopped talking and remained silent until the maid had left.

"Do you smoke?" asked the friend. Then she went on quite freely, "I smoke a lot. It's a release for me, but I do it when my husband's not around. He doesn't like women to smoke." The friend lit the two cigarettes. "I once saw you in a public place take a pack of cigarettes out of your purse, light one, and smoke it at your ease. I envied you. Aren't you afraid of what people might say?"

The visitor wanted to answer, but her friend stopped her.

"My husband indulges in all the vices. So do all the men of the family, depending on their particular tastes. I've been waiting to see you for some time. Twice I was told you had gone on a trip, once for business and once for pleasure. Which one of your trips did you enjoy more?"

"The trip home to my own country—"

"Home . . . home . . ." The friend interrupted her. "Do you feel you have a home country? Do you know your home country? I . . . I . . . I'd like to know where *my* home country is, so I could go there. I hope it does you good. Are you happy when you talk about your home country? What's happiness anyway? How can one feel happy talking about a home country? I feel a dreadful darkness around me. We all exploit each other. Our family is a group of enemies. I'm tired of all the hatred. I want to love, to be allowed to love . . . I want love . . . I want to . . ."

The maid came in, and the friend stopped talking and remained silent until the maid had left with the two coffee cups.

"I'm worried . . . I'm worried that the maid has concluded from what I was saying that I want *someone* to love . . . Maybe she'll think I love someone other than my husband . . . I'm worried that she'll assume I want to cheat on my husband, or that I'm already cheating on him. She doesn't know I'm cheating myself by living with him when I hate him. As for him . . . if he could cheat on me, if he could manage not to be afraid of my father, the minister, he'd cheat on me with the maid. I'd like to announce what I think of my father in the newspapers, to see what my husband would do then—"

This time the visitor interrupted her friend. "Will you go on living like this?" she asked.

"What can I do? Commit suicide? I wish I could write a letter and say everything in it, everything. A letter that would be published in the newspapers, so that people would know. But who would publish such a letter? They're afraid of my father, the minister. My husband, the minister's son-in-law, would burn it. My husband's family would spread rumors that I was an evil woman, that I had tried to hide my sins, and that this was the reason I had committed suicide. My family . . . they would get a doctor's certificate to show that I had died a natural death. They'd even stop me enjoying death! But what about me? I don't live a natural life, so don't I have the right to refuse to live? Don't I have the right to let people know this?"

"Suicide isn't the only course of action," the visitor said. "There are a thousand different ways to express refusal. Try to show your rejection of this kind of life in some other way. For example . . ."

Suddenly the husband came in. He rushed over to greet the visitor and declare how proud he was to see her and salute the struggling working woman. He regarded the visitor as an exemplary woman, because she had been assertive and established herself.

"I wonder if you're really proud of women like me," the visitor said. "Do you really mean it? Would you like your wife to be like me?"

"My wife . . . my wife's a different sort of person. She's supported and protected. Her father's a minister; her husband's . . ." he laughed loudly, "a director-general. She has a well-established family around her. Why would she need to work and struggle?"

The visitor stared at her friend, silently urging her to say something, to make some sort of statement, just to utter one word. She waited, but the silence continued. She offered her friend a cigarette, but she refused it, saying that she didn't smoke.

The husband settled into his chair, then called the maid and asked her to make him a cup of coffee. Her friend jumped up from her seat mechanically and cried, "I'll make it myself. You like the coffee that I make!"

When the room was empty except for the husband and the visitor, she got up and walked to the door. She had no intention of saying goodbye to her friend, who was busy making coffee for a husband she despised.

Back in the kitchen of her own house, the visitor found several bundles of clothes. Her maid, dressed in her best clothes, was sitting on a chair, waiting. She looked around, unable to understand.

"I'm leaving, madam," the maid said.

"Leaving? Without a reason? What's happened?"

"My honor's the most important thing to me," said the maid.

She didn't understand this answer.

"But who's offended your honor?"

"Your husband. He asked me about his telephone book. When I told him I didn't know where he'd put it, he screamed at me, saying over and over again that I was to get it, even if I had to dig it out of the ground. He accused me of lying and stealing. He shouldn't be taking it out on me like that. I'm not his wife."

"But where will you go? It's almost ten o'clock at night and you're a stranger in this city!"

"There are plenty of hotels, and I'll contact my children. There are men in my family who can protect me."

She didn't say to her, "Then why are you working as a maid when you're so old? Why aren't your children supporting you?" All the events of the day were jumbled in her head. She didn't know where to start.

The packages and bundles of clothes were moved out of the house. She heard the sound of the door closing behind the maid, but she continued to stand there, undecided. Should she admire the maid or be angry with her? Should she go after her or respect her decision?

When she finally went down the steps and reached the street, the maid had already disappeared into the long dark street. She stood motionless, contemplating her surroundings, overwhelmed by the whirl of events.

A female cat passed by. It stopped and stared at the woman standing in the dark street. Then it strolled on, its long tail hanging, relaxed, behind it.

It was a dirty, skinny cat, and obviously hungry. She called out to it, but it didn't turn around. It crossed the street and jumped over a broken wall around a vacant lot.

There was no sound of a male cat calling its mate in the vacant lot, and the lonely, dirty, hungry cat wasn't mewing either.

Sun, I Am the Moon

Hanan al-Shaykh

❀❖❀

*T*he goat coughed from shortness of breath. It stamped the ground, and the bag covering its udder shook. Mud dust rose, reaching its mouth and nose, and it coughed harder. Qamar,[4] dressed in black, rushed toward the goat and hugged it. The goat yielded to her, as though it were again a young one that needed its mother. It huffed and puffed against the chest of Qamar, who kept shaking her head and saying, "I'm sorry. May God grant you forgiveness." She looked at the sky but could not see anything. The sun's rays were everywhere, spread like fire. Everything was silent. Some of the thinly scattered trees were dead, the thistles dry, the hills barren. Qamar lay her head on the goat's back and said, "God tortures you and me. Why? I don't know. Maybe I annoyed Him last year when I picked a red fig and ate it during the fasting period, thinking that no one would know. I thought even He couldn't possibly see me through the thick whirls of dust. I completed my fast, but God must have known." She sighed, still clinging to the goat, and asked it consolingly, "And you? What have you done, poor thing?" The goat gazed at Qamar with pleading eyes, then moved its head, opened its mouth, and yawned. Qamar's slender frame rose, and her little toes were revealed. She pulled the big black cloak over her head, exposing her waist, which looked like that of a child of ten. She readjusted her cloak to cover both her head and body. She bent down and picked up some dry leaves, placed them in her dress, and folded the edges of the dress. Then she took a box of matches from her breast pocket, ignited the leaves, and brought the goat close to the smoke, saying, "Come on, precious. Come on, sweetie. Sniff and cough. Inhale and cough, so that the cough will go away completely." The goat neither sniffed nor coughed. Qamar stood glancing around, occasionally wiping the beads of sweat that had appeared on her forehead and ran down her neck. Then she raised her face to the sun and said, "Sun, I am the moon. Have some sense of shame and go down!" She smiled at her words and resumed her activity, bringing the goat close to the smoke and saying, "Come on, precious. This will cure you. Sniff and cough."

The smoke thickened. The goat began to cough, producing a strange noise that convulsed its entire body. Qamar embraced it and stroked its back, whispering, "I wish you could give me your cough. Maybe that would drive the old man away from me." She lay down for a moment, tucking her hand like a pillow under her head, which rested on the little stones. Suddenly she jumped to her feet, held her breath, and stood silently. Her eyes turned in every direction, and then froze. She saw the tail of a small viper vanish into a hole between two stones under the fig tree.

The following morning, Qamar left the mud house, preceded by the dry, disjointed cough of the goat and followed by a middle-aged woman. Qamar walked through narrow alleys, leaving behind houses tightly packed together and barefoot children playing with a cloth ball. Those who might walk through these dusty roads would never dream that they would soon encounter hills, trees, and fields. Qamar bent down, searching for dry leaves, which were sparse. Perhaps the night winds had swept them away. She began to pluck off green leaves, placing them in her dress. After she had piled them on top of one another, she took the box of matches from her breast pocket and ignited the leaves. Then she pulled the goat and said, "Come on, precious. Sniff and cough."

The older woman was wearing a wrap with blue squares that looked like a bedspread. She walked behind Qamar, clearing her throat noisily, and then squatted on the ground. She tried to break the silence with another little cough, which was followed by a spit, saying, "When will you stop wearing black clothes? Be sensible, Qamar. Wearing black is a bad omen. Yes, it really is a bad omen. Your mother and father are still young, and your brothers are small children." Qamar contented herself with biting her lips. She rose and glanced around before bending down to pick up a dry branch. She broke it with her thin hands and used it to poke the pile of leaves, which had almost ceased to burn. Then she blew on it a couple of times. When the fire finally came alive and spread in the veins of the leaves, she straightened up. Her face was flushed, small blue arteries protruded in the middle of her forehead, and a thin mustache appeared above her mouth, despite her dark complexion.

She stood silently, watching the two stones under the fig tree. Only when she saw a little head peek out of the hole and then vanish did she move. She drew near the woman, who was still squatting down on her heels. When the woman saw Qamar approaching, she felt she could broach the subject again. "What did you say Qamar?" she asked. Qamar stopped biting her lips and sighed, "God will provide." The woman was familiar with Qamar's reply. She extended her hand toward the ground and ran her palm through the dirt. The blue stone in her ring glittered, and the silver bangles on her wrist jingled. She picked up a twig, peeled it, gnawed on it, and then spat out the bark. No sooner had Qamar added "God will provide" than the woman, whose pupils were obscured by the darkness of her small eyes, said, "My God, I don't understand you. You're like my daughter. If anyone upsets you, tell me and I'll kill them. I know that Fatima is a wicked woman, but she's afraid of me. Tell me if she does anything to you, and I'll persuade Qahtan to divorce her. My name is not Zamzam if I don't make him divorce her." She lost her balance as she waved her hand threateningly. She readjusted her wrap to cover her head, after her sharp features and devilish eyes were revealed. Qamar continued to stand motionless, biting her lips and sobbing. But the woman's words encouraged her. She focused her eyes again on the hole between the two stones under the fig tree. Moving closer to the goat, which was still coughing, she stroked its back. Then she picked it up in both arms, hugged it, and left.

On the third day, Qamar appeared to trip over her feet as she walked quickly, with the goat behind her. She didn't pause for breath except when she arrived at the two stones under the fig tree and saw the hole. The goat was still coughing. Qamar loathed the goat's cough this morning and felt no sympathy for the animal. The goat's cough only added to her confusion. She stood there, her heart beating frantically. She lingered a long while before the two stones and the hole between them and the shadow of the fig tree. When the viper emerged, she held the goat by its neck and pulled it away, stumbling. She removed her black cloak and carelessly dropped it on the dusty ground. Her breathing quickened, which intensified her confusion. She undid the piece of cloth wound around her waist, where she had hidden a medium size straw box. She lifted the lid, removed an egg and a piece of paper with some lard, and placed them on the ground. The goat drew near and tilted its mouth toward the box and the egg. Qamar grumbled and pushed the goat away with a light blow on its head, then dragged it quickly to the trunk of a branchless tree. She undid the rope, which was also wound around her waist, and rushed, stumbling, to catch the goat and tie the rope to its neck and then to the tree. She walked a few steps away, then returned to make sure that the rope was securely fastened around the goat's neck.

She glanced around before she reached into her breast pocket and took out a container made of flat tin plate. She knelt down in front of the goat, untied the bag covering its udder, and milked it with strained fingers. When she saw that the milk was trickling partly onto the ground and partly into the container, she uttered, "In the name of God, the Compassionate, the Merciful. May God curse Satan." She tied the bag around the goat's udder and rose, holding the container. She tried to walk calmly, but her pounding heart increased her confusion. She stumbled and cursed Satan again, watching over the container of milk, until she arrived at the two stones under the fig tree. She hesitated before placing the container there, her eyes searching the hole. She straightened up, glanced around, and then bent over a dry thistle, pulling at it. The thistle was stubborn and firmly rooted to the ground. Its thorns bloodied her hands, but remained solidly planted in the dirt. Qamar didn't wipe the sweat that had begun to drip from her nose, forehead, and cheeks. Her hands trembled as she held the box of matches and tried to light a matchstick that had become wet with sweat. She glanced around her. Everything was quiet. The goat resumed its disjointed cough. Once again, Qamar rubbed the matchstick against the edge of the box, which was still dry. She gasped when she saw the fire and threw the matchstick on the thistle, which was consumed in no time. She hurriedly took out another tin container from her pocket. Using her finger, she scooped the remainder of the lard that had melted in the paper, and placed it in the container. She felt a burn from the heat on her finger, so she put it to her mouth and licked it. Then she broke open the egg into the container, which she continued to hold with the edge of her dress. When she saw the bubbles of egg white appear, and its smell filled the air, she removed the container from the thistle and placed it near the container of the goat's milk.

She retreated quietly and stood at a distance from the two stones, unable to distinguish between fatigue and fear. Were her feet tired or were they trembling? The lower part of her belly contracted, and when she breathed, she felt pain in her chest. Meanwhile the scorching sun raged above her. She stood there for quite a while, her eyes riveted on the empty space between the two containers and the two stones. When the tin of the two containers remained the only thing glittering in the sunlight, Qamar thought to herself: Maybe this is for the best. If the viper emerges and creeps toward the bait, what will I do? I'll surely flee. I won't be able to extend my hand toward its yellow body. It looks like its skin is covered with mercurial material, and I won't be able to touch it. The viper is cunning. It's inside, oblivious to the smell of the milk and egg. If it sees the two containers, will it know that this is a trap? Or does a viper not think like humans?

But Qamar's eyes popped in disbelief. The viper poked its head out before creeping outside. The farther it crept, the more intensely she trembled as she observed the traces that its body left on the white mud. "I must swoop down on it now," she said to herself, her hand on her heart, the sweat oozing from every pore of her skin. The viper drew near the two containers. Sticking its tongue out, it licked the milk, then the egg, then went back and forth between the milk and the egg. "I must swoop down on it now," she repeated, trying to work up the courage by recalling the suffering that she would endure tonight, and every single night, if she didn't swoop down on the viper at once. She approached it from the back, exactly as she had seen her brother Hilal do. Now! Her body poured with sweat, and she trembled and shook like a leaf. As though hypnotized, she reached out and grabbed the viper's tail from the back, just as she had heard her brother say: "The first grip is everything, because it shocks the viper. After that, seizing it by the neck is easy." To Qamar's utter amazement, the viper's neck was in her hand, and its tail was striking against her as she brought it to the straw box, threw it in, then shut the lid tightly. Holding the box with one hand, she rushed to untie the rope from the goat's neck with the other, and to wind it around the box. After she had placed the box gently on the ground, she collapsed beside it, hiding her face in her hands and sobbing loudly. How did she do it? The strongest men here dared not look at a viper, let alone catch it. The men's stories usually told of catching hyenas and fleeing at the mere sight of a viper's eggs! Had she not seen Ahmad with her own eyes, lying like a corpse on the ground, when his brother wanted to force him to get down from the tall, solitary fig tree, and cried out: "Snake, snake!" Suddenly the answer hit her: It's God who caught the viper. He forgave me. She raised her tearful eyes to the sky, and saw nothing but the sun. He caught it. It was God. She was unable to get up, as if the sobbing had paralyzed her. The fear tightened her chest, gripped her heart, and possessed it, as if what was twisting in the box was unreal. She got up, frantic with fear. With chattering teeth and trembling knees, she wrapped her black cloak around her body and the straw box. Then she walked with stumbling steps, followed by the goat and its cough.

In the evening—like all other evenings—Qamar sat silently, her hand on her cheek, between Qahtan's first wife, Zamzam, and his second wife, Fatima. The scent of burning incense filled the room. She heard Fatima's children frolicking in the next room and wished that she were among them, playing. She heard Fatima saying with an affected smile, which made her full face look as round as a sunflower, "Are you really only sixteen, Qamar? My God, you look older." Qamar didn't reply; instead, she moved her hand from her cheek, dropped it onto the reed mat, and began to scratch at it with her fingernails. Fatima continued, "Just sixteen years old, a damned girl, and you make the man want you every night. Maybe you have something we don't. Or maybe your mother has taught you how to attach a man to you." She laughed until her body shook. She reached for the incense and stirred it with one hand, while toying with her toes with the other. Zamzam intervened, shouting, "Shame on you Fatima. What does Qamar's mother have to do with this matter? I promised Qamar that if you open your mouth and say one word, then you'll see." Qamar was silent, as if waiting for the last torture of the night to come, so that the fatigue and fear of the day would vanish. Fatima went on, "The goat is still gasping for breath."[5] Zamzam turned to her and screamed, "What do you mean?" Feigning innocence, Fatima raised her penciled brows and replied, "Nothing. I swear. It seems that the grass smoke didn't help it." Qamar shuddered, wondering whether Fatima might have seen the straw box. She always went into her room and fiddled with her things. No. If Fatima had seen the straw box, she would have broken into loud wails. She breathed in relief and sat trembling as she waited for the last wave of fear. Zamzam yelled, "May God curse your face. Fatima al-Zahra[6] must be turning in her grave at the thought of you bearing her name. You're a sly, heartless woman. I went with Qamar and saw with my own eyes. You're afraid. I told you a hundred times. Qahtan won't divorce you. He won't throw you out. He may marry ten women, but he won't divorce any of them. He's devout, and fears God and his Prophet. Leave Qamar alone." Silent, Qamar confronted successive waves of tension, fear, and trembling. She buried her face in her hands. Zamzam turned to her and said, "What's the matter with you, girl. You seem tired. Go to sleep." Fatima laughed and, slapping the palms of her hands together, said sarcastically, "Go to sleep? And what will the man do? Don't you hear her voice when she cries out every night, 'Mama, come.' She cries out a hundred times, a thousand times, 'I'm tired. Mama, come.' And the person who comes is Qahtan with his stick, not her mother."

Qamar continued to bury her face in her hands. She didn't want to hear Fatima's words or to remember what would happen tonight, like every night for the past few months, ever since she had been married off to him. She heard Qahtan's slow footsteps approaching from the men's sitting room. His hoarse voice was calling her now: "Girl, Qamar, come here, so we can go to sleep." She didn't rise but rather began to scratch at the reed mat harder, wishing that her fingers would cleave to it. His voice electrified her again: "Girl, let's go to bed." Qamar remained motionless, looking pleadingly now at Zamzam, now at Fatima. Zamzam rose and left as Qamar's eyes, brimming with tears, begged her for help. Fatima rose, staring jealously at Qamar. Her steps fell heavily under her great bulk as she entered her children's room. Qamar stayed rooted to the spot, her heart pounding, her throat dry from swallowing so hard, her eyes riveted on the colorful reed mat. She turned her face when she saw his coarse, bare feet with the little white hairs on the toes and the wrinkled, thick flesh, looking like animal paws. She felt the edge of the stick poking her head. She jumped to her feet and ran screaming and sobbing. He hurried after her, shouting, "Girl, don't scream. The children are asleep."

As she did every night, Qamar ran to the room that was empty, except for a wardrobe and a bed, under which she would hide and wait, painfully wait. Each night, she tried in vain to find a solution when she saw the edge of the stick searching for her to poke her. She would begin by sobbing and screaming, then she would bite her lips and pinch her breast. But tonight her pain was accompanied by a terrible fear. The stick was poking her forcefully while she, crouching under the bed, tried to dodge its coarse, pointed edge. She attempted to grab it, but he pulled it with a force incompatible with his sixty years. He resumed his poking, while she continued to evade him. Then he craned his neck to look under the bed. When she saw his loathsome eyes, white beard, pallid complexion, and nearly toothless gums, she asked God for mercy, convinced that the man was Satan incarnate. He craned his neck only once. That was what happened every night. He had told her many times that he could not bend down to look under the bed because of the pain in his back. Therefore, once she forced him to bend down, he would curse her incessantly, unable to control his anger from the resulting back pain. Then the pokes he gave her with the stick became unbearable. He would poke her as if she were the wall. Now he was threatening, poking her more savagely. Qamar retreated to the other corner. She reached for the straw box in order to push it, but her hand froze, and her heart was in her mouth. She must bring the box close to the stick. Must. Even with her scream she could push the box and turn it over, so that the viper would escape and twist itself around the stick. Then she would shout, "Okay, Qahtan. I give up," which would make Qahtan pause for the first time to catch his breath. Then, when he recovered the stick, he would scream in fear and pain. But Qamar's fear overcame her courage. Her frozen hand moved—but it hid the box in the corner.

Her plans and dreams of sleeping alone from this night on vanished. As she crawled from beneath the bed, she said in a choked voice, "Okay, Qahtan. I give up."

The Dreadful Sea

Zuhur Wanisi

❦

When the old woman placed her hand gently on the shoulder of her daughter-in-law, Fatima, whom her son, beyond the sea and absent for months on end, had married, it was as if she had opened a wellspring of emotion that burst out suddenly into hot tears. The tears flowed freely, flooding the young wife's face, as if in an effort to wash away the cares and sorrows that lay deep down in her tormented soul. Nevertheless, tears that are shed freely can be comforting and therapeutic. There is a big difference between such tears and those that are shed in secret and fear, the fear of malicious joy and pity. How cruel are piteous glances coming from eyes that are jealous even of her food and drink and clothes!

"My God, what do you lack? True, your husband works abroad, but he doesn't forget you. He sends you and your child a lot of money, as well as the nicest clothes. Thanks to this, you have a good life. You don't lack anything."

"I don't lack anything. . . ." It appeared that Fatima didn't lack anything—according to the concept of need prevalent among the neighbors and relatives in this little mountain village. Even her mother-in-law was often influenced by such attitudes, which the village women, both old and young, continually displayed.

"What good does it do me to have my husband at my side day and night if we barely have enough to eat and clothe ourselves? The little children we have borne want food at every mealtime and clothes in every season. What pleasure is there in the smell of arak and the expression of hardship with which my husband approaches me every night? It's as if he's not making love but war against the phantoms of poverty, misery, and suffering, and against all the circumstances that had brought him into existence!"

141

The woman who spoke these words was Fatima's close friend. Fatima frequently contented herself with her advice and heeded it. But with the passage of the days, Fatima couldn't help thinking that her beloved husband—the son of her dear paternal uncle—didn't want to return. An irresistible force was keeping him there, beyond the damned sea. She said to herself, "I see the sea every day telling the sky many long and fantastic stories, of which we know nothing here. Perhaps they are the truth, and whatever the village people say is utter nonsense because it stems from personal feelings of sympathy, envy, or pity.

"Several years of my youth have been wasted. I am now twenty-two years old. I have a child who constantly calls for his father, with no response. Am I really awake or is this all a dream? Even the postman, that man to whom we are grateful for bringing us news, rarely shows up. It would suffice if I could hold a letter to my heart and touch it with my lips, for I'm one of those who can neither read nor write. This is not unusual. Everyone in the village is like me—men and women—except for one youth, who is burdened with solving the problems of all the village people in this matter. His skills have made him the most beloved and respected person in the village."

Fatima wiped her stream of tears, feeling relief. The old woman was reciting the afternoon prayer in one of the corners of the wide courtyard. The sun had started to turn away from the high courtyard wall. When Fatima entered the hut, it appeared darker than it had at any other time. She groped her way to a mattress on the floor where her beloved child slept. His crimson lips were parted, and dribble oozed down his chin and wet his little pillow. She gazed at him affectionately as she knelt down before him. He seemed to be sleeping peacefully. And why not? What could a two-year-old child understand? The important thing was that he still enjoyed suckling at his young mother's breast. Why should she wean him? What was the point of it? Was she going to bear another child? She felt peaceful when she nursed him, often recalling one of the happy occasions that she had shared with her husband during the rare times they had spent together.

"Isn't my child the fruit of one of those happy moments? Isn't he the connecting link between me and my absent beloved? Doesn't he feel the same way, despite the distance that separates us, when he imagines me nursing his child?"

A week earlier, the old woman had said to her, "Wean the child. He's become a man. He eats everything. There's no need to nurse him anymore."

Perhaps the old woman was right. But . . .

The child didn't awaken from his sleep, despite her many kisses.

Fatima rose to gaze at the things that filled the small hut. There was a stone bench with a mattress that usually remained tidy, for she hated sleeping on it. She preferred to sleep on the floor with her son. When she slept on the stone bench, she became more keenly aware of her husband's long absence. There was also a wooden trunk the sides of which were decorated with birds and flowers in yellow and red. She polished it every day, and the colors remained bright. She knew how many birds there were, how many flowers, and even the number of the small radiant leaves.

She opened the trunk carefully, as if touching a dear person whom she was afraid to hurt. As far as she was concerned, this trunk contained the life she wanted. It contained beautiful clothes that she could don only for her husband, for they were his gift to her. It contained splendid jewelry that she enjoyed wearing only for him. It contained his pictures, and letters, and those precious, intimate items that were for them alone. It contained the past, present, and future. It contained the youth which is lived only once, and which, therefore, we must live fully. Fatima slowed down a little, her hand resting gently on these objects. Then she proceeded to take out a pretty, striped dress. She spread it out before her and ran her hand over it tenderly. Then she held it up to herself as she stood before a suspended mirror, which reflected only the face and part of the bust.

It was truly a lovely sight of a mature and feminine woman with a slender figure, full bosom, and long, beautiful hair that cast translucent shadows on her even more beautiful face. Her face was flushed intensely red from the tears that had flowed so freely earlier and that had washed away much of the pain, leaving behind a state of pleasant resignation. Resignation to everything, even to the pain that would definitely return with every sunrise. She dropped her hands with the dress and heaved a deep sigh from within. Here she was, having derived no joy from life except those few brief hours, kept secret from the eyes of her mother-in-law and her husband's relatives, whose faces were always clouded with gloom. A few brief hours for which she was now paying very dearly. It was enough to be considered one of the married women rather than one of the village spinsters. She was called by a man's name, even though her only connection to that man was the memory of a few brief hours of sensual pleasure devoid of any meaning, except what she mistakenly attributed to it.

You, Fatima, are a woman, and every woman is you. There are no differences among you. You are all a vessel into which we pour what exceeds our needs in this life. And if you leave, Fatima, there are plenty of other Fatimas. None of you has an advantage over the other, except for the extent of your obedience and the number of children you bear, and how nice it would be if all of those children were boys. . . .

"Is the other person, the one who prevents him from coming back to me, also a woman, merely a female?"

"Yes. That's how it is, Fatima. Perhaps the names differ, but the reality remains the same. She, too, is merely a vessel. She replaces you there. She may be slightly or much more beautiful than you. But in the eyes of this young, strong, and muscular man who is called your husband, she's a female. There's no difference between you and her, except that she's nearer and available. She can respond to the persistent desire in your husband and in other women's husbands."

No, she definitely appeared to be different. Fatima had often heard that the women there, beyond the sea, never surrendered what they had caught in their snares, and her husband was a precious catch! The African sun had inflamed his soul, body, and features, while the Arab soil had infused his character with generosity and courage, especially before foreigners, and foreign women in particular.

The village people told Fatima the following: "Foreign women, despite being nonbelievers in our religion and that of our forefathers, are still permitted to be wives to our Muslim men, and the children they bear are considered Muslim, even if their names are like those of the nonbelievers, and even if they attend Mass with their mothers every Sunday."

They told her many things, all of which emphasized that what her husband did abroad was within his legitimate rights, granted to him by the canonical law of Islam as well as by custom and tradition. There was no cause for self-questioning, bewilderment, or even blame. As for protesting, that was not one of women's rights, and we were born women . . .

It's enough, Fatima, that you look after the cold walls in your house, and obey the ceaseless demands of your mother-in-law. It's as if she's attempting to compensate for the lack of authority she suffered in her youth by ordering you around. It's enough that you look after this child who bears your husband's name. Your husband, who is not really a husband, will protest when he returns and finds him a man. He'll protest even more angrily—against you—when he finds that his son doesn't measure up to his expectations, that he refuses to obey him, and that he doesn't kiss him on the head with every greeting. He is his son, his flesh and blood, even though he knows nothing about him—his upbringing, nature, desires, dreams, and needs for affection, sympathy, and care. Woe to you, Fatima, if you think of disobeying, and if your soul and empty days and lost youth yearn to protest! In that case, you must say farewell to your son forever. They will tell him that you were dead and buried, and that you were a disgrace that befell him and the entire family.

Yes, the village people told her many things. That was the reason that her only solace came through these hot tears, which she shed in agony. The tears were the balm she applied to the pangs of total deprivation, even of the right to protest.

It was a new and happy day when Fatima heard that Muhammad, the neighbors' son who lived abroad with his wife, had returned to the village late at night for a short visit with his family. Muhammad surely brought a lot of joyous news from her husband. But why didn't her husband come as well?

"No, Fatima. There's no need to ask such questions. Just praise God for the news that you'll receive through Muhammad."

Fatima didn't sleep a wink; instead, she entertained pleasant dreams. Suddenly she created all kinds of excuses for her absent husband: "He surely works hard and slaves away for my sake and our son's sake. No doubt he suffers loneliness, homesickness, and longing for his son, whom he has never seen. He naturally wishes to see him every day. He certainly imagines him to be a handsome, well-behaved, and happy boy. How can it be otherwise when he's his father and I'm his mother and both of us are attractive and charming?"

Muhammad came, lavishing smiles upon everyone in the family. He held her little son in his lap, playing with him and kissing him, while saying over and over again, "Amazing! God bless you. He's become a man."

Fatima's glances were glued to the man's lips as she poured his coffee.

The old woman could almost dance with joy as she listened to the man repeat time after time: "He's fine. I saw him just yesterday. He accompanied me to the airport. He's in good health, and sends his greetings to each and every one of you."

Fatima was tired of these generalities because she didn't hear what she wanted. But what she wanted fell into the category of "shamelessness" and "immorality." How could she allow herself to present the question that had rendered her sleepless all these months and years?

"Didn't he tell you when he's returning to us?"

The guest remained indifferent. He made no attempt to reply because Fatima had silenced the words on the tip of her tongue. Insurmountable barriers restrained her. The question had melted away along with everything else that was melting away every moment in her soul, spirit, and heart.

But the guest, Muhammad, finally spoke. He said many things without altering his tone of voice, as if he were imparting joyous news or relating perfectly natural events. He didn't realize that his words were deeply affecting Fatima's soul and instantly turning her life upside down, for her expression never changed. She didn't have that privilege. Many feelings at that moment prevented her reaction, not the least of which was her wounded dignity.

"Al-Tahir married a foreigner and has a daughter by her. He says, 'Don't worry about me, for I intend to visit you in the summer. As for Fatima, if she wants, she can stay, and if she doesn't, I won't stop her from returning to her father's house. But my son must remain with my mother, so she can raise him.'"

After saying farewell, the man departed.

The mother received the news with a certain sense of pride. So, her son was capable of marrying a European as well . . .

And did Fatima go away? No, of course not. She didn't return to her father's house because she couldn't bear to leave her two-year-old son. The days and months passed, while Fatima imagined that everything that had happened was a dream, that the coming days would bring her love, happiness, and respect, and that this dreadful sea would dry up one day and diminish the distance between her and her absent beloved.

Woman with a Story

Mayy Ziyada

~~~~~~~

*E*very person has a special story. Relatives and distant relations tell it to each other in their various dialects; they understand it according to their different mentalities, and weave a host of tales around it. Most often, one recounts the basic story about one's chosen victim, then adds, "He played this trick on me!" and "There was the saga with my colleague, and that episode with someone else," and so on. The narrator is lavish with this story, explaining it, going into great detail about it, embellishing it. And the others listen in amazement, tut-tutting and invoking the Almighty. They poke fun and jeer, as if neither they nor anyone before them had ever done anything like what is being related to them. Naturally, when they apply the rules to others, they don't see how lax they are in judging themselves. Yet the golden principle of loving your neighbor and treating others as you wish to be treated yourself is still a golden principle. There's no getting away from it.

When judging others, people don't follow the criteria they apply to themselves. They judge according to the rigid texts that make up the moral code, using these as ammunition against each other. If faults are put up for auction, it's an auction where competition to determine the lowest bidder is precluded. The speakers, whose capacity as such makes them righteous, pure, and saintly, turn to this severe code with the look of executioners. Just as the arithmetic table that the Greek Pythagoras invented provides us with a ready reckoner, so the moral code provides us with a way of reckoning up the evil deeds of God's servants, and judging them. It's a ready reckoner whose sublime numerals are above any dubious deduction!

I used to encounter Madame Gh. B. frequently in various places: at church, at concerts, and in department stores. I rarely walked through the streets of the Ismailiyya quarter, such as Qasr al-Nil, Imad al-Din, al-Maghribi, al-Madabigh, and Sulayman Pasha, without seeing her pass by, so that it seemed she must live in one of these districts or nearby. If I was with a friend or companion, up would go the cry that women usually utter—and men too, with due respect to our honorable gentlemen—when a woman with some distinguishing feature passes by: "Look! Look!" And Madame Gh. B. had more than one distinguishing feature. She was known for her beautiful voice—I heard her sing at two concerts—and she dressed elegantly, in the most up-to-date clothes. In fact, she was among the first to popularize the latest fashions in Cairo. And she was known as a beauty.

I used to watch her from a distance, attracted to her by that special thing that is in all human beings. It's not their clothes, or their facial features, or the way they move, or their silence; it's something indefinable, something that differs with each individual. Some observers of physiognomy maintain that it's located between the eyes; others say it's in the pupil of the eye, or around the mouth, or in the line of the lips, or in the tilt of the chin. I only know that it's there, and that it's the greatest definer of what we call the individual's "personality." With some people it's very strong and has a great impact. It seizes the onlookers, and after that they can never forget this personality or its possessor.

Once the words "Look! Look!" have been uttered, there inevitably follows a story about the subject under scrutiny. That's how I came to hear many stories about Madame Gh. B., stories that made me think a lot about her. I wondered what she was really like. What should I believe from all the gossip? My preoccupation with her increased as the stories about her mounted. I was like the man who was introduced to a celebrity and said, "I've heard all the bad things people say about you, and I couldn't wait to get to know such a formidable person."

Her eyes were the thing that stuck most firmly in my mind. They were ever changing. Sometimes they looked like the eyes of a woman in pain, a long-suffering woman; and sometimes they were contemplative, avoiding all the show of life. Sometimes they had an unfathomable look: they stared straight ahead, piercing through objects into space, as if watching the signs of an invisible hand in the air. And sometimes they seemed like the eyes of a gregarious person who enjoys the usual festivities and is quite content with them, not imagining that anything better exists. At these times they shone, happy, as if life had given them their fill of quiet delight, and was realizing its highest hopes through them. But I liked them when they became dull and the light in them went out, as if she had aged fifty years in two weeks. Then I would meet her another time, and in her rose-colored dress, with her hat fluttering around her face, she would seem like a child, anticipating all sorts of joys from life.

One day the cream of the city's amateur musicians gave a concert in the big festival hall at the Shepherd Hotel. Two famous instructors supervised the organization of the concert. One was Mrs. K., the most talented of the foreign singing teachers. She held recitals at her home, and those who studied under her and moved in her circle—the finest singers of Cairo—flocked to them. The other was Signore F., who had lived in the city for years and had numerous students from various colonies of foreigners. He regularly performed such miracles on the piano that the number of his friends and admirers grew steadily.

At this concert, Madame Gh. B. sang. But I couldn't find anyone who could tell me anything about her—perhaps because most of the people present were amateurs. Every time a performer played, or a singer sang, they all rushed to congratulate his or her relatives, thus guaranteeing that they would also be congratulated when their children sang and played. The woman didn't have any family, yet her singing created a big stir and provoked loud applause, which she accepted with simple silence. A deep, jet-black flame appeared in her eyes; she had the look of a woman who was neither young nor old, like a statue, with unchanging features and unvarying posture.

I thought about her for a long time that evening, and from all that I had heard about her I pieced together a sad story. I said to myself, "What a waste! Why does this woman pretend not to know her true self? Why doesn't she forget she's beautiful and rise to the level I'm sure she merits?"

The following morning, Signore F. came to give me my piano lesson. Instead of arriving at eleven o'clock, which was the appointed time, he arrived at ten minutes to noon. He came in, rubbing his hands, his eyes shining behind his glasses. I grumbled, "Signore, you don't care about my time! You've ruined my morning. In fact, you've ruined my entire day!" He laughed; it was a laugh which began moderately but ended in a sound like the chirping of birds. "I'm not a mathematics teacher," he said. "I'm not obliged to come at the appointed time." And he rubbed his hands again, citing a French proverb to the effect that some confusion is necessary for the enhancement of art.[7] "But my time—" I said. He interrupted me, "The lesson! The lesson!" And so for a long hour the neighbors were treated to that special noise of a student practicing and repeating as the teacher looks on.

When the hour came to an end, and the labors were over and peace restored, I demanded my due. If Signore F. was satisfied with his students, he would play whatever they requested. The reward I requested that day was a piece of Russian music that he had played the previous day.

He sat at the piano, and before he started playing, we talked about the concert and exchanged views about the voices of the singers, eventually arriving at Madame Gh. B.

"Is she one of your students?" I asked.

"No, no. She's one of Mrs. K.'s students. She's been to her house several times."

"Sometimes they call her Madame and sometimes Mademoiselle. Is she married or single?"

He sighed and said, "Poor woman!"

"What's so terrible about her life that it makes you feel so sorry for her?"

"Who wouldn't feel sorry for a woman who has beauty, intelligence, and goodness, who's been given everything she needs to be happy, and yet has had nothing but misery in life?"

"What misery?"

"What? Don't you know her story?"

"I know little bits here and there. You can't really get a clear picture of someone's life from what people say."

He sighed again, and his fingertips hurried over the musical scale, as if he were releasing some of his grief, or looking for a new way to tell an old story. Then his expression clouded, and he said, "Her father was a judge in the mixed courts.[8] He was very learned and intelligent, so he taught his daughter and gave her the best education. When the time came for her to be married, the same thing happened to her as happens to a lot of girls. Her parents chose a fiancé for her, a foreigner, and she had no say about him. The fiancé was quite handsome, so she didn't object. She was content, like many of her sisters, to receive the customary gifts of clothes and jewelry, and to attain a certain measure of freedom and independence. So she was married and had a magnificent wedding, to which the most prominent people from the European colonies were invited. It wasn't long before the husband claimed what had been agreed as a dowry."

Signore F. stopped talking. A look of mingled shame, compassion, and contempt clouded his face. After a moment of silence, he continued, "Many women make men unhappy. Many women tear marriages apart and break people's hearts. But if a woman is not a wicked person, then she's really unfortunate. However much she rises up in her own eyes, however much she's liberated from her chains, and however much those who defend her rights exaggerate in raising her to a man's level, her life, her entire life, remains in the grip of this being—this man—whose equal she claims to be. In reality, she's nothing but what he wants her to be. If he's free and noble, he makes her free and noble. If he's low and mean, he debases and humiliates her. She's his plaything; she's his slave; something he need show no restraint with, whatever the situation. Men who have a conscience are frightened by this authority over women, this power. It's a power that scoffs at changes in politics and society, because it's stronger than either of them, and more deeply rooted—in nature itself. So they refrain from marrying out of fear of themselves."

His comments were important, but they irritated me—I wanted to hear the rest of the story. So I said, "Then what happened?"

"What happened is that this imposter had a secret relationship with another woman and needed money, and marriage was the easiest way to get it. After three weeks, he disappeared."

"How did he disappear?"

"He left the house and never returned. For the first few days, his wife went mad, thinking he had died. Weeks went by and the news that he had gone off with his first wife started to spread. So they sent people out to look for him in his own country, Italy"—and here Signore F. swallowed hard because he was Italian—"but the efforts of the police were in vain. They found no trace of him, either in Italy or in any other country in the West. Shortly after that, the father of this woman, who'd been cheated out of her youth, love, money, and standing, had died. She became lonely and poor. The church refused to annul her marriage because the man hadn't married his first wife in church; it was a marriage by agreement only. There's a legal penalty for this, but how can the law reach someone who's vanished? Even if the church annulled the woman's marriage, people would still have their suspicions about her, because the one who's wronged is more vulnerable to suspicions and speculations than the wrongdoer, especially if the wronged person is a woman and the wrongdoer is a man. That's why people watch every move she makes. She's settled on their tongues and become a tasty morsel for their chitchat. Even if she were to spend her days fasting, praying, and living the life of an ascetic, they wouldn't give her her due. No matter how high a price she paid them, they wouldn't sell her that illusory regard with which they flatter people of power and wealth and authority, or those who are good at duping them. What purpose does this woman have in life? She's not divorced, so she isn't free to spend her time as she wants; and she isn't chained, so she can't console herself by breaking her chains. It's a crippled sort of life. The man made her miserable, just as he has crippled many other women before her and made them miserable."

"But how is it that she didn't see through his deception during the engagement?

"I don't know why she didn't realize. And her family didn't notice anything either."

"Perhaps he was sincere when he married her, but kept thinking of the other woman. Perhaps she was very beautiful."

"Those who know her say she's an old gray-haired woman and are amazed that this bright, elegant man should be content with her—even as a servant." Signore F. lowered his head and remained silent for a while. Then he continued, "But youth and beauty don't have any bearing on these matters. People look for beauty in the salon, in the theater, in society, and on the street, and a pretty woman usually attracts more attention than a plain one. But the effect of her looks doesn't go beyond this—history proves my point. The most recent historical example is that of the crown prince of Austria, whose murder set off World War I. He was the one who turned away from all the Austrian archduchesses and their dazzling beauty, and rejected all the princesses in the ruling dynasties, and abdicated from the throne and the crown to marry a woman who was the least graceful and beautiful of all. That was the Countess Sophia Chotek, a lady-in-waiting to one of his female relatives. After her marriage, she became the Duchess of Hohenberg, and was killed with him in the tragic incident at Sarajevo."

Signore F. settled himself in his seat and began to play a sad, stirring piece by Beethoven: The Funeral March of the *Eroica* Symphony.

Yesterday in a garden on the outskirts of Cairo, I saw the woman with the story. I understand now why the expression in her eyes changes. While I don't yet fully understand what the words "crippled life" mean, I do realize that life prepares circumstances for some people that they never dreamed of, and if they were to dream of them, they would try to eliminate them, even if it meant walking on thorns and burning coals. I have learned that in that upright figure, in that body which expresses strength and pride, there is a heart once wounded by true love. But today it is tortured by a cancer with roots spreading to all its corners, that deep-seated cancer which cannot be eradicated: contempt for life and lack of trust in people.

The Persian Rug

Hanan al-Shaykh

When Maryam had finished arranging my hair in two plaits, she put her finger to her mouth and licked it, then passed it over my eyebrows and sighed, "Oh, your eyebrows are so untidy!" She turned quickly to my sister and said, "Go and see if your father is still praying." No sooner had my sister gone than she came back and whispered, "He still is." She stretched out her hands and lifted them to the sky, imitating him. I didn't laugh as usual, and neither did Maryam. Instead, she picked up the scarf from the chair, covered her hair with it, and tied it hastily at the neck. Then she carefully opened the cupboard and took out her handbag. She put it under her arm and reached out her hands to us. I held one, and my sister held the other. We understood that we had to walk on tiptoe, like her. With bated breath, we went out through the open front door. As we descended the stairs, we looked back toward the door, then toward the window. When we reached the last stair, we started running, not stopping until the long narrow lane had disappeared from view and we had crossed the street. There Maryam had stopped a taxi.

Our behavior was prompted by fear. Today we were going to see my mother for the first time since her divorce from my father, and he had sworn he would never let her see us again. This was because just hours after their divorce, news had come that she was going to marry the man she had loved before her family forced her to marry my father.

My heart was pounding. I knew this was not because of the fear and the running, but because I was worried about the meeting, and the confusion I expected to feel. I was reserved and conscious of my shyness. However much I tried, I couldn't show my emotions, even

154

to my mother. I would be unable to throw myself into her arms and smother her with kisses, or hold her face in my hands, as my sister would do, and as it was her nature to do. I had thought a long time about this, ever since Maryam had whispered to me and my sister that my mother had returned from the south and that we were going to visit her secretly the next day. At first I thought I would force myself to behave just like my sister. I would stand behind her and imitate her blindly. But I knew myself too well. However much I tried to force myself, and however much I thought in advance about what I should and shouldn't do, when the time came, I would forget what I had resolved to do and stand looking at the floor with a deep frown on my face. Caught in this situation, I wouldn't despair; I would beg my lips to open into a smile—but it would be of no use.

When the taxi pulled up at the entrance to a house with two columns topped by two lions of red sandstone, I felt a surge of joy and momentarily forgot my fear and shyness. It delighted me that my mother lived in a house with an entrance flanked by two lions. I heard my sister imitate the roar of a lion, and I turned to her enviously. I saw her stretching up her hands in an attempt to grab one of the lions. I thought to myself: She's always so uncomplicated, so full of joy. She remains joyful even at the most critical moments. Here she is now, not the least bit concerned about this meeting.

When my mother opened the door and I saw her, I found myself unable to wait and rushed forward, throwing myself into her arms before my sister. I closed my eyes, and all the joints in my body seemed to fall asleep after a long period of insomnia. I smelled the same old scent of her hair, and discovered for the first time how much I had missed her. I wished she would come back and live with us, despite the loving care that my father and Maryam were showing us. My mind wandered, recalling her smile when my father agreed to divorce her, after a religious sheikh had intervened because she had threatened to douse herself in petrol and set fire to herself if my father wouldn't divorce her. I felt dazed from the smell of her—a smell I remembered so well. I realized how much I had missed her, even though when she had left us, with tears and kisses, we had gone back to our game in the narrow alley by our house while she had hurried off behind my uncle and climbed into the car. When night had come, for the first time in a long while we didn't hear her quarreling with my father; silence had reigned over the house, disturbed only by

Maryam's sobbing. She was related to my father and had been living with us in the house ever since I could remember.

Smiling, my mother ushered me aside so that she could hug and kiss my sister, and hug Maryam again, who had started to cry. I heard my mother say tearfully to her, "Thank you very much!" She wiped her tears away with her sleeve and, gazing at my sister and me again, exclaimed, "May God keep away the evil eye. How big you've grown!" Then she put her arms around me, and my sister put her arms around my mother's waist, and we all began to laugh when we discovered that we couldn't walk like that. We reached the inner room, and I felt certain that her new husband was inside, because my mother said with a smile, "Mahmud loves you very much and wishes your father would let me have you, so that you could live with us and become his children too." Laughing, my sister answered, "You mean we're going to have two fathers?" Still dazed, I put my hand on my mother's arm, proud of my behavior, of having escaped from myself, from my fettered hands, and from the prison of my shyness—all without any effort. I called to mind the meeting with my mother, how I had spontaneously thrown myself into her arms—something I thought was utterly impossible—and how I had kissed her so hard that I had closed my eyes.

Her husband wasn't there. I gazed at the floor, then froze. Confused, I looked at the Persian rug that was spread on the floor, then gave my mother a long and hard look. She didn't understand my look. She went to a cupboard, opened it, and threw me an embroidered blouse, then she opened a drawer in the decorated dressing table, took out an ivory comb painted with red hearts, and gave it to my sister. I stared at the Persian rug and trembled with resentment and anger. Again I looked at my mother. She interpreted my look as longing and affection, because she put her arms around me and said, "You must come every other day, and you must spend Fridays with me."

I remained frozen. I wanted to push her arms away. I wanted to sink my teeth into her white forearm. I wished I could reenact the moment of meeting: she would open the door, and I would stand as I should, staring at the floor with a frown on my face. My eyes were now glued to the Persian rug; its lines and colors were etched on my memory. I used to stretch out on it as I did my homework, and find myself examining its pattern. Close up, it looked like slices of red watermelon, one next to the other. When I sat on the sofa, the slices changed into combs with fine teeth. The bouquets of flowers around the four sides were purple-colored, like a cockscomb. At the beginning of every summer, my mother would put mothballs on the rug—as on the rest of the rugs—then roll it up and place it on top of the cupboard. The room would look dull and sad without the rug, until autumn came, when she would take it up to the roof and spread it out. She would pick up the mothballs—most of which had dissolved from the heat and humidity of the summer—brush the rug with a small broom, and leave it on the roof. In the evening, she would bring it down and spread it out on the floor, and I would feel overjoyed. With the rug's bright colors, life would return to the room. But a few months before my mother's divorce, the rug had disappeared after being spread out on the roof in the sun. When my mother went up in the afternoon to fetch it and didn't find it, she called my father. It was the first time I had seen his face redden with anger. When they came down from the roof, my mother was in an irate and agitated state. She questioned the neighbors, who swore, one after the other, that they hadn't seen the rug. Suddenly my mother exclaimed, "Ilya!" We were all speechless—my father, myself, my sister, and our neighbors. I found myself shouting, "How can you say that? It can't be true!"

Ilya was an almost blind man who frequented all the houses of the neighborhood to repair wicker chairs. When our turn came, I would see him, as I returned home from school, seated on the stone bench, his red hair shining in the sun, with a pile of straw in front of him. He would stretch out his hand and work the rush with an ease that made weaving seem like the motion of a fish slipping unharmed through the meshes of a net. I would watch him insert the rush in a hole deftly and skillfully, coil it around, and take it out again, until he had formed a circle on the seat of the chair, just like the circles before and after it. The circles were all even and precise, as though his hands were a machine. I was amazed at the speed and dexterity of his fingers, and at his posture: he sat with his head inclined as though he were using his eyes. Once I doubted that he could see nothing but dark shadows, and I found myself squatting on the ground looking up at his rosy-red face. I saw blurry eyes under his glasses, and the white line that went through them pierced my heart. I hurried off to the kitchen, where I found a bag of dates on the table. I put a heap of them on a plate and gave them to Ilya.

I continued to stare at the rug as the image of Ilya, with his red hair and red face, flashed into my mind. I saw his hand as he climbed the stairs by himself, as he sat on his chair, as he haggled over a price, as he ate and knew he had finished everything on the plate, as he drank from the jug and the water flowed easily down his throat. When he came one midday, calling out "Allah!" before knocking and entering—just as my father had taught him, in case my mother was unveiled—my mother rushed at him and asked about the rug. He didn't say anything, but made a sound like weeping. As he walked off, I saw him stumble for the first time, almost banging against the table. I went up to him and took him by the hand. He recognized me by the touch of my hand, because he said to me in a half-whisper, "Never mind, girl." Then he turned to leave. When he bent over to put on his shoes, I thought I saw tears on his cheeks. My father said, "God will forgive you, Ilya, if you tell the truth." But Ilya walked off, supporting himself on the rails of the stairway. As he descended the stairs, he took an unusually long time to feel his way along. Finally he disappeared from view, and we never saw him again.

The Dream

Aliya Mamdouh

❧❀❧

He left the nightclub, descending the stairway step by step, and looked carefully around him. Passersby, with full or close-cropped beards and wearing old clothes, gazed at him mockingly.

The music sounded like loud wailing to him, while the dancer's seductive movements aroused his erotic feelings and fantasies. He was slightly thirsty. He had gulped down so many glasses of arak that he had lost count. The thirstier he felt, the more unsteadily he walked. He began to hum softly. He didn't know what spoiled the atmosphere. Was it the music or the dancer's clothes, the stripping act or the customers, the man or the arak?

He was unaccustomed to frequenting nightclubs and didn't know what happened inside them. It was a world that he could not afford to explore, a world that he feared, even hated. He walked farther away from the nightclub, entering dark streets and alleys that smelled of mud and dirt. Were it not for his fear, he would have returned to the nightclub at once. But he felt a raging thirst now, and his wife would be worried. At this moment, he dared not do anything.

This moment was like a dream that he was afraid to entertain, but equally afraid to relinquish. The blood flowed hot through his veins, and the dancer's lips, which seemed to dominate the pavements and alleyways, looked lewd and defiant.

He didn't stumble as he made his way home. He wanted to walk with his eyes shut so that he could conjure up the image of the dancer's body, shoulders, and lips. He knew for certain that he would never see her again.

He wasn't thinking only about the fervor of his virility. Uppermost in his mind was this dancer's life. Did she have moments of

159

self-doubt like him? When he reached this point in his thinking, his house appeared before him, dark. Here he would find relief from his inner turmoil.

His wife lifted the blanket from her face and looked into his eyes. He was sad and confused. She got up and put on her veil, moving the blanket aside. The room was narrow, the bed small, and the floor bare. The window let in ice cold air. He was still standing in the middle of the room, gazing at her. Her face and neck were covered with the threads of a black veil embroidered with cotton fringes that hung slightly over her forehead. He remembered the dancer's teeth; they were white and small.

"Did you have supper?"

"No. I'm still hungry."

He looked at her in alarm. "Wrap a shawl around your shoulders."

She shivered a little, and he realized that he loved her. His anguish had partially subsided.

She moved before him, making some noise with the dishes.

"Where's Aziz?"

"He slept at my mother's. Tomorrow's a holiday."

"Come over here. I don't want to eat now. Listen. I want to see all the clothes that you've got from the day we were married until now. I want to watch as you put them on, one by one, until you get warm."

His tone of voice frightened her, but she approached him anyway and glanced at him again. Sparks of desire emanated from his breath, nostrils, and the quiver of his mustache. He didn't touch her but kept staring at her.

"Why don't you go to sleep? You're a little drunk."

His intoxicated voice rang out: "No, no. I'm happy. I want you to be happy too. I'll sit on the bed and watch you wear all your clothes."

It seemed to the wife that her husband was slightly ill. Faced with his stubborn resolve, she gave in to his will. She brought out a big bundle from under the bed and began to open it.

"Let me see your clothes. I'll choose for you."

"Are we going out this late at night?"

"Yes, for a while. Doesn't it make you happy?"

She fell silent and stared at her clothes for a long while. Then she picked up the bundle and placed it before him. The smell on his breath had filled the bed, the room, and her nostrils.

"Do you think I'm mad?"

She looked into his eyes, trembling. "No, no. God forbid! But you're tired."

He started to take her clothes out of the bundle: a patterned, rust-stained dress, closed in the front, another dress with an open back, and several faded underclothes. He suddenly realized how poor they were.

"Wear these two dresses one on top of the other."

His wife began to put on the first dress. She stood in the middle of the room, filled with questions. Her breathing became somewhat more regular. She readjusted her veil.

"Walk around the room a little. Sing any song you like."

Her limbs and knees were trembling with fear. "I love you. I love you," she said, "but I'm afraid of you. What do you want? I'm sleepy and you're tired."

His voice grew louder: "Take off the veil first."

He rose to his feet slowly and stood face to face with her. She lifted her hands to her head, removed the veil, and left it hanging around her neck. He touched her hair with his fingers. It was shiny and clean, and smelled of henna. It was parted in the middle and arranged in two braids.

"Where's the comb?"

She quickly handed him the comb. He undid the braids on her shoulders and ran the comb through her hair. Her face reddened as she looked at him in astonishment. He threw the veil onto the floor and moved away a little.

"Walk around the room. Let your hair fall down the sides of your face."

His voice rose higher than before: "Do as you're told!"

The woman couldn't bring herself to obey his last order. She brushed back the hair from her face, and awaited new instructions from him.

"Now take off the first dress."

He rose to his feet to help her again.

"And the second one as well."

He stood staring at her, as if seeing her for the first time.

"Now take off your nightgown."

An interval of silence passed, during which she glanced at him furtively. This was her only man. Nakedness made her shy. Didn't he realize that? She remained transfixed, reluctant to undress. He drew closer to her. It seemed to him that she had shut her eyes. The light irritated him a little. The dancer danced in dim lights, shaking her shoulders, bosom, and legs. She continued to move back and forth for a long while as she undressed before the customers. His wife's face was as swarthy and lovely as ever. He wished she would not open her eyes. If the dancer died in one of her dance sessions, would her body tremble like this? When she threw away her bra, she first turned around for a while and exposed her back to the customers. The music erupted from all the corners of the nightclub, tunes he had never heard before, with musical instruments unknown to him.

"When she shuts her eyes, it will look like she's lifeless."

The dancer took several steps forward and continued to undress. He could not see her body completely. The lights blurred his vision, forming circles, squares, and triangles of multiple colors. The music kept rising and falling. He was bewildered, not knowing how to quench the fire raging inside him, not wanting to speak with anyone. He continued to feel a sense of humiliation and disappointment.

He proceeded to remove his wife's nightgown, and she reluctantly submitted to him. As he pulled the nightgown off her head, her hair became disheveled and the expression changed on her face and in her eyes. She appeared before him in her underclothes, a woman at once trembling, angry, lonely, and distant.

She collapsed on the floor on top of her clothing, mute. Painfully shy about her naked body, she lowered her head and averted her eyes. Her posture reflected her awkward situation. She was a simple woman at peace with herself. He stood bewildered. The events, moral laws, and dreams crowded into his mind, throwing him into utter confusion. In his outward appearance, he seemed to be writhing in pain. He beat his head with his fist and flung himself upon her chest, weeping loudly.

Pharaoh Is Drowning Again

Sakina Fuad

❦

he sea. I sail your waters to the end of the world. I came from you as a drop, as a tear from your eye. Why was crying created from tears? So that I would fall as a tear? A tear on a night of love, misery, or revenge. Any night. A man and a woman and a tear. And a creature dying and living, carrying the sin of one night. Life in its entirety is the sin of one night. Damned are the nights that produce human beings. They drink in the nights consumed with anxiety. Misery flows in the marrow of their bones. A nasty shock occurs at every moment. The sensation of pain resides in the folds of the brain. Creatures afflicted with madness, anger, agony, and grief, and ground down by the crush, the chase, and the fleeing.

From where? And to where? And when will the drop return to the sea? I don't know.

The voice of Abd al-Wahhab the singer cries in the distance, carrying all the sorrows of the night.

The sea . . .

Moses struck the water with his stick. The water receded, and a road was opened up beneath the feet of those fleeing.

I was one of them. I hid amid the exodus of the wretched, and veiled myself with their nights so I could flee. I shared their dreadful ordeal. We descended to the bottom of the parted sea, crawled, and fled. The waves protected us. The waves were like mountains on either side of us. It was a moment in which the whole world became still. The sea held its breath. Had it breathed, the mountains of its waves would have collapsed on those in flight. The sea held its breath and clutched its waves to its heart. We crossed to the other bank. We flung ourselves onto the ground to catch our breath, to nurse the wounds, and to soothe the pain with the sweetness of salvation.

The sense of terror . . .

The sight of Pharaoh standing on the other bank with his armies of men and chariots, his arrows sharpened and poisoned . . .

The flight . . .

But where to? There is no escape. Pharaoh is our fate. He is always behind us.

"The fugitive will find a way on dry land."

There's no end to my good mother's proverbs. Life consists of pleasing proverbs on my mother's tongue, and other women's tongues.

My mother is a person from the generation of proverbs. Her meaningless words are killing me. As soon as they ring out in my ears, I feel as if they chop off my head and blow out my brains. I yell at her, and at myself, and at the whole world.

I run away . . .

"Taxi!"

"Where to? What's the address?"

"Take me as close as you can to the sea."

The taxi takes off at full speed. My mind races ahead of the speeding car to the water. My innermost feelings are a sea raging and beating against the shores of my body. I head off from wherever I may be sitting, and sail away. The horizon has no limits. The world has no end. I came into the world at the moment of beginning. Everything was water, and I was a drop, carried along by the current, gliding on the surface of the universe. The earth and the sky were still joined together. I was at their meeting point. I climbed up to the sky and down to the earth. I chose the sea, so that traveling and the horizon would remain my limitless world. I could ascend to the sky and flow on the surface of the earth. There were no limits and no fetters, no bridges and no walls. We were all drops, swimming incessantly. When did the journey of misery begin?

The drop was covered with white foam. The foam assumed the shape of a beautiful woman. Her first name was Aphrodite. The name changed, and the shape changed too, but she remained a woman. The body is only the first prison cell. After it, there are millions of other prison cells.

"Where to?" The driver asks again.

And I'm still traveling alone, competing with the speeding car, searching for a time that is free of our cares and sorrows; looking for a place that doesn't possess me, nor I it; a place that I come to as a guest and leave without grief; a place that doesn't know me, nor I it.

The silence takes me back from the sea to the earth. The silence means we've come to a stop.

"Whereabouts?"

"This is the place."

I look closely at the number, at the building, at the faces. Everything is exactly as it was before. I stare at the driver. How did he know my address? How did he find out where I live?

I ask him.

He assures me that I gave him the address when I flung myself on the car seat. I don't argue.

A lot of things have come to an end, including the age of arguing. We've entered the age of silence. Everything is done by force of habit. All actions take place without the intervention of our will. We eat. We drink. We sleep. Children are born. We kill, and hate, and love. Even love. What was the meaning of this word in your time, you, the old people? Words are scarce. We can no longer bear the additional burden of words. Machines operate and think and plan. The radio is the only machine that sometimes speaks. There are modern devices that pick up vibrations from space. Our engineers work away, and receivers break through new barriers every day. Voices are received from space, and we hear all those who have left us. I have no longing for anyone. I've often asked about the meaning of this word. They say longing is a cold that bites at the depths of the heart. Longing is a maddening desire for something. These words belong to the age of words: my heart is nothing but a pump drawing blood.

Something happened this morning.

What was it?

In a vibrating, staccato voice, the radio broadcaster announced:

"Our instruments have managed to pick up signals—muttering and whispering—from the uppermost reaches of space. Reception is still poor, but the voices have confirmed that they are from our planet, from earth. Everything is still very vague. We are trying to overcome engineering problems, but the few words that have reached us are ones of greeting to you."

For the first time ever, longing was born in me. My blood's pump trembled; the monotonous routine to which it had worked, year in, year out, broke down.

The cold that bites at the depths of the heart . . .

I yearned for something . . .

My yearnings were submerged in a feeling of alienation. I had no idea what *he* wanted, or what I wanted. I listened to the program. Instruments had been used that were more sensitive than any known before. No penetration of space had ever reached these voices before. This was the first time *they* had said that they left us simply to dissolve in space as souls, and then observe us. I threw myself to the floor under this sophisticated piece of equipment. My ears vied with the instruments in trying to reach out into space. I searched for something.

These mutterings and buzzings and silences and tears were all *his*. I heard his tears and silence and coughing as he met the morning with his old, bare chest. He died far away from us. They said it happened in obscure circumstances. His pointed words killed him. In an age when only sickly words are spoken, he was surrounded by sugar-coated words. But he was not one of those who spoke them.

I've never seen him. I know him as if he breathes in my soul, and I wear his face, with all its sharp features.

My mother tells me I was born a few days after they took him away. Yet I know him. His image often appears to me. I meet him on all my journeys. There is no shore I visit without seeing him there as well. His roaring laughter is soundless. He beats his broad chest and waves his fist. One day the time for our meeting will come. And today I hear him. My heart is heavy with longing. Its fuse can explode at a touch. The sand from every shore of every sea in the whole wide world will no longer be enough to extinguish the fire.

"Where to?"

To whom is my question addressed? I can't see the taxi driver. When did I get out of the taxi? How long does it take to climb these twenty floors with their five hundred stairs? I don't count them in minutes or numbers, but in the words that are gnawing at my heart and that I'm chewing over. I finally reach the last floor. People, houses, cars are like little toys fulfilling the daily routine. At the end of the day, the puppets are turned over, face down. The game at night is called sleep. At dawn, the key is stealthily turned, and the machines are wound up and begin to gyrate. I've released my daily scream. Who will release me from my key? Who will demolish the prison cells? Who will make me a human being again?

My heart is overflowing with longing. The face of my father, whom I've never seen, accompanies me. I wait for his voice in the coming vibrations. I thirst for it. I touch all the seas of the world, and they turn into crystals.

I want a drop of water.

My apartment is on the first floor. I won't go back there. I've made the decision for the thousandth time. I climb up and down the five hundred stairs every day, struggling with the decision and fleeing from my chained will. The turning of the key in the elegant door puts an end to everything. There it is: the air-conditioned apartment, the colorful walls, the soft white bed on which dreams roam and stretch and yawn. The plushness and lushness of the bedroom are enticing. My husband conducts his important conversations on a number of colorful phones. Everything is soft, alluring, and entwined in fine spider's webs. The expensive pictures are imported from Paris. He draws his money from an enchanted well. His hobby is to collect the rare—in art, love, and food.

He laughs mockingly. Whatever is left of my strength, after the exertion of climbing the stairs, fails at the sight of his triumphant expression. My dead resolution finds its resting place in his eyes. With one glance, I've become part of the picture. The comfort and softness possess me. The silence, the stillness, the smoothness drag me to the bottom of the earth. I sink under its layers. The spider's webs wrap my feet together, twisting my steps around each other. I whirl around from room to room. The tombstones of furniture rise higher every day. I recite the verses of the Fatiha.[9] The reciting voice rings out in the silence. The walls close in. They move, advance, press together. They turn my body into a flat, dry surface, a leaf preserved for millions of years between the pages of a book made of brick, concrete, and iron. My heart is overflowing with longing. I rewind the recorded program. I listen. My ears reach out into space searching for him, for his roar, for the blow he struck into the air in order to crush them, for the spit he spat at them when they took him away. He spoke his words at the right time. Words that are not spoken at the right time and place are decaying corpses.

My lifeless body rises from the bed and relieves itself. My husband makes love to me skillfully, as skillfully as he handles everything else that I know nothing about.

The cup of tea, the rocking chair, the long bathrobe, and the bed are all still warm. I tremble and watch his briefcase. The briefcase moves away, carried by his hand, and vanishes. I, and the other things in the picture, go into a state of waiting.

I tidy up again, but without deviating one step from the framework of the picture. The tombstones of furniture rise higher every day. I pace the floor among them, reciting the verses of the Fatiha. I lift the silk covers. There is not a scratch on the furniture. The covers are lifted only to be patted gently and to have the dust brushed off them. His hobby is to visit auctions and bring back the rarest things. He visited our house and handed his money over, and I was added to his purchases and the collection of rare things. My features have become the same as theirs. Words have lost their value. Silence is no longer a condition around us; silence is a living creature inhabiting our depths and smothering every ember there. Everything is done by force of habit or through fear of him. Pharaoh runs his kingdom with great skill: the maids are sent to the market and the wives are kept behind closed doors. Pharaoh is a god who rules by divine right. The queen ascends a throne of fog; a puff of air from the master's mouth blows the throne away, and he seats another woman on his right or left. Ownership has corrupted everything. Sincerity has vanished, and relationships have lost their intimacy. Pharaoh does not speak. Pharaoh has become one of the machines of our time, operating, pushing buttons, managing.

This morning is unlike any other morning.

Why?

Penetration into outer space brings back all those who have left us. Penetration into the layer where souls live is happening for the first time. I've recorded the program. I play the recording again at the lowest speed, searching for him among them. Everything strong belongs to him, the laughter, the roaring, the stupefying silence.

He says his words there. I long for him. I long for words. I long for a place that doesn't possess me, nor I it. I move, I run, without limitations, without chains. I dwell on the surface of the whole world, taking and giving. I turn into a drop of water. I flow into the vast sea.

The sea . . .

Pharaoh is standing on the other bank. His scream reverberates. I must go home, or else he'll come down to get me.

Pharaoh sinks to the floor of the parted sea.

The wounds dry out. The pain subsides. I stand upright on the shore of the wretched. I turn into a giant rebel, killing and burning.

The waves roar. The sea releases the breath it has been holding until we cross. Its mountains explode as raging waves, submerging Pharaoh and his armies. His men beat the water with their hands; their chests fill up with brine; their remains float on the water.

The world becomes still, empty, clear.

We are at the moment of beginning.

I'm still moving as I sit on the ground, watching the sea: the movement of the water takes me on a journey across the whole world. My heart is a bird that has left my breast to flutter on a horizon where the earth joins the sky. My body is a ship that stops at harbors to take provisions, then continues its travels.

I will not return . . . until the sea has swallowed all the Pharaohs.

Part Five

Childbearing

The Spider's Web

Ihsan Kamal

ore than a week had passed since Ghada had first noticed the spider's web. She had been greatly surprised to
discover it while lying on her bed with her eyes wide
open, as she was accustomed to spending half her time in bed awake.
She would stare at nothing, gazing at the ceiling without seeing it.
She would think about her personal, and seemingly endless, tragedy,
which she inevitably pondered day and night.

Sometimes she whispered to God, "Is it difficult for You, O
God, to grant me a child? You give others dozens, and nothing
is hard for You, if You want it. You, then, simply don't want it. But
why? You have wisdom in everything. What is the wisdom in my
childlessness? Perhaps Your wisdom is hidden from me, and I must
search for it." Yet despite all her searching and pondering, she could
not resolve her dilemma. She therefore resumed her supplications:
"One child, O Lord, with whom my husband and I would be delighted, and with whom we would reinforce the bonds of love that
exist between us—or rather, that existed between us." She frequently
asked herself, "Is it possible for him to continue to love me after
I have deprived him of the joy of fatherhood?" Then she would
protest—against no one in particular, for no one had leveled an accusation at her, but she felt that it was always present in people's
hearts, eyes, and words. And so she would defend herself: "What
fault is it of mine? I never spared any effort. God knows how I long
and wish for a child from the bottom of my heart!"

Her husband often said to her, "Drop this matter. I personally
no longer think about it. What would having a child—or children—
accomplish? Would they work miracles for me, or for the country?
Would they right any wrong? If they don't arrive, that's God's will."

172

But she didn't believe him. She was certain that it was merely his delicacy and decency that prompted him to try to alleviate her suffering. He repeatedly reassured her, "Nothing matters to me in this world except you. You mean everything to me. You're the best thing that ever happened to me. As long as we're together, I couldn't wish for anything more." She would smile inwardly and think to herself: He's really a prince. He does everything he can to ease my pain and anxiety. But I wonder how much longer this can last. Certainly, the day will come when he'll run out of patience, when he'll begin to fear that he'll miss the chance of having children, when the silence in his house becomes unbearable. I wonder when this day will come. Will it be sooner or later? And how will he let me know that he has despaired of me? Will he be kind and warn me before he leaves me? Or will he ultimately explode in frustration?

She was so engrossed in thought that she was unable to sleep. She tossed and turned in bed and shut her eyes, but sleep escaped her. She then opened her eyes, but saw nothing, not even the reflection of the sunlight off the windows of the cars passing through the street, a reflection that flashed swiftly across the ceiling of her room and then vanished. She was unaware of the spider's web until one day when she noticed that one of these reflections did not glint like the sun's golden rays and, though it moved, did not disappear quickly. She wondered what sort of shadow it was. When she looked closely, she discovered that it was not a shadow but a spider's web. She was extremely surprised. For one thing, it looked completely different from any other spider's web that she had ever seen. The spider's web with which she was familiar was usually as small as a piaster, black, and so dirty that it aroused a feeling of revulsion. By contrast, the one she saw on the ceiling was quite large, dark gray, and of a texture similar to that of a sheer fabric like chiffon. It was so gauzy that it fluttered in a mere puff of air. Moreover, the very presence of the spider's web surprised her. She was meticulous about cleaning her house, so much so that she received the praise and admiration of her female relatives, inspired jokes among her girl-friends who thought her obsessive, and was criticized by her enemies who searched for faults: "After all, what does she have to keep her busy? Does she have an infant at the breast or a baby who's crawling?"

The size of the web indicated that the spider had not spun it in a single day. So how could she account for her failure to notice it earlier? Searching for a possible explanation, she attempted to distract herself from her persistent problem with humor. The spider could have worked throughout the night, in addition to its normal hours, to earn overtime! Or perhaps the housing crisis had affected spiders as well, so that four or five of them cooperated in spinning one web! But her attempts at joking were unsuccessful. Suddenly she gasped as she remembered a phrase that I'tidal, the daughter of her husband's paternal uncle, had used when one of the female relatives was advising her, during a large gathering that included many of them, to content herself with the three children that she had borne and to begin taking the contraceptive pill. I'tidal replied that she had thought of it after the birth of her first two babies, but that her husband loved children and wanted more. Of course this was because he loved her, and because children reinforced the bonds of marriage. She then added, "A house without children is more fragile than a spider's web!"

Ghada gasped when she remembered these words. She stared again at the spider's web on the ceiling. It was so thin and delicate that it swayed in the slightest breeze and seemed about to fall apart. She said to herself sadly, "Is my house more fragile than this spider's web? True, the gentle breezes have not destroyed the web yet, but now it's the end of summer. In a few weeks, autumn will set in with its strong winds. Will the spider's web be able to withstand them? And after the autumn, winter will come, bringing heavy storms. How awful the winter storms are!"

She wondered whether I'tidal had meant her with these words. There was no doubt about that. She had often heard from several female relatives that I'tidal—with her mother's blessing—had aspired to be married to Sa'id, Ghada's husband. Despite her subsequent marriage, I'tidal continued to hate Ghada and envy her and wait for an opportunity to speak ill of her. The day when she had made that foolish remark—and it was not the first time that I'tidal had spoken thoughtlessly—she bit her lip in a theatrical gesture, as if she wanted to correct a mistake, and looked in Ghada's direction. But her tactless demeanor revealed that she was referring to Ghada.

She thought of getting up to fetch the ceiling duster in order to remove the spider's web, but her body would not respond. She had no inclination for work or for any other activity. She made excuses about being tired after her morning exertions and felt that she should rest for a while. As soon as she had refreshed herself with a nap, she would tackle this task. But after arising, she forgot the entire matter, until the afternoon of the next day. When she lay on her bed to rest and looked up and saw the spider's web, she cried out, "Good heavens! I forgot about it all this time!"

Once again she could not rise, so she postponed the task until she had rested her exhausted body. As usual, she was unable to sleep, and began to amuse herself by watching the spider entering and leaving its web. She wondered what it was doing. Undoubtedly, it was working on enlarging the web. "What a greedy creature!" she muttered. "All this area is not enough for you? You have approximately until five o'clock, when I get up from bed." She thought that the spider was not only greedy but also impudent, because it chose to dwell in her bedroom, and above her bed at that! Was it challenging her? Wouldn't it have been more appropriate for the spider to spin its web in one of the corners of the kitchen, or in the little room that was opened only rarely, when one of the female relatives stayed with them as a guest? She had intended to turn that room into a nursery for the children who had not arrived, and who apparently would never arrive. How strange is Fate, which makes a mockery of, and amuses itself with, human suffering! Many of her female acquaintances and friends complained bitterly of the side effects of the contraceptive pill. But when they stopped taking it, they became pregnant, despite every precaution, and had to resort to doctors and folk prescriptions to rid themselves of an unwanted pregnancy. Why would a person who wanted a child be deprived of one, while the person who did not want a child would be given one?

She tried in vain to steer her thoughts away from this subject. In ancient times, it was said, "All roads lead to Rome." Today, she could say, "All subjects lead to my childlessness." She did not forget the spider after rising from her bed, but she did nothing to remove it. Was the sight of the spider entering and leaving its web so comforting to her that she desired its presence? Or had she reached a stage where she refused to make any effort to care for a house that was doomed to collapse sooner or later? Perhaps she sympathized with the spider as an ally that participated with her in weakening the foundations of her house. Or perhaps she had lost her enthusiasm for everything. No one, not even she herself, knew.

As the days passed, her depression and withdrawal increased, despite Sa'id's attempts to brighten her outlook. How earnestly she wished she could respond to his exuberant high spirits! What had come over her? One day she said to him, "Praise be to God for creating me with a heart big enough to contain all my love for you!" Indeed, she had not ceased to love him as much as she had during their engagement and the first years of their marriage.

In reality, Sa'id's love had not changed—or rather, the outward manifestations of his love. She ardently wished she could penetrate his hidden depths in order to discover his true feelings. Was it still love or had love turned to pity? She had always known him as a river of tenderness. How happy his tenderness had made her—she, who had deprived the father in him of a child! Her mother's love and care lacked—she didn't know why—tenderness. Today, his outpouring of tenderness no longer made her happy. She was obsessed with the thought that this river would one day change its course toward another woman who would give him what she herself could not, despite all the doctors' reassurance that there was hope. But now the years were passing and the hope remained unfulfilled.

Whoever said that it is easier to suffer a misfortune than to wait for it to happen was right. The spider kept enlarging its web despite her decision to remove it within the hour, a decision the spider was unaware of. God seemed to be more merciful toward a spider than toward a human being. She believed that if the spider had known about her decision, it would have died of grief before she even touched it with her ceiling duster. And she? She lived waiting for Time to finish sharpening its sword of misery for her. She continued to work all day like a robot without a soul, until Sa'id returned from his work and approached her with longing. She received his longing with apathy, and deep down in her heart was a persistent question: "When will you do it? What are you waiting for? Why don't you hurry up and relieve my tension?" One day she even asked for a separation. That was more honorable for her. But he flew into a rage and warned her, with a pained voice, not to mention this topic ever again.

After lunch she went to bed, but she could not sleep. Her eyes remained open, gazing at the spider's web in strange indifference. The indifference increased daily, until more than a week had passed since she had first noticed the spider's web. She made no attempt to remove it, although she thanked God that neither Sa'id, nor any of the close female relatives who sometimes went into the bedroom to repair their makeup, had seen it.

That day the telephone rang. She hurried from the kitchen to answer it. I'tidal's mother was on the line, asking her to convey her thanks to Sa'id for his efforts to reconcile I'tidal with her husband Mu'min, and to ask him to cease these efforts, which were regretfully fated to fail. I'tidal's husband had repudiated her the previous day, claiming he could no longer bear the disharmony in their married life, which he blamed on her extreme stubbornness and endless badgering. Ghada could only utter one sentence: "It can't be . . . It can't be . . ." Then she replaced the receiver without adding a word.

Before returning to the kitchen, she hurried, as if hypnotized, to fetch the long-handled ceiling duster from the utility room. Then she rushed to the bedroom and brushed the ceiling clean, moving the duster back and forth several times to eliminate any trace of the spider's web.

Man and Woman

Rafiqat al-Tabi'a

❁❁❁

*T*he two of them had been stretched out together since the early hours of the evening. As the night wore on, the light of the bedside lamp grew brighter around them. She was contrasting her dream with the miserable reality of the world.

"We are, then, a man and a woman, weaving love from old times. But neither your smiles, which I cherish, nor my whispers, which you desire, nor my kisses, nor your hugs, nor our dreams together, can equal a single tear plucked by pain from the wide eyes set in this sad face, a face drained of all excitement.

"I loved to look at your picture every day, and memorize your features bit by bit. But one picture which I cut out recently, and the message written under it, have made me forget my joy with you. It was as if I had been brought back to the misery in which every human being is born, to the spontaneous cry that was in my mouth at birth, on the day when my only hope in life was the gentle touch of the midwife's hands!

"Who are you from now on? Who am I? In my handbag I carry your love letters and your picture. In your wonderful smile, which I adore, lies the image of the wide-eyed child we used to dream of equally. *This* child, with the short message written under his picture, has eyes that cry without tears. Perhaps he is the child I often wished you would give me one day, and now I've grown afraid of the mere thought of it. I'm a lost human being. I don't own even a tiny plot of land here, or anywhere; and if I do one day, what will it be worth when the time comes and I have to take your beautiful child in my arms and flee with him from terror, only to face ruin and death? Should I run with him to the south, to the blazing hot sands to bury him, his wide open eyes, eager for life, sealed by the sandy storms?

Or should I flee with him to the north, to drown him, the black lock of hair on his forehead plunged in the raging waves, his mouth filled with killer fish? Or do you want me to go east with him, to step on barbed wire that will sink into his soft, dark-skinned flesh, while barking dogs and roaring weapons chase after us, and whirls of dust cover and suffocate us? I can see myself now, before the dark-skinned child is born, gathering up all the clothes that I possess and dragging my feet around in search of a safe hut to shelter our child, a hut in which we would not be exposed to the howling winds that could blow away any fuel I had collected to warm my child's winter. I see myself struggling to find a tent of reeds to protect us from the midday summer sun, which could dissolve our child's nerves and dry out the blood of hope from my veins. I imagine the fog surrounding me in a strange, snowy territory, where I am utterly lost. I don't own even a tiny plot of land for my child, and your love isn't enough to fill with kindness and affection the vast world containing all the misery I now see in the eyes of the dark-skinned child, who cries without tears.

"I no longer want a child. Hunger would kill him little by little. You would die in a short, fateful battle. And I would spin around with him in a whirlpool of never-ending sadness. I don't want to give birth to a life and then kill it with my own hands. I don't want a child, born by me, to lead the life of a vagabond. I don't want to have to endure the pain suffered by an innocent creature who, if it were not for me, would not have been thrust by the fates into the agony of this world, which is threatened with hunger and nakedness and vagrancy. It is a world that smiles on millions of powerful people, while at the same time, and with the same calmness, sinking its poisonous claws into thousands of millions of faceless people. The child with the short message under his picture is dead. He was hungry, uprooted, sick. And with him my desire to give birth to a child has died forever.

"A dark-skinned child died, his feet burned by blazing sands, as he searched for a place of refuge like the one snatched from his parents. The death of a helpless child renders me sleepless, makes me abstain from you sometimes, shows me how insignificant the hours are that I previously regarded as glorious.

"The picture of the homeless, hungry orphan crying without tears has made me relinquish my dreams before I start breathing life into them with you. Nothing will happen. We—you and I—will bury our dreams in their cradle with our own hands before the war buries them, or the earthquakes, or before the tyranny of material-ism kills them. After all, what are we but two repeated images!

"We are what is perhaps an inferior copy of the millions of copies which time has annihilated. A man and a woman, you and I. Behind us are poor huts where the sick live, and in front of us tall buildings inhabited by hypocrisy. You and I are an insignificant link in the chain of time. It will not miss us. We used to dream of a future that never came, and build on a past that we couldn't remember. As for our present, the present is this picture of a lost child, with no hope of find-ing a resting place, with no aspiration to feel even a false touch of af-fection from hands like mine or yours, with no expectation even of a mouthful of dry bread made from withered seedlings of wheat.

"We are like the picture of the child I stumbled on, and the mes-sage under it. You plug your ears so as not to hear the misery in his voice. I shut my eyes, dreaming of a wonderful life, trying not to see the ugliness of life in our gloomy present. Yet our child is the child in the picture. Why couldn't this child be ours? We bore him in olden times, before we were born ourselves. We bore him when we lived as a clearer copy in this world, before we died, and our souls returned to this miserable life in these two bodies we have grown accustomed to.

"Don't you remember you told me one day: 'When I was a child I used to feel older than my years?' Why couldn't it be that your soul was older? Perhaps your soul was previously the soul of that father who died, unwillingly abandoning his poor son.

"Our child, then, has existed since olden times. We wished in vain to give birth to him again through our dreams. What pain, my darling, did we suffer to have him? What misery? Perhaps you will never love me again. My task had ended even before it began. My dream had died before it was born!

"It was as if my soul had grown old before all its youth was ex-hausted.

"I shall not give birth to a child, when there are poor children already everywhere, in the picture, and in reality, wandering in the desert, lost in woods, hungry in forests, ill in huts, orphaned and lonely on the shores of oceans and seas. I shall kill my dreams, my darling, and bury them before they take hold of us and lead us to in-crease the sadness of this world, to rob it of the mouthful of food be-longing to a poor child who is already alive, in order to put it into the stomach of a child we used to dream of!"

Half a Woman

Sufi Abdallah

❧❦❧

Her heart beat wildly and she felt a surge of joy that set her body quivering. Her eyes roamed over the scene around her. Could she notice anything? Could she sense the droves of people and the crush around her? No, not at all. As the car made its way through the streets, her longing was almost leaping out from her heart, pushing her forward, as if she felt the car was moving too slowly and she was struggling against a desire to jump out and run off . . . to where she would meet him!

She paid the driver and rushed to the elevator. She ran into the apartment—the door was ajar, as it always was when she came, because he knew her regular arrival time—and looked around for him. In an instant she was in his arms, and he was holding her tightly, and whispering ecstatically in her ear, "My darling . . . My darling . . ."

Rubbing her cheeks against his chest, she began to whisper with the same yearning, "Rushdi . . . Rushdi . . ."

They fell into the trance of the meeting. Each was totally absorbed in the other, and everything became still around them, except for the passionate sighs, like smoke rising from a fire raging inside her. When they had calmed down a little, he pulled her by the hand to the sofa and put his arms tenderly around her, touching her, as though afraid that she would dissolve from between his arms, or that, after all the time he had missed her and whispered secrets to her and embraced her apparition, he would discover that she was a mirage. He stretched out his fingers gently and lifted her chin. Their eyes met. It was a passionate, love-crazed look.

"What are we to do?" he cried out.

Yes, what were they to do? How could they possibly go on living like this? How long could she hold out against the burning flame of this love? She wondered whether she could manage to lead a double life. She wondered whether she had the strength to carry on with this comedy her whole life. Today she would make the break between her past and her future! Today she would say her last word to him! Today she would bring down a thick curtain on ten years of her life, ten years during which she had been the model of a faithful wife and devoted mother . . . until she had seen *him*.

How had he managed to rob her of her mind, her heart, and her being, and turn all the values that formed the fabric of her life into nothing? How had he managed to stifle all her motherly feeling, making love of life and the self and the desire for freedom and pleasure sweep away everything else? Was this what people called the irresistible power of love? Then there was no hope for her, no hope for life. She wondered what fate was lurking in wait for her, and what had come over her that she could change into the opposite of who she was.

Had she had an unhappy life?

She didn't know. They had married her off at eighteen to a successful businessman of thirty-five: handsome, daunting, and self-possessed. He respected her and treated her kindly. She hadn't felt any change in her life, except for those intimate encounters that she experienced with her husband at set times, without finding any fulfillment or meaning in them. She became the mistress of a great villa, having grown up in a large family. Her husband's behavior was steady; the times at which he slept, woke, sat, stood, and ate never varied. She never heard an improper word from him; his actions were marked by kindness, gentleness, friendliness, and calmness. She had lived with him for ten years, and in that time had borne him Samih and Najwa, a boy and a girl, the delights of her eye and the focal points of her life. She was the exemplary wife of the successful businessman, slim, calmly beautiful, and self-assured. Her movements, just like her gestures, were careful and deliberate. She lent grace and beauty to the parties given by her husband; she was an excellent housekeeper, a model mother, and an obedient wife, devoted to her good husband.

Her life flowed along in a single, unchanging mode, although in recent years the volume of her husband's work had grown, and the number of business trips he undertook at home and abroad had increased. His business had expanded to such an extent that she rarely saw him. The children grew bigger and went to school. She had less say in their supervision, because daily care of them was entrusted to a German nanny born in Cairo. The nanny obstinately refused to let anyone come between her and her children—as she called them—even if that person was their own mother, and even if seeing them gave their mother more joy and happiness than anything else on earth.

And suddenly Rushdi had burst into her life! She had met him at a party where her husband was the center of attention. It wasn't the first time she had seen him. In fact, she had often seen him: he was a well-known figure in literary and musical circles. But she couldn't remember his ever having caught her attention, or her ever having thought about him separately from the other people she had met. Even when she had greeted him, she had merely nodded from a distance. She couldn't remember ever having shaken his hand. So what on earth made it impossible, on that particular day, for her to take her eyes off him? What new feature in him had attracted her? And why had his eyes constantly searched her out, not letting her escape, as if he were trying to hypnotize her, plunging with her into the abysm, making her realize how heavy her body felt, how worn her nerves were, and how much she wanted to relax!

Things moved quickly after that day. They moved in a way that made her forget herself and her life and her husband and her children, until she could no longer see anyone but him. He had opened her eyes to the secret of life—a secret closed to every woman, so that she should discover it with her husband, the man who held sway over her life.

Rushdi was the man who had made her aware of her femininity, and then she had lost her equilibrium and good sense; she had surrendered control of her life to him.

What would happen to her husband if he lost her? He would be sad for a while, then he would be whipped up into the whirlwind of work and forget her, like a phantom that had passed through his life and vanished. He wasn't even aware of her existence; she was like a piece of furniture that he was used to seeing in its usual place. If he found the place empty, he would feel a lump in his throat, but it wouldn't be long before he consigned her to oblivion . . . And what about her children? How could her heart ever agree to leave them? With whom would she leave them? In fact, they had grown and didn't need her anymore, and there was someone there to look after them and to provide them with the necessities of life.

She wondered whether she was deceiving herself. Was it possible for her children to replace her with that nanny? Had her affection so dried up that she thought the necessities of life were all that those two little darlings wanted in the way of care?

Perhaps they would be sad when she left, but they would surely forget her: the hearts of children are easily impressed and quick to forget. It would be better to leave a good memory of their life together in their minds, before the pangs of love made her lose her equanimity and vent her frustration on them—if she let Rushdi slip from her grasp.

In any event, she couldn't continue to live like this, now that she had tasted the sweetness of love. And even if she wanted to, Rushdi wouldn't agree to it. He was mad about her. He presented her with a choice: either they ran away together and got married, once she had demanded a divorce from her husband, or else he would leave the country and wander about. Jealousy gnawed at his heart and tortured his soul when he pictured her with someone else. He wouldn't be happy until she had become his, heart and soul.

What should she do? She was caught between two fires: her children and her love! But could she face life after him, if she let him go?

No, no, she couldn't face it. Nor could she manage to lead a double life. And if she didn't enjoy herself now, how miserable life would be then! She would be no more than the remains of a woman; every mouthful she ate, every garment she wore would be pathetic!

Yes, she would be the remains of a woman. Any woman who lost her heart, nerves, and feelings was nothing but remains! A body without a soul, a creature crawling but lifeless! That frightened her. The years she had already lost were enough for her to want to start anew, before she wasted the blossom of her youth and the fragrance of her life.

The children were asleep, and her husband was away on one of his trips. She told the nanny she would be away for three days at her aunt's in Tanta, and then she left, carrying a suitcase with some of her clothes in it. She urged the nanny to take good care of the two children until she returned.

She left in a hurry, as if someone were chasing her. She flung herself into the first cab she found and told the driver to hurry to the station in time for the eight o'clock evening train.

Rushdi had gone to Alexandria two days earlier to make preparations for a long stay. Although the hard thinking of those two days had exhausted her, she had become all the more convinced that she had no life without him and that it was futile to think of turning back. That time had confirmed to her beyond doubt that it was impossible to break the relationship, whatever the consequences.

The short hours of the journey seemed like an age. Her thoughts focused on a single unchanging point: the moment of meeting—although she couldn't avoid feeling pangs of guilt now and then, as she imagined her children facing the new day without jumping onto her bed and delighting her with kisses and hugs and laughter. Would they be sad? Would they suffer? How long would it be before they stopped missing her and forgot her?

The train stopped. He was waiting for her, as usual, burning with longing and lovesickness and passion. As soon as they were ensconced in his car and she was wrapped in his arms, she forgot the children, and the house, and the whole world.

They spent the night locked in each other's arms, as if time had stood still, as if the world would end within the hour.

As she dozed off, she was startled by a picture flashing across her mind. It was her daughter, Najwa, jumping onto her bed to give her the morning hug. But she couldn't respond; she was as stiff as a corpse. She could see her and hear her, but she couldn't speak to her. The girl let out a resounding scream, "Mama! Mama!" then broke into tears.

She opened her eyes, alarmed. She sat up in bed and looked around, baffled. Where was she? Where did she belong?

A thin thread of morning light penetrated the wooden shutter and slid into the middle of the room, which was drowned in darkness. She turned around, and there he was, snoring happily and contentedly, his lips parted in a faint smile.

The events of the previous day crowded into her mind. Without thinking about it, she got out of bed, took off her nightgown, and hurriedly put on her clothes. Then she collected her things, threw them haphazardly into the suitcase, and wrote a hasty note on a scrap of paper:

"Happiness was not made for people like me . . . Forgive me . . . My children are calling me . . . You wouldn't be happy living with half a woman . . . I know you . . ."

She looked at him one last time, with an expression that was both sad and determined. Then she went out and slowly closed the door, leaving behind dreams that were unattainable, given the inescapable reality that summoned her.

Heir Apparent

Ramziya Abbas al-Iryani

Khadija touched her belly anxiously while muttering supplications that this time she would give birth to a boy and make her husband, Masoud, happy.

His words coursed through her body and wounded her.

"How barren your soil is, Khadija! Six girls one after another. If you had given me one son to watch over his sisters in my old age and after my death, then life would have been easier."

She tried to placate him.

"There's no distinction between girls and boys anymore. They all go to school and get jobs."

"Believe me, mother of my daughters, girls cause a lot of worry and trouble."

Then he added with affected calmness and indifference, "You remind me, Khadija, of our land. The only thing it generously bestows on us is qat."[1]

"You baffle me. Is it my fault that I'm just the soil? What you sow, you reap. Take care to sow crops other than qat and you'll see what the land produces for you. But all you care about is hurting me and your daughters."

Khadija moaned from the pain as she tried to forget her sorrows by recalling beautiful memories and by occupying herself with tidying the house. But the pain refused to go away.

She said to herself, "What a pity, Khadija, if you have another girl in your belly. Masoud will remain angry with you for one or two whole weeks because of his bad luck.

"I pledge a dozen candles and half a pound of incense for the saints and holy men, a celebration for the Prophet to be held at home in the first week after giving birth, and a thousand riyals for

186

the recitation of the Koran in the big mosque. The important thing is that Muhammad will arrive."

She had chosen this blessed name for her son. Masoud would surely approve of it, for he only cared about the child being a boy. The name did not matter to him at all.

That sharp pain had persisted in her back since the previous night. Her belly was burning like an oven full of flames. She had been pregnant six times before and had never experienced such pain.

The midwife who assisted the neighborhood women in childbirth always shouted joyfully, "There is no god but God!" when she saw her, declaring that this time her pregnancy was different. Her complexion was pure, her belly round, her voice clear, her eyes bright, and her walk light. And soon the boy would arrive.

How happy it would make her to hear the midwife announce Muhammad's birth! The pains of childbirth would vanish and she would give a celebration deserving of Muhammad. On the day of the boy's circumcision, Masoud would slaughter a big lamb, and they would invite all the family and neighbors. Blessed be her sisters, for they would prepare a feast to honor the boy and present his father favorably.

She could no longer suppress her screams. The labor pains got closer and closer together, and her body convulsed from the excruciating contractions, which felt like they were splitting her body in two.

She screamed in pain. Masoud woke up startled. The awaited time had come, and fate was approaching.

He rushed out of the house to seek help, and returned at once with the midwife. She proceeded to assist Khadija, who had collapsed.

"I've been pregnant six times, Umm Ali, and never before have I experienced this pain."

The more she screamed, the more Masoud feared for her life. He insisted on taking her to the hospital. Perhaps there she would get something to ease the pain.

He felt his limbs stiffening when the doctor informed him that his wife's condition was critical, and that only God, the Benevolent, could save her.

He waited a long time, his heart pounding.

The nurse came out with a gloomy face.

"Congratulations. It's a boy, and . . ."

He jumped to his feet with childish joy, and headed for the operating room. The sound of his son's crying rang out, rising higher and higher.

The nurse grabbed him. "Where are you going?"

"To see my son and his mother. Have you told her? Let me share with her our joy over Muhammad's birth."

"His mother . . . his mother asked about the sex of the child before she breathed her last."

At that moment, he wished he had been told that the baby was dead and the mother alive.

"She died? It can't be! How did she die? How could she leave six little girls, and a newborn child who hasn't yet opened his eyes to the world . . . and me? Who will look after them?"

He broke down in tears as he burst into the delivery room, utterly incredulous. The doctor led him to her.

Choking his tears back, he held her cold hand with longing.

"Come back to us, Khadija. I don't want a boy. I want you. Your daughters need you. They have no one to look after them but you. Your baby may not survive without your tender breast and merciful hand.

"How will I return to your six children without you? They don't understand the meaning of death and life. All they want is your presence. Will you abandon them? Will you abandon your own flesh and blood?"

The baby's crying grew louder and louder, and Masoud's sobbing became more anguished. They all tried to release his hands, which were grasping at the body lying prostrate on the table. Meanwhile the nurse approached with the newborn child to put him in his father's trembling arms.

The Newcomer

Daisy al-Amir

❧✦❧

What were her mother's eyes concealing? Was it what she had always feared? Their eyes had not met the entire day. Which one was ashamed of the other?

According to her grandmother, her mother was forty years old. She was capable of bearing another ten children.

When the ninth child was born, and the joyful shrieks of the female neighbors announced to the father that he had another son, she had decided not to congratulate her mother and had avoided seeing the new baby. Seven days later, she had warned her mother, yes, *warned* her, that she should stop bearing children, or else she would no longer shoulder the responsibility for the costs. She would travel away, emigrate, commit suicide. But her mother could not muster enough courage to tell the father, and in the next five years, three more children had arrived.

How proud she had felt while she was attending school, and how disappointed when she had to leave school and go to work. The family had grown and needed more income. She was the eldest daughter, and her father's salary was not sufficient to provide for everyone.

Her eldest brother was preoccupied with the political struggle. He ardently wished to complete his studies and find a job, but political activity was the fastest way, he claimed, to earn money. "Tomorrow the regime will change and justice will prevail. Then the exploiters will learn a radical lesson on how to treat others." But tomorrow never came. Instead, a policeman came to arrest the brother on the charge of participating in an organization that sought to overthrow the regime. When the brother, dumbfounded by this accusation, swore that he had done nothing but say these

189

things to his mother to reassure her about the future, the mother confirmed that she had repeated the words only to her female neighbors. Then she remembered that the son of one of these neighbors worked for the police. And so, through a casual remark picked up by a female neighbor, the brother was taken into custody pending investigation. He was tortured in an attempt to obtain a confession from him concerning his comrades in the secret organization.

Several months later, he was released from prison with a broken leg, one eye missing, and the other eye damaged. As a result, the number of siblings whom the sister had to support had increased.

The next two brothers were more careful than their eldest brother and never talked about their activities. They actually began a secret operation that required them to be away from home most of the time. They returned only when they had nothing to eat.

Despite the hardships, the family, for whose sake the father and the eldest daughter toiled, continued to grow—thanks to the father—and his daughter had to bear the brunt of the burden.

Today, the mother kept her eyes averted. Was it because she was ashamed that she was expecting again? Did she have to carry out her threat to stop her mother? But did she have the courage to threaten her father too? If she left the house, wouldn't her father go after her and kill her, spilling her blood in front of spectators, proud that he washed off his daughter's disgrace? Or would her two brothers the fighters intercede on her behalf? And if her eldest brother could walk, wouldn't he follow her and drag her by the hair back home?

Exploited animals get daily fodder from their masters whereas she . . . she was exploited and still had to provide the daily fodder for herself and for the others! They would need even more fodder, if what she read in her mother's eyes meant another baby.

Her father always rebuked her younger sisters when he saw them standing in front of the mirror. He toiled and slaved away while they . . . they did nothing but stand idle in front of the mirror. The girls often awoke with his death threats ringing in their ears, and slept dreaming about the knight who would rescue them, whereas she . . . when she awoke, she rushed to work, and when she went to bed, she eavesdropped on her parents, afraid that there would be a newcomer, and that the numbers of male fighters and female workers would increase.

One of her brothers, whose exact place in the succession of siblings she no longer remembered, had declared war on them. He let his hair and beard grow and started a new life. He would come home late and devour whatever food the mother had hidden for him. Then her father's shouts would ring out, rebuking, denouncing, and threatening the mother, who would make an effort to appease him. And she feared that the price of appeasement would be a newcomer.

What were her mother's eyes concealing?

Should she go to her and ask for an explanation? Should she demand that her mother tell her honestly and courageously?

If the answer confirmed her fears, how would she react?

One of her brothers had managed to escape the dire home circumstances and traveled to a faraway place. He wrote that he would return shortly. He would return with a small fortune that would release them from their worries. They expected that he would return within a few months. The months stretched into years, and his letters with the promises became increasingly irregular. In hours of despair, she believed her brother's letters. She forced herself to believe them. But when her father boasted about his absent son, she finally acknowledged the enormity of the illusion that they all had created, lived in, and anticipated.

Sometimes she wished that she could read what was *not* written in those letters, so that she could disabuse her mother and father of their false hope.

What were her mother's eyes concealing? If there was another baby on the way, however innocent it was, she might kill it. Suddenly she realized that she hated everyone around her. She wanted to love them. Why was she forced to hate them?

She went to her mother, held her by the arm, and turned her face toward her. The mother's eyes were lowered. She stared at her and screamed, "Look at me. Look me in the eye. Tell me the truth. What are you concealing? I'm the first person who deserves to know the truth, because I'm the one who has to bear the consequences. Come on, admit it! You've been a coward long enough!"

The mother raised her eyes submissively, and looked her daughter in the face.

"It wasn't me who accepted the offer of marriage for your sister. It was your father," she said fearfully.

Part Six

Self-Fulfillment

International Women's Day

Salwa Bakr

✧◊✿◊✧

When the headmistress entered the classroom, Uthman, the teacher, shouted enthusiastically, "Stand up!"

The girls and boys rose to their feet amid a murmur of voices, while Uthman glanced around the classroom, ascertaining that his order had been promptly obeyed and silence observed. He constantly told his students, "Standing up means all of you shut up. Everyone keep quiet. It means that if I throw a pin on the floor, I will hear it drop. Is that understood?"

After the teacher had satisfied himself that the whole class was standing completely still, he said in a calm but haughty voice, "Sit down."

The students proceeded to sit down, as they had been a few moments earlier. Meanwhile the teacher greeted the headmistress and offered her his chair, which stood behind his desk facing the young students, so that she could sit and examine his daily lesson plan book. As soon as he saw her poring over his lesson plan book, he turned toward the blackboard and wrote in large, ungraceful script, unbefitting a teacher of Arabic: "Woman and Life."

The headmistress began to read in the teacher's lesson plan book an elaborate speech about the importance of women in society. He had prepared this speech in celebration of International Women's Day. She noticed that the teacher had not forgotten to mention the wives of the Prophet, God's prayer and peace be upon him, and famous Arab women of the past, among them the poet al-Khansa, and Hind, daughter of King Nu'man, and Zubayda, wife of the Caliph Harun al-Rashid.[1] She disregarded his omission, or perhaps ignorance, of Zarqa al-Yamama.[2] She had already realized from her twenty years' experience in primary school education that he would inevitably conclude his speech with the well-known verse of the poet Hafiz Ibrahim: "The mother is a school; if you prepare her, you prepare a nation with a strong foundation."[3] At that point, she smiled and raised her head from the lesson plan book to listen to what the teacher was saying to his students. As she gazed at him, she noticed the thick, coarse hair on his head, which was easily distinguishable at a distance, even if Uthman were to stand at the farthest corner of the schoolyard. She paid attention as he recited:

"A man came to the Messenger of Allah and said, 'O Messenger of Allah, who is most entitled to the best of my friendship?' The Prophet said, 'Your mother.' The man said, 'Then who?' The Prophet said, 'Your mother.' The man further said, 'Then who?' The Prophet said, 'Your mother.' The man said again, 'Then who?' The Prophet said, 'Then your father.'"[4]

One of the boys, Usama Abd al-Fattah, didn't give Uthman time to say anything more. He shouted from his place at the back of the classroom, "Excuse me, sir. Muhammad Mansur is holding his private parts. He badly needs to pee."

The teacher's ears reddened and the headmistress turned her eyes away from his face to bury them once again in the lesson plan book, pretending to be engrossed in reading. Meanwhile the children's bursts of laughter grew so loud that they frightened away two sparrows that had alighted on top of one another at the edge of the classroom window. Before long, the sounds of laughter were restrained and stifled, as the teacher's face darkened and his forehead knotted in anger and warning. Silence reigned when he bellowed, "Shut up, you jackass."

But Usama Abd al-Fattah was truthful, enthusiastic, courageous, and insistent on rescuing whatever could be rescued. He continued to speak in order to defend his assertion. "By Almighty God, sir. He needs to pee very badly. Look, he wet his pants a little."

As she could no longer feign ignorance, the respected headmistress smiled to soften the atmosphere. The teacher swallowed his anger and forced a smile, signaling to Muhammad Mansur to go to the bathroom.

"Hurry up, you awful brat. And don't you dare be late!" he yelled.

Then, wishing to change the subject, he leaned toward the headmistress and told her in a low voice that he was very strict with the students about using the bathroom during class time, because they were extremely devilish and made excuses about needing the

bathroom to play truant. He then explained to her that he had prepared all the lessons for the following days of the week, and that he
had devoted today's lesson to topics befitting the occasion of International Women's Day, in accordance with the instructions he had
received from the school administration. But the headmistress mo-
tioned to him to continue the lesson so as not to waste class time.

In fact, she was worried and preoccupied with her own problem.
She wished that one of the officials would visit the school on this special day so that she could tell him about her problem. While Uthman
was teaching his students that girls should be polite and well behaved
so that they would grow up to become distinguished women, the
headmistress was praying that a miracle would happen and the First
Lady would visit the school. Gentle, compassionate, and humble, the
First Lady would surely listen sympathetically to her problem, if she
inquired of her: "Is it acceptable to you, madam, that a woman of my
age and my position has to ride public transportation each day and
expose herself to extreme harassment in order to get to work? The
matter of my transfer to a school near my home is very simple and in
the hands of Mr. Abd al-Hamid Fakry, the undersecretary of state.
But he insists on my staying at al-Nur school for an unknown reason,
although he has been informed that I'm responsible for looking
after a household, a husband, and four children at different stages of
schooling. This is the reason that I appeal to you to solve this problem for me, as I'm extremely upset and perplexed by it."

After that she would present the First Lady with her request,
which she had handwritten in a beautiful script. The First Lady
would take it from her with the utmost kindness and gently ease her
mind. She would then give it immediately to the undersecretary of
state, who would surely accompany her on her inspection tour of
schools on a day like International Women's Day, and he would sign
the request for transfer promptly.

The respected headmistress was unable to continue her day-
dream to the point where she would shake hands with the First Lady
and express her deepest gratitude, because Uthman had a loud voice
no less coarse than the hair on his head. She was forced to relinquish
the request for transfer and the First Lady's handshake and the signature of the undersecretary of state, when the teacher's voice rose
higher as he said, "Women comprise half of society. God enjoined
upon men to treat them well. It was said in olden times . . ."

One of the girls, Fatima Mitwalli, didn't hear what was said in olden times, because she was busy writing to her classmate, Aisha Mar'i, on her school desk: "I'll act like Muhammad and wiggle about, and you'll say to the teacher, 'Fatima is holding her private parts. She badly needs to pee.' Then all the children will laugh and the teacher will say to me, 'Get up, girl, and go to the bathroom.'"

Aisha liked this idea, especially as she was a bit of a trouble-maker and enjoyed imitating the boys in all their actions. Perhaps it was because she was the only girl among three siblings. Or perhaps it was because she loved to outdo the boys, particularly in running and playing physical games. As she was slightly reckless and occasionally inclined to adventure, she stood up promptly and said, "Fatima, sir, is holding her private parts. She badly needs to pee. She wants to go to the bathroom but is too ashamed to ask."

Like a thunderbolt, the teacher rushed to the place where Aisha stood, to pounce with the thick palm of his hand on her temple, curses vying with saliva to flow out of his mouth. Denouncing her as an ugly, impolite, and ill-bred girl, he ordered her to leave her place and stand with her face toward the wall. Then he threatened her with a day blacker than Chinese ink, after he had uttered the conditional clause, "God willing."

The headmistress was slightly annoyed, because Uthman seemed extremely violent with Aisha. She had no idea at all that one of the reasons for this violence was perhaps that, while speaking of olden times, he kept thinking about the best way to punish his wife and discipline her, because of her bad behavior toward his family. Should he give her a good beating until he heard her bones shaking, or should he abandon her in bed and withhold her allowance until she repented and recognized that Allah is the Truth?[5] But when the image of his wife with her shapely legs, full white buttocks, and flirtatious laughter appeared in his mind, he felt that the latter solution would make him nervous and harm him in one way or another. He couldn't control his anger and slapped Aisha across the face. The headmistress thought of whispering to the teacher to remind him that hitting was legally forbidden by the Ministry of Education. She thought the slap was very hard. Perhaps it injured the little girl's ear. However, she decided to postpone this matter until after the end of the class, deeming it was better to soften the atmosphere and say something in her capacity as the distinguished educator, headmistress of the school. So she addressed the students, taking care that her voice would sound wise and calm:

"We all know that we must be polite, our expressions respectful. The words used at home are different from those used at school. It's inappropriate to use vulgar expressions at school or on the street. A girl must be polite, her voice low. It's shameful to touch any area of impurity in the human body. A girl is forbidden to touch an area of impurity or to let her hand come near it, regardless of the reason."

Then she turned to Fatima, pinched her ear lightly, and demanded that she apologize to the teacher. As she walked out of the classroom, heading for another one to make sure that the teacher complied with the instructions of the Ministry of Education on International Women's Day, she was thinking of the necessity of hurrying home from school to prepare lunch. Meanwhile Uthman was scratching himself between the thighs with satisfaction. As for the students, they began to breathe a sigh of relief because the school bell started to ring, announcing the end of the class.

The Filly Became a Mouse

Layla Ba'labakki

ﾟ❀ﾟ❀ﾟ

*M*y skin was still flabby. I ran my fingers over my neck. I felt the pulse of my green, protruding veins. I pulled my dress tight around my chest, closed my eyes, and raised my face toward the ceiling of the room.

I started to feel the weight of the cloth on my knee again. I lowered my head and buried my chin in the dress enveloping my shoulders. The dress clung to my back. Suddenly I smelled a certain scent and lost consciousness. I became . . . (a white filly proceeding slowly on the bank of the river. She cranes her neck in the open air, and her head touches the pure sky. She observes the river meandering through the trees, grass, distant mountains, houses, and valleys. She shakes her neck, and a white cloud lifts her up and lands with her on the water's surface. She listens to the frogs singing in the ponds near and far, and watches the colorful butterflies dancing. She says inwardly that if she hadn't been born a filly, she would have chosen to be a butterfly, reigning over the prairies and the sun's rays and the face of the moon.

One day the filly was drinking from a spring. She was returning from a journey to regions where it had snowed. She had seen a new world, bright and shiny, in which the trees transformed into candles set on mountaintops. The houses looked like children clad in white fur coats with red hats.

These images were still fresh in the filly's memory as she drank. She thought the water was delicious when she heard cautious footsteps approaching. Out of the corner of her eye, she saw a man. She didn't know what prevented her from jumping with fright or kicking him. She smelled the man. The smell penetrated her nostrils and seeped into the bottom of her heart. The filly let the man come

closer and closer to her, lay his hand on her back, stroke her, wrap
his arm around her long and erect neck, and take her with him to
the city.)

When I opened my eyes, my face was turned toward the ceiling, on which the image of the filly had vanished. I rubbed my temples with both hands, and my ears began to throb. The intense
whiteness of the ceiling was dazzling, so I searched its corners,
where darkness had gathered. My gaze then fell upon the edges of
the six windows along the three walls. I paused for breath. The chill
of fear crept slowly into my joints. For the first time I noticed that
the windows were narrow, very tall, and covered with iron grilles.
They were not fitted with glass. Attached to them on the outside
were two wooden shutters that reached the ground. They were fastened with rusty screws and painted a faded, flaking green. Dust
penetrated the edges of the windows and collected inside the room.
On the bare, light-colored tiles stood a big round table which, from
the vantage point of the chair on which I was curled up, appeared to
have no legs. The chaise longue seemed as if it were creeping on the
floor. At that spot, I discovered the man who was with me in the
room. It was the same man who was with the filly. From the ceiling,
the room looked like an underground cellar, dark and cold.

When I saw the man, the room turned into a bottomless pit
inhabited by rats. I was a mouse, and the man was the owner of the
house. I lost consciousness once again. I became . . . (a little mouse,
slightly bigger than a cricket, lean and sticky. Her body is flabby and
hairless, her nose red, her glazed eyes pale yellow. The mouse lives
in the man's old chair, which he had inherited from his father, as his
father had from his grandfather. She leaves her nest when the man
turns off the lamp. She fearfully steals away to the table and eats the
remains of the man's supper. She drinks the dregs of his coffee and
sleeps under his arm. The man squashes her and almost chokes her
to death whenever he moves in his sleep.

During the day, the man sets a trap. Each day he brings a wooden
box containing a hook and a pin, into which he inserts a piece of bread
dipped in butter. He places the trap behind the door, then under the
table, then on the chair, then inside the cupboard, eventually moving
it throughout the house. The mouse thinks to herself: If only the man
knew that to get rid of me he must loosen his grip!)

I laughed. I imagined I was a mouse with a transparent body
jumping in the air, on the furniture, and on the nose of the man,

who chased after her in order to kill her. I laughed and the man—my husband—raised his nose from the magazine and looked at me frowning, amazed, even derisive. He muttered, "Christine Keeler—what a woman!"[6] and buried his nose again in the pages of his magazine.

I stopped laughing and looked at him. He was reclining on the chair with his feet resting on the edge of the table between the ashtray, the half-full bottle of water, the empty glasses, and the silent transistor radio. He was dressed in a green-and-white striped terry bathrobe, opened from chest to waist. The skin of his chest looked darker than that of his stomach, then grew darker the farther it was from his stomach. His head seemed to stand apart from the rest of his body, as if it belonged to someone else whom he had met at a party with liquor and bleach-bottle blondes. At dawn, as the two men prepared to leave, they took their heads from the clothes rack in the hallway. One of them mistakenly took the wrong head, and neither man knew the other's name and address.

I laughed again at this thought. The man—my husband—moved his borrowed head and his features became visible for a fleeting moment. The face made no sound. I was no longer smiling when it disappeared again behind the magazine. I remembered that I had encountered this face before. When? Where? What had changed in it?

It was difficult to travel back in time, to the past. I closed my eyes, as though I were passing through a long, dark tunnel, and arrived at a moment seven years earlier.

Summer was approaching, just as now. I met him at a girl-friend's house. When I saw him, I whispered in her ear, "This is the man of my dreams!" He walked up to me and asked me where I came from. I told him I was from here. He asked me why we had never met before. I told him I had been in Europe, traveling between capital cities, learning ballet. I had come to spend the summer with my mother, and I intended to return. His voice faltered when he inquired why I had chosen this type of art, which is foreign to our country—the sun, the soil, and the dark, black heads.

I told him a long story about a five-year-old girl whose mother had held her by the hand one afternoon and taken her for a walk. The sun was pale, the alleys cold, and the windows of the houses shut. They stopped in front of an old brick house, and her mother rang the bell. The door opened and an old man whose face was wrinkled and extremely white peeked out. He stretched out his slender,

long-fingered hand and shook her mother's hand. Then he ruffled
the girl's hair and moved along, as she walked with her mother
ahead of him. He seated her on a chair and sat down as well, and
then she received her first piano lesson. Meanwhile her mother sat
in a corner with her eyes closed, weeping floods of tears that
streamed down her chest.

I told him that the piano lessons had delighted me in the beginning. It was like an amusing game in which I took pride, for I
was the only one to possess this skill among my little friends. I told
him that my mother was a foreigner who had lived with my father
for thirty years, dreaming of her distant country and longing for it.
When my father died, her dreams died with him, so she transferred
them to me. Once again, she took me by the hand and led me to a
small house belonging to a woman who spoke her language. This
was when I received my first dancing lesson.

I told him how my mother had sold her rings and bracelets to
send me to Europe, and how she had sold her furniture so I could
stay there, and how she had mortgaged the plot of land in my
father's village so that she could visit me in Paris and take me to
Rome. Her hair had turned gray as she kept smiling, while my hair
had grown long and dark. I had excelled at dancing, and now we
were both looking forward to my participation in a performance at
the Paris Opera the following autumn.

He said nothing. He took me by the hand, walked me down
the stairs of my girlfriend's house, and roamed the deserted streets
of Beirut with me. He brought me to a house with a garden. He
didn't ring the bell, and the door remained locked. He seated me by
a tree trunk without uttering a word.

I told him how I felt *there* the way my mother felt *here*, longing
for this land, for the blazing sun that scorched the skin and made it
sweat, for the sad songs, for the stars that sparkled in pitch-black
nights, for the belly dance, for the silver bracelets, and for the barefoot people. I told him that I couldn't live without dancing, that if I
didn't dance, I would suffocate. I was a stranger here and a stranger
there.

He still did not utter a word. He put his arms around my waist
and drew me close to him. His breath brushed against my ear, and
I imagined that a spring had burst from the tree trunk and gushed
over my face. I buried my head in his chest, and saw stars dangling
on the branches. He clung tightly to me, wrapped his arms around

me, and asked whether I felt happy. I replied that I felt as if I were walking naked in the wilderness while raindrops were falling on my body and everywhere pieces of wood were igniting calmly and casting a red and blue glow. He said that I was a stalk of sugar cane whose time had come to be harvested. The stalk was lost, looking for a fertile soil in a hot country in which to be planted. He said that if I fed him this sweetness, he would cut his arteries and give me his blood as a gift. And if I married him, he would let me dance, dance, dance. I could go on dancing between heaven and earth until the end of time.

I married him, and my mother died of grief.

I became pregnant with my daughter, and the thought that I had caused my mother's death vanished from my mind. She was no longer desperate or sad or disappointed in me. She was coming back to me in another body, and I was carrying her in my blood just as she had carried me. I would suffer the pains of childbirth so that she would forgive me my sins. And, indeed, my daughter bore a striking resemblance to my mother.

In order to return to dancing—he had promised that I could after the birth of my daughter—I had to lose some weight. I would never forget that morning. I was stretched out on my bed, being massaged by a masseuse, when my husband opened the door. He pushed the masseuse away and threw her out of the house. He screamed that he would not permit any woman in his house to spread her legs in front of men, that I should learn how to be a mother before I opened a school for hopping up and down, and that I should learn how to be a housewife before I attended to entertaining other people.

Now. Now. In this room on the mountain, he was in front of me, slowly turning over the pages of his magazine. I pulled my silk dress tight around my chest and felt its soft touch on my warm body. Now I was unable to think about that morning. I had said nothing then. I had lain motionless on the bed for many hours, until the sun had set and darkness descended. I had not screamed, wept, or moved. Something within me had been smothered and slain, although it was a bloodless death. I had withdrawn within myself, and devoted all my time to my daughter. I breast-fed her, washed her diapers with my own hands, embroidered her dresses, and taught her how to walk and speak.

And I had crawled. For five years, I had crawled with my face down.

And now, just now, I met this man—my husband—again. A few minutes earlier I had been lying on the same chair where he was now seated, with him on top of me. I had watched his movements on my body. Five years had passed with his entering and leaving my house, eating and sleeping with me, while I remained in a state of unconsciousness—long, heavy, and dry. Now I would wake up. Wake up.

I opened my eyes wide and discovered a few gray hairs on his temples. On the table, between his feet, I saw a glass of water and in it a red rose like the ones sold at a nightclub entrance. I saw a pack of menthol cigarettes. I sniffed the air and smelled in the room the scent of a woman who comes to him secretly, in the dark. I gave a mocking, joyful laugh. My husband frowned and asked me angrily, "What's the meaning of this hysterical laugh? Are you crazy?" I told him to put the magazine down and look at me. He became confused and obeyed me. The magazine fell from his hands, and he watched me in bewilderment as I tore the dress from my body and remained curled up, naked, on the chair. I repeatedly said to his face, "Don't take your eyes off me. I'm starting to move again now. I was a filly once, and you transformed me into a mouse. I'm no longer bewitched. The magician has lost his magic wand. Look, I can move my hands and feet. I can get off the chair. I can walk and stretch. I can again become a filly."

I began to dance before him, as if in a trance. I watched my own movements and kept asking myself, "From where did I summon this courage? How did I regain my courage?" The sweat oozed from every pore of my skin. My daughter turned around me, laughing happily. He said I was deranged. Deranged. I slowly came to a stop. I picked up my daughter, went into my room, and stood with her in front of the mirror. For five years, I had not looked at myself. I put on my clothes, while my husband continued to read his magazine, took my daughter in my arms, and went far, far away.

Restoration

Umayma al-Khamis

❦❧❦

When she took a quick peek at herself in the mirror, she saw a scene of inner collapse. She hastily turned away from the mirror and went to where the women had gathered. She alluded to the price of her dress, pushing up a sleeve to show off a diamond-studded gold watch. She spoke of a recent promotion at work, and how her superiors admired her management style. She then shifted the conversation to three suitors who had come one after another to her parents' home to ask for her hand during the previous month. She also didn't forget to mention the names of the hotels she had visited during the previous summer. She danced spontaneously and flirtatiously. She walked to the dinner table slowly and coquettishly. After dinner, she applied her lipstick, gazing into a mirror with a gilded frame. In the mirror, she saw the scene of inner collapse again . . .

Waiting for Hayla

Umayma al-Khamis

❧❀❧

"Hayla is coming," the maid announced as she stood at the living-room door. Her cheeks were flushed and her nostrils flared.

At that moment, I felt a surge of enthusiasm, and the gathering became restive.

"How do you know? Did she call?" the hostess asked.

"Yes. She will ride in the first car available to her."

The gathering became animated, and the receiving line of women moved with anticipation. Some of the vitality permeated my body and removed the lethargy that had crept into it and that two cups of coffee had failed to expel from my blood. I became excited, and the melancholy of the gathering vanished into the air, which was circulated by a tireless electric fan.

In the interval preceding Hayla's arrival, we touched lightly on her personal life. I learned that her eldest son had joined the navy, that her daughter had come out of the postpartum period, and that her husband was rumored to have taken another wife, especially after his recurrent trips to India.

The bell rang forcefully. The groups of little children scattered among us dashed to the door. The women craned their necks, and a hush fell on the gathering. The hostess rushed toward the women's entrance to receive Hayla.

The gathering was filled with the hubbub of voices as Hayla circulated among the guests, exchanging greetings. Meanwhile a woman appeared from another room to pick up her cloak.

I began to scrutinize Hayla's face, trying to link her with snippets of gossip I had picked up about her, snippets that were exaggerated by my expectations. But she was busy greeting those in the receiving line. I only noticed her voice, which resembled the cooing of an old pigeon.

When my turn came to greet her, I was overly eager and cordial, as if I wanted to tell her that I had known her for years. But her reserve made me suppress my hearty laugh, so that her feelings would not be offended. I withdrew within myself, observing the scene in silence. Meanwhile Hayla proceeded to mingle with the other women. The phone rang. The children quarreled about who would pick up the receiver. The maid appeared and snatched it from them.

"Latifa is coming," she announced with less enthusiasm than before and less flush in her cheeks.

A state of joy reigned again over the gathering. Even Hayla herself shared this joy with us.

Because Latifa came quickly, I was unable to pick up tidbits about her before her arrival. However, her demeanor revealed clearly that she was a teacher: her tone of voice was loud, her manner of shaking hands assertive, and her skirt practical and worn. She was also in the habit of repeating an anecdote twice, first to narrate it, and the second time to clarify it.

The gathering started to quiet down, and the fan resumed circulating the turbid air.

"Where's al-Jawhara?" the hostess asked in a dignified, calm voice. Then she whispered to her unmarried daughter, whom we could refer to as the "young lady": "We cannot serve dinner before al-Jawhara arrives, but she's definitely coming, for her husband closes his shop at ten o'clock in the evening."

"By the time he gets home and then brings her here, she'll surely be late," the young lady replied.

"Why don't you send a driver to fetch her?" asked one of the inquisitive—and also hungry—women.

The hostess looked at her with a mixture of contempt and rebuke. "My married daughter does not ride in a car unless she is accompanied by a close male relative,"[7] she said emphatically.

At ten minutes to eleven, al-Jawhara arrived with her children and a bag full of feeding bottles for her infant.

As soon as she came, the daughter-in-law signaled discreetly to the hostess, informing her of al-Jawhara's arrival. Then the hostess announced, "Dinner is served."

We rose in relief. We were no longer waiting for anyone—or perhaps we had not been waiting for anyone after all.

We had been merely amusing ourselves by tossing names into the jaws of Time—lest it assail and devour us.

The Closely Guarded Secret

Sahar al-Muji

❦

She hid it carefully after she had wrapped it in an old shabby rag as a disguise. No one would think that anything of value was folded in this rag. Perhaps it had no value. But that was merely what they said, and she didn't believe them. She would look at it after midnight, when everyone had fallen asleep. She would sit with it under a pale light, so that nobody would notice them whispering to each other. It would be a disaster if they found out what she was doing. However, she was smarter than all of them, and so no one discovered the matter.

When she got married, she took it with her in the same old rag. Naturally, things became more difficult. The man seemed to know that she was hiding something. He would give her doubtful and suspicious looks, follow her around, watch her every move, demand an accounting of her simplest actions. Why was she doing things this way, instead of another?

But she hid it carefully and guarded it ever more closely. It was the only thing in the whole world that was hers alone. She was fond of it and lived with the guilt.

She hid it because she feared that the others might harm it. She was smarter than all of them. She led them to believe that she lived as they wanted, while she lived as she wanted.

The years passed, depriving her of her black hair, her upright posture, and several relatives and friends. Nevertheless, she was still attached to it, hiding it, and preserving it from harm. The years went by, and no one discovered her secret.

209

I Will Never Forfeit My Right

Mona Ragab

She arranged her papers in a big file that contained her legal
case, and put her identity card in her handbag. As usual,
she put the picture of her little boy in the center of the
handbag.

At nine o'clock sharp, she stood waiting by the door of the
courtroom where the judge would preside, armed with her papers
and an unshaken belief in the justice of her case. When the minutes
passed agonizingly slowly, she was overcome by fatigue, so she leaned
against the staircase of the big courthouse. At her side she placed the
cane that she had been using for several months, the exact number of
which she could not remember.

Since morning, the courthouse hall had been filled with a sad
procession of women who had dropped exhausted in the middle of the
battle. There were women of all ages, sizes, and appearances. Some
were dressed in dusty black robes, others in ornate modern dresses,
and still others in rags that reflected humiliation and deprivation.

No, her spirits would not flag for lack of a chair to sit on. She
would not be intimidated and would courageously persist in her
demand.

She had learned that in the following week her former husband
intended to travel with her little son to another Arab country. He
wanted to make her suffer because she had dared to speak. He wanted
to deal her a fatal blow because she had voiced her desire to express
her humanity.

No . . . but she was here, and she would not budge until the
judge listened to her case.

But . . . all those women were waiting, and leaving, and
returning . . .

All of this was unimportant, for she was certain of her right. What judge would rule that a child should suffer by becoming a stranger in a distant land? Or that a child should fall victim to a tyrannical father who imagined that in this way he was avenging his manliness on a mother who insisted upon her right to work?

Nevertheless, the air was infused with sadness, the dust of anxious waiting floated in the corridors, and the tearful eyes bespoke degradation, having been suspended so long on the swing of uncertainty.

When the fat, exhausted bailiff called out her number, she stepped forward with alacrity fueled by hope. She opened the door and entered, to stand opposite the judge, who was surrounded by some of his assistants.

He signaled to her to present herself: her name, her occupation, and her case. She was in floods of tears as she spoke.

"Your Honor, I am an Egyptian woman. I have a small business—and a legal case. I had to make a choice: either to live with him and lose my humanity, or to leave him and live in dignity."

The grave man stared at her in amazement. His eyeglasses had slipped off his nose from the sharpness of her words. He glanced at the papers, and then gazed at her again, as though he had not seen her tears. In the file placed before him, he found documents proving that the child was her son, that he was five years and two months old, that she was divorced, and that her son had been staying with his father for the past nine months.

"Woman, stop crying and tell me your story," said the judge, who was overburdened with thousands of pending cases.

She spoke: "I had to decide whether to live as a body without a head, or as a complete human being; either to be his wife and live with him according to his conditions, or to be a divorcée and live alone, in isolation. I've chosen to use my mind rather than lose it. So here I am today, a divorced woman."

"Be quick. What do you want?"

"He took my child away from me."

"Be brief. What exactly do you want?"

"I'm devoted to my work and to my child."

"Why did he take your child away from you?" asked the judge.

"Because I said 'no' to him after I realized that the Middle Eastern man wants his wife to sigh rather than think," she replied.

"Hurry up! I have no time," said the judge.

"I want to speak. Who else but you can listen to my case?"

"Call the next case," the judge said to the bailiff.

But she continued: "He's traveling away with my child in a week. Tell me, Your Honor, who appointed him a judge? He's a self-appointed judge and executioner! He wants to place my child's head in a guillotine next week. That's why I ask you to expedite your ruling in my son's custody case."

"Calm down," said the bailiff. "The judge, as you can see, has a pile of files of other plaintiffs before him."

"I won't be another sacrificial lamb that you offer to history. I won't hide my dignity in the bottom of the trunk, and I won't vanish like smoke in the wind. I will continue to cry out for prompt justice, and I won't rest until justice is done," she declared.

"Call the next case," the judge said to the bailiff, ignoring her.

"But he's going away with my son in a week's time," she protested. "My son will be torn from my bosom, and his father, proud of his sham victory, will tell him tales about his imaginary heroism. My little boy will live a miserable life in a distant land. Who will listen to him when he cries out, 'I want my mother' "?

"I will make my ruling tomorrow," the judge said, without further comment.

She left, sobbing. She was so upset that she unknowingly bumped into the women who were sprawled on the floor of the courthouse hall since early morning. Finally, one of them screamed at her, "Look where you're going! Haven't we suffered enough?"

The judge did not deliver his verdict on the following day. She learned from the court clerk that the judge was overburdened with thousands of cases each day. He faced mountains of files that he had to read during the week before he could rule on the cases.

"The matter is not in my hands. Come again tomorrow," the bailiff said sympathetically.

When evening came, she sat alone, weeping like a frightened rabbit. She jumped to her feet when she heard interrupted knocks on her front door.

She opened the door and threw her arms around the little boy who had walked such a long way to see her. Her cane fell to the floor. She had been using it to support herself after she had suffered a depression that had affected the muscles in her back and rendered her incapable of moving for four months.

Overcome by cares and sorrows, she collapsed on the floor and lost consciousness. The neighbors took her to the nearest hospital, where she lay surrounded by glass tubes, syringes, and rows of medicine bottles with costs unknown.

When the doctor came to transfer her to the intensive care unit, the loud weeping of a little boy could be heard. His trembling hand was clutching a lock of her hair as he anxiously awaited a single look of recognition from her.

Homecoming

Fadila al-Faruq

⚜

*A*t last, I was returning from my long journey, liberated from my exile. More accurately, soon I would be liberated from it, and be certain that I had left the foreign country which I had previously chosen out of love, conviction, and "blindness" as my future. I wondered whether I would be overcome by a fit of maddening joy that would make me bend down and kiss the ground at the airport, or was such eccentric behavior reserved for leaders and celebrities? Would I dash toward the taxi stand and hire the most expensive driver who would take me in the shortest time to my small neighborhood? There, I would rid myself of all the ugly images that used to surround me. I would surely not see an Arab woman sitting on the sidewalk and exposing her body to whomever would pay her more because she could not afford the bus fare home, despite all the purchases that she had stashed somewhere. I would then breathe my full share of clean air, unlike the air that I had breathed furtively and shamefully from mouths that deeply offended my dignity.

During my daily routine at work, I often encountered unpleasant tourists—fellow Arabs—who disgraced the streets with their behavior. I would wither in a moment of grief at the sights, swallow my bitterness, and silence my raging protest. After all, I was not one of those reformers. I was not a prophet. I didn't possess King Solomon's magic ring. I had barely enough strength to stand all day in Monsieur Pernand's shop.

"I'm going back to my country, Monsieur Pernand." That was what I had told him, so he would give me my salary before the end of the week. He smiled and said in a sarcastic voice in French, "I will miss you, Brunette." The wicked man had never called me by my name since the day I had come to work for him, although he knew very well that my name was Fatima.

Strands of memory and the vicissitudes of life seemed to overwhelm me. I felt that the plane was suspended in midair, unwilling to advance toward my homeland. I could no longer bear the throbbing heartbeats of yearning and joy when the flight attendant leaned toward me and said, "Madam, please fasten your seat belt. The plane is going to land in a few minutes."

In a few minutes, I would throw myself into the arms of this rough country, and the pleasure of descending would remind me of the swings that I played on in my childhood.

The past was always with me, as if my experiences away from home were testing my love for my country. Here I was now, tired of having been tested and fearing the result.

"Have you come to spend your holiday here?" asked the taxi driver, interrupting my reverie.

"No. I've come back for good," I said.

He laughed, then fell silent for a while. I imagined that he had forgotten me or found it difficult to continue the conversation with me. But he surprised me again.

"Go back to where you came from. This country is not meant for human beings."

"God protect me from you!" I replied and frowned. Then I grumbled to silence him. He surely could not understand the residual fear that paralyzed my steps at the first indication of disapproval for my presence here.

He didn't notice my frown, and my grumbling meant nothing to him. He continued to chatter as I broke into tears when my old neighborhood appeared in the distance. Familiar scenes embraced me, welcoming me, despite the many changes that had taken place. And all those children! How reckless my people were! They bred like rabbits, perhaps because their hours of sleep greatly exceeded their hours of wakefulness. People crammed the streets, as I threaded my way among them. I climbed the old staircase leading to our house, and opened the door, which had no lock. Suddenly my mother stood before me, as if she had anticipated my arrival, and was waiting to embrace me.

Until that moment, I had not known the taste of a mother's tears, but here I was now, sharing her tears and melting away on her scented chest. Then I vanished among the children of my brothers and their wives. I felt as if the sweat dripping from my body was dark, poisonous, reeking of repression, exile, longing, pain, and joy all at once. Resting on my mother's bed, I surrendered again to her scent, and childhood memories came flooding back to me when she squeezed my hand and spoke words that were music to my ears: "I forgive you, my little girl."

As I was falling asleep for the first time in many long years, I heard a voice saying, "Is she going to stay with us despite our cramped living conditions?"

"You're happy with her presents, but not with her being here?"

"I don't mean that, Auntie. She has lived most of her life in France, and her nature and way of thinking must have changed. How will she endure the human misery here?"

Then the discussion became angry, throwing me into utter confusion. A chill began to creep slowly into my body. My mother's scent filled my lungs. Her voice argued on my behalf. I was dazed, and my heart fluttered, for my dream was cracking. Voices interrupted each other, rising higher. My dream was collapsing. A child's cry rang out. My dream was shattered. Monsieur Pernand, with his small round glasses, smiled wickedly, then laughed, then burst into guffaws. My dream turned to rubble. Sleep escaped me. Weariness overwhelmed me. My mother's scent wafted against my skin as she bent over me, removed a piece of gum from her mouth, and stuffed it in my ears.

Bittersweet Memories

Zabya Khamis

*I*t was a long journey, starting in a Western industrial city and ending in this particular airport. A long journey—but its difficulties began right here. Everything at the airport contributed to the oppressive atmosphere: the long lines of Middle Eastern workers, the male odors in the humid and putrid air, the presence of police everywhere, and the lines of passengers, who looked like a herd of sheep being led to the slaughterhouse.

Here was al-Jawhara, coming home. She was returning without an escorting male relative and without a black cloak. She had laughed a lot during the flight, consumed two cans of beer, and enjoyed a long conversation with a young European man who was seated beside her. He inquired about the climate and the environment in her country, the night life, the secrets of the palaces, the amputation of hands, the flogging, the executioner, and the beheadings that he had heard about from time to time. He sighed deeply— it was a world beyond his imagination.

Her being a native of this country amazed him. His amazement became mingled with fear when she warned him not to talk to her with such directness at the airport. He shouldn't look at, shouldn't speak to, and should avoid the women of this country altogether—or else he would suffer dire consequences, the least of which would be dismissal from his job, but it might go as far as his beheading or flogging.

Patrick was twenty-six years old. He had traveled over most of Western Europe by train and by motorcycle. He had been unemployed for a long time after completing his university education. He believed in the total liberation of women and in multiple sexual relationships. He saw in socialism and the principles of anarchism the salvation of the world. He enjoyed drinking beer and red wine, as well as roaming freely in crowded streets. He was offered a contract to work in this country and decided to accept it immediately, having a keen interest in both the petrodollars and the new experience. This country, as far as he was concerned, was a mysterious world known only through pictures of camels and veiled women, stories about the Organization of Petroleum Exporting Countries, and the conflict with Israel.

Al-Jawhara seemed to him like a houri who had emerged from the tales of the *Arabian Nights*, wearing Western clothes and jewelry. She was Scheherazade, liberated in the Western sense of the word. He was astonished to see a woman from this country with two arms and short hair, dressed in pants and an elegant shirt. He thought all women in this country looked like black tents in which nothing moved except a pair of lizard eyes, always downcast. How was he to know that he would be dazzled by al-Jawhara? She was a different kind of houri, one who looked like any European woman he knew, except for her Middle Eastern features.

They entered the passport control area for both citizens and foreign nationals. Al-Jawhara stood in the citizens' line. Men, in white flowing robes, occupied the front of the line. In the rear stood the women, looking like black tents, with their children running around them. Al-Jawhara seemed out of place. Harsh looks assailed her from every side. She bit her lip. This was her first visit home in six years. She had heard a lot about her country by following the news. She hated the idea of returning, but in the end she returned. Now she faced several hours of waiting in this line, unnerved by the oppressive atmosphere, the heat, the children's screams, and those weapons in the hands of the police. There were Bedouins armed with clubs everywhere.

Finally one of the customs officers shouted, "Come here, woman!" He inquired why she was standing in the citizens' line. She started to explain. He interrupted her in exasperation. "Give me your passport. Come on!"

She gave him the passport. He examined the name and the number closely, then stared at her sternly.

"Are you al-Jawhara So-and-so?"

"Yes."

"You're the daughter of So-and-so?"

"Yes."

"Where's your cloak?"

She didn't answer. She looked around, slightly frightened and angry. He was trying to provoke her, as if this was a perfectly natural thing to do. Who was he to ask her all these stupid questions?

"Where's your husband? Where's the close male relative escorting you? Don't you have a family that you're traveling alone?"

She told him that she had been studying abroad, that she had obtained her master's degree, and that this was the first time she had returned after a long absence.

"Step aside and wait!"

"What about my passport?"

"I told you to step aside and wait!"

She stood waiting, and the waiting lasted a long time. Meanwhile she observed how the customs officers questioned other passengers. It was not with the same harshness that she had received, but still with a lack of civility.

She wondered whether they knew who al-Jawhara was. Did they find out about her student activities? Her talks with Arab socialists? Her contribution to Palestinian revolutionary songs? Her visit to Dublin? Did they know her views on women's liberation? On sexual liberation? On the ruling family? Were they aware of her academic distinction? Of her visits to Palestinian refugee camps? Did they discover that she had donated blood to the rebels of El Salvador? Or that she had a Cuban male friend? Or that she had secretly attended meetings of the international socialist movement?

Al-Jawhara began to dread her memories.

She felt that she was merely a piece of luggage subject to search.

In the past, the authorities had not feared women as they did now. Seized by an overwhelming fear, they had started to search, arrest, and even torture them. They had detained some of her female friends, and stripped others of their passports and official documents. They had also canceled study-abroad programs for many female students. They did not bother to justify their actions, or to bring charges, or even to prove their charges.

Voices of protest rose within al-Jawhara: What about basic human rights? Where are the international organizations for justice? The resolutions of the United Nations? The reports on the social conditions in her country? She asked herself all these questions, choking back her anger. A few beads of sweat, which she tried to wipe, ran into her eyes.

Where was her country? Where was her homeland?

To what was she returning? To the humidity, the oppressive atmosphere, open sewers, male odors, police, armed men, identity papers, and the club in the hand of that Bedouin who was waiting for an opportunity to use it. She was nothing. Absolutely nothing.

She was merely a travel document[8] and a female who had to conceal herself behind a cloak. She mustn't move any of her facial features except the two lizard eyes; she must lower them.

One of the customs officers called out her name: "Al-Jawhara!"

She replied. He gave her the passport after fixing her with a shameless stare of lechery accompanied by an expression of contempt.

And Al-Jawhara proceeded to the baggage claim area.

Part Seven

Customs and Values

Tears for Sale

Samira Azzam

I don't know how it was possible for Khazna to be a mourner for
the dead and a beautician for brides at the same time. I had
heard a lot about her from my mother and her friends before I
had the opportunity to see her for the first time—when one of our
neighbors died. Not yet fifty, this man was already consumed by disease, and so it came as no surprise when one of our female neighbors
said to my mother, without sadness, "He has passed away, Umm
Hasan. May misfortune never befall us."

I got the feeling that I was about to experience a colorful day
full of excitements, and it pleased me. I could take advantage of
being a neighbor of the deceased man's family and sneak inside with
the other boys and girls of the alley to stare at the dead man's waxen
face, to watch his wife and daughters weep for him, and see the
female mourners rhythmically clapping their hands and chanting
phrases they had learned by heart.

I took one of my little girlfriends by the hand and together we
managed to sneak through the visitors' legs and find a place not far
from the door, where lots of other children had gathered, keen, like
us, to get acquainted with death and experience a few adventures.
There we stayed—until a big hand pushed us aside. It was the hand
of Khazna, standing, tall and broad, in the doorway. She quickly assumed a distressed look, stretched out her fingers and undid her two
braids, then took a black headcloth out of her pocket and tied it
around her forehead. She gave a horrendous scream, which filled
my little heart with dread, and forced her way through the women
to a corner in which stood a vessel containing liquid indigo. She
rubbed her face and hands with it, making herself look like the
masks that vendors hang up in their shops during festivals. Then

222

she came back and stood by the dead man's head, gave another scream, and began to beat her breast violently and roll her tongue, uttering rhythmical words that the women repeated after her. Tears were already streaming down their faces. It was as if with her screams Khazna was mourning not only this dead man, but all the dead of the village, one by one. She stirred sorrow in one woman over the loss of her husband, and in another over a son or brother. You could no longer tell which of the women was the mother of the deceased, or the wife, or the sister. If the women flagged in their efforts, exhausted, Khazna delivered a particularly sad eulogy, followed by a horrendous scream. Then the tears gushed out, the weeping grew louder, and the grief intensified. Khazna was the pivot in all this, with an indefatigable tongue, a voice like an owl's, and a strange ability to summon up grief. The reward was in proportion to the effort, and Khazna's reward was such that it awakened in her an inexhaustible spring of grief.

I still remember how, when the men came to carry the deceased to his wooden bier, Khazna begged them to proceed gently with the dearly departed, to be careful, and not to hasten to cut his ties with this world. This went on until one man got fed up with her chatter, pushed her away, and, with the help of his friends, forcibly carried off the deceased. Then the black handkerchiefs were raised in farewell, and the women's requests followed each other in quick succession, some sending greetings to their departed husbands, others to their mothers. Khazna then filled the whole place with a wailing that rang out clearly above the voices of the dozens of screaming women. Only when the funeral procession moved off and the bier, on which the dead man's fez wiggled, was slowly carried away by the escorting men, did Khazna quiet down. Then it was time for the women to rest a little from the sadness that had overwhelmed them. They were invited to help themselves to some of the food set out on a table in one of the rooms. Khazna was the first to wash her face, roll up her sleeves, and fill her big mouth with anything she could lay her hands on. As I stood among the little children who had slipped in, I noticed her hiding something in the front of her dress. Sensing that she had been spotted, she gave a tired smile and said, "It's a little bit of food for my daughter Masouda. I got the news before I could prepare anything for her to eat. And eating the food from a mourning ceremony is rewarded in the hereafter."

That day I understood that Khazna was different from any other woman. She was a necessity for death even more than for the dead. I was unable to forget her big mouth, her fearful hands, and her loose, curly hair. Whenever I heard that a man was dying, I would run with my friends to his house, prompted merely by the wish to see something exciting. I would then relate the adventure to my mother—if, that is, she had not run there herself. But I would be distracted from the face of the dying man by the sight of Khazna, and my eyes would be glued to her, watching her hands as they moved from her breast to her face to her head in a violent beating which seemed, like the words she intoned, to have a special rhythm that penetrated the wounds of the bereaved family and made the visitors feel the grief.

Some time passed before I had the opportunity to see Khazna at a wedding. I could not believe my eyes. She had the same black curly hair, but it was combed and adorned with flowers. She also had the same ugly face, but the powders made it look completely different from the face painted with indigo. Her eyes appeared bigger because of the kohl that she had used to circle them. Her arms were loaded with bracelets (who said trading in death was not profitable?). Her mouth was constantly open in laughter; now and then she shut it halfway to chew a big piece of gum between her yellow teeth.

Then I realized that Khazna had to do with brides as much as she had to do with the dead. Her task began on the morning of the wedding day. She depilated the bride with sugar syrup and penciled her eyebrows, at the same time initiating her into her sexual duties in a whisper—or what she thought was a whisper. If the bride blushed, she laughed at her and winked, reassuring her that in a few nights she would become skillful at lovemaking, and that she could guarantee it if the bride kept applying the fragrant soap to her body and the oil to her hair. These were items that the bride could fetch from the chemist or buy from Khazna herself. In the evening, the women arrived together, perfumed and beautifully adorned, and gathered around the bride, who sat up on a platform. Then Khazna's trills of joy tore asunder the sky above the village. She played a prominent role in the dance circle, going around joking with the women, saying obscene things that made them laugh. When, amidst the winking of the women, the bridegroom came to take the bride away, Khazna undertook to conduct them solemnly to the door of their room, where she still had the right to keep guard. I didn't quite understand why Khazna was so eager to stand at the newlyweds' door, waiting nervously and inquisitively. Whenever the signal came—after a short wait or a long one—she uttered a piercing trill of joy, which the bride's family had obviously been eagerly awaiting. When it came, the men twisted and twirled their mustaches, and all the women stood up simultaneously and uttered proud trills of joy. Then Khazna left, content in eye, soul, stomach, and pocket, the women wishing that she, in her turn, would rejoice at Masouda's wedding.

Masouda's wedding was something Khazna looked forward to. It was also the reason that she collected bracelets and provisions. After all, she had no one else in the world except this daughter, and it was to her that everything she earned from the funerals and weddings would pass.

But the heavens did not want Khazna to rejoice.

It was a summer that I was never to forget. Typhoid ensured it was a season like no other for Khazna. The sun did not rise without a new victim, and it was said that Khazna mourned for three customers on one day.

The disease did not spare Masouda, invading her bowels. Death took no pity on her, despite Khazna's solemn pledges.

The people in my village woke up to the news of the little girl's death. Their curiosity began where the life of this poor girl ended. How would Khazna mourn for her daughter? What kind of eulogy would her grief at the loss prompt her to deliver? What sort of funeral ceremony would throw the neighborhood into a state of agitation?

Curiosity and sadness got the better of me, and I went along to Khazna's house, together with scores of other women rushing to redeem some of their debt to her.

The house had only one room and could not contain more than twenty people. We sat down and those who could not get in remained standing in a circle at the door. My gaze swept over the heads, searching for Khazna's face, because I didn't hear her voice. To my utter amazement, I didn't find her weeping. She was silent, speechless, lying on the floor in the corner of the room. She had not wrapped a black browband around her head, or painted her face with indigo; she was not striking her cheeks or tearing at her clothes.

For the first time, I saw the face of a woman who was not feigning her emotions. It was the face of a woman in agony, almost dying from agony.

It was a mute grief—grief that only those who had suffered a great misfortune could recognize.

Some women tried to weep or scream. But she looked at them in dismay, as if she loathed this affectation, so they fell silent, utterly amazed. When the men came to carry the body of the only creature for whom Khazna might express her feelings without hypocrisy, she did not scream or tear at her clothes, but instead looked at them distractedly. Then she walked off behind them like someone in a daze, as they headed toward the mosque and the cemetery. All she did there was lay her head on the earth to which the little body had been entrusted, and let it rest there for hours—God alone knew for how many hours.

People came back from the funeral ceremony with different versions of what had happened to Khazna. Some said she had gone so mad that she seemed rational. Others said she had no tears left, because all those funerals had exhausted them. And there were even people who said that Khazna did not cry because she was not getting paid for it.

There were only very few people who preferred not to say anything, and leave it to Khazna—in her silence—to say it all.

Misfortune in the Alley

Ramziya Abbas al-Iryani

᚛᚛᚛

*D*arkness descended on the street before the electricity was restored. There was a flurry of haphazard movements, and rapid footsteps could be heard, as people hastened to return home. Children's voices rang out in one of the alleys that branched off the street. It was a long, narrow alley covered with dirt and scraps of paper, and strewn with garbage from the houses on either side.

The children gathered in circles and groups, happy with the silence of the adults, who sat motionless, waiting for the lights to come back on. The women went home to prepare candles so that they could make supper for their children and coffee for their spouses who returned from the smoking den—a popular haunt known for its large variety of qat,[1] each kind of which was attributed to the particular village that cultivated it.

"May God's curse be upon the person who invented the electricity!" exclaimed a man who was sitting in front of one of the houses.

"On the contrary. May God bless him!" his wife replied angrily. She was standing in front of the window on the second floor.

The man jumped to his feet, startled by the voice that answered him unexpectedly.

"Why bless him? The electricity has made women lazy and—"

"Lazy? Does the electricity do women's work? Or else what do you mean?"

"Each time the electricity fails, you go to bed and snuggle down between the covers, using the power outage as an excuse. Meanwhile the children go hungry and the adults feel lost. Do you deny that, Safiyya?"

227

"What can I do? Buy me an oil lamp and a butagas stove, and I won't have another excuse!"

The voice of a child crying interrupted them. He had stepped on a piece of glass while playing with his friends. It was followed by a louder voice, which was shouting and asking the people of the alley for help. A misfortune had befallen this person. Safiyya could not identify whose voice it was. She rushed out of the house to find out what had happened and began calling out to Hasan, the baker's son. Before she could ask him, he hastened to tell her that Samira, Hajj Abdallah's daughter, had vanished. She had fled, and there was no trace of her.

Safiyya straightened her veil and hurried to join the crowd that had gathered in front of Hajj Abdallah's house. She wanted to hear the entire story from his wife, Latifa, who was telling it over and over again.

"Did you see her yourself, Latifa?" asked Sayyida, the alley's dressmaker, who had dropped everything to learn what had happened.

"Yes, I saw her myself yesterday talking to a cab driver. And the other day I saw her getting out of the same cab," Latifa replied.

"Have a heart, Latifa! Samira is a poor orphan, and what you say can ruin her reputation!" Safiyya shouted with all her strength as she pushed her way toward Latifa.

"Shut up!" Latifa interrupted her sarcastically. "You're the cause of our misfortune. Whenever I advised her father to discipline her, you yelled and behaved arrogantly, and I was made to be the one at fault when I'm her aunt and—"

With her shrill voice, Nuriyya the baker intervened to defend the runaway girl: "Samira cannot be blamed if she ran away today. You beat her every day, so she became fed up with her life. The housework and the care of your children are upon her shoulders. And any mistake on her part or your children's part, she is held responsible for—"

"What do you mean by 'if she ran away?'" Latifa cut her off angrily. "Are you hiding her in your house while her father is searching for her like a madman?"

Fatima the henna painter shouted at the top of her voice, "I wish she had run away to our house! But God will take care of her and ease her way. The drops of blood that trickled from her nose and mouth yesterday are still visible on the stairs. Surely you haven't forgotten that you pushed her down the rooftop stairway? I was watching from my window with my own eyes. May the worms eat them if I'm lying!"

"And do you know why she pushed her?" Zahra the peddler insisted on having her say. "Because she stayed too long on the rooftop hanging out the washing of her aunt and her aunt's children!"

Maryam, one of Safiyya's neighbors, exploded with anger as she shoved people aside in order to be in the center. "And today you accuse her of running away to finish what you started. Maybe you chased her away from home. God alone knows what you've done to her!"

Latifa screamed, asking everyone to bear witness on her behalf against what the women were saying, for they were fabricating lies about her and treating her unjustly.

Suddenly a hush fell on the scene. Samira's father appeared amid the crowd. He looked disheveled, and his shawl hung askew. This event was a great misfortune to him. His world had collapsed. He was not capable of sustaining such a heavy blow.

He stood bracing himself before the women, who cleared the way for him in front of his house, and then formed a circle around him to hear what he had done. He looked to the right and left in humiliation and dejection, the tears silently running down his face. This misfortune was more than he could endure. Facing death was easier for him than having to stand like that. The comforting words he heard from here and there seemed trite and hollow to him. He wished that the women would hold their tongues so he could collect his thoughts and find a way to resolve this predicament or, more accurately, this calamity. He gazed at his wife, hoping she would give him a clue to his daughter's whereabouts. He tried to quiet down everyone in order to explain the steps he had taken to search for her, but his voice failed him. An eerie silence fell on the crowd. Even the children were speechless with fear, holding fast to their mothers or clinging to their friends. Everyone hushed except Latifa, who broke the silence with her malicious, vengeful voice.

"There is no use looking for her anymore. I saw her riding in a cab with one of the young men and fleeing. I pleaded with her. I reminded her that her poor father would be extremely distraught about this. I tried to go after her. Death before dishonor. There is nothing to be done."

With stammering, desperate words, Hajj Abdallah yelled at her, "Shut up woman! I'm sick of your fabrications. I've hated my life since the day you entered my house. Your flattery and insincere praise of my daughter in my presence made me believe you were behaving like a mother. Your hypocrisy killed my daughter. I used to believe you and go to extremes in punishing her. You broke her spirit and destroyed her life. God alone knows what you had done to her until she fled. God alone knows what is fated for her. And you, my neighbors, you are responsible for what has happened. None of you told me what went on in my house during my absence. Why didn't you protect her from injustice? Why did you join in an alliance to oppress her? Are these the duties neighbors have toward one another? What have you done other than whisper and gossip about what goes on in my house? Has any of you thought of stopping this unjust woman? What—"

While the poor father was fumbling for words, the light suddenly flashed and the electricity was restored to the alley. Everyone fell silent, even the father, who was astonished to see the large crowd that had gathered. It included the inhabitants of the neighboring alley as well, for the news had spread, and people hurried to come, either as spectators, sympathizers, or participants. All eyes were riveted on the father, now overwhelmed by pain and distress.

It was easy to see in the alley after the lamps above the doors of the houses were lit and rays of light filtered out through the windows overlooking it.

Suddenly they all heard a strange noise coming from the stack of firewood in front of the baker's house, which was adjacent to Hajj Abdallah's house. Everyone was startled except the father, who approached it slowly, staring at the firewood as if he had found a glimmer of hope. He extended his hands toward the stack of firewood and began to scatter it about. Then they all heard him scream in joy mixed with astonishment. He stood rooted to the spot, as if he had found himself. He had found his daughter crouching among the spiky pieces of firewood, blood dripping from her hands and legs!

He turned toward the crowd and shouted hysterically, "My daughter! She didn't run away! Come and see. Here she is! Come on, girl. Come out to show them that my honor is well protected, and that shame did not and will never enter my house!"

He opened his arms to embrace his trembling, frightened daughter, who could not believe that she would escape punishment.

Her tears of fear and pain mingled with the father's tears of joy. Latifa stood as if nailed to the ground, watching what was happening in bewilderment and humiliation. The crowd stared at her in contempt and malicious joy. Words merged with sounds, and she could no longer make out what was going on around her. The voices of the adults blended with the noise of the children, who had become tired and sleepy. They had been standing there for a long while, trying to keep up with the grownups in following what had occurred in their alley. Now all they wanted was to return home so they could fill their empty stomachs and go to bed.

Questioning

Fawziya Rashid

t that moment, on a night long ago . . .

A sea of ghostly, dust-covered faces turned toward you. Your mother's face was behind the door. Her lips were calling up a spirit that was said to be of an older sister of yours, one whom you never saw again after that night. All eyes were ablaze. She was asleep. In the dark of night, the wrinkled hand wanted to take advantage of her drowsiness, which seemed to melt her into the bed. Between you and her small face was now the distance of a dream, or the distance of wakefulness, or woods inhabited by creatures from an unknown region.

They dragged her as she moaned in fear. Her extreme drowsiness made her collapse between their hands.

Behind the closed door, you heard a man's voice, like your father's, saying to her in disappointment mingled with anger: "Speak up. Who is he?"

Her voice sounded choked with fear, and she made no reply. Then another voice broke the gloomy silence. You listened reluctantly, wishing you could deliver her from the people who besieged her behind the door.

With a trembling voice, your sister uttered a name. You heard the name, and your alertness heightened.

"I didn't do anything. I was playing with him," she said feebly.

"He is a boy, and you are a girl."

On that rainy night, they gathered around the samovar. No one dared to ask where she was.

However, later you heard muffled sobbing and disjointed

words coming from the circle of women assembled in the courtyard of the house.

"She was young . . . The boy deceived her . . . Honor and the family . . ."

All you knew was that she had disappeared forever.

You are secretly peeking into the women's public bathhouse. There are indistinct bodies emanating steam. It's a dream or something like a dream. What has brought these women here? Your wide open eyes turn around searching, but you can't find her. However, you hear a whispered conversation in the evening before you go to sleep. You've been told a lot of things about women, but you are constantly haunted by the crooked furrows in the faces of those who snatched the sleep away from your little sister's eyes.

Now you see nothing but nakedness moving in the steam, women swaying with desire, and the figure of a housewife chasing after you. You had stolen into her house at random, and were shocked by her lewdness, so you turned and fled as fast as you could.

You've seen plenty of things in your neighbors' houses and behind fences belonging to men who veil the faces of soft-skinned women.

And now:

You remember that girl who was several years older than you. At times you burst into an anguished cry, and at other times you wish you could grab hold of those who had hurt her and cut off the arteries pulsating in their groins.

Why did they make her vanish into the night? Why can you no longer hear her chatting and playing in the shade of the old tree in that thick forest?

You remained alone in the house. You and your parents.

They were getting older, while you were approaching the age of overwhelming virility.

Sometimes you saw them together without understanding the meaning of those flirtations. He would approach her after removing the clothes from the lower part of his body, while she seemed tired or annoyed, until the moment came when she drifted into his ecstasy in silence. You later learned that this was part of the very nature of life, and that a woman should not give herself easily, even to the master of her house. Neither of them suspected that you were not yet asleep. Why, then, had they banished that little girl for a similar act?

The virtuous woman does not accept the flirtations of love even if she does not know the significance of such intimacies.

Where had she vanished? Years later, you were told that she was afflicted with a critical fever that took her life on a rainy night.

Which land was it that the little soul had passionately loved and into which she had vanished on that rainy night? The wound caused by her departure had not healed. It was said that the litter of genies on springtime evenings assumed the form of stars, which the little girls frolicked with after vanishing from earth into heaven. It was said that she was there among the girls, playing with the outpouring stars and blazing lights.

She was in a different world, one that was devoid of sadness and filled with unimaginable happiness.

It was also said that there was always someone who departed to the bliss of heaven as long as happiness on earth was incomplete.

What puzzled you for a long time was that she was summarily condemned to oblivion for a common, everyday act in which all people engage secretly.

The Dinosaur

Emily Nasrallah

❧

*T*he stranger asked her how old she was. She smiled mysteri-
ously, like the Mona Lisa, and did not reply.

"I think you're in your mid-thirties," he said.

Her heart fluttered at his words, not at his glances.

"I'm pleased with your estimate," she responded jokingly.

He persisted in addressing the subject of age.

"Thirty-six years . . ."

She laughed until tears flowed from her eyes. She would not let
him ridicule her, treat her the way men treated women: first they
tested the waters, then they advanced step by step, regardless of the
distance or the degree of unfamiliarity.

As a middle-aged woman, she knew herself, and courageously acknowledged her age. She also knew that she had achieved remarkable
success over the passing years. She had not wasted her time. When she
looked back on her choices, she had no regrets. She had used her head
in confronting questionable situations. Now she was facing a stranger
at a surprise party in a house far away from home. As she was finding
her way in this new society, something like a "magic box" opened before her eyes and puzzled her deeply. She did not know how to deal
with this man, or whether she could apply her usual standards to him.

As usual, she resorted to a traditional pattern of behavior with
which she felt comfortable: first she considered the situation carefully, then she trod cautiously and slowly, so that she would neither
lose her bearings nor stumble into a trap.

She smiled as an image imprinted on her mind from her village
days occurred to her. She remembered a saying that she frequently
repeated on such occasions: "You can take a girl out of the village,
but you cannot take the village out of a girl's heart."

235

What a naive village woman!

If the man addressing her had spoken Arabic, he would have detected her accent. Her accent was rural, mountainous, and pure. But the stranger spoke a foreign language, devoid of the "cracking sound" of the guttural consonant Q, which distinguished her speech from that of her acquaintances in the city.

He didn't realize that she was arming herself before every new situation with a weapon she had inherited from her grandmother: her composure and reserve.

"The lightheaded girl is a joke to everyone."

"Girls' hearts are like locked trunks."

"A girl is not like a boy, and what's permissible for him is not permissible for her."

Why was she reciting this litany of advice now? She wanted the fog of the new atmosphere to envelop her, so that she could forget her roots, the place, and the time, and let herself go . . .

She asked herself: "What would happen if I let myself go just once, for a try? Just like that, if I forgot my composure, and my sense of self, and my bashfulness, and the trembling of my lips and fingertips. What if? . . ."

(If she were thirty-six years old!)

The stranger was still gazing at her questioningly. It was as if he could think about nothing but age.

"Why are you preoccupied with age?" she asked him with a boldness that astonished her.

"I test my intelligence."

"Is that your only goal? Then you're the most intelligent man I've ever met!"

He was completely taken aback by her reply. After her initial surprise, she began to consider what other odd things might happen.

She observed the man for quite a while. He was holding a drink, sipping a little, and smiling. The smile shifted from his lips to his eyes, then spread across the creases of his face.

Creases . . . wrinkles. She found the word for the folds that had begun to cling to her eyelids. His face was wrinkled around the mouth and the eyes and above the brows, where a rebellious lock of his thick, chestnut-colored hair had fallen. Suddenly it seemed to her that similar wrinkles were rising from within her chest, just as the earth's crust rises from the heart of subterranean volcanoes, and spreading over her face and body, to accumulate layer upon layer. She was unable, even subconsciously, to count the number of layers.

She began to move so that she could get away from this man.

"Where to?" he asked abruptly.

"I remembered something important."

"Are you coming back? I'll be here, waiting for you."

She fled from him to the nearest mirror. She brought her face close to it and began to scrutinize her features as never before.

This was her old familiar face. Dreadful wrinkles had not completely taken over. Her face seemed relaxed and smooth, and bore clear marks of joy and wit.

Her feeling of aging, then, was groundless. She would remain thirty-six years old.

She ran the comb through the front locks of her hair, sweeping them back to reveal her forehead—high, smooth, and proud, like a watchtower above her eyes.

"I'm a narcissist," she whispered to the mirror.

It seemed to her that the mirror replied, "And what woman doesn't go through a narcissist stage?"

"You've reassured me!" she said to the mirror, bidding it farewell. Then she returned anxiously to the parlor, uncertain of how she should conduct herself. Should she avoid this man or continue the game until the end of the evening?

This was a game, nothing more, she reminded herself, and its utmost limit was the end of the party.

He didn't allow her to pursue her thoughts. He intercepted her halfway to the parlor, saying, "I was worried that I wouldn't find you."

She didn't know how the words escaped her. "But you're not alone here!"

"Yes, I'm alone," he whispered, and gave her a seductive look.

"How strange!"

She meant nothing in particular, but he caught her remark.

"And what's strange about it, madam?"

"I thought you were escorting a beautiful woman, and that you were in your own country, and among your acquaintances."

"The greatest loneliness can be experienced among family and acquaintances," he said, lowering his head.

"That's merely philosophizing. I don't think that a man like you can remain alone."

He surprised her with a daring look. "A man like me? How do I strike you?"

"Pardon me. I didn't mean to analyze your personality, but—"

"Let's put the 'but' aside. You're right. For a while, a few years ago, I wasn't alone. I escaped loneliness twice. The first time was with a beautiful girl not yet twenty years of age, when I was twenty-five. We fell in love with each other at first sight, and our love resulted in a happy, though brief, marriage."

Anger began to well up inside her. What devil had led her to this situation? Would she have to spend the entire evening listening to accounts of this man's adventures? She looked around her, searching for rescue, for someone to emerge from the closely packed and joyful crowd, for a single person to stand by her side and deliver her. But she was disappointed.

He continued, "I lived with Doris for one year during which I discovered that we were two conflicting planets. We agreed to separate. But when a man is accustomed to living with a companion, being alone is awfully depressing. The days become dismal and dreary. Life flowed along in this mode until I met my second wife, Marlene. I was already older, and so I decided not to make the same mistake again. It seemed to me from the beginning that Marlene, who was nearly thirty, was a mature, delightful woman. I said to myself, 'This time I will not rush. We're both mature, so our relationship should have a solid foundation.' Everything about Marlene was alluring and attractive—her smile, her eyes, her poise, and her lively mind. It seemed like a paradise. I didn't think it strange when she objected to sex before marriage. I believed that each woman has her own style of seduction and arousing passion. Perhaps she wanted to set a fire in my blood so that she would later quench it with water sweeter than honey and more intoxicating than wine.

"I stood miserably at the door to her garden on the wedding night, and the following nights, during which time I discovered that Marlene, whom I had chosen to be my bride, was still a virgin. A virgin! Can you imagine? No man had touched her before. My garden turned out to be deserted!

"I shook with fear and aversion, and withdrew to the threshold. Only after I had closed the door and retired to my separate bedroom, did I regain my composure.

"For as long as I live, I will never forget her appearance when I approached her. She began to tremble like an autumn leaf. Her muscles contracted, and the veils of seduction fell away. Suddenly, her body seemed to have been transformed into a wasteland of weeds and thorns. Her lips parted in an attempt to say something, to apologize for a crime she had not committed, but I didn't wait around to listen. Passionless, I left her lying on the bed and walked away, with her virginal ghost chasing after me."

The stranger paused to collect his breath, and his eyes remained riveted to her face. She could almost see her reactions in them—her amazement, unspoken questions, and . . . had the man told her the story topsy-turvily?

What had he told her?

What kind of crazy confession had he made to her? And why had he chosen her, the only Middle Eastern woman in a large crowd of unfamiliar Westerners?

She began to doubt the soundness of his mind.

She thought to herself: In a few moments I'll say farewell and never see him again. I'll forget him and everything he has told me. I won't concern myself with whether the story was true or a figment of his imagination, whether he told it accurately or topsy-turvily. Such matters will be rendered irrelevant by my scheduled departure, early in the morning, to continue my journey through the continent of curiosities and wonders: America!

The stranger kept repeating between one sip of drink and then another, "A woman living in the late twentieth century who is still a virgin? What a scandal!"

She made no comment.

The words, like sharp blades, stuck in her throat. She began to move backward very slowly. She wasn't afraid of him, but she feared that his words would provoke her to reveal opinions she would rather keep to herself.

She feared that she might ask him, "Where can Marlene be found? Marlene, that rare breed of woman who may become extinct like the dinosaur in your country."

Moreover, she feared that his words would provoke her to make a comparison between two situations: two women, two men, and two worlds. Tonight she was attending a dinner party—a trivial social event at which the guests could forget their troubles, avoid any analysis of psychological and social problems, and disregard the issue of refugees from seemingly civilized nations.

She feared that she might tell the stranger that his account was the opposite of a story she had heard in her own country a few days earlier. The story originated from a woman whose tongue was sharp and in whose social gatherings there was always a mention of scandal. Instead of voicing any of these thoughts, she heard herself saying, "How strange!"

"What do you mean?" he asked.

"I . . . I'm a stranger, sir. Don't you notice my accent?"

She meant to say, "Don't you notice my amazement? Don't you see that we cannot stand in front of the same mirror?"

Again, she preferred to remain silent. She gave him a brief handshake and said her farewell.

"I'm sorry to leave you on your own, sir. Thank you for taking me into your confidence."

"But . . . but . . . won't we meet again?" he stammered, taken by surprise.

"Maybe, at another time, in another place," she replied with a smile. "But now I'm going on with my trip to see the famous sights of your country."

She really meant to say, "I'm going on with my trip to search for the vestiges of the dinosaur."

Moonstruck

Hadiya Sa'id

The Face of the Moon

There is no moon in London. But I've seen it. What do we know when we say "I"? When I say "I," I don't know my inner self, I don't know myself. I saw my true self at night just as I saw the moon. It happened unexpectedly while that man was bringing me home. We were returning from a concert. He escorted me from the train station to my landlady's house. It was a seven-minute walk along a wide street, across a bridge, and past a pub before reaching my alley. The pub was called Sunrise. I would pay attention to the name on my way home, but ignore it as I left for work. In the company of that man, I almost passed the pub. Then I lingered for a while, not because I wanted to have a drink with him, but because he suddenly said, "Look! Do you see the moon?"

It was a round disk, like his face. Before I raised my head to gaze at the moon, I had thought that men's faces were all either elongated or square.

We drew near the edge of the bridge, before the courtyard of the pub, with the moon above. I saw it and saw myself with that man, alone, in the darkness. That meant I was free. Freedom is attained when your entire family is gone and a stranger in a foreign country escorts you home. How did the moon arrive here for me to see? I left it in our village in northern Iraq. We lived in a little valley, and our house was at the foot of the mountain. I left the moon above my mother's grave, which was a mound of earth under which lay the severed limbs of her body. The fighters said, "Pray for her quickly and then leave." The moon remained there along with her scent. It seemed that the moon had caught up with me. However,

241

were it not for this man, I wouldn't have seen the moon. He was warm. I felt the warmth of his flesh. My shoulder touched his arm. He had a luxuriant head of hair and a clean-shaven face. A heavy scent of violets and carnations wafted from him. He talked endlessly, as men do, and said many things, which I immediately forgot. As I opened the door of the house, which was hidden behind a cypress, I could only remember the face of the moon. And I kissed him.

The Shadowless Tree

A cypress has no shadow. The man became its shadow. He said to me, "How sweet you are today!" I thought, after entering, that perhaps I wasn't sweet yesterday, and that I wouldn't be sweet tomorrow. I thought of him wiping the strings of his violin and handling it with care as he stored it in the case and hastened to meet me after I left the conservatory for the day. He used to surprise me by waiting behind a cypress in the parking lot. The cypress was smaller than the one by the door of my landlady's house. I found myself one day waiting for him behind it when he was a bit late. The students were gathered around him. They were fond of him. I remained distant from him and from them. He usually saw me only at the office. He sometimes went out with me and escorted me home if we stayed late at a party in which he performed or listened to music selections that we liked. When the train traveled at high speed, the trees along the railroad swayed backward, obliterating the reflection of his face in the window. The trees were bare, like his soul, which he said he had unveiled to me.

It occurred to me that he had dreamed of becoming a great musician and had ended up as a professor at the conservatory. I thought he was better off this way. Wagner was a devil. He stole Liszt's daughter when she was someone else's wife. Chopin was ill and oppressed, even by his lover. He could have burst with love of music and died, like my brother. My brother left our village to pursue his music and traveled to Baghdad and London. He became a musician in the emigrant circle and then a professor at a conservatory. When we fled our village and came here, I tried to complete his mission and bring his music to the people. I went to the conservatory to study and also to defend his music, but they chose what they believed was suitable for me: silence and clerical work. I hummed one of my brother's unappreciated tunes for the man. He said, "Nice," then fell silent. I knew that he was preoccupied, and I didn't want to torture him with the artistic legacy of my ill-fated family. We were not precisely under the cypress, but near it. It was shadowless. At the door, after I hummed and before I opened my handbag and took out the key, his kiss landed, as if it had dropped from the tree. It wasn't a fruit but a tune, which I carried between my lips. I kept my song in my heart, and went inside.

The Sudden Thud

The morning has no memory. The morning begins with a news bulletin of political events, crimes, and music. A small television speaks in one room, and a radio sings in another. Tony Blair quarrels with John Major. There is a lot of bloodshed in Bosnia. A madman makes music under Clinton's window. Yeltsin's eyebrows are ugly. Advertisements: Call this number and get a collection of compact disks and cassette tapes. Selections: classical music and Elvis Presley and the best of the sixties. You can return the merchandise if you don't like it.

Conchita, the Italian, doesn't like the classical music of the morning, and Natalie, the Frenchwoman, hates the melody channel. Conchita is afraid that her mistress will dismiss her because she arrives late to pick up the children in the morning. Natalie silences her. She wants quiet, because today she will take her examination for the first certificate in English. She limits me to one minute for washing my face and less than that for brushing my teeth. The dentist says three minutes, at the very least. He doesn't know that Maria, the Slovakian, occupies the bathroom for half an hour. She pretends to be in the shower while praying that the authorities will renew her residence permit. One bathroom is not enough for four female immigrants. The upper floor, with all its four rooms, is not enough. The landlady, a Kurd from Iran, lives on the floor below. She's a good woman, but moody. If she shows understanding today, I'll excuse myself for paying only part of the rent. My relatives, who are under siege, need the money more urgently than she does. The man I'm going to meet on my way to the conservatory will bring them the money, and also some medicine. Who is left among them? Our Kurdish landlady weeps sometimes, like me, but compulsively. The volume of the radio in her room is high this morning. On other mornings, she deprives us of hot water. "Don't be late back." "What do you think of this bridegroom?" "It's a safeguard for girls to get married." "Western women don't care if they become spinsters. They sleep with men and don't wait. Don't they confide in you?" Her loud voice rises like a stone above the pop music and acid jazz that Conchita is listening to, above my baggy pants, which I forgot to put in the dryer, above the sounds of our quarrel. "The telephone bill!" she yells. The toast is spoiled. Natalie has eaten the cheese. Maria is still in the bathroom. The train leaves in ten minutes. I need five minutes to run to the station, and three more minutes for my teeth, hair, and blouse. I'm not going to make it. The train has probably left, and I must wait another quarter of an hour. I'm late. The morning news bulletin is repeated. Our quarrel is repeated. The landlady's voice rings out again. There's a sudden thud against the ceiling of the glass porch. A roof shingle has fallen on it directly above my head. Where's the moon? Where's the tree? When I say "I," my thoughts wander, and I miss the train.

A Moment of Truth

Khayriya al-Saqqaf

❦❦❦❦❦

*T*hose were spring days . . .

Just like the days which had gone before. She wasn't very interested in measuring the time—the months, weeks, or days, the hours, minutes, or seconds.

She stood for a few moments, caught in the scheme of time, near a wall on which a huge clock was hanging.

It was a clock like those magnificent ones made in previous generations—old, wooden, with an air of authenticity and gravity, and matching the shadowy awesomeness of the house.

She looked at him. She thought for a long while why it was that she never tried to talk to him.

He was fifty years old. He sat on a swivel chair, wearing a flowing robe. His head was covered with a piece of cloth the color of which she couldn't make out, because it was faded with age; it was neither round nor oblong, of a hue tending toward black. His eyes looked out from behind a pair of thick glasses. He was holding a book between his hands.

She thought to herself: I go away and come back at night or in the daytime. A week passes, or a month, and I always find him sitting in the same position, with the same book between his hands, open at the same page. I remember growing up and seeing him just like that, as if he were one of the ornaments in the house; but while some of the ornaments have been changed or rearranged, and some have even been lost, he remains just as he was! And behind him the big round clock still hangs on the wall. It, too, has stopped at one particular point: it always says five minutes and twenty-five seconds to five!

She had come on one of those spring days. She sat down slowly beside him, and began to speak to him.

"Why do you regard time as motionless, whereas it constantly marches on and consumes your life?"

He didn't answer. He remained silent, mute.

"How is it that spring passes and summer comes, then autumn ends and winter begins, and one year goes by and is followed by another, while you continue to sit in the same place, in the same clothes and shoes, with the same glasses on, holding the same book?"

Again he didn't answer and remained silent.

"Has time stopped at five minutes and twenty-five seconds to five? Or perhaps you think of the world as nothing but a book between your hands, a book called 'Life Is a Moment'?"

She asked her questions without expecting any reply, then she got up to leave.

But for the first time ever, he cleared his throat and moved in his chair. It came as a shock to her, because he had never done this before. Testing his voice with one low cough and then another, as though he were trying it out for the first time after a long period of imprisonment and silence, he said:

"It seems to me that you haven't grasped the meaning of the passage of time. That's why I didn't answer your question before. *(You stupid girl. You'll understand as time goes on.)*

"I didn't bother to answer your second question because it isn't worth the trouble. *(You stupid girl. Perhaps you don't understand the eloquence of silence!)*

"As for your third question, the first part is beyond you, because you don't know the significance of the hour and its minutes and seconds; and the last part came to an end the very moment I spoke."

And he fell silent. He froze. His pulse stopped.

She shook him, screamed, slapped his face with the palms of her hands.

She stared at him, shocked. He didn't move.

She backed away, terrified.

She asked herself: "Could he have been a real man after all, a normal human being? What was it that he wanted to say and I didn't understand? Perhaps a man reaches a stage of contentment with his personal philosophy, then withers and dies. And when he reaches a stage of profound comprehension of it, perhaps he cannot realize his own value unless he attracts someone's attention and interest. At that point, does he perhaps not care if he lives or dies?"

She looked at the clock.

She was utterly distraught. She saw that the clock had moved forward one more second: it was now five minutes and twenty-six seconds to five.

She backed away, petrified, slapping her hands against the wall.

The Future

Daisy al-Amir

❧✲❀✲❧

*S*he paid for the dress hurriedly, not even sure whether it
fitted her, but aware that it was made of a thick material
suitable for spring or autumn. It was now midsummer, she
thought. Perhaps there really was an autumn or a spring coming, but
would she see it arrive? Would there be a spring or an autumn? Last
spring and autumn had not happened. Time had stood still, as it had
stood still during all four seasons of the year. Not so the fighting,
which never stood still, annihilating every minute, every whisper,
every emotion, every, every, every . . . She hid the dress quickly in
the bag. She didn't want to admit to herself that she was committing
a crime by buying a dress while the war of destruction assailed everything. Two whole years of weeks and months? No. No. She could no
longer concentrate. She could no longer calculate the number of
weeks that were in those many months, or the number of days, or
minutes, or seconds. She was like everyone else, waiting every moment for news, news that was not too distressing, or news that made
no mention of the massive destruction and the deep darkness.

She had bought the dress at the apartment next to hers. She
hadn't had to cross a single street or go down a single flight of stairs.
The woman who lived next door sold clothes.

The shops no longer opened for business. When she had contemplated buying a dress, she felt that tar would be thrown at her
and her house, the sort of hot burning tar that was thrown at the
houses of dishonorable women, so that every passerby on that road
would know that the house pelted with tar was inhabited by an im-
moral woman. Then her hair would be cut off and her house burned
down and . . . She touched her hair with one hand, and clutched the
bag that concealed the dress with the other.

The dress was for the autumn, and it was summer now. Those who had managed to stay alive were either imprisoned in their houses, or else heroes. They had been lucky—or were cowards—not to have been hit by a sniper's bullet or a rocket that had gone astray, accidentally or intentionally, or not to have been kidnapped at a roadblock, or slain in the cause of religion. What other ways of dying could she recall, old and new, common and rare, which people had known over centuries of human civilization?

How could she have bought a dress when minutes ago she was wondering how she could possibly get hold of bread for the next few days? If the days actually came, would the fuel she had be enough for lighting and cooking? Would there be a night when she didn't suffer hunger cramps? Had she really bought a dress, when there were hundreds and thousands of people with no roof to shelter them, and hundreds more longing for a mouthful of bread, and hundreds beyond that who were now corpses, flung about and consumed by death?

Lebanon was dying. Newspapers and news broadcasts the world over began with reports about the fighting in Lebanon. Everybody tried to diagnose the disease, and everybody knew what it was—but there was no remedy for the chronic ailment.

Wouldn't it have been better if she had saved some of this money rather than buying a dress? On the other hand, if she had kept the money in her bag or in her cabinet, or if she had hung the dress in the wardrobe, could she be certain of holding onto either of them? The whole place—property, money, people—was a target for plunder. So what difference did it make whether she bought a dress or saved the money, since everything could be looted? The dress that she had bought—where had the woman who sold it got hold of it? How did these dresses, displayed for sale, come into her possession? Were they purchased? And those who traded in dresses, did they buy them, import them, or make them themselves? There were constant reports of theft from warehouses and banks and firms and private houses.

Armed people were fighting for a national cause and dying willingly as martyrs; other armed people were fighting to steal. How could you tell one from the other? Who was stealing from whom? And who was protecting the possessions of those who were not armed? The fighters thought themselves entitled to steal and plunder. What did the armed faction in defense of the national cause do when they saw the other armed faction plundering and stealing? Was it not in the national cause *not* to let the country be plundered? Was it not in the national cause *not* to deprive individuals of their possessions as they were deprived of their souls?

The dress she had bought was paid for with money that she had earned by the sweat of her brow. So was the dress she was wearing, and there was no shame in it.

Other people . . . other people deserved to have hot burning tar thrown at them and their houses, so that every passerby would know that true shame must be put to the flame and made public. She ran her hand over the bag containing the dress, smoothing it out. It was no longer folded. She had the urge to tell someone that she had bought a dress from a vendor who didn't sell stolen goods, and that she had bought it with honestly earned money. She wanted to scream at the top of her voice, "I didn't steal! I didn't steal, and I never shall! And I'll wear the dress next spring or autumn!"

Next spring or autumn? She no longer waited for anything anymore. She didn't know what season it was. Why think of the seasons and wait for the next minute, when in an instant the end might come . . . the end . . . death.

If she had only one moment left, wouldn't it be enough to enjoy herself and vent her anger by buying a dress with honestly earned money from an honest garment seller? What did it matter whether she wore the dress or not? What mattered was that she had derived joy from buying it. Save the money for the future? Was there a future? Would she still be alive the next morning?

She wanted to feel that life was going on. She wanted to experience the desire to possess. She wanted to prepare for days to come. And so, suddenly, she felt she wanted to live, to prepare for the future, for the autumn or the spring, and have a new dress to wear. She didn't want to feel that she might die at any moment. Were these excuses to get rid of her feelings of guilt? Buying a new dress when people were dying from hunger, and the bombs and rockets were falling everywhere? Death was waiting for her at every corner, and she was clutching the dress, as if by clinging to it she was clinging to life.

Lebanon was dying and calling for help, while the whole world . . . the whole world, one way or another, was plunging a new knife into it, administering a new, deadly poison to it, and burying it more deeply. Political leaders the world over were plugging their ears with new wax, and reaching out to plunder. They sent provisions that never arrived, and delegations that made empty promises, sold the truth or concealed it, and told lies.

All this was happening in Lebanon, while she was busy buying a new dress for an autumn that she knew would never arrive?

The seller of the dress said that she was forced to trade at home because her husband and children had stopped working. In this way, she tried to make a living. Even the seller felt compelled to justify her garment business by her need for sustenance, whereas *she* had bought a dress for an autumn that would never come! Could the dress save her from hunger? Could it avert the sniper's bullet, or a rocket, or a bomb, or explosives? Could it abolish the darkness she was afraid of? Could it eliminate the fearful waiting in the autumn or the previous summer? She folded the bag so that its volume would not attract attention. She folded it again, reducing its size still further. Perhaps that would help her forget that she was carrying a dress in the bag, a dress just for her.

A car filled with fighters passed through the street. They shot into the air to frighten people, but she wasn't afraid.

She was accustomed to the bullets, explosives, rockets, and darkness, and at the same time she wasn't accustomed to any of them. She was still alive, in spite of all the dead, wounded, and mutilated people whom she saw and heard about, or whom she didn't see and hear about. But did she have the right to buy a new dress on the pretext that she was still alive? And would she be able to keep it? Would her house remain safe from looting? Would she be able to get to a doctor, or would the doctor be able to get to her, if she fell ill? If she were wounded? If she got hit? Would the armed people at the roadblock give her the chance to explain that she might die if she didn't get to the hospital? And the fighters? What did the word *death* mean to them, when they had experienced death every day, every hour, every minute for the past two years? What significance did the individual have—whether he or she remained alive or the death toll increased by tens or hundreds or thousands? When did the individual's life ever have significance in the eyes of the fighters who were exposed to death all the time?

But the fighters who were exposed to death had a barricade and weapons with which to defend themselves.

Weapons and fighters and commanders and leaders and presidents and parties and followers and organizations—they approached and avoided each other, supported and fought each other, cursed and praised each other, and she . . . she was one of thousands of individuals who didn't belong to any of these groups. How could she overcome her fear of the moment, of the hour, of the day, and of recent memories?

Would she see the next day arrive? Would a new dawn break? Would a new sun rise after the long dark night lit by rockets? And what about *her*? So she had bought a dress for the autumn. What kind of season was that which they called autumn? The seller of the dress had said that it was suitable for spring or autumn. Which of these seasons was nearer at hand? Which season's days would she experience as they really were, without having the world, and the house, and the sky shut off around her?

A bomb fell on the entrance to the building. She wasn't afraid. She didn't panic. She didn't run away. She stood motionless, observing the broken glass and listening to the cries of fear. Where did this courage come from? Was it from the future she was holding in a bag hidden under her arm? The residents of the building were hurrying to the shelter. She stood at the top of the staircase, watching them racing each other and screaming, with their little children in their arms. She couldn't tell whether the children or the adults were more frightened. Which of them would still be alive the next minute, and which was death waiting for? And she . . . she touched the dress. Her soul was profoundly sad, unable to find a justification for buying a new dress.

The bombs came thick and fast, piercing the walls and windows. She descended the dark staircase, holding onto the railing, and reached the shelter door. She didn't know what made her stand motionless there, instead of rushing inside with the others.

She touched the dress and felt reassured. And yet, who could explain to her at that moment why she had bought the new autumn dress? And if anyone asked her about it, how could she explain that she felt reassured holding her new spring dress?

Another bomb fell, followed by rockets. The screaming and crying intensified. She held tightly to the bag with the dress. The fighters came into the building, wearing combat clothes. They had long beards, and on their shoulders they carried a variety of weapons. One of them rushed toward her and shouted, "Get into the shelter! Can't you hear? Can't you see? Why are you standing there like a statue? The shelter's the only safe place!" He raised his Kalashnikov and shot into the air. The panic increased, and the sound of the screaming grew louder, but she remained motionless. The fighter became angrier. He approached her, yelling, "I told you to come down! Get into the shelter! What are you doing there? Start moving! What are you clutching so nervously? Give it to me and come down!" She held the bag with her autumn-spring dress more tightly and didn't reply. Terrified screams rang out again, and he yelled again and shot into the air. He looked at her furiously and advanced toward her. But then she shouted, "This is my future, my autumn, my spring. I'm hanging on to it, and what I'm most afraid of is that you'll take it away from me!"

The Gallows

Suhayr al-Tall

❦❦❦❦❦

Y ou have no choice: either you come out or you succumb to decay that will eat away your skin, which is floating in that black, sticky liquid.

You won't be able to resist those dreadful gunshots for long. Let your skin, which aches from the constant pressure, stretch out. Let it breathe something else.

Are you afraid of the darkness? You drift in it, and it dwells within you. But you're not the only man in the darkness. All those who preceded you, and whose screams reach you, resisted for a long time inside their shells, which are filled with a sticky liquid like yours. In the end, they came out.

You're coming out now. You're advancing. That dense, dreadful, dark mass will not frighten you. You're its little part that hasn't yet cleaved to it. You're approaching. Here you are now, cleaving to it, and vanishing in its crush.

The deafening noise is merely the echo of your screams. You're equal to them now, a little part of a huge, gelatinous mass, flowing in every direction.

Don't let the little details distract you. They are nothing but a reflection of who you were. Do you see a dim figure dressed in rags? That's you. Or a female figure with a prominent bosom like a cannon ball about to be launched? That's you, too. Haven't I told you not to look at the details around you?

You want to know your whereabouts? The place is indefinable now.

The gelatinous mass is flowing everywhere. It is divided and scattered about, but it will definitely meet at some point where it will be completely reunited. Then you'll know where you are.

Why do you trouble your little head with looking around you? No matter what the capacity of this head is, you won't be able to see more than the range of half a circle. You want to see what's behind you? You never can. Look ahead, straight ahead, for only what you actually behold with your own eyes is a certainty. As for what's behind you, it's nothing more than something behind you; it may or may not exist.

You are gazing at the large open space in front of you. Good. And you see the gelatinous mass accumulating around you. Good. You've certainly arrived. You're in the square now. The square? Yes. In every place where a mass like the one you're part of happens to be formed, there must be a square. Around this thing that is called a square, there is what I conventionally call a city. But the city is not an integrated whole. The square serves to divide one entity into two, a city into two cities. Each one is different from the other. You'll be persistent and inquire about other justifications for the existence of the square. Don't find it strange if I tell you that the square is the place where the two cities are united, where everything commingles. Never mind the feelings of loathing and hatred that some people have toward others. Never mind the amazement of some people at the reality of the existence of others. This is true, for every city has its own story, world, and dreams. You'll be amazed when you discover that the only thing that the two cities have in common is the desire to annihilate each other.

And the square?

That's the neutral zone, the only place possible for everything to merge together. All the emotions dissolve in it to become one desire upon which everyone has agreed. This desire is the devilish secret, the fire raging in the blood, the constantly erupting volcano, the insatiable thirst.

You are amazed? How amusing. Look deep down in your soul and you'll see. Face yourself. Do you see that blood-red fluid mingling with the darkness of your inner depths? It begins as a small stream, but it quickly turns into a raging torrent. Here it is, flowing as saliva at the corners of your mouth. Why? You'll know later.

Why does the silence surprise you?

It's the echo of your silence.

And the approaching noise? It's one of the forms of the devilish secret, which has started with the appearance of blood-red saliva at the corners of your mouth. The sounds of powerful blows will not frighten you. They are invisible and inaudible in the darkness. And now you are a part of the darkness spread around you.

Obscure figures are advancing now. They come near you, touch you, and then move away. You feel something weighing you down. Your feet have been shackled to all the other feet with a thick steel chain.

The blood-red saliva overflows, covering your face. It dulls your senses, transforming the pressure of the steel on your feet into a pleasant numbness that permeates the pores of your skin. You don't feel the splitting of the great mass, but you watch your other half from behind the resulting void in the square. Open your eyes wide, and you'll see, despite the blood-red saliva and the dark shadows, the reflection of your other half, fastened with that steel chain, at the edge of the square.

The obscure figures have faded into the distance. There is a special event for which preparations are in progress. The echoes of strange voices pierce through your saliva into your ears. But you don't turn your face because the fire in your blood begins to flare up. The shadow of your other half appears to you from within the tongues of the flame in the void. The rites of the devilish secret proceed toward the middle of the square. The noise grows louder. You advance farther. A huge edifice looms up ahead of you. The noise gets still louder. The tongues of the flame rise higher. Your blood-red saliva blurs your vision, propelling you toward the edifice in the middle of the square. You climb up to it, feeling a pleasant numbness. Numbly, you surrender your body. You don't know that what you've surrendered to is nothing but a big gallows. The noose, which will soon tighten around your neck, is a gigantic phallus.

Part Eight

The Winds of Change

The Breeze of Youth

Ulfat al-Idilbi

The grandmother saw her granddaughter arranging her hair in front of the mirror and said: "Where are you going? To the university or to a wedding? Since when do schoolgirls do their hair and put on makeup? Everything's so different nowadays. How much tighter are you going to make your clothes? Have you no fear of God? You, schoolgirls! Your troubles affect us all! God has kept the rain from us, so prices have gone up again, and He's inflicted locusts, and epidemics, and foreigners on us, and removed compassion from people's hearts. All of that because of you, and you haven't learned your lesson! But you're not the only one to blame. Your father's guilty as well. He doesn't listen to me; he doesn't put his foot down and make you behave. Yesterday's men and today's are worlds apart! When I was your age, my father once saw me making myself pretty in front of the mirror—and I was already a widow and the mother of a child. He took me by the hair, slapped me hard, and said to me in a tone so harsh I still remember it: 'Who are you making yourself pretty for, you wicked girl? I won't have daughters who spend hours in front of the mirror, understand?' Since that day, I've never had my hair done or put makeup on my face. God have mercy on him! He knew how to raise daughters. As for your father, he'll regret it when regret will be no use. Whoever said 'The worry over a daughter lasts from the cradle to the grave' was right."

But the girl, who was already eighteen, paid no attention to her grandmother's chatter. She continued, unhurriedly, to dress in front of the mirror. As soon as she had finished, she put her books under her arm and bounded down the stairs, three at a time, humming a popular song.

258

When she came out into the street, she saw a group of her classmates. She exchanged greetings with them, then joined the group, blending in. She walked with a spring in her step, the wind playing with the thick tresses of hair that hung down around her shoulders. Meanwhile her grandmother stood on the balcony and watched her from a distance, anger and envy simmering in her heart and burning in her eyes. She was contrasting her own life, lived under the burden of traditions and restrictions, with the free, unfettered life, enjoyed by the girls of the new generation. Suddenly she said to herself, "What are we compared with today's girls? What have we seen of this world? May God never forgive you, Father, and never be kind to you. You nipped my youth in the bud. You deprived me of everything, even the pleasures of reading and writing, which many of the girls of my generation enjoyed. My God, I don't understand. What benefit did you derive from all this?"

She pulled over a chair, sat down on it, and began to reflect. The sight of her granddaughter, of that ebullient youthfulness, stirred distant memories in her. The days of her childhood and youth came flooding back to her. Are memories of childhood and youth not like moist breezes that blow over a dead land, suddenly turning its dry stalks green and transforming its thorns into roses and lilies?

But for her, there was only one such moist breeze. As she sat there, the memory flashed through her mind, and suddenly she was fourteen again, wearing a white, shapeless robe, and such a thick veil over her face that she could hardly see through it. Escorted by her mother to buy new shoes, she was stumbling along the narrow alleys of Damascus. They arrived at the Hamadiyya bazaar and went into a shoe shop. A young salesclerk, who appeared to be the shop owner's son, received them and skillfully began to display his merchandise, enumerating its qualities. A pair of black patent shoes took her fancy.

She sat on a chair to try them on. The salesclerk knelt down in front of her to help her put them on; her mother, meanwhile, was busy selecting another pair for herself. Suddenly the salesclerk ran his hand over her leg, then held her foot between his hands and squeezed it a little. He whispered sweetly, "Praise be to the Creator! I have seen many things in this shop, but never before have I come across such tiny, delicate feet!"

His daring touch sent a shudder through her body. Excited and confused, she pulled her legs away from him and dropped the edge of her robe. He lifted his head and stared at her with a sweet, enticing smile. But how could he see anything through her thick black veil?

She, on the other hand, could see every bit of him: he had a round, dark-skinned face, thick black eyebrows, and shining eyes. It was as if their shine had bored through the veil and settled on her eyes. She had to lower them and mutter, "May God preserve him for his mother."

When she left, carrying her new shoes under her arm, he followed her with a look that devoured her completely. She began to walk proud and erect at her mother's side. Until that moment, she had been completely unaware that she possessed beauty capable of provoking the praises of the Creator.

Hardly had she moved away from the shop when a young man with features just like those of the salesclerk came toward her. Her hand stretched down spontaneously and lifted the edge of her robe, as if she were afraid it would get dirty from the filth on the street. Her shapely legs were revealed.

But the stupid young man didn't see what had been exposed for him! Instead, an ugly old man with a big nose and protruding eyeballs saw her legs. He screamed at her in a hoarse voice exactly like her father's: "Drop the edge of your robe, girl. May God damn all girls so that of every hundred only one will survive!"

She felt as if a bucket of hot water had been poured over her. She dropped the edge of her robe and walked, shrunken, behind her mother until they reached their home.

It was the twenty-seventh day of the month of Rajab.[1] In the interval between the sunset prayer and the evening prayer, her father sat in the middle of the large living room, and all the family gathered around him. In a humble voice he started to recite to them the story of the Mi'raj.[2] Before long, he got to the passage that says: "When the Prophet, peace be upon him, was in the Fifth Heaven, he asked to see Hell. Among the things he saw there were women hanging by their hair. He asked, 'O my brother Gabriel, what is the matter with those women who are hanging by their hair?' And the angel answered, 'Those women have shown their attractions to men.'"

At that moment, it seemed to her that her father was casting a penetrating glance in her direction. Her heart began to beat wildly when she remembered how the salesclerk had flirted with her, how she had behaved toward the young man, and how the old man had rebuked her. The image of the women hanging by their hair appeared in her mind, and she was seized by an overwhelming fear. In her heart, she repeatedly asked God for forgiveness. She performed the evening prayer, then retired early to think the matter over. She came to the conclusion that she had not intended to entice anyone at all. The salesclerk had praised the Creator for the beauty of His creation when he had seen her legs. Was it wrong, she wondered, for God's servants to praise the Almighty God, the maker of slender legs and tiny, delicate feet?

On this basis, which seemed quite logical to her, and in spite of her shapeless robe and thick black veil, she began to allow herself to resort to diverse tricks to show her charms whenever she walked past a dark-skinned young man with shining eyes.

Two weeks passed, and then one morning her mother surprised her with a question: "What's the matter with you? You look so somber and distracted. You spend so much time on your own, and you're eating and sleeping very little."

She became confused and made a flimsy excuse to her mother to divert her attention from what was going on inside her. Deep in her heart, she wished she could confide in her. But what could she possibly tell her? About the intense yearning for the dark-skinned face and the shining eyes? Or about the persistent desire for the daring touch and the sweet whispers? Oh, how she longed to see her admirer, the salesclerk, once more. The passion of love tormented her until she could bear it no longer. His handsome image appeared in her mind day and night, and his sweet whispers rang in her ears continuously. On some nights his apparition accompanied her until morning.

But there was no way to see him again, not before those damned shoes were worn out. She took the shoes and examined them closely. They were very strong; it could take a whole year to wear them out.

A whole year? What an eternity! She would never be able to endure it.

She thought a little, and suddenly her face lit up. She hurried back to her mother and said with an air of dismay, "Mother, my little brother took one of my new shoes to the park and threw it into the canal. The water swept it away!" She began to sob. The mother went to her wrongly accused son, who was too young to explain himself, and punished him. Then she returned to her grief-stricken daughter and stopped her tears by promising that they would go to the same shoe shop the next day. Perhaps the salesclerk would agree to make one new shoe; if not, they would buy a whole new pair.

When they were on their way to him, she was filled with great hopes and sweet dreams. She said to herself, "Last time, he praised God. But this time I will provoke him to say the words 'There is no god but God' and 'God is the greatest.'"

But when they entered the shop, he was not there; he had gone away on business, and his father had taken his place. For the first time in her life, she realized that she was ill-fated.

She was ill-fated, there was no doubt about it. On the evening of that very day, her father received from the ugly old man with the big nose and the protruding eyeballs a bag containing one hundred gold pounds: it was payment for his daughter's hand. The old man had been taken with her beauty when he had met her accidentally on the street and rebuked her for raising the edge of her robe. He had followed her to find out where she lived, and on that ill-starred night he had come to ask for her hand because he desired her. Her father welcomed him and gave him his word, but insisted that the old man should pay him the bride price before he left.

That day marked her last contact with love and the beloved!

These pictures from the remote past sprang up one after the other in the old woman's mind. When they had reached their sorry conclusion, her eyes filled with tears, and she heaved a deep and fervent sigh for her lost youth and long life, which now seemed drab and worthless to her. She choked with grief. She shook her head a number of times and looked into the distance with a wandering glance, as if she were reading the long book of her life. On the opposite balcony, she noticed the figure of an attractive young girl. She wiped her glasses, put them back on, and peered hard at the figure. "My goodness!" she said. "That's our neighbor, Umm Anton. I really thought she was a twenty-year-old girl! If it hadn't been for her purple shawl, I wouldn't have recognized her. Umm Anton is much older than I am, but she still wears makeup. All women do that except me! Why don't I try it—even just once?"

No sooner had the thought occurred to her than she hurried to her granddaughter's room and started fiddling with the little drawers that contained the granddaughter's cosmetics. She finally managed to open them, and what she saw dazzled her: jars and bottles of all shapes and sizes, objects made of thin, shining metal with ivory handles, and pretty lipsticks in various shades of red—some light, some dark, others with a yellowish or bluish tinge. There was also a scissor-handled instrument with an end like half a circle. She had once seen her granddaughter do her eyelashes with it and had mockingly said, "I hope you stab your eyeballs with it, and die for the sake of beauty."

No, that instrument was terribly dangerous. She couldn't and shouldn't use it. Nothing she inspected appealed to her, except a bottle with a sticky white liquid. She turned it upside down in her hand, saying to herself, "This must be the solution that the hairdresser applied to my face on my wedding night. It really has a magical effect." She smeared it on her face, looked in the mirror, and muttered, "By God, I'm much prettier than Umm Anton!"

After that she picked up a small bottle containing a shiny red liquid. She was taken with its shine. When she opened it, a sharp smell drifted to her nose, but she took some of the liquid from the bottle anyway and applied it to her cheeks and lips. Suddenly, an ugly face was staring at her from the mirror. Its ugliness startled her, and she began to back away, step by step. Oblivious to where she was putting her feet, she stumbled into a marble statue that her granddaughter had placed near the mirror, and fell to the floor. The statue fell on top of her, hitting her head, and she lost consciousness.

The following morning at the riding club, her eighteen-year-old granddaughter was puffing away on an expensive cigarette and saying to her friends, "I don't know what happened to my poor grandmother yesterday. When I left her in the morning, she was fine, giving me her usual lecture. But when I came back from the university, I discovered that she had gone into my room while I was away, which is unlike her, and had broken a statue—*Venus, the Twentieth Century*—which a friend had sculpted, using me as a model. It's a shame. It was a wonderful piece. She had fiddled with my drawers and left them all untidy. She had smeared her face with a whole bottle of expensive hair oil, and she had painted her cheeks with nail polish. Her face is so wrinkled that it was impossible to get it off. And all the time she was raving about a dark-skinned young man with thick eyebrows and shining eyes. Whenever she saw me, she uncovered her old legs and asked me, quite seriously, 'Have you ever seen anything more beautiful than these?' and 'Don't you think I'm prettier than Umm Anton?'"

One boy with a malicious sense of humor remarked, "Who

knows? Perhaps memories of your grandmother's youth came flooding back to her yesterday and affected her mind!"

   This prompted a peal of laughter from the girls and a guffaw
among the boys.

A Successful Woman

Suhayr al-Qalamawi

❦❦❦

lthough it was an extremely cold day, the hairdresser's salon was crowded with women. The sounds of their voices and movements mingled with the smell of dye, soap, and creams, creating a strange, suffocating atmosphere in the cramped space. The hairdryers, the number of which was multiplied by the mirrors on the walls, contributed to the crowding. Despite it all, Naima managed to come and go nimbly and tirelessly.

She had learned the skills of hairstyling by practicing in this salon, and had acquired numerous customers who insisted that no one but Naima should dress their hair. At first, she would constantly look at herself in the various mirrors. At times, she thought her gentle, dark-complexioned face beautiful, and at other times ordinary. But she always seemed contented, especially if she was working on a customer. When she finished dressing the hair, she felt proud of her accomplishment, as if her face were the signature that she affixed to this excellent piece of work. Gradually, she stopped seeing the signature; it sufficed to see what was under the signature—a head that was not particularly striking, but which, at any rate, demonstrated her creative talents.

Abbas, the son of the salon's owner, had liked and admired Naima. He had begun to regard her with sympathy as she, a somewhat naive village girl, strove not only to master her work but also to excel at it. This sympathy eventually turned to love, which was obvious to anyone who worked in, or frequented, the salon.

On this day Naima was busy dressing the hair of a fat, blonde, blue-eyed woman with an impudent voice. The woman was all dressed up and wore an expensive diamond ring that she deliberately flashed in front of everyone in the salon. She laughed with affected gaiety as

265

she foolishly tried to instruct Naima how to arrange a lock of hair hanging loosely over her wide forehead.

Naima had learned that artistic beauty was one thing, and individual taste another. Her skill in reconciling such discrepancies was the secret of her success. But this young woman, the corpulent Miss Buthayna, could not be pleased at all. The reason for this problem was obvious to everyone: Abbas had begun to look attentively at Miss Buthayna, and she encouraged him in a shameless and outrageous manner.

Abbas thought that Buthayna was not ugly, although she was not pretty; that she was not boorish, although she was not refined; and that she was not queer, although she was not natural. He made inquiries about her and learned that she was the daughter of a merchant from the province of Sharqiyya[3] who worked in the vegetable market. He was extremely wealthy, because he had supplied the provisions to the army during the war. Buthayna was his daughter by his first wife. He had married another woman of about the same age as Buthayna, after God had made him rich, and after his wife of old, hard times no longer knew how to conduct herself in the grand mansion and the fancy car. Life became unbearable between his daughter and his young wife. The men who came to ask for Buthayna's hand didn't measure up to his new social status; they were after her money. For some reason unknown to the father, no acceptable suitor, such as a government employee, presented himself. More importantly, the father had no time to look into this matter.

Therefore, he contented himself with giving his daughter the gifts of a diamond ring, a private car, and a bank account of several thousand pounds for her trousseau. He then busied himself with settling disputes, enjoying the maladies of affluence, going to doctors, and attending as many parties as possible.

When Abbas's attention toward Buthayna, although merely superficial, increased, she thought it could develop into love. She encouraged it, and eventually she achieved her goal. Naima was a major obstacle in the beginning, so Buthayna often picked a quarrel with her to get Abbas to interfere and be obliged to humiliate Naima out of respect for the customer. Whenever she humiliated Naima and won her own conciliation, she felt joyful and triumphant.

On this day Naima tried her utmost to avoid this situation, despite the fact that she had dressed the hair of numerous customers, for it was Thursday, and it so happened that there were three wedding celebrations. But Buthayna was determined to force a confrontation. Abbas said, "We are at your service, Miss Buthayna. This hairstyle is absolutely perfect for you, and it's the latest fashion." But Buthayna retorted, "Look how this lock of hair covers my eye!" Abbas repeated, "It doesn't matter. That's the style, and there's no face it suits better than yours." Then he began to fix her hair and called Naima to assist him, but this time she retreated to the back, suppressed her anger, and refused to lift a finger.

The noise faded away, and laughter rang out. Naima stood defeated and miserable, looking at Abbas, who barely turned his face toward her. She glanced at the other women, and sensed their mocking smiles, but even these failed to comfort her.

That was the last contact Naima had with Abbas's salon. She told him frankly that evening that he had abandoned her in order to marry a rich woman who would help him with his business. She also said that she would never again dress Buthayna's hair, nor anyone else's in his salon. Abbas was indifferent, although he made kind remarks.

That night, Naima cringed like a frightened kitten on her grandmother's chest. She was her only relative in Cairo since the day she had left the village, longing to escape from the tyranny of her uncle after her parents' death. She wept bitterly, telling her grandmother, between tears and sighs, everything that had happened. Her grandmother held back the tears, both hers and those of her granddaughter, who was the only kin she had left in the world now that her daughter, her only child, had passed away.

"Enough, my little girl," the grandmother said. "If only you had married the son of your paternal uncle and had lived among your relatives, instead of all this worry and toil. How strange! I lived with your mother for almost a year, and I hated the village just as you did after you had grown up. My God, how strange!"

Naima showered her grandmother with kisses and slept like a calm child in her embrace. Two days later, she surprised her when she said, "Let's go to the village."

Despite her surprise, the grandmother wanted nothing more. When she inquired about the reason for this sudden decision, Naima replied briefly, "You are right, Grandmother. Women like us are better off living within our means, and a little will suffice. Whatever the family decides is better than being humiliated by a stranger."

Throughout the train journey, Naima thought about village life—peaceful, simple, and respectable. It was the kind of life that her relatives had wanted for her when they had suggested that she marry her uncle's son. But she was not in love with him, and she had rejected a life that would place her at anyone's mercy. She wanted to live by the sweat of her brow and on her own money, rather than the money that someone else would be gracious enough to give her. She wanted her independence, and the freedom to express her individuality. She also wanted a husband of her own choosing. And here she was now; she had entered the workplace and suddenly all the arrows had been directed at her, and she was unable to defend herself before Abbas. He had raised her hopes and made her believe that he loved her. Then he had sold her off like a slave. But she would not be defeated. She would live happily in the village.

The beauties of nature met her eyes and set her mind at rest. She entered her uncle's house, in which she was raised, and was surprised to see that it was completely different from what she had imagined. A few days later, she discovered that the rampant neglect around the house left everything bordering on chaos and dirt, that the relatives' conversation was utter nonsense quickly arousing anger or ennui, and that their way of thinking was incomprehensible and unbearable. Their only saving grace was that they were good-hearted and well-intentioned. Her cousin had married a girl who had rapidly become a fat, bloated woman. Within five years, she had borne him three girls whose little faces were nearly covered with flies, and whose dirty bodies were fertile ground for germs and open invitations to disease.

At night, life became intolerable. She heard coarse and offensive remarks about trivial matters, and when she went to bed, she was disgusted by the casual attitude toward bedbugs. She did not sleep a wink, and was ridiculed if she complained.

As it happened, she could not bear this existence and urged her grandmother to leave. The grandmother, after years of living in Cairo, did not need urging. She, too, felt disappointed. Naima reasoned that the room they had in the city was small but clean, the work exhausting but pleasant, and though Abbas had let her down, she could find another man. Anyway, why should marriage be her goal? She could work at another hairdresser's salon and contact her customers, and they would follow her wherever she went. She would never go hungry.

One salon's owner welcomed Naima, and then another one, and before long she had again established herself. A few years later, she used her savings to buy a hairdressing salon from a Greek who returned to his own country. Today she owned a salon, just like Abbas, only it was more successful than his, although Buthayna, whom he had married, had spent all the money that her father had given her for her trousseau in decorating Abbas's salon. But why make comparisons? She was not comparing anything, for she no longer cared. Now she was busy putting aside money because she had realized that she would not continue to be successful all her life. Since she had no husband or children to support her in her old age, the thought of saving for her retirement was uppermost in her mind, and she no longer paid attention to anything else.

The years passed. One day she ran into Abbas. He was astonished to see the change that had come over her features: her naive, calm, and contented face had transformed into the hard, greedy face of a businesswoman. Where was the girl whose heart would rejoice at a glance from Abbas's eyes, and whose dreams would be filled with happiness and love at receiving a small gift from him? They observed each other closely. How much he had changed too! Where was the old touch of chivalry in his demeanor? How could his proud expression have become so meek? Was this Abbas or merely a distorted image?

Their meeting unsettled Naima for a few moments. Was she still in love with the Abbas she had known? Was there time to think about such matters? The clock in the square struck eight, and she had to collect the day's earnings from the salon's cashier.

Naima hurried to catch up with the cashier before he left the salon. Her only lingering thought was that she had merely five thousand pounds left to pay off the loan on the building that she had purchased.

In Need of Reassurance

Radwa Ashour

❧❀❦

*T*he door opened slowly, and Amm Abd al-Qadir appeared, asking for permission to enter. When Dr. Qasim nodded, he entered, followed by a man unknown to me. Amm Abd al-Qadir was the policeman charged with guarding the small entrance to the college. He could be seen all day sitting on a wicker chair, his jacket fastened by a leather strap fitted diagonally across his chest, twisted around his right shoulder, and connected to a wide belt with a metal buckle. His cloak, whether of white cotton during the summer or of black wool during the winter, was old and worn. It hardly reflected the air of authority, power, and fear associated with a policeman. Moreover, his kind small eyes, friendly features, and thick, white mustache imparted noticeable gentleness to him.

"This man is the grandfather of a female student in your department. He asked me to put him in touch with one of the professors," Amm Abd al-Qadir explained.

As he turned to leave the office, he said to the man, "Rest assured. They will help you." Then he greeted us and departed.

The guest extended his big hand to Dr. Qasim, who was sitting behind his desk, and said, "I'm Fahmi Abd al-Sattar, the father of a martyr, and my granddaughter, Nadya Ahmad Fahmi Abd al-Sattar, is a student here. Do you know her?"

Dr. Qasim asked him to sit down and wait until he had completed some paperwork and was ready to listen to him.

The man sat beside me. I, too, was waiting for Dr. Qasim to finish his paperwork so that I could get his comments about the portion of my master's thesis that he had read.

The man looked old, despite his stout body. He had a round face and dark complexion, that coffee-brown color peculiar to the people of Upper Egypt. He wore an old suit and held a coarse cane in his hand.

Dr. Qasim raised his head. "Yes, what can I do for you?"

"I'm Fahmi Abd al-Sattar, the father of a martyr, and my grand-daughter, Nadya Ahmad Fahmi Abd al-Sattar, is a student here," the man repeated himself.

"In what year?"

"In the first year."

"I don't teach first-year students, but I'm the head of the department. What's the problem?"

The man smiled in embarrassment. "No, praise be to God, there is no problem. I just want to be reassured. Does the girl attend classes? Is she industrious? Does she behave well? I need to know!"

Dr. Qasim grinned and said in a tone that sounded ironic only to those who knew him well: "You'll know at the end of the year, when the results of the examinations are announced!"

But the man repeated without smiling this time: "I need reassurance *now*. True, I've brought her up properly and spared no effort, but . . . Did I tell you that she's the daughter of a martyr? When her father died in battle, her mother was pregnant with her. My granddaughter, Nadya Ahmad Fahmi Abd al-Sattar, who is a student in your department, was born in November 1967, and her mother, may she be honored by God, never remarried, although she was seventeen years old at the time. Did I tell you that she's working now in the United Arab Emirates?"

Dr. Qasim began flipping through the papers on his desk. He had started to lose interest in what the man was saying and stopped listening to him.

"I'm from Upper Egypt. I said to Nadya, 'Knowledge is light, but morals come before knowledge, and modesty is an ornament. Talk with your male colleagues, that's all right, but respect the prescribed rules of social conduct. Don't raise your eyes to any male colleague. Keep your eyes lowered, for seeing is temptation, daughter, and be—' "

"What exactly do you want from me?" Dr. Qasim interrupted him.

"I told you, sir. I want one thing only. I want to be reassured about my granddaughter!"

"How?"

Dr. Qasim spoke sharply and impatiently, and I feared that if the meeting continued, it would end with the man's expulsion from the office. I was picturing to myself this unfortunate scene when three students knocked on the door and entered, carrying a poster that they wanted to show Dr. Qasim. He read it and laughed, then turned to me.

"Camellia, listen to this attractive advertisement for the trip to Port Said:

> The free city opens its arms to you.
> Port Said is a sea of commodities.
> Come with us to swim and shop!"[4]

Dr. Qasim continued to laugh as he signed the advertisement and returned it to the three students, one of whom asked me whether I was going on the trip. I said that I hadn't yet decided.

No sooner had the students left than the man began speaking again. For a moment, it seemed that Dr. Qasim was surprised by his presence, and that he had completely forgotten that he was sitting in the office.

"I mean, for example, if you could give me the class schedule and the lecturers' names, sir, I would be able to—"

"The schedule is posted in the hall. It shows the class times and the lecturers' names."

I volunteered to show the man where the schedule was posted. He followed me, and I took him there. I left him to copy his granddaughter's class list, and stood chatting with some fourth-year students. When he had finished, he came over to me and stood a few steps away so that I could finish my conversation. I noticed that and asked him whether he wanted something else.

"In the schedule, first-year students don't have classes on Wednesday, but Nadya goes to the university every Wednesday," he said.

"In which group is Nadya?"

"In your department."

"I know she's in our department, but I'm asking if she's in 1-A, 1-B, 1-C, or D, E, or F? The first year is divided into six groups. In which group is Nadya?"

"I don't know."

"How did you copy her schedule? There are six different schedules for first-year students."

He hesitated a moment before replying. Leaning toward me, he said in a low voice, "Forgive me, I'm in my seventies and I didn't notice that. In any case, I'll copy all six schedules, and later I'll ask Nadya which group she's in."

He paused, then continued in a whisper, "I'm seventy-seven years old, and my wife, Nadya's grandmother, is seventy. Nadya's father was killed in battle before she was born. Nadya's mother went to work in a foreign country so that she could give her daughter a respectable life. This is a great responsibility, and I don't want to spare any effort."

I was about to utter some casual words to reassure him before leaving, when I saw a tall, dark-skinned girl approaching us with a bright and somewhat astonished smile.

"Hello, Grandfather. What brought you here?"

Nadya had a friendly face and a slightly childish air, which was reflected in her simple clothing and long black hair, tied in a ponytail with a thin, blue ribbon.

"Nadya, which group are you in?" the grandfather asked.

"1-C, Grandfather. Why?"

"I came to copy your schedule so I will feel reassured by knowing when you have classes. But I discovered that the first year is divided into many groups."

The girl's face registered sudden seriousness, which gradually turned to a frown. I saw tears in her eyes as she protested, "But Grandfather—"

"But what?" he interrupted her. "I want to know everything so that I can protect you and take care of you properly."

The girl bit her lower lip and remained silent for a moment.

"Excuse me, Grandfather. I have a lecture," she said abruptly.

She walked a few steps away, then turned toward us and added, "By the way, Grandfather, there's a trip to Port Said, and I want to go."

"To Port Said?"

"Yes."

"No, Nadya. There's no need for trips. No need."

"But Grandfather, I want to go! I *will* go!"

Then the girl left us. The grandfather leaned toward me and asked in the same low voice, "Are you going on the trip?"

"I don't know, but rest assured that even if I don't go, several female teaching assistants, colleagues of mine, and several professors will go."

"As long as she's not under my supervision I need to be reassured. However, a trip to Port Said would give Nadya an opportunity to get to know her country, and also . . ."

His voice dropped to a whisper, as if he were talking to himself, "Yes, she'll get to know her country and also see some of the land where her father fought and for which he died in battle."

I left him and returned to Dr. Qasim's office to listen to his comments about my thesis.

When I left the college two hours later, the old man was sitting on a wicker chair next to Amm Abd al-Qadir, and the two of them were chatting together.

"I thought I should wait for Nadya until she finishes her classes so we can go home together. We live far from here and it's a long journey," he explained to me.

I left the college, thinking about the trip to Port Said. I finally decided to go. I said to myself, "It's an opportunity to rest as well as to buy shampoo and nylon stockings."

Short and Sassy
Nafila Dhahab

❦❦❦

She walks with a spring in her step as she roams freely in the streets. Everyone around her delights in staring at her dress, which does not cover her knees. Curious eyes devour her naked legs and gape at her hair, which is short, too. She smiles, remembering the words that her mother used to say to her whenever she combed her hair: "A woman's beauty lies in her hair." Her mother acknowledges that the hair attracts men but disapproves of her short dress sometimes. What's the difference? she wonders.

She recalls how one hot day she went to the hairdresser and asked him to cut the tresses that attract men. She saw him run his fingers through her long flowing hair and bite his lip in regret.

"Why do you want to have your hair cut? It's beautiful—"

"Do as I say. Cut!"

He reluctantly obeyed the order. She grinned when she saw the scissors open slowly and nibble at her silky locks. The hair fluttered in the air like soft feathers and fell to the floor soundlessly.

The passersby around her hurry along, their feet barely touching the ground. Good heavens, what's the matter with them? she wonders. An old man comes toward her, exclaiming as he passes her, "That's the end of the world. We can no longer distinguish between a man and a woman." Is there a difference? she thinks to herself. The difference is only in the eye of the beholder.

People crowd at the bus stop and the taxi stand. They cannot afford to be one moment late. Time is short! The restaurants are packed with people who have numerous requests. They want to enjoy everything. They want to have cars to drive to work so that no time is wasted. They prefer to eat in restaurants because they don't have time to go home and wait for the meal. Everything tempts them, especially beauty, wine, love, and erotic passion.

They want to savor all the delights of this world. Life is beyond their control; it is in the hands of Fate, which does whatever it wishes with them.

When she saw Uncle Ali bringing two chickens to slaughter for the feast day, she was astonished.

"Why did you buy two chickens when you have no children?" she asked.

Stroking the chickens' feathers, he said with a smile, "Have I got another life to live? Life is short, and I want to eat until I have my fill."

"Yes Uncle Ali. Life is short. Enjoy your chickens!"

Money tempts them. Captivating sights make them lose all self-possession. They crave everything because life is short.

They constantly seek pleasure. Whenever they come close to attaining their hearts' desires, they ask for more. But when they are defeated, they are overcome by despair. Eventually they resign to their lot and say, "Praise be to God that life is short."

Time is short, but the glances linger for a long while on the short dress! There is never enough time for work and sleep, but plenty of time for staring at a short dress . . .

The Collapse of Barriers

Samiya At'ut

❧❀❧

*T*he minutes passed slowly. I took a cigarette from my shirt pocket and lit it. I continued to look at her, smiling.

"Please extinguish the cigarette. The oxygen may not be sufficient for us," she said.

"Are you so afraid?" I asked.

She raised her eyebrows and stared at me in amazement.

"Aren't you afraid?"

"I have nothing to worry about except my life, and it torments me that I'm going to lose it near such beauty."

"You're insolent!" she retorted and turned her pallid face away. She was trembling. I smiled inwardly.

I began to enjoy the situation. I was undoubtedly a wicked man—I was happy with what was happening. However, for the sake of the beautiful hair falling down in a cascade over her shoulders, I extinguished the cigarette.

"Are you pleased now?"

She didn't reply and remained silent for a few moments. She took a handkerchief out of her handbag and wiped the sweat on her forehead.

"When will they come? I'm beginning to suffocate. Push the bell button once more. Try again, please."

"Okay, though I've done it numerous times since the elevator got stuck. I even banged on the door with my hand. It's no use."

"Is this my end? I had a premonition this morning that my day was ill-fated. I expected to meet my death under different circumstances—an earthquake, a car accident. I never thought that I would suffocate while I'm completely aware of my approaching end."

"Are you sad?"

"Should I be happy?" she replied in a sad voice tinged with irony.

"I think you should count your blessings."

"Why?"

"Because you're young, beautiful, and seem to be prosperous."

"Are you satisfied with your life?"

"From the day I was born, I haven't enjoyed a day like today."

"You're a complicated man, maybe even crazy."

"No, rather realistic. My dream was to speak with a girl twice your age and half your beauty. Now something even better has happened to me."

"You frighten me with such talk. You're admitting that we're going to die. I don't want to die!"

A silence followed.

"Do you have a family?" she asked.

"Yes."

"Do you work here?"

"I'm the elevator operator. Didn't you notice my clothes? But what about you? What brought you here?"

"I wanted to sign up for a trip to Europe for the upcoming holidays because I'm exhausted."

"Ah . . . ah . . ."

"Are you making fun of me?"

"No, but the situation . . . I'm beginning to feel shortness of breath," I grumbled.

"And I'm almost suffocating . . ."

She let the handbag drop onto the floor and leaned against one of the walls. I looked at the reflection of her pale face and sweaty forehead in the mirror. She broke into tears.

I tried to allay her fear. I reached out and stroked her shoulder. I touched her face with such excitement that for a moment I thought that the flow of blood in my fingers would leave marks on her cheeks. The silence had a stronger presence between us.

I almost wept. From fear for her? For myself? I didn't know. I pulled myself together, with effort, and asked her, "What's your name?"

"Hanan."[5]

"It's as if the tenderness of the whole world is reflected in your eyes."

"And the emptiness of the whole world is reflected in your eyes!"

No sooner had she said this than the elevator began to move.

She shrieked with joy, jumped like a child, laughed like a woman. She was beside herself with happiness. Meanwhile I was groping for words to express my desire to see her again. When she noticed that I was silent and gloomy, she calmed down. Looking at herself closely in the mirror, she fixed her hair and straightened her clothes. Then she picked up her handbag and said, "The fifth floor, please. Hurry up!"

She spoke tersely. Her tone was that of a master.

The Beginning

Salwa Bakr

❦❦❦

*T*he chiming of the clock interrupted the moanings of the songstress, whose voice rang out from the radio as she crooned, "My love. Oh, honey."

As the clock chimed, she opened the jar of apricot jam, after she had managed to find the can opener. Her husband had left it in the study two days earlier, after opening a can of imported cherries. She muttered to herself, "My goodness, it's already one o'clock!"

She then hurriedly removed the cake from the oven, so it would cool, and began to wash the remaining bowls and dishes in the sink. While doing so, she remembered that she had forgotten to add salt to the vegetables, which were still in the oven. So she stopped washing the dishes, dried her hands, and took out the pan quickly to salt the vegetables. The hot pan burned her hand because she didn't wear the oven mitt. She ignored the stinging redness that appeared on her palm. She was thinking of the necessity of scrubbing the bathroom sink, once she had finished cooking. She put the pan of vegetables back in the oven and ran to the living room to dust the plastic flowers in the vase. She had started to brush them with a feather duster when one of them fell out. When she bent down to pick it up, she felt as if her body was about to split in two from severe pain and exhaustion. Her attention was drawn to the voice of the songstress, who had come to the point in her song where she wished she were with her beloved in the happy nest of matrimony. She ran angrily to the radio to turn it off, and thought of throwing herself onto the Asyut-style chair beside it. But then she said to herself, "Finish everything first, because if you're overcome by fatigue when you sit down, you won't be able to get up again." Her resolve seemed to infuse new energy into her

280

exhausted muscles. She began to rub her hands with the water pouring out of the faucet as she filled the bucket for mopping the floor. No sooner had she started mopping the floor than she heard the squeaking of the apartment front door, and her husband's approaching footsteps. She turned around, formed an appropriate smile on her face, which was framed by her long, loose hair, and greeted him affectionately.

He took off his eyeglasses with one hand, raised the forefinger of the other, which was coated with a fine layer of dust, and said disapprovingly, "The television screen is all dusty!"

He then went into the kitchen and lifted the covers of all the food bowls. She told him that she was almost finished with the cooking. He observed her closely as she tried to fasten her hair with a big clasp, while the smell of cooked food wafted around her. The image of a fourth-year female student flashed into his mind, wearing a light blue dress and a perfume that announced her arrival before her footsteps. She had come to ask him, "Is it true that you deleted chapter four, Professor?" Her words sounded musical to him, just like her footsteps, as she walked off and the clicking of her stiletto heels against the floor resounded in his ears: *tik . . . tok . . . sol . . . mi . . . tik . . . tok . . .*

He couldn't bear the pungent odor of spices rising from the cooked food and hastened to leave the kitchen. She followed him into the bedroom, recounting the pains that she had taken with her superior at work until he had given her permission to leave two hours earlier than the official time. She had gone home quickly to prepare everything, after she had done the shopping at the market. Raising her arm in the air and moving it about several times, she declared, "I carried almost ten kilograms on my way home. My shoulder felt like it was going to fall off!"

He gazed at her and noticed again that she was rather short in stature. Instead of paying attention to her account about doing her utmost so that her cooking would come out well and she would make him proud in front of the head of his department, a voice rose from within him and rang in his ears: *tik . . . tok . . . sol . . . mi . . . tik . . . tok . . .* So he replied indifferently, "Clever woman. Good work. Now prepare my clothes, because I need to take a bath quickly before the guest arrives."

"A bath?" she exclaimed disapprovingly, then added, "No. I want to take a bath first, because my hair takes longer to dry."

She also felt angry, because she needed a bath first not only to give her hair time to dry but also to relax her exhausted body and get rid of the cooking odors. Since six o'clock in the morning, she had not rested at all. She had waited for the bus and squeezed herself onto it amid the usual rush to get to work on time. From work she had gone directly to the market, only to return to the kitchen with her heavy load. And now it was already one o'clock and she had not yet finished her housework. She wanted to rest her feet, which were swollen from standing so long, and close her eyes for a while. But she kept staring blankly at the floor as the image of her old friend, whom she had accidentally met on the street a few days earlier, appeared in her mind. In her slender figure and white pants, she looked like a twenty-year-old girl, although she was exactly her age, well past thirty. The friend kept laughing, that delightful laugh coming from a tranquil mind, as she stood staring at her.

"You, Muna, need to go on a hunger strike for a year, so that your body will again be slim and attractive, and you will look as you did in the good old days!" she said to her teasingly.

At that moment she felt sad about the good old days, when she had been the prettiest and slimmest girl in the neighborhood where she lived with her family. But after her marriage and the hellish whirlwind of married life, her body had thickened into the shape of a huge perch. Although she was annoyed by her friend's words, because they were true, she didn't let it show, and said proudly that her husband had obtained his doctorate and had become a professor at the university. But her friend paid no attention to that. Instead, she began to talk about her beautiful daughter, the small apartment she had purchased with difficulty but always strove to decorate, and her desire to pursue higher education again.

Her musings were interrupted by her husband's angry voice.

"Hey, you forgot to iron my gray shirt, and I want to wear it for lunch!" he yelled.

"Oh, I really forgot to iron it in the crush of work. Iron it yourself while I take my bath."

He exploded with anger. He cursed her, and accused her of being neglectful and stupid. She flew into a rage and accused him of being insensitive and inconsiderate. Then she lost her self-control and added, "My God, you have no shame!"

As usual, he jumped from his place and attacked her, slapping her hard across the face. She felt a blow on the head, and then her friend's derisive words about the necessity of going on a year-long hunger strike resounded in her ears.

She didn't burst into tears as she had always done when this happened. She didn't withdraw to a corner of the apartment to weep bitterly, until her eyes swelled, for him to come later to pat her on the back and stroke her hair and say, "I'm sorry." Then he would embrace her and pledge his love for her, and the incident would end in a reconciliation, with him on top of her. After that, he would invite her along with her brother and his wife to the cinema or to a restaurant on the Nile, where she would chat with her brother's wife about fabrics and shoes, while he and her brother chatted about soccer, imports, and exports. At the same time, their insolent male eyes would follow every passing woman, undressing her completely and examining her from head to foot, including the most intimate parts of her body . . .

No, she didn't behave as she had always done, for she was fed up and exhausted. Things had come to a head. The image of her friend in her white pants, tightly drawn over her slender body, was dancing in her mind like an unruly mare, and the rhythm of her revealing words was playing a derisive tune in her ears. The tune continued to resonate, madly repeating itself over and over again. Then she heard a loud bang. The blow didn't strike her ears, but rather her husband's head, which she had hit with the marble statue of Aphrodite that stood on her dressing table. The statue was the closest thing that she could lay her hands on.

The beautiful Aphrodite fell to the floor, her arms, head, and body smashed. The blow drove her husband mad, and he attacked her like a wounded animal. He pulled her by the hair violently, pinned her to the floor, and punched her in the back with his thick fist. She gathered her strength, recalling five years of marital repression, and inserted her nails into his thigh, furiously cursing him and his forefathers. He moved away a little, bracing himself against the pain, and then continued to beat her. He reached out to grab her neck, but like a wounded lioness, she anticipated him with a punch on his bulbous nose. The punch was hard enough to cause a nosebleed. He gasped at the salty taste of blood running down his lips, and collapsed in tears on top of the statue of Aphrodite.

She was astonished to see him like that. It was the first time she had ever seen him crying. She never thought it possible for him to cry. Her rebellion subsided. She felt disgusted, and had an urge to vomit. In this posture, he looked just as he did during their love-making. Her hatred toward him surged when she recalled that as soon as he had had his fill of her, he would turn his back to her, light a cigarette, and puff on it with delight. Then he would roll over on his stomach to sleep, and begin to snore loudly.

Her friend's voice and derisive words resounded again in her ears. She gazed at her wedding picture, which was hanging on the wall above the bed. Her eyes swept over the heavy, dark-colored furniture, which her father, mother, and eldest sister had chosen. She felt that the pieces of furniture were becoming heavier and darker, causing a tightness in her chest that impaired her ability to move.

She ran out of the bedroom, removed her light slippers, and took her shoes out of the hallway closet. She loosened her hair from the clasp, and walked calmly toward the apartment front door. She opened it, went out, and slammed it shut behind her. His voice mingled with the chiming of the clock, which announced the end of another hour.

A Moment of Contemplation

Nuzha Bin Sulayman

*T*he seashore was almost empty, except for a few workers charged with maintaining cleanliness and safety. The sun was about to set after casting a golden glow over the surface of the vast sea. I sat down on one of the rocks. They were scattered in the sand, witnesses to the lives of generation upon generation of human beings. Perhaps these rocks had known many people before me who had come here with their hopes and sorrows after wearying of the hustle and bustle of city life and its daily problems.

I was absorbed in watching the waves, which had calmed after a stormy day, and in reflecting on the universe and the greatness of the Creator. I was almost lost in contemplation, which seemed an infinite realm to me, by posing question after question, most of which couldn't be answered. It was only a loud quarrel between two male workers cleaning the seashore that brought me out of my private world.

After a while, I realized that the two people were neither cleaners, as I had assumed, nor were they both men. Rather, they were a man and a woman from among those who frequented the seashore, and what went on between them was not a quarrel, as I had thought, but a passionate embrace accompanied by shrieks of joy. Perhaps I had projected my personal feelings onto them. I was upset, and so I imagined everyone around me to be in a similar state of mind.

The man and the woman began to advance slowly toward me. In the pale light of the late afternoon, they first looked like two ghosts; it was difficult to discern their figures from a distance. When they drew closer, I saw a couple in their youthful prime, dressed simply in sporty clothes. They were walking hand in hand on the golden sand, which they probably loved as much as I did. Some of the expressions of blame that they exchanged in the course of their conversation were audible.

"It's your fault!"

"No. You're responsible for everything that has happened."

"Many years were lost. To hell with the years!"

"What matters now is that we're back together. Let's start over."

Their shouts rang out again, expressing joy, and they began to run like children in ecstacy. I was taken by surprise when they addressed me.

"Good evening, madam. Please share our joy. I'm Sa'id and she's Latifa. We've been in love for seven years. Tomorrow morning we're going to the office of the marriage official, and our happiness will be complete."

"Congratulations, Sa'id. Congratulations, Sa'ida."

"No. My name is Latifa."

"Yes, I know. But I hope that you'll be *sa'ida*,[6] too."

She laughed, and they continued to run toward the pier, where Sa'id had parked his motorcycle. They rode away and soon vanished from sight in the direction of the city.

A cool ocean breeze brushed my face after this brief encounter had brought me back to reality. I wondered why I was here at the seashore, crouching motionless like the deaf rocks, and why precisely at this hour, for it was unusual for me to be out so late.

I then remembered that a minor marital dispute, which occurred a few hours, rather than years, earlier, had sparked my rebellion and brought me to this place. I considered the seashore to be a just judge: I would tell him my story, and he would stand on the side of the oppressed and treat me fairly. I thought the matter over and almost laughed at its triviality. It seemed to me unworthy of all this fuss and nervous tension. I whispered softly to myself, "Perhaps it was all my fault, or at the very least I was partly to blame."

Perhaps the pressure of juggling a job and a family had made me edgy. I didn't give myself or my husband a chance to understand or look logically at what had happened, and see that such an ordinary and simple problem did not justify this overreaction.

I said to myself, "Regardless of whether I was wrong or both of us were wrong, what good are the principles we've learned from our culture, customs, and traditions if we are unable to show patience and tolerance, especially toward those who are the nearest and dearest to us and most deserving of good treatment?" A little misunderstanding caused all this trouble. I made a mountain out of a molehill. Unable to deal with the situation, I rushed out of the house and flung myself into the car and drove unknowingly to this seashore, which many people like me used as a refuge in times of distress.

I rose to my feet and brushed the sand off my clothes. I then got into my car and drove to my house, where I found my husband and Sawsan, my cat, waiting for me.

I Will Try Tomorrow

Mona Ragab

❀❀❀

Barefoot and on tiptoe, I steal away like a thief fleeing with his loot. My notebook, in which my pen has been suspended for ages, is under my arm. The idea has completely captured my imagination. It has become an obsession, and there is nothing left to do but commit it to paper. I've been trying to write for several nights, but my weariness and overexertion have prevented me.

The pressure of time and innumerable obligations works against me, but I've grasped the idea, and it won't elude me. I'm not going to let this golden opportunity slip through my fingers. No one has noticed me yet—everyone is still asleep.

All I have to do is avail myself of this long-awaited opportunity to the utmost. I'll write the idea quickly and release a waterfall that yearns to inundate the barren land! It's useless to try to silence the hot hammer that is pounding on the gate of my fortress in order to liberate what is imprisoned behind it. I'll let the words flow freely, and later I'll polish them little by little. Nothing matters as much as this moment, which has presented itself to me, when no one asks anything of me, when the silence receives me with open arms, and the white sheets of paper invite me to write. The moment begins now and will continue for a while, but the important thing is to commence.

The extremely humid air makes me retrace my steps to the bathroom to wash my face several times. I close the door quietly, afraid that I might awaken somebody, and it causes a squeak that startles me. I rush through the long hallway to snatch an hour before the precious minutes slip away. Finally I get to the study. I open the windows, and a moist dawn breeze brushes my face. The Nile

288

sways to and fro with its silver rays, and green leaves dance on its surface, as yet undisturbed by the fishing boats and the irksome rounds of the river-bus.

My imagination paints the picture of a young woman standing at the water's edge, staring at nothing. I open my notebook and begin to write: "She met him, and he started speaking to her in a tone of voice that electrified her in the midst of the deep silence." Here it is; the story is born. "She fell in love with him, not knowing how or when . . ." I hear a voice shattering the silence of the unfolding dawn, a cry that is rising higher and higher: "Mama!"

I throw the pen away and run in alarm to the bedroom. My little son has awakened and wants his feeding bottle. I prepare it quickly for him, so that he will not make noise, though I know that he likes to drink it very slowly. I wait submissively while I cuddle him tenderly to lull him to sleep. When he finishes his bottle, I put him in his bed and hasten to leave on tiptoe. Then a scream pierces me from the other side of the room.

"Mama, I want to drink."

My daughter, who is older, always complains of thirst and cannot bear the intense heat.

"Mama, the mosquitoes bit me. Bring me something to soothe the itch."

I quickly calm her down with an ointment that I apply to her legs.

"Sit beside me, Mama."

I sit slowly and wearily on the edge of the bed.

"Don't go away, Mama. I had a terrible dream. The pictures of the slain children in Lebanon haunt me. I'm afraid to sleep alone."

"You're a big girl, sweetie," I reply. "You're now seven years old. What will we say to your little brother if he sees you frightened like this?"

"But I feel so hot, Mama. I want to get up so we can sit together on the balcony."

With feigned firmness, which I display to achieve my goal of completing what I had begun to write at my desk, I say to her, "No, sweetie. It's still dawn. Try to get some sleep."

"Then tell me a story so I will fall asleep."

I tell my little girl a story that I forgot I had told her a month ago. Despite her tiredness, she interrupts me angrily.

"I want a *new* story."

I collect my thoughts to tell her a new story. Our voices wake my son, who stands up and begins to jump in his bed.

"Mama . . . The ball . . ."

He calls out to me to play with him. I fetch him his little ball to play together. Then, in resignation and submission, I put him on the floor to amuse himself as he pleases.

The neighbors are awakened by the sounds of our early noise. The milkman arrives, and I go to open the door for him. The garbage man arrives, making a din, and I go to open the door again. I prepare our breakfast, some food for my little boy, and a sandwich for my girl. I postpone writing the story that I had started, and console myself over the loss of yet another opportunity to put pen to paper and bring my idea to fruition.

Notes

Introduction

1. For an overview of Arab women writers, see Miriam Cooke, "Arab Women Writers," in M. M. Badawi, ed., *Modern Arabic Literature* (Cambridge: Cambridge University Press, 1992), pp. 443–62.

2. Virginia Woolf, *A Room of One's Own* (New York: Harcourt, 1981), p. 4.

3. Ibid., pp. 41–42.

4. Evelyne Accad, *Veil of Shame* (Sherbrooke, Quebec: Editions Naaman, 1978), pp. 31, 159.

5. For transcripts of the trial, see Elizabeth Fernea and Basima Qattan Bezirgan, eds., *Middle Eastern Muslim Women Speak* (Austin: University of Texas Press, 1988), pp. 280–90.

6. For additional details on al-Tall's trial, see Fadia Faqir, ed. *In the House of Silence* (Reading, U.K.: Garnet, 1998), p. 13.

7. Zabya Khamis describes her prison experiences in her volume of short stories, *Ibtisamat makira wa-qisas ukhra* (Kuwait, 1996).

8. Yusuf al-Sharuni, citing Nabila Ibrahim, in *The 1002nd Night* (*Al-Layla al-thaniyya ba'da al-alf*, Cairo, 1975), pp. 10–11. Translation mine.

9. Fatima Mernissi, *Doing Daily Battle*, trans. Mary Jo Lakeland (New Jersey: Rutgers University Press, 1989), p. 13.

10. Ibid., p. 14.

11. See also Joseph T. Zeidan, *Arab Women Novelists: The Formative Years and Beyond* (Albany: State University of New York Press, 1995), pp. 88–91.

12. Salwa Bakr, "Writing as a Way Out," in Fadia Faqir, ed., *In the House of Silence*, p. 39.

13. Evelyne Accad, *Veil of Shame*, pp. 14–15.

14. In Khannatha Bannuna, *Al-Sura wa-al-sawt* (Casablanca, 1975), pp. 87–92.

15. Ross Parmenter, "The Pothook," *The Plant in My Window* (1949).

16. In Alifa Rifaat, *Distant View of a Minaret and Other Stories*, trans. Denys Johnson-Davies (London: Quartet Books, 1983), pp. 61–76.

17. Nawal al-Saadawi, "She Is Not a Virgin," translation and analysis in Dalya Cohen-Mor, *A Matter of Fate: The Concept of Fate in the Arab World as Reflected in Modern Arabic Literature* (New York: Oxford University Press, 2001), pp. 143–48.

18. Raphael Patai, *The Arab Mind* (New York: Charles Scribner's Sons, 1983), p. 29. A compelling story depicting the tragic fate of a mother who bears only daughters is "A New Year" by Mikhail Naimy; in his volume, *A New Year: Stories, Autobiography, and Poems*, trans. J. Berry (Leiden: Brill, 1974), pp. 23–32.

19. Ghada al-Samman, "Another Scarecrow," translation and analysis in Dalya Cohen-Mor, *A Matter of Fate*, pp. 200–10.

20. Abd al-Qadir al-Qutt, cited in al-Sharuni, *The 1002nd Night*, p. 15.

21. Yusuf Idris, "Yusuf Idris yuqaddim katiba jadida," *Al-Shumu'*, 3 (May 1986), pp. 86–87. Translation mine.

22. For an English translation of this story, see Saddeqa Arebi, *Women and Words in Saudi Arabia: The Politics of Literary Discourse* (New York: Columbia University Press, 1994), pp. 82–83.

23. Al-Sharuni, *The 1002nd Night*, pp. 14–15.

24. See also Roger Allen, "The Arabic Short Story and the Status of Women," in Roger Allen, Hilary Kilpatrick, and Ed de Moor, eds., *Love and Sexuality in Modern Arabic Literature* (London: Saqi Books, 1995), pp. 88–89.

25. Qasim Amin, *The New Woman*, trans. Samiha Sidhom Peterson (Cairo: American University in Cairo Press, 1995), p. 2.

Part 1

1. The Waqfa is the most important rite of the pilgrimage to Mecca. It involves solemn standing on Arafa mountain, where a special sermon is delivered. On the following day, all Muslims celebrate the Feast of Sacrifice or the Great Festival.

Part 2

1. A casino is a restaurant or nightclub, without the Western component of gambling, located especially alongside the Nile in Cairo and the Mediterranean coast in Alexandria.

Part 3

1. The word *stella* (Latin for "female star") is used here for the Arabic word *najma*.

Part 4

1. An Egyptian proverb runs, "Marriage is like a closed watermelon" (i.e., you can't tell how it's going to turn out).

2. The reference is to the construction of the Aswan High Dam, completed in 1970.

3. According to Muslim tradition, it was Ishmael who was ordered to be sacrificed to God. When Abraham complied and proved his true faith, a sacrificial ram was sent down from heaven to take the place of Ishmael.

4. The name means "moon."

5. In Egyptian and Lebanese Arabic, the verb *shahaq* ("to gasp") also means "to exert influence by means of the evil eye." It should be noted that in Arab folklore, the jinn often show themselves disguised as animals, including goats.

6. This is the epithet of Fatima, daughter of the prophet Muhammad.

7. In parallel, a famous line by Nietzsche runs: "One must still have chaos in oneself to give birth to a dancing star." (Zarathustra's Prologue, in *Thus Spoke Zarathustra*, tr. Walter Kaufmann).

8. A system of civil courts presided over by Egyptian and foreign judges, with jurisdiction over residents of foreign nationality. They operated in Egypt from 1876 until 1949.

9. The first chapter of the Koran, which is recited, among other occasions, at funerals, or when remembering the dead, or on visiting a grave.

Part 5

1. A shrub native to Arabia whose leaves act as a narcotic when chewed. *See also* part 7, n. 1.

Part 6

1. Al-Khansa (died *ca.* 665) is considered the greatest early Arabic elegiac poet. Hind (died *ca.* 602), daughter of Nu'man III (the last Lakhmite king of Hira), was a Christian who founded a monastery in Hira. Zubayda (d. 831), wife of the Caliph Harun al-Rashid, was known for her noble character and charitable works.

2. An Arab woman who lived in the Hejaz before Islam. She was famous for her blue eyes and very sharp eyesight. Owing to her ability to spot the enemy from far off, she was employed as a scout by her warring tribe.

3. Egyptian neoclassical poet (1872–1932), dubbed *Sha'ir al-Nil,* "the poet of the Nile." This famous verse is quoted from his poem "Madrasat al-banat bi-Bur Sa'id" (The Girls' School in Port Said), which he recited upon visiting the school on May 29, 1910.

4. This famous tradition, attributed to the prophet Muhammad, gives the highest place of honor to the mother. See, for example, Maulana Muhammad Ali, *A Manual of Hadith* (Lahore, n.d.), pp. 373–74.

5. A colloquial Egyptian phrase used to admit wrongdoing. It equates wrongdoing with straying from the path of Islam.

6. A London call girl who was involved in a sex and espionage scandal with British War Secretary John Profumo and a Soviet military attaché. Both Profumo and British Prime Minister Harold Macmillan resigned from their offices in 1963, when the scandal broke.

7. In Saudi Arabia, women are forbidden to drive automobiles. When traveling, a woman must be escorted by a close male relative to whom she cannot be married, for example, her father, brother, or uncle.

8. In Saudi Arabia, a man may bar his wife, minor children, and adult unmarried daughters from leaving the country without his permission. To travel abroad, a woman must have the written consent of a male guardian.

Part 7

1. An evergreen shrub (*Catha edulis*) of Arabia and Africa, the leaves of which are used as a stimulant narcotic when chewed or made into a beverage. In Yemen, chewing qat is a way of life. It is estimated that three-fourths of Yemeni adults chew qat leaves each afternoon for a period of five hours, and that people spend about one-fourth to one-third of their cash income on qat. The heavy use of qat in Yemen is seen as a hinderance to agricultural development and as a cause of social and economic stagnation.

Part 8

1. The seventh month of the Islamic calendar.

2. The miraculous midnight journey of the prophet Muhammad from Jerusalem to the seven heavens, believed to have taken place on the 27th of Rajab.

3. Egyptian province in the northeast of the Nile Delta.

4. The announcement contains puns in the words *sea* and *free*. "Free city" implies both "liberated" from Israeli forces, which occupied the eastern bank of the Suez Canal after the Six-Day War of June 1967, and "a tax-free" industrial zone, declared by President Sadat following his "Open Door" policy of 1975. While this change has brought prosperity to Port Said, it has also resulted in profiteering and rampant consumerism.

5. The name means "affection" or "tenderness."

6. Sa'ida is the feminine form of the name Sa'id, which means "happy."

About the Authors

Sufi Abdallah was born in al-Fayyum, Egypt, in 1925. She attended English, French, and Italian girls' schools, and was tutored in Arabic at home. She began to write short stories in 1942, and won a literary prize in 1947. She has worked as editor for Dar al-Hilal publishing house in Cairo, and has contributed numerous short stories, articles, and synopses of foreign novels to several of its popular magazines. She has also edited a column called "Your Problem" for the women's weekly magazine *Hawwa*. A prolific writer of fiction, she has published fourteen volumes of short stories, five novels, three books of plays, two critical studies, and many translations from world literature.

Nura Amin was born in Cairo in 1970. She took a degree in French literature from Cairo University in 1992. She now works as a film, theater, and literary critic for the magazine *al-Hilal* and the newspaper *al-Ahali*, and as a lecturer at the Academy of Arts. Her first volume of short stories appeared in 1994, and she has since published two more volumes, a novel, and a critical study of modern Egyptian drama.

Daisy al-Amir was born in Baghdad in 1935. She received her B.A. from the Teachers' Training College in Baghdad and also studied a year in London. In 1960 she went to Beirut, where she first worked as a secretary at the Iraqi Embassy, and later as director of the Iraqi Cultural Center. In 1985 she returned to Iraq for a period of five years, after which she spent a year in America before moving back to Beirut in 1991. She is a writer of short stories, of which she has published seven volumes since 1964. A selection of her stories, *The Waiting List*, is available in English translation.

Radwa Ashour was born in Cairo in 1946. She received her B.A. in English literature from Cairo University in 1967, and her Ph.D. in Afro-American literature from the University of Massachusetts in 1975. She is presently professor of English literature at Ain

Shams University. A novelist and short-story writer, she began her writing career in the late 1970s with two critical studies. Since then she has published five novels, a volume of short stories, and a memoir of her stay in America. Her novel, *Granada*, is available in English translation.

Samiya At'ut was born in Nablus, Palestine, in 1957. She took a degree in mathematics from al-Mustansariyya University in Baghdad. She now works at the Arab Bank in Amman. She is the author of four volumes of short stories, the first of which was published in 1986.

Samira Azzam (1927–67) was born and raised in Acre, Palestine. She lived most of her adult life in Iraq and Lebanon, where she worked in journalism and broadcasting. A writer of short stories, she produced five volumes, the first of which appeared in 1954, and the last posthumously.

Salwa Bakr was born in Cairo in 1949. She took a degree in business management from Ain Shams University in 1972, and a degree in theater criticism from the Institute of Dramatic Arts in 1976. She has worked as a government rationing inspector for several years, and then as a film, theater, and literary critic for various journals and magazines. She began to write short stories in the mid-1970s, and her first volume appeared in 1985. Since then, she has published six more volumes, four novels, and a play. A selection of her stories, *The Wiles of Men*, and a novel, *The Golden Chariot*, are available in English translation.

Layla Ba'labakki was born in southern Lebanon in 1936. She studied literature at the Jesuit University in Beirut, but interrupted her education to work as a secretary in the Lebanese parliament. She began her writing career as a journalist on local newspapers and magazines. Her first, highly acclaimed novel, *Ana ahya* (I Am Alive), was published in 1958, and a volume of her short stories, *Safinat hanan ila al-qamar* (A Spaceship of Tenderness to the Moon), came out in 1963. The stories landed her in court on charges of obscenity and harming public morality. Although she was eventually acquitted, she stopped publishing works of fiction after 1964, and has since written mostly articles for newspapers.

Hayat Bin al-Shaykh was born in Tunis in 1943. She received her elementary and secondary education in the Tunisian capital and has worked in broadcasting and journalism. She is the author of three volumes of short stories, the first of which appeared in 1979, two novels, and a book of poetry.

Nuzha Bin Sulayman is a Moroccan writer. She has written two volumes of short stories which were published in Casablanca in 1995.

Nafila Dhahab was born in Tunisia in 1947. She studied law at the University of Tunis and graduated in 1970. She has written three volumes of short stories, the first of which was published in 1979, and several books for children.

Fadila al-Faruq is an Algerian writer. She has worked in broadcasting, presenting a popular program called "The Havens of Creativity" on Algerian radio, and also in journalism, writing a weekly column called "A Woman's Whispers" for the Algerian magazine *al-Hayah*. Her first volume of short stories was published in 1997, and her first novel in 2003.

Sakina Fuad was born in Port Said in 1943. She graduated in journalism from Cairo University in 1965. She started to work as an editor for the *Radio and Television* magazine, and became its editor-in-chief in 1982. She has written two novels and five volumes of short stories, many of which have been dramatized for Egyptian cinema and television. Her critically acclaimer novella, *Laylat al-qabd ala Fatima* (The Night Fatima Was Arrested), won her the cinema-story prize in 1985. A number of her stories have been translated into European languages.

Ulfat al-Idilbi was born in Damascus in 1912. She is the doyenne of Syrian women writers. Having married at a young age, she could not pursue her formal education beyond the secondary level and is largely self-taught. She began her writing career during the early 1950s, and won a BBC prize for short stories in the Arab world. Her works of fiction include five volumes of short stories and two novels, *Sabriya: Damascus Bitter Sweet* and *My Grandfather's Tale*, both of which are available in English translation. She has also published two books of essays and a critical study of the *Arabian Nights*.

Ramziya Abbas al-Iryani was born in 1954 in the village of Iryan in Yemen. She received her elementary education in the village school, and her secondary education in the city of Taiz, graduating in 1973. She took a degree in philosophy from Cairo University in 1977, and then pursued a career in the Ministry of Foreign Affairs of Yemen. In 1979 she became the first female diplomat in the Yemeni foreign service. Her first work of fiction, a novel, appeared in 1969. Since then she has published four volumes of short stories, a historical novel, and several books for children.

Ihsan Kamal was born in Egypt in 1935. She is a founding member of the Egyptian Writers' Union and the Story Club. A prolific writer of short stories, she has penned ten volumes, the first of which appeared in 1965. Many of her stories have been dramatized for Egyptian cinema and television, and some have been translated into European languages.

Umayma al-Khamis was born in Riyadh in 1964. She received her higher education in the Saudi capital, where she attended the College of Arts for Girls at King Saud University. She has written three volumes of short stories, the first of which was published in 1993, and numerous articles for local newspapers and magazines.

Zabya Khamis was born in Abu Dhabi in 1958. She studied at the University of Indiana, obtaining her B.A. in political science and philosophy in 1980. From 1982 until 1989 she worked toward her Ph.D. at the University of London. In 1987 she was arrested in Abu Dhabi and jailed for five months without trial as punishment for writing allegedly transgressive poetry. In 1989 she moved to Cairo, where she currently works for the Arab League. A poet and short-story writer, she has published nine books of poetry, three collections of short stories, and two volumes of translation from world literature.

Colette Suhayl al-Khuri was born into a Catholic family in Damascus in 1937. She received her elementary education in a convent school and her secondary education in a French school in Damascus. She studied at the University of Damascus, obtaining a degree in French literature in 1972. She has worked as a lecturer at the University of Damascus. A poet and writer of fiction, she has published eight novels, four volumes of short stories, and two books of poetry originally written in French.

Nadiya Khust was born in Damascus in 1935. She studied at the University of Damascus and took a degree in philosophy. She then went on to Moscow University, where she wrote her dissertation on the influence of Chekhov on modern Arabic literature, earning her Ph.D. in 1970. She works in journalism and broadcasting. She has published five volumes of short stories, four novels, and several critical studies.

Aliya Mamdouh was born in Baghdad in 1944. She took a degree in psychology from al-Mustansariyya University in 1971, and then worked in journalism. From 1983 until 1990 she lived in Morocco, serving on the editorial staff of several newspapers and magazines. Her first volume of short stories was published in 1973, and she has since written another volume, three novels, and a book of essays. She currently lives in Paris, where she works for the Arabic press. Her novel, *Mothballs*, is available in English translation.

Sahar al-Muji is an Egyptian writer. Her first volume of short stories came out in Cairo in 1998, and she has since published another volume and a novel.

Buthayna al-Nasiri was born in Baghdad in 1947. She studied English literature at Baghdad University, obtaining her B.A. in 1967. She began her writing career in the mid-1960s by contributing short stories to local newspapers and magazines. Her first volume of short stories was published in 1974, and six more volumes have appeared since then. In 1979 she moved to Cairo, where she currently runs a publishing house. A selection of her short stories, *Final Night*, is available in English translation.

Emily Nasrallah was born in 1931 in the village of Kfeir in southern Lebanon. She received her secondary education in Shoueifat, and then studied at Beirut University College and the American University of Beirut, earning her B.A. in education in 1958. She has worked as a teacher, lecturer, and journalist. Her first novel, *Tuyur Aylul* (September Birds), was published in 1962, and won her three literary prizes. Since then she has produced seven more novels, seven volumes of short stories, four books for children, and three books of essays. One of her novels, *Flight Against Time*, and a volume of short stories, *A House Not Her Own*, are available in English translation.

Suhayr al-Qalamawi (1911–97) was born and raised in Cairo. She belonged to the first generation of Egyptian women to graduate from the university and enter the sphere of academic life. She attended the American College for Girls in Cairo in 1929, and then studied Arabic literature at Cairo University, earning her Ph.D. in 1941. She joined the Department of Arabic at Cairo University, and worked her way up from lecturer to professor to chairperson, serving in that capacity from 1958 until 1967. In 1935 she published *Ahadith Jaddati* (My Grandmother's Tales), the first volume of short stories by a woman to appear in Egypt. Her writings include two volumes of short stories, ten critical studies, and many translations from world literature.

Mona Ragab was born in Cairo in 1953. She studied at Cairo University and took a degree in economics and political science. She is currently cultural deputy editor of the leading Egyptian newspaper, *al-Ahram*. She has written five volumes of short stories, the first of which appeared in 1985. Some of her stories have been translated into European languages.

Fawziya Rashid was born in Bahrain in 1954. She has worked as a journalist on the Bahrain newspaper *Akhbar al-Khalij*, and has written numerous articles for the Gulf and Arab press. She began to write fiction in 1977, and both her first volume of short stories and her first novel appeared in 1983. Since then, she has published two more volumes as well as two more novels. She currently lives in Cairo.

Alifa Rifaat (1930–96) was born and raised in Cairo. Having married at a young age, she could not pursue her formal education beyond the secondary level and was largely self-taught. She began to write short stories when she was seventeen, and from 1955 until 1960 she published under a pseudonym. Owing to her husband's opposition to her work, she stopped writing for more than a decade. Following his death in 1974, she was free to resume her literary activities and began to publish under her own name. Her writings include four volumes of short stories, the first of which came out in 1975, and a novel. A selection of her stories, *Distant View of a Minaret*, is available in English translation.

Nawal al-Saadawi was born in the village of Kafr Tahla in Egypt in 1930. She graduated from the Faculty of Medicine at Cairo University in 1955, and then worked as a physician in both the countryside and the city. In 1967 she became Egypt's director-general of health education, a post from which she was dismissed for writing *Al-Mar'a wa-al-jins* (Women and Sex, 1972). Her activities on behalf of Arab women's liberation landed her in jail in 1981, when Anwar Sadat was president of Egypt. In 1993 her name appeared on a death list issued by a fundamentalist group, and she went into exile in North Carolina for five years. A leading feminist writer, she has published a large number of books, both fiction (novels, short stories, and plays) and nonfiction (social studies and memoirs). Many of her books have been translated into European languages.

Hadiya Sa'id was born in Lebanon in 1947. She took a degree in literature from the Arab University in Beirut in 1969. Her first volume of short stories appeared in 1978, and she has since published four more volumes and an award-winning novel. In addition to works of fiction, she writes scripts for documentary films for television and the screen. She currently lives in London, where she works as a journalist.

Khayriya al-Saqqaf was born in Mecca in 1951. She received her B.A. in Arabic literature from King Saud University in Riyadh in 1973, her M.A. in education from the University of Missouri in 1976, and her Ph.D. from Imam Muhammad Bin Saud University in 1988. She currently works as a lecturer at the Girls' University College of King Saud University, and as editor of the women's section of the leading newspaper *al-Riyadh*. She writes short stories and articles, and gives radio talks and public lectures. A volume of her short stories was published in Riyadh in 1982.

Sharifa al-Shamlan was born in 1946 in Zubayr, a town near the Saudi border with Iraq. She took a degree in journalism from Baghdad University in 1968. She currently lives in the port city of Dammam in the eastern province of Saudi Arabia, where she is the head of the institution of social services for delinquent women. She has written three volumes of short stories, the first of which was published in 1989, and numerous articles for local newspapers and magazines.

Hanan al-Shaykh was born in Beirut in 1945. She received her elementary and secondary education in Beirut, and in 1963 she went to Cairo to study at the American College for Girls. In 1967 she returned to Beirut and worked as a journalist on the leading daily *al-Nahar*. Later she moved to the Arabian Gulf, where she lived for several years. The Lebanese Civil War prevented her return to Beirut, and in 1982 she moved to London, where she currently lives. Her widely acclaimed novel, *The Story of Zahra*, published in 1980, has been banned in several Arab countries because of its frank treatment of sexual and political topics. A writer with a worldwide reputation, she has published six novels and two volumes of short stories. Most of her works are available in English translation.

Rafiqat al-Tabi'a is the pen name of Zaynab Fahmi, a Moroccan writer born in Casablanca in 1940. She is presently the principal of a girls' school in Mohammedia. She has written three volumes of short stories, the first of which was published in 1969.

Suhayr al-Tall was born in Irbid, Jordan. She took a degree in philosophy from Amman University and then worked as a journalist. She is currently editor of the Jordanian newspaper *Sawt al-Sha'b*. Her first volume of short stories was published in 1982, and the second, entitled *Al-Mishnaqa* (The Gallows), in 1987. The title story of her latter volume, which is included in this anthology, landed her in court on a charge of offending public sensibilities. After a long and bitter trial, she was convicted, fined, and sentenced to short imprisonment. She has published two critical studies since then.

Najiya Thamir (1926–88) was born in Damascus into a family of Tunisian origins. She attended schools in Baalbeck and Damascus, where she was exposed to both French and Arab cultures. She lived in Tunisia from the age of twenty until her death, working in broadcasting and journalism. She published four volumes of short stories, two books of plays, a collection of essays, and a book for children.

Layla al-Uthman was born in Kuwait in 1945. After graduating from a local high school, she did not pursue a university education and is largely self-taught. In 1965 she began to work in broadcasting and journalism. Her first volume of short stories appeared in 1976. One of the leading women writers of fiction in the Arabian Peninsula, she has published ten volumes of short stories, two novels, and a book of poetry. Some of her short stories have been translated into European languages.

Zuhur Wanisi was born in 1936 in the Algerian town of Constantine. She took a degree in literature and philosophy from the University of Algiers and then worked as a teacher and journalist. In addition, she pursued a political career: she joined the Algerian struggle for independence between 1954 and 1962, was a member of the Algerian parliament from 1977 until 1982, and became the first female minister in her country when she was appointed to the Office of Social Affairs and National Guidance in 1982. She is currently editor of the women's magazine *al-Jaza'iriyya*. She has written four volumes of short stories, the first of which was published in 1967, and two novels.

Latifa al-Zayyat (1923–96) was born in Damietta, a coastal town in Egypt. She received her elementary and secondary education in local schools, and then studied at Cairo University, obtaining her Ph.D. in English literature in 1957. A political activist and feminist, she was twice imprisoned for her political views. At the time of her death, she was professor of English literature at Ain Shams University. Her writings include a play, two novels, two volumes of short stories, three critical studies, a book of essays, and her memoirs. Her first novel, *The Open Door*, and her memoirs, *The Search: Personal Papers*, are available in English translation.

Mayy Ziyada (1886–1941) was born in Nazareth to a Palestinian mother and a Lebanese father. She received her education in Nazareth, Ayn Turn, and Beirut before moving with her family to Cairo in 1908. She became a prominent figure in the cultural life of Cairo, and from 1914 until the late 1920s she hosted weekly salons that were frequented by the leading Arab intellectuals of the day. A pioneer woman writer of fiction and poetry, she published widely in Cairo and Beirut presses, and corresponded intimately with the Arab-American writer Gibran Khalil Gibran. In 1936 she suffered a severe depression that cut short her literary career. Her writings include speeches, essays, prose poems, short stories, biographies of women, critical studies, and many translations from world literature.

Dalya Cohen-Mor, the editor and translator of these stories, has earned her Ph.D. in Arabic language and literature from Georgetown University in Washington, D.C., and her M.A. in English language and literature from the State University of Utrecht in the Netherlands. A literary scholar and anthologist, she has published two volumes of translation and is the author of *Yusuf Idris: Changing Visions.* Her most recent publication, *A Matter of Fate*, which explores the belief in destiny in the Arab world as reflected in modern Arabic literature (New York: Oxford University Press, 2001), was selected as an outstanding academic book by *Choice* magazine.